Phage lowered her arm and stared at Kamahl.

He stood a hundred paces away, his staff grounded in the sand. Druidic robes ruffled in the wind. Beneath gleamed his barbaric armor. If anything, his new devotions had made him more muscular. He would be a formidable foe, except that he hoped not to kill but to save. That was his weakness.

Phage shrieked and ran toward him.

EXPERIENCE THE MAGIC

MAGIC
The Gathering®

ONSLAUGHT CYCLE · BOOK I

ONSLAUGHT

J. Robert King

ONSLAUGHT

Cover art by Ken Walker
First Printing: September 2002
Library of Congress Catalog Card Number: 2001097174

9 8 7 6 5 4 3 2 1

US ISBN: 0-7869-2801-8
UK ISBN: 0-7869-2802-6
620-88618-001-EN

U.S., CANADA,
ASIA, PACIFIC, & LATIN AMERICA
Wizards of the Coast, Inc.
P.O. Box 707
Renton, WA 98057-0707
+1-800-324-6496

EUROPEAN HEADQUARTERS
Wizards of the Coast, Belgium
P.B. 2031
2600 Berchem
Belgium
+32-70-23-32-77

Visit our web site at **www.wizards.com**

For Denise R. Graham

THE UNHEALING WOUND

*J*eska clutched the wound in her belly and curled up in a soft bed of soil. Centuries of humus had made this a lovely place to lie, a likely place to die.

Jeska didn't want to die.

She wasn't home. Instead of her people, tawny-skinned and golden-eyed, she was among mantis folk. Instead of her brother Kamahl, who had carried her across the continent to be healed, she was tended by an ape-faced horse-man.

"It's all right. It's all right," Seton soothed. "This is a place of ancient power. It will heal you, if any place can. . . ." Already, the mantis folk had told him she would not live. "The infection has gotten under your skin, that's all. It's just skin deep."

Jeska shook her head in denial and pain, and ferns clutched her thrashing hair. All around her, trees twisted into the sky. Birds and bushbabies and other things stared down from the green fronds and sent forth strange whoops of laughter.

Kamahl said she would be healed here. He hadn't said she would die.

She would die.

Jeska let go of the unhealing wound and gripped the arms of the centaur. Her fingers stained his flesh red and black. "Tell me what I must do. You are a druid, a healer. How can I live?"

Seton glanced up, seeking the support of the mantis folk. They were gone. They had withdrawn. He looked longingly at the forest, as if he wished to join them. "I should bring back your brother."

"No! Don't abandon me. It's bad enough to die among strangers, but to die alone . . ."

"It's going to be all right—"

"For you! Oh, what I would trade to be in your skin instead of mine. Tell me what I must do to live."

His simian face was grieved as he stared down at her. Then there was something else—terrible pain. Seton shuddered and reached up over his shoulder. He gasped a breath and blood poured from his mouth. Eyes fixed in horror, he toppled forward onto her.

Jeska shoved at him. "Seton! What's happening! What are you doing?"

A new voice came, a woman's voice. "He saved your life—if you have the will to claim it. Do you, Jeska? Will you embrace a nightmare to live?"

Jeska stared over Seton's still shoulder but could not see who spoke. Her own strength failing, she said only, "What must I do?"

CHAPTER ONE

IMAGE AND TRUTH

*F*or some, pit fighting was about killing. Just now in the pit, a gigantipithicus ape and a griffon tore each other apart. The air shimmered with feathers and fur, and the stands boiled with cheers. Avid faces peered down in concentric rings from the height of the arena. The crowds loved killing.

Ixidor shook his head, averting his eyes from the arena gate. He did not wish to see the fights as they were. He wished to see them as they should be. His hands flashed through a series of paper disks. Each showed a contingent of noble warriors arrayed for battle, striking blows, deflecting attacks, advancing, falling, fighting, prevailing. In pen and ink, Ixidor had rendered the scenes with such clarity they sank away from the page as if to imprint themselves on reality. Shortly, these images would become reality—and victory. Image magic.

For Ixidor, pit fighting was about art.

He paused in shuffling the disks and reached out to his partner. His hand settled on her knee and his eyes on her figure. She was more perfect than any art. Beautiful, brilliant, bold, garbed in white robes and bedecked in jewels—she was everything he was not. How Ixidor, a gawky artist with jutting jaw and unkempt hair, could be the companion of this gleaming angel, he would never know. Perhaps she needed him. After all, a work of art needed an artist.

"The avens aren't ready," Nivea said as if in a trance. Though she grasped his hand, her mind was faraway, tapping other creatures. "We can't count on them for this fight."

Ixidor's angular face split in a bemused grin. He fished a disk from among the others. It showed a contingent of bird-men advancing with pikes foremost. Crumpling the thing, he threw it to the floor of the prep pen. "Avens've been worthless for a couple of seasons. I'm not going to waste time with them anymore."

Nivea smiled—not because of his words, but because of another summoning she prepared. "Still, the Order refugees are raring to go." Nivea herself had once been part of the Northern Order before it was decimated. "They'll be enough."

Deftly, Ixidor moved the appropriate disks to the top of the stack. He closed his eyes, imagining the armor he would grant the Order soldiers. Nivea would summon warriors to the pits, and Ixidor would wrap them in image magic. She commanded reality and he illusion. They had not been beaten yet, and today would be no exception.

Though her mind still moved among magical mercenaries, Nivea's attention had shifted. "How much will we make . . . if we win?"

"*When* we win," corrected Ixidor, "we'll make plenty."

"Plenty enough to quit the pits?" Nivea asked. The visionary light had left her eyes, and she fixed them on Ixidor. "I hate all the killing."

Ixidor flashed her a winning grin. "I know, but we don't kill, my dear. We subdue."

"What if we *get* killed?"

He kissed the back of her hand. "We can't get killed, not while we're together. Who can stand against us? None so far."

"So far," echoed Nivea.

"Come on." Ixidor stood and stretched. In one hand he held his paper disks, and in the other he held the hand of Nivea, lifting her from her seat. He drew her up beside him and wrapped her in his arms. "Look in my eyes. What do you see?"

Nivea stared. "Confidence. Cockiness. Courage."

"Look closer."

Her gaze grew more intent. "I see myself."

"Yes. As long as you are in my eyes, I am complete. As long as I am in your eyes, you are complete. How can any of these half-hearts compete with us?"

The worry left her face, and the smile that formed there was radiant. "You always know what to say."

"You mean I'm always right."

She shook her head ruefully. "I mean you *almost* always know what to say."

Ixidor laughed, and Nivea joined him. This was as much a part of their pre-fight ritual as preparing their magic. They could not truly fight together until they could laugh together. The sound of it tuned their souls.

Beyond their laughter came an agonized shriek from the griffon. The crowd roared ecstatically, and the death bell tolled. The gigantic ape bowed amid a flurry of lost-wager stubs. Pit vermin scuttled out and dragged away every shred of the bird-lion.

Before the ovation could die down, the gate before Ixidor and Nivea swung open, and the two emerged onto the pit floor. They lifted their hands together to hail the crowd, and they laughed.

The clamor united Ixidor and Nivea, no longer two entities but one. Some teams were sundered by that roar—each member fighting as if alone and dying the same. Not these two. Ixidor and Nivea were utterly amalgamated.

They were crowd pleasers, despite the fact that they rarely killed. Crowds loved beauty almost as much as blood, and to watch Ixidor and Nivea fight was to watch beauty.

Ixidor turned, gazing out at the pit. It was a deep, black well, ringed round by tiers of seats. Spectators bunched out like violent flowers. Faces lit with anticipation, human and inhuman—elfin, aven, centaur, barbarian, simian, and unnatural combinations thereof. All shone with the same bloodthirsty light.

"We belong here together," Ixidor said, his heart pounding.

"We belong together," Nivea replied. She pivoted and bowed before the roaring crowd.

The cheers fell suddenly away, as if choked by a killing cloud. Ixidor felt a dark presence at their backs. Still clinging to Nivea, he turned. Together they saw.

From a dark prep pen, their adversaries emerged. The first was a tall, lean man. Pallid skin stretched across his knobby skull. Blood-red eyes smoldered in sunken pits. Yellow teeth clenched in a crescent grin. The man wore black robes that swayed as he lurched forward. He seemed a marionette—long limbs quivering, feet clumsily pounding sand. He planted a gnarled staff beside him and halted, leaning on the ancient wood. From the staff hung small skulls that rattled against each other, momentarily masking the approach of the other creature.

It shifted in the dark pen, a noise like sand sliding over metal. Scales glinted above coiling muscles. The creature advanced into the arena, seeming to drag the darkness with it. Only then did Ixidor realize that it *was* the darkness.

"A giant serpent," he whispered to Nivea.

"Undead," she replied.

A side-winding snake, as large around as an elephant, looped its coils out across the sand. It welled up behind the simpering wizard, and its cobra-hood spread to eclipse the stands.

Though the crowd had gone momentarily silent at the arrival of this great menace, now hisses and murmurs told of wagers withdrawn and new stakes offered.

Ixidor's hands worked quickly, drawing a few new disks from pockets in his jacket and replacing others. He spoke through a tight smile. "Any of your Order cronies know how to turn undead?"

She shook her head. "Nope." She stared at the massive serpent, a wall of black sinew. A vermillion tongue lashed out, tasting the air. "I don't suppose you have any illusions that smell?"

"I have a few that stink, but not the way you mean," Ixidor said.

"Now we're staring down death," Nivea pointed out. "Do you still think we belong here together?"

He squeezed her hand. "We belong together. Let's do this."

Releasing his grip, he lifted the disks and fixed his eyes on the images there. Ink lines pulsed and began to lift from the pages. Hatch marks turned to true shadows. Image strained to break into reality. The moment the bell tolled, the disks would fly, and the images would emerge.

Beside him, Nivea grew still. Her vision retreated inward. With her mind's eye, she gazed out across the world. In the far north, she had once fought beside Captain Pianna of the Order. Now captain and Order both were decimated. In place of honorable battle, Nivea and her comrades had only dishonorable blood sport. Still, it was a living. She tapped the warriors who had granted her summonation rights. Each would receive a share of the purse—if he or she survived. Otherwise . . . there were the pit vermin. With inward eyes, Nivea called them. Riding on lines of light, they answered the summons.

The bell tolled. The match began.

Nivea took a staggering step back, her arms flung wide. In the space before her, motes of light twinkled into being. They seemed stars in a wide cluster but then lengthened into stalks of light. One by one the stalks swelled to take solid form: twenty warriors in the leather and canvas armor of the Order. They bore bone-tipped pole-axes and hook-ended swords. These warriors fought as a unit, striking hard and fast, straight at the foe. Digging toes into sand, the Order contingent charged.

They had not taken two full strides before Ixidor cast a spell. Hurling the first of many disks from the stack in his hand, Ixidor spoke an evocation. The words tore away the whirling paper and left only the lines across it. Ink unraveled in the air. Black and white schematics flung themselves out around the warriors. Drawings overlaid armor of canvas and bone.

Ixidor's magic took hold only just in time.

The marionette man lashed clawlike hands down through the air. His fingertips lanced black fire. It cut down across the warriors and would have sliced them to pieces except for their shimmering protections. Failing to bring forth blood, the spell shot into the sand. There, it *did* find blood—old stains from former duels. Dark flames coruscated. Heat melted the sand to glass and spun it up into the air. A razor thicket of glass formed before the charging troops.

They couldn't stop. They smashed into the glass. It shattered and spun about them. Any exposed flesh was laid bare. Cheeks, eyelids, lips, knuckles, all were flayed. Still, the warriors did not stop. Oozing red, they charged through and sank their pole-axes into the flank of the undead serpent.

Shafts gored black scales. Bone blades clattered amid desiccated ribs. Hunks of rotting flesh fell away. Roaring, the warriors twisted their weapons and yanked. Gobbets of corruption came away. The withered organs of the monster gaped within.

Undead things did not need organs to live. The serpent did not even recoil from the assault, bringing its titanic tail around to smash the troops. Triangular scales rattled above creaking bones. The rotten bulk impacted.

An Order warrior was flung through the air to crash against the arena wall. Another snapped like a twig and fell in a crumpled mass. Two more died beneath the tail's crushing weight. The rest climbed out of the tail's path, clambering up the snake's heaving sides. It was the wrong retreat.

The snake's head darted down. Its mouth splayed gray fangs. One pierced a warrior from crown to gut. Another caught the armor of two men and dragged them into the jaws. A comrade who tried to save them was hurled away by the thrashing head. With a crunch of the creature's jaws, four warriors died.

"That's almost half!" shouted Ixidor. He frantically flung a disk that bled blue lines in the air. A net of power wrapped the other warriors and dragged them from harm's way. "Any more troops?"

Nivea's eyes were intent, though she focused on distant places. "I'm bringing in the avens."

Growling, Ixidor remembered the aven disk he'd crumpled in the prep pen.

The marionette man spoke the words of a wicked spell.

Ixidor snarled. "I'll take the wizard."

Reaching to the center of the stack, he drew out a circle scribed with wild vortices. His wrist flicked. The disk sliced through the air. Halfway to the wizard, the paper flashed away. Ink lines whirled into true cyclones. A bundle of spinning storms swarmed the marionette man. Winds picked at his limbs and flung them akimbo. The spells forming before him dissolved. He lost his footing. Kicking frantically, he spun away from the arena floor. A twist of Ixidor's hand sent the wizard up to crack against the serpent's jaw. The great snake reeled. The white-faced man tumbled behind it.

"Here's your opening!" Ixidor called.

Nivea stood with arms wide. A contingent of avens winked into being before her. The bird-warriors were a mixed group—some with humanlike heads, others with the heads of eagles, some land bound on raptor legs and others already flapping into the air for battle. Whether with mouths or beaks, they emitted the same shrieking cry.

The sound mounded up through the arena, and the crowd added its own roar. Since the destruction of the Northern Order, it was a rarity to see nomads and avens fighting side by side. The match, especially against so vile a foe, harkened back the glory days of the Order. The sight energized the crowd.

On sand and wing, avens rushed the undead serpent. Talons clutched scales and tore them out. Beaks dived through ribs to pull out organs. Wings beat at the serpent's darting head to confuse it, and one aven rammed his pike through the snake's eye.

Amid pumping wings, Ixidor's disks whirled. With utter precision, they cracked upon the backs of the avens. Magic ambled out across them. Blue power annealed pinions into wings of steel. Rock hard, avens pummeled the serpent with their bodies. They punched through flesh and bone and tore out the other side.

In moments, the undead beast was riddled with holes. Its scales hailed down. Its ribs cracked loose and augered into the sand. Its lashing head flailed on a crackling neck. Avens and Order warriors swarmed the monster, dismantling it.

"Not bad for an improvisation!" Ixidor called out.

"Not good enough!" Nivea answered.

Suddenly, the black beast was gone. It did not vanish but dissolved to a cloud of ash. Avens that had perched on it took startled wing. Order warriors dropped down through spinning clouds of white. Ixidor feared at first that they would suffocate in the ash, but something drew it rapidly away. A great roar came from behind the cloud, draining the ash into the marionette man. His body absorbed the strength of the giant serpent.

"Soul-shift!" Nivea warned.

The marionette man leaped forward. Gone was his loose-jointed gait. His body, which had once seemed bones and skin, now bristled with muscles and power. No longer were his eyes sunken, but they bulged like bowls of blood. His crescent smile had grown wider, teeth jutting in fierce triangles. Powerful arms lashed out, and black lightning cracked from fingertips. Each bolt traveled with a will, seeking avens in the air and warriors on the ground. Where the jags of power struck, fighters fell.

Their souls were ripped right out of them. An Order warrior lay boneless, his hair burning. An aven flashed to a skeleton, her flesh turned to drifting smoke. One by one they fell until all of the summoned soldiers were reduced to charred ash.

"Got any more?" Ixidor called out.

Nivea only shook her head, face white with dread.

The black wizard cackled. He lifted his hands above his head. Ebon energy crawled into the air and formed a killing dome. Even the spectators high above leaned back, lest some stray bolt end their lives. In the sudden silence, the mage's shout was clear to every ear:

"Bow then, or be destroyed. You are finished!"

Ixidor and Nivea traded grave stares. Every eye in the pit watched the undefeated pair. Thousands of wagers and millions of coins waited on their decision. There was only defeat or death. Which would they choose?

Shaking his head angrily, Ixidor flung away his unused disks. They whirled out across the smoldering sands and landed, inert.

Beside him, Nivea sighed, and the glow of summonings vanishing from her eyes.

A sound, half growl and half sigh, rolled down from the stands.

"May we approach to bow?" Ixidor asked sullenly.

Blood-red eyes fixed on him. The man's crescent smile grew somehow sharper. "Of course."

Over sand stained in blood and pocked with soot, the two fighters walked. Ixidor reached out to take his partner's hand. Nivea squeezed fondly. They spoke to each other in tones no one else could have heard.

"Why did it take you so long?" Nivea hissed.

Ixidor sniffed. "It was like you said, the serpent could smell a deception. I had to wait until it was gone before I could cast the false death."

"What about the ones killed first?" Nivea asked.

"None of them were killed. That was a minor illusion, and a bit of acting on their parts. No, my dear, they're quite fine. Look." He nodded gently past the black mage, toward the wall of the arena. Shadowy figures shifted across the cut stone. Ixidor's remaining disks, lying in an arc behind the mage, had set up an illusory curtain of magic, behind which the avens and Order warriors advanced. No one in the crowd or the arena could have seen them. Even to Ixidor they seemed only wavering air, like a desert mirage. "They're all alive and ready."

Nivea gritted her teeth. "I hate the killing."

Ixidor smiled tightly. "We don't kill, and none of our people get killed."

"So far. . . ." They had reached the marionette man.

He towered above them, preternaturally tall. His muscular arms were crossed over his chest. The black shocks from his fingers still whirled, flinging his cloak back behind him. "Well? Will you bow, or will you die?"

Ixidor's eyes blazed. "Before we bow, I must remove one final illusion." He lifted his hand, and before the mage could counter, simply snapped.

In a tight circle around the man, a shimmering curtain of force dropped to the sand, revealing twenty warriors of the Northern Order and the full contingent of avens. Four men grasped the mage's burly arms and forced them up beside his head. A fifth man rammed a squelching helm down on the mage's head and cinched the arm loops tight. The largest aven grasped the wizard's belt and hoisted him high on flapping wings. The once-fearsome necromancer now seemed no more than a trout in the claws of an eagle.

It all had happened in a breath of time—the gasp drawn by the crowd when they saw the living warriors. Now those full throats bellowed in joy. It was a strange sound. The crowd was unanimous for Ixidor and Nivea. Even those who had lost a fortune knew a good show when they saw one. Noble warriors and ignoble illusion—what better show could there be?

Ixidor beamed, clutching Nivea's hand and lifting it high in triumph. Side by side, they bowed to their adoring fans.

All the while, their foe wriggled impotently in the grasp of the bird-man.

"One of the things that's great about not killing them," Ixidor said through his fierce smile, "is it takes the judge awhile to declare a victory, and we get all that time for bows."

Nivea wore a sideways grin. "You enjoy this too much."

"You do too."

Only then did the death bell toll—a symbolic death for the necromancer, but a real victory for Nivea and Ixidor. The crowd's shouts grew to an ovation that rattled the rock walls of the pit. The best sound of all, though, was the roar of coin—gold and silver and electrum—from the coffers of the Cabal into Ixidor's own lock box.

"Enough to quit the pit?" asked Nivea hopefully.

Looking around at the two contingents, Ixidor said, "Not with all these mouths to feed. Next time we fight, it'll be enough. I'll make sure of it."

CHAPTER TWO

WHERE SPIRITS DWELL

*S*ister . . ."

Jeska had been here, just here, within the hut of Seton. Now she was gone, along with those who had tended her. Tracks led away—nantuko and centaur, but no human tracks. They must have taken her out of the hut to heal her, taken her to some sacred spot. . . . They must have been desperate.

Kamahl glowered at the empty hut. He had crossed a continent to save his sister, only to leave her for one final fight. Kamahl's sword had slain his old foe, and his neglect might have slain his sister.

Dragging his armor onto his massive shoulders, Kamahl set off to follow the tracks. They wandered through undergrowth, into a cathedral of ancient trees, and down a long slope above a holy stream. A mass of aerial roots made a palisade on the banks. The tracks ended there.

Jeska was gone. So too were the mantis men who had worked to heal her, and her protector, Seton.

No, he remained, or some part of him.

A hoof lay in the dirt on the opposite side of the tree.

Eyes pinned to the hoof, Kamahl circled the vast tangle of roots. His tan skin looked almost crimson amid the green. Rounding the corner, he saw a second hoof lying beside the first. The legs attached to them were skeletal. Bleached fur stretched across fetlocks and cannons. One more step, and Kamahl glimpsed the whole equine form.

The centaur had been stabbed in the back. His corpse was horribly gaunt. His pelt had been sucked in over ribs and spine. The skin across his chest was tight like the head of a drum. Lips and eyelids and nostrils had widened grotesquely, fixing his face in a silent scream. It seemed that the knife in his back had drawn out his insides, and he had imploded.

Kamahl stood in silent reverie. His armor dragged him down, the weight of war. He knelt beside the body, and deep grief moved through him. He and Seton had fought side by side in the pits. They had become comrades and even friends. Seton had suffered a terrible fate, and in defense of Kamahl's sister. What worse fate did she suffer?

"Sister . . . Jeska . . ." Kamahl closed his eyes and clenched his hands on his knees. He had caused it all. He had struck the unhealing blow across Jeska's gut, the blow that even mantis druids could not heal. If she lived, no doubt the wound remained. If she had died, no doubt she had died at his hand.

Kamahl's armor was suddenly too heavy. Red and massive across his shield arm, it was like the claw of a crab. He reached up and undid it. The plates slid to crash on the forest floor. Once, the armor had counterbalanced Kamahl's huge sword. Now it too was gone.

The sword. The damned Mirari sword. It had killed dozens in the pits and hundreds in Kamahl's homeland—and Jeska herself. He hated that sword. If Kamahl still had it, he would have broken it and tossed it away. It was too late for that, though. The sword had found its final resting place, buried in another unhealing wound.

"Laquatus." Kamahl scrubbed the stubble of his shaved head.

Instead of tending his sister, Kamahl had battled Laquatus. He had driven his sword down through the merman and spiked him to the forest floor. There could be no more fitting end for the Mirari sword than that—a grave marker. Once, it had led Kamahl into murderous warfare. Once, it had driven him to slay endlessly. Now he was done with killing. The Mirari sword marked not only Laquatus's grave but Kamahl's own.

What was a barbarian without a weapon? What was Kamahl without killing?

He lingered there beside Seton, where his sister had lain. The old Kamahl would have snatched up his sword and gone out for revenge. The new Kamahl knelt. He was a changed man. A strange stillness filled him. He had never been still in his life. Always before fire had burned within. He had channeled its fury, had ridden the power of chaos. Now the fire was quenched, the chaos diverted. Stillness reigned.

Kamahl did not feel peace but panic. How could he live in utter stillness?

But it wasn't utter stillness. Even beneath his knees, there was movement. Growth. The power of the forest was not like the power of the fire. It was slow, patient, inevitable—creative rather than destructive. Kamahl sank his fingers into thick tufts of grass. Hot air breathed from the blades. Cool water moved through the veins. Smooth roots sank through crumbling soil. The grass trembled with life.

Kamahl's breath softened. He listened, felt, sniffed. Stillness deepened around him, and the whispers of life grew to shouts. Always they had spoken to him, but he had never heard. Now he listened.

This is not our true voice, they told him—not in words but in significances. This is the sound of travail. This is the sound of your sword buried in the heart of the wood.

Kamahl trembled. His sword had claimed one more victim. To spike Laquatus, he had pierced the ground. The Mirari sword, which had wreaked such havoc in Kamahl's own homeland, now stabbed the heart of the Krosan Forest. He had seen the ravages begin—rampant growth in the grove around the sword. Trees thrust up into the sky. Vines swelled and tangled. Flowers budded and burst in wide glory. These strange mutations hadn't come from Laquatus. They came from the Mirari.

Kamahl had to rise, to act. His damned sword called him again.

It almost hurt to move, to break the stillness. Still, Kamahl stood. He had listened to the forest and could not ignore its plight. Let him draw the sword and heal the wood. If he was to save his sister, let him begin by saving the forest.

Kamahl turned and strode back the way he had come. Soon the trail became difficult. The forest shuddered and groaned with startling life. Vines snaked along the ground and fattened. Leaves sprouted and rattled while the ancient boles that bore them cracked, grew, and cracked again. The rampant growth had spread far indeed.

Pausing, Kamahl stared forward, past pitching treetops and undulating carpets of moss. He glimpsed the royal ziggurat at the heart of the forest. At its base lay Laquatus, pinned by the sword. It was the epicenter of the growth wave. Kamahl climbed toward it.

He plunged into a thicket. It deepened around him. Burrs scratched along his limbs, and thorns lengthened to pierce his skin. Branches doubled and redoubled. Kamahl wished for his sword to hew inward, but the impulse immediately felt false. Kamahl could not take the heart of the forest by violence. He was part of the wood now.

Wrapping fingers about a pair of branches, he drew them

steadily aside and stepped between. Tendrils twined around his wrists. They released only grudgingly as he struggled through the thicket. Thorns ripped his wolfskin cape to tatters.

Kamahl escaped the thicket, but the forest floor was no more forgiving. Roots writhed across the ground, grasped each other, clawed and dragged at his boots. Stumbling over one jealous root, Kamahl barged against a swollen tree. Bark grated his bare arm and opened a series of abrasions.

It seemed the forest would demand a blood toll to let him pass. Kamahl was prepared to pay. It was absolution for what he had done to Seton, to Jeska, to the very wood.

A great willow reared up before him and tossed its ugly head. Branches lashed the ground, ripping away humus. They would rip away Kamahl's skin just as easily. A single man could not battle a whole wood.

Kamahl knelt. He dug his fingers into a deep carpet of moss. The voice of the wood clamored to him again, but this time he did not listen. He only spoke. "If ever I am to right the wrongs I have done, I must survive to do so." He said the words quietly, as if to himself.

Someone or something heard.

Through lashing branches and thrashing roots, a path formed. It seemed like a part in thick hair, rising straight up the hill toward the ziggurat.

Kamahl shivered in wonder. He was becoming part of the wood, and it was becoming part of him. He rose and picked his way up the slender trail. He could not have taken the forest by violence, but he now walked a peaceful path inward.

To either side, chaos ruled. Trees grew so massive they lay down like giant strands of hair. Some stretched for miles and continued to grow. Around them, briar thickets mounded. New shoots rammed their way up into sunlight, thickened, and flowered.

The growth wave struck more than just flora. A line of beetles on a nearby log split their skins and emerged larger to split again. A crow followed them up the log, growing as they grew. It feasted on the smallest bugs, its black wings bristling wider with each beakful. The last beetle it snatched up was the size of a cat—and the crow the size of an eagle. Deeper in the wood, a stoat fled an encroaching bramble. The creature's legs lengthened. Soon it seemed a lanky wolf, and then a shaggy pony.

All this mutation came from the blow Kamahl had struck. He leveled his eyes up the narrow way. Even the royal ziggurat was warping. It had become a mountain of tangled wood. Formed of four ancient trees in five tiered terraces, the ziggurat once had lifted hanging gardens above the forest floor. Now the four trunks had nearly fused, and their bough clashed brutally. Foliage choked the one-time gardens, and massive caterpillars gnawed everywhere.

Ten more strides brought Kamahl to the tumulus where he had stabbed Laquatus. The ground had mounded up like an infected boil, but the source of that infection . . .

"Where is Laquatus?" Kamahl paused and stared.

The body and the sword were gone. At the peak of the tumulus opened a narrow hole. He strode to it and looked down a deep black well. It shook violently, the epicenter of the tremors. Kamahl squinted down the shaft. Something glinted there, something unmistakable.

"Mirari."

Kamahl had chased that bauble across the continent. He had been rid of it. To take it back was to doom himself. To leave it was to doom the forest.

Kamahl knelt. He reached down into the shaft. His hand slid easily over the familiar hilt. The Mirari burned feverishly, violently. Kamahl tightened his grip. He took a deep breath. It would be simple. He needed merely to pull it out. One simple move would change everything.

The sword did not move, but something within the sword did. The Mirari beckoned. It would end these torments and make all those unhealing wounds inconsequential. He needed only to draw the sword and Kamahl would transcend all that was trivial.

His hand tightened. It was best for the forest and best for him.

Kamahl released his hold. He drew his arm from the hole and sat back on his heels. The Mirari reflected his own wishes, the very impulses that had nearly destroyed him. He could not draw the sword so long as he *wanted* to draw it. His heart thundered, and his breath came in rags.

All around, the forest convulsed in torments of growth.

Despite the turmoil within and without, Kamahl calmed his mind. His consciousness sank to inner levels. He sought stillness and the mind at the center of stillness. The forest spoke in inference and impulse, in the running of sap. Only in stillness could Kamahl hear it. He reached a place of such quiet that the forest seemed to roar.

This all had been a test. The forest sought to know his mind about the Mirari sword. It wanted to know if he was truly done with the blade, for the blade was not done with him.

"I am done," said Kamahl, as much to himself as to the wood. "I wish never to touch it again, but I will draw it and break it if it will save the wood."

Take the sword.

Kamahl reached into the hole. His hand settled in its accustomed way around the hilt. The soul of the Mirari trembled. He tightened his fingers. Instead of drawing the blade, though, he was drawn by it.

Kamahl left his body. It seemed a cicada husk crouched above the hole. The contact of skin to metal to root had conveyed his soul into the millennial root bulb. He entered the forest mind.

It was not a consciousness so much as a vast place, the ideal forest. Suffused with plant and creatures, it was vital. Air lived. Ground lived. Water lived. There was no blue sky, for the blazing sun lived immanently—in glowing stamens and fox fire and infinite eyes staring out of darkness. There was no sea except omnipresent dew and ghostly mist. All was forest. All was life.

This was the inner stillness, deeper than meditation, deeper than thought.

Kamahl breathed. Air tingled in his lungs and suffused him. Myriad leaf-shapes filled his eyes, receding upward to white and downward to black. Warm and humid, the forest air clung to him. He wished never to leave.

Yet into that place of utter quiet intruded a single disquieting thought.

"Jeska."

Kamahl suddenly returned to his body. In fact he had never left it. He had not been drawn down into the forest mind but had let the forest mind rise up into him. The quiet place, the ideal forest, was within him. In its stillness, he had gained strength enough to battle legions.

Kamahl stood. He left the sword where it lay. It was too dangerous to draw. He no longer needed it, for his power came from within.

The forest had granted him a great boon. It would keep the sword within a knot-work of roots. Never again would the Mirari decimate a land, and if it made the forest grow bountifully, it was a willing sacrifice.

Kamahl had begun this rampant growth and could not end it, but he would serve the forest as its champion. It had saved him and imbued him with power. Now he must go save another.

"Jeska."

* * * * *

Kamahl reached the forest's edge. He had walked unafraid among plunging boles and spiraling vines, but now, he felt fear.

Beyond a ridge of saw grass lay a nowhere place—a dune desert. It was the utter antithesis of the forest. Nothing lived in it. There was only sand and sky. Once, scrub trees and creosote bushes had clung to the clay soil, but sandstorms from the north had buried them. Only endless and undulating dunes remained beneath a swollen sun. Night would come soon.

It was a place of terrible emptiness, but it lay between Kamahl and his sister.

He had known it would be here. He had provisioned himself with water-root, which would provide both food and drink for his journey. He had fashioned palm leaves into shields against the merciless sun. At his belt hung the shell of a freshwater clam, a tool for digging daytime shelters. He needed but one thing more— a weapon, one that drew on the strength of the living forest.

Kamahl retreated to the tree line. Absently, he raised a hand to a nearby bole, clutched the vine clinging there, and pulled it free. Plucking away the sucker stalks, he rendered the vine into a long whip. He lashed it once experimentally. The tip whistled angrily by, wrapped a sole head of saw grass, and cut it off. Kamahl had learned to use a bullwhip during his weapons training but always had preferred straight steel. No longer. A whip could steal a man's feet without stealing his life. Still, it would not be enough.

Kamahl hunted among the trees, seeking precisely the right staff. He found a likely branch, though it was long dead and as fragile as clay. Another bough proved too short, a third too narrow, a fourth too crooked.

All the while, the blood-red sun sank toward the west. Forest shadows lengthened, and the sea of sand cooled. It was time to set off.

Kamahl drew a long breath and laughed gently. He had been too easily drawn back into the weary ways of time. The sun's swallowing course made no difference to him. Nor did the acquisition of a simple staff. He would set out not because he must, but because he would.

Hands dropping to his sides, Kamahl walked with silent patience toward the desolation. The water-roots rapped gently against one leg and the makeshift whip against the other. His boots pressed deep prints among the saw grass, and then he was out onto the sand. Already, the air felt different around him—dry and unforgiving. With each step, his forest home drew farther back, and solitude sank more strongly over Kamahl.

The chuff of his feet in the grit became a bleak rhythm. Somehow, the desert seemed louder than the forest. Kamahl struggled to find his quiet center, the ideal forest within. His consciousness descended past the sound of night breezes, beneath the argument of thought, and down to that perfect place. A sigh escaped him as his soul settled in.

Something jabbed his foot—hard—and he fell facedown in the sand. Kamahl rolled to his feet, snatched the whip from his belt, and sent it lashing out in an arc where he had passed. The vine snapped angrily in thin air. No one stood nearby. Whistling through its arc, the whip circled back around and landed limply in the sand.

Something had tripped him. Kamahl retraced his steps. A small knob jutted up from the sand. It looked to be a white stone cracked in half, with a flower inside. Kamahl knelt, pulled the shell from his belt, and began to dig. Another small stone appeared, and another—they turned out to be the tough husks of a desert plant. More digging uncovered a whole cluster of the flower pods, and beneath them a thick, stout staff.

Kamahl smiled. It was a century plant—a desert agave that bloomed once every hundred years. It stored up its life essence for a whole century, produced a long, straight shaft, and topped it with a profusion of seed-bearing flowers. The plant had been buried by sandstorms, yet it reached out of them. There could be no more vital weapon for Kamahl.

Bowing his head in thanks, Kamahl reached down into the hole, grasped the pod, and yanked. With agonizing slowness, the shaft eased from the sand. Kamahl had cleared only a foot of it before he had to stop and pant. He grinned through the grit.

What did time matter to him?

The stars appeared and scratched across the sky to midnight. At last, the shaft came clear. Kamahl lifted the sandy thing high—straight, stout, and strong. It would be perfect. Only one final act remained.

Kamahl whirled the shaft, watching as the seeds of the doomed plant leaped away among the stars to plant their life anew.

CHAPTER THREE

UTTER DEFEAT

*I*xidor worked feverishly, but not at his table. His quills and ink sat quiet beside sketches for the next battle—plenty of illusions to keep any foe jumping. Ixidor had put aside paper disks for metal disks—a different sort of image magic.

Crouching beside the fireplace, Ixidor fed three more wax-soaked logs into the blaze. With blackened fingers, he closed his jury-rigged furnace and pumped the bellows. Each breath of air stoked the heat. It radiated through the metal plates and made the river-stone chimney crackle. Ixidor watched in delight as the thin pewter wire resting atop the grate melted away.

He clapped his hands and rubbed them excitedly together. Donning a thick glove, he picked up an iron skillet filled with more pewter—shavings and shards from a cup he had owned—and gingerly slid the skillet into the upper compartment.

"What are you doing?" came a voice behind him

He pivoted, nearly falling, and set his knee down. "Nivea. I didn't know you'd come in."

She stood above him in their small apartment, her arms folded over her chest and one eyebrow lifted. She looked beautiful, as always, but also a little severe as she stared at the smelting process. "I know we're short on coin, but you're not melting down my jewelry again, are you?"

Ixidor spread one hand innocently on his chest and left a black handprint. "You wound me, my dear. I would not rob you of your jewels, though even finest gems look shabby next to your eyes."

Her skepticism only deepened. "What are you up to?"

"Art," he said brusquely, and he turned back to the fireplace.

Nivea dropped her arms from her chest and approached, irritation replaced by curiosity. "Really, what are you doing?"

Still wearing the thick glove, Ixidor drew the hot skillet from its slot in the front grate. The pewter had melted into a thin, smooth pool of metal. Ixidor carried the skillet to his table, where thick pads waited. He set down the molten metal, doffed the glove, and picked up a slender pair of tongs. With them, he plucked a gold coin from the table top and lowered it to rest flat upon the pewter.

"I'm making money. It's a sort of sculpture, really—"

"You're counterfeiting? Here, in Aphetto? Why don't you just cut your throat?"

"Don't be so dramatic," muttered Ixidor. He set another gold coin into the hot metal, this time turning its obverse side downward. "I'm not going to be actually spending the money. It's just security."

"What security is money you can't spend?" asked Nivea.

Ixidor positioned a third coin, and a fourth. "Security for a bet. I'm going to turn ten gold coins into a thousand—lead ones, at any rate, with golden pigment. With solid bets, I'll turn a thousand into a hundred thousand."

Nivea circled around to stare him in the eye. "Why are you doing this?"

Only then did he pause. "How else will we make enough money to quit the pits? How else will we be able to travel to our undreamed land?"

Nivea seemed to stare beyond him, as if over the horizon. Her eyes were haunted. "What happens if the Cabal finds out?"

"They won't find out unless we lose."

"What happens if we lose?"

Ixidor did not answer, only setting another coin into the hardening metal.

* * * * *

It was a match day like any other. Beasts and warriors fought across blood-stained sand. Crowds gawked in avid rings up to the heavens. Bookmakers laid odds. Bets coursed in tortured channels.

Ixidor had placed five different high-stakes wagers, each of which would pay off only if he and Nivea won the match in a certain amount of time or in a certain fashion. Between the prize purse and any single payoff, Ixidor and Nivea would be able to retire from the pits. If they won every bet, they would be set for life.

The partners waited together in the prep pen. Ixidor worked a final fidgety adjustment to his stack of disks. Nivea mentally prepared aven and Order warriors for summoning.

It was a match day like any other, except this time Ixidor and Nivea weren't laughing.

"Make sure we have enough fliers," Ixidor said as he flipped through the disks. "A flier saved us last time."

Nivea's eyes remained on distant places. "A flier that I brought . . ."

"You almost didn't have *any* avens."

Nivea's focus shifted to her partner. "Don't worry about the warriors. They'll be there. Worry about your illusions. You can't fool everybody."

Ixidor scowled, and his chin jutted irritably. "If you're talking about the fake coins, you won't be so critical when we win a fortune."

"I'm not talking about the coins," began Nivea slowly. She started to pace, rubbing her thumbs across gnawed fingernails. "Not *just* the coins. I'm talking about everything. Nothing is real to you, not warriors, not coins, not spells. You make fun of me because I dream about escaping to some faraway place, but you're the one living in a false place, surrounded by illusions. You call it art, but it's just lies."

Ixidor stopped flipping though the images before him. Nivea had struck the truth. She always did. Under her blazing glare, he was defenseless. The bloodthirsty cheers of the crowd gave him an out. "This isn't the time to talk—"

"When is the time?" She gestured over her shoulder at a minotaur warrior crouching beneath a rain of blows. "This may be the only time we have."

"All right. Let's talk. You're so keen on truth. The truth is that you are the reason we're fighting in the pit. If it weren't for you and the fall of your self-righteous people, I'd still be telling fortunes with these cards—"

"Don't turn this on me—"

"You're the reason I'm trying so hard to get us out of the pit—"

"This isn't about me. This is about lies and deceptions—"

"My lies. My deceptions. All right. You knew that when you met me. I was an unabashed charlatan. I read your fortune just to meet you. Now I'm an artist."

"What's the difference?"

"You. You're the difference." He stowed the disks in his jacket pocket and took her hands. "I never liked the world as it was. I never wished to live in reality. I made up worlds that were truer and more beautiful. You are the only *real* thing I ever cared for. Everything else is a lie, but you aren't."

She pulled her hands free and turned away.

The crowd roared.

"The false gold is meant to buy you a real paradise. The false spells are meant to bring about real magic. The lies that I call art are the only way I know to change what is into what should be."

"I know," she said quietly.

"Once we win, I'll give it all up—the illusions, the lies. This is our last deception. If we win, we won't have to lie again."

She glanced over her shoulder, and a weak smile formed on her lips. "Once we win."

The minotaur in the arena went down. The pit thundered with delight.

Ixidor took Nivea in his arms. They could not go into battle this way, divided and shaken. He had to wipe this all away, somehow. "Let's just think of the coins as practice."

"Practice?" She stared, red-eyed, at him.

He nodded deeply. "Yes. Once we have our paradise, we'll need to mint our own coins. I'm thinking your face should grace the coins."

She smiled wryly. "Knowing you, you'll carve one part of me for 'heads' and another part for 'tails.'"

He laughed, and she joined him.

"I thought the reverse side should hold my own profile," Ixidor said grandly, "but perhaps that would make the coins too valuable to spend."

"Too valuable?" she asked, slapping him lightly. "Yes, it would take a lot of gold to depict that chin."

They both laughed and wrapped each other in an embrace. The death bell tolled. They were one again, and only just in time.

The gate to the prep pen swung open. Vermin scuttled across the pit, gulping down small pieces of minotaur and dragging larger scraps away. Other beasts kicked sand over blood trails. The victor, an aged gigantapithicus on a massive chain, exulted in the crowd's ovation. Some of the younger spectators threw tomatoes—sanguine signs of approval—which bathed the beast in red juice and pulp.

Ixidor studied the gory figure. "Are you ready for this?"

Nivea peered at his face as if to memorize it. "What choice do I have?" He turned toward her, and she added, "Yes, I'm ready."

Hand in hand, the undefeated partners strode out the prep pen and into the loud ovation of the crowd. Ixidor held their hands high and gave a brilliant grin. Nivea smiled broadly as well, though the look was forced. It did not seem to matter. The spectators greeted them with redoubled excitement. Here were two winners, two showstoppers.

As Ixidor turned them, gesturing grandly, he felt the old thrill pounding in his heart. This was where they belonged, here before the roaring throng.

The adulation suddenly hushed as the prep pen on the opposite side of the arena slowly opened. Massive hinges voiced their lament, and the gates swung wide. Darkness filled the prep pen, and something moved within. The crowd strained to see.

"Whatever it is," Ixidor said through his stage smile, "it's the last thing we'll have to fight, ever."

Nivea winced slightly as his hand wrung hers.

The thing emerged—a woman, thin, lean, tall, and young. She wore a body-suit of black silk marked across the stomach with a jagged red line. She carried no visible weapons. Her hair was short and spiked, the same color as the suit, and her face, throat, and hands were pale.

The crowd burst into laughter. In their awful silence, they had expected something more ferocious and imposing—an angry bear, a squad of lancers, a necromantic legion—but a single, unarmed, unarmored woman? They jeered her. Who was she to challenge the undefeated duo of Ixidor and Nivea? Who had even heard of this woman, this Phage, before?

Ixidor grinned eagerly. "This may well prove easier than we thought."

Nivea was grim. "Can't we quit now? Can't we be done and walk away paupers?"

He drew her to his side and kissed her. "Come, my love. One last fight and we are done."

The starting bell tolled and laughter died to silence.

Ixidor and Nivea assumed their ready stances. Ixidor drew the disks from his jacket pocket and held them poised before him. Nivea withdrew into her mind and pulled upon the lines of magic she had secured to her warriors. She started her spell, and brave beings slid through the ether toward her.

For her part, the adversary, Phage, stood still, one foot slightly ahead of the other.

"Bring them in. Let's get to this!" Ixidor said.

Nivea shuddered. Her hands flung wide, and she took a step backward. White energy leaped from arms and spine, forming a nexus before her.

Ixidor lifted his first disk and hurled it at the focal point of energy. The disk struck. The nexus broke open, its corners peeling back. Through the extradimensional space charged a contingent of Order warriors. They emerged at a run, their war cries sounding muffled within the breach but welling to full force. Pikes glinted in the charge, arrowing toward the black-silk breast of Phage.

Still she stood, no weapons drawn, no spells forming. She seemed not even to see the charging warriors. Her eyes were as black as a shark's.

Ten warriors emerged, and into their backs Ixidor sent more

disks. Each struck, flashed, and sent a scintillating barrier of armor around the fighter. Ixidor hissed to himself, "It'll be a massacre."

Phage seemed unprepared to meet them. Her hands remained at her sides.

The crowd roared their delight.

The first warrior charged in, pike ramming into Phage's belly. The blade sliced into the silk suit, transfixed her spine, and jutted out her back. Phage did not stagger or scream but only stood as the shaft followed the head right through her body. The warrior continued the charge, his hands ramming through the wound as well and ripping out her back. He kept running beyond her as two more pikes tore into her body.

Still, Phage stood unmoving.

"She sees through the illusion," Ixidor hissed to Nivea.

"How?"

"I don't know. Call off the charge!"

"It's too late!"

Phage's arms, once so still, swept suddenly outward. The charging warriors dissolved into thin air. Phage's hands came down, one to either side, and struck where nothing was. Her fists rose, gripping air and wrenching. Pikes appeared in her grasp. She hurled them—one, two—in rapid succession directly toward Ixidor and Nivea. Even as the shafts flew, trembling with the force of the throw, Phage grasped empty air again. This time, men appeared—the two pikemen whose spears she had taken. Her touch had stripped away their cloaking illusion, and she hurled them before her to the sand.

That was all Ixidor and Nivea had time to see. They fell to their faces, the two pikes whirring by just overhead. Side by side the heavy spears embedded in the wall behind them, their shafts quivering.

"Get up! Here come two more!" Ixidor shouted. He grabbed Nivea's arm, shoved her to her feet, and scrambled after.

A pair of pikes sliced through the air. Their erstwhile wielders spilled on the ground beside the first pikemen, who writhed as if with broken bones. One blade skimmed Nivea's arm, scribing a long red line. The other would have taken Ixidor's head if he hadn't ducked.

The clamor of the crowd was nearly deafening.

Phage dispassionately ripped two more weapons from the air and sent them tearing toward the running pair. She hurled pikemen onto the writhing pile. Only then did Ixidor see that the men did not suffer broken limbs but missing ones. Each had lost an arm. They rolled, gripping their gory shoulders in their remaining hands.

The tableau had distracted Ixidor. He glanced up too late.

A pike angled in to split his head. He hadn't time to dive away. Steel flashed and struck. Ixidor winced. The pike toppled, and its haft smacked against his arm. The weapon dropped to the sand.

Nivea stood smiling. She held another pike. Its blade was notched where it had deflected its mate. "I made a good grab."

"A very good grab." Ixidor snatched up the fallen pike. "Now we've got something to fight with."

"Side by side." The partners advanced, pikes leveled.

Phage did not spare them a glance. Instead, she finished off the remaining warriors, each relinquishing his pike, then his illusory cloak, then his arm. Phage worked with the deadly agility of a black widow. She hurled spear after spear, the blades shrieking as they split the air. The crowd shrieked as well.

Ixidor set his teeth. His pike leaped outward and batted the first spear down into the sand. Nivea's weapon simultaneously downed the next. They struck together for the third and fourth, creating an impenetrable wall of steel. Pikes clanged away from them.

The ovation shook the pit to its core.

"More illusions?" Nivea asked.

"What's the point? She can see through them," answered Ixidor. "More warriors?"

"We've already lost ten friends in this fight. I'll not toss more on the mound."

"You don't need to. We can defeat her, you and I. Together, no one can stand against us," Ixidor said.

Nivea muttered, "What if we must kill her?"

"We'll never have to fight again," Ixidor replied, "and she deserves it. Just look at our friends."

Nivea nodded grimly. The partners advanced.

Phage had stepped away from the mound of dying pikemen but made no move to engage her opponents. She stood, hands at her sides, shark eyes staring beyond them.

"I'll strike first," Ixidor said.

"No, together."

"You've already saved my life," Ixidor insisted. "Let me repay my debt."

Without waiting for her response, he lunged, swinging the pike as if it were a long axe. The head surged down toward Phage with speed enough to split her from skull to navel.

The crowd's cheers dropped to a communal gasp.

With both hands on the haft, Ixidor muscled the blade down toward Phage's brow.

Phage caught the blow in one slender hand. Her grip was implacable. She yanked, as she had done to the other pikemen just before ripping away their arms.

Unlike the pikemen, Ixidor released his hold.

Phage pulled the weapon away, quickly reversed it, and hurled it at Ixidor.

Futilely, he flung himself backward.

Once again, Nivea saved him, her pike intercepting Phage's in midair.

Ixidor crashed to his back on the sand.

The strike cost Nivea everything. While her weapon tangled with the other pike, her back was toward Phage. The silk-garbed woman stepped up behind her and wrapped her in a strange embrace—a killing embrace. From arms, hands, hips, and legs, rot spread onto Nivea's body. It was not mere gangrene but a living virulence that voraciously ate flesh. Gray skin and muscle sloughed from bone, which in turn went to ash.

Nivea flashed one final, desperate look to Ixidor. "Remember me!"

"Nivea!"

Her face rotted away. Her eyes dissolved to nothing. In mere moments, the rot had swept through her hair and down to her toes.

She was gone, utterly gone.

Ixidor meant to fight. He flipped over to rise, to charge, to kill, but his legs wouldn't move. It wasn't cowardice that made him weak. He wished nothing more than to kill or die. It was horror.

One moment, Nivea was there. The next, she was gone. It was as though the world had disappeared beneath Ixidor's feet.

The death bell tolled once. Once for Nivea. An amazed hush filled the stands. Half of the undefeated pair was dead, and the other half was down before the novice.

Clutching the sand, Ixidor raised an animal shriek and struggled to rise, at least to get off his groveling belly. He lurched to his side, to his back, not wanting to grant Phage the victory—

The death bell tolled again, now for Ixidor. He was too late.

The crowd surged to its feet, a thousand fists in the air. The bellow of triumph filled every mouth.

The roar struck Ixidor and curled him like a pill bug. He crouched at last in true surrender.

Nivea was gone. His world was gone.

Carrion vermin swarmed out across the arena. Barbed legs flung sand as they went. They tore into the pile of dismembered warriors.

The bristly beasts swarmed past Ixidor. Some took experimental nips from him but found that blood still ran beneath his skin. He didn't care.

A dementia summoner bounded from a prep pen, her braids flying gladly in the air. She came up beside Phage and bowed deeply to the crowd. A voice above, magically amplified, announced the winner—"Phage, champion of the Cabal by trainer Braids."

Again came that crushing shout. Ixidor crouched beneath it like a man trapped in pelting hail. Everything ceased to exist. Only numbness remained.

* * * * *

They had moved him out of the pit, they must have, but Ixidor could not remember it. He seemed forever to have lain here on the floor of his apartment.

Legs moved past—human legs, booted. Cabal officers ransacked the place. His disks lay in disarray. In one corner, counterfeit coins made a gleaming pile. Ixidor's clothes had been ripped down from hooks and tossed to the floor or seized for payment. Nivea's jewelry—

"No!" Ixidor screamed and lurched up. He got his feet beneath him and glimpsed the gold and jewels. A meaty hand slammed the case closed, and another crashed down on his head.

* * * * *

Again he crouched on his belly in the posture of surrender. This time, though, he was bound hand and foot and gagged and strapped to poles that dragged through sand. Grit covered his skin and scratched his eyes. Squinting against the glare, he saw two giant lizards ahead of him. They lumbered across the hot sand. Harnesses on their backs creaked as they dragged the travois forward. A couple Cabal stewards walked to either side of the beasts, applying sticks to their necks.

Ixidor tried to croak, "Where am I?" but the gag allowed only a moan.

One burly steward glanced back with annoyance and began upbraiding his comrade. An argument ensued, ending only when the other steward retreated, drew a knife, and cut the leather thongs across the travois.

Ixidor tumbled off, hands and feet tied, gag firmly in place. The sand was hot. It burned his face as he flopped against it.

Ahead, the lizards kept up their slogging pace. They dragged the travois away across the dunes.

Ixidor chewed viciously at the gag. His teeth ground together. At last, he bit through and spit out the sodden rag.

"Where am I?" he shouted.

The stewards and their giant lizards were gone.

Ixidor gulped a deep breath. "Nowhere."

CHAPTER FOUR

SIBLING RIVALRY

*O*nce in a previous life, Kamahl had approached Cabal City. It had been the glorious capital of pit fighting, and he had been a barbarian spoiling for a fight. Now Cabal City and Kamahl the Barbarian both were gone.

A new Kamahl approached a new Cabal city: Aphetto. The settlement inhabited a deep, wet canyon carved by a winding river. The waterway was no longer even visible, trickling through black depths two thousand feet below the cliff where Kamahl walked. He made his way along one of many overhangs. Stone shelves jutted above the snaking heart of the canyon. Mists from below draped each level in gray curtains of moss.

Kamahl strode toward the city's main gate, atop the cliff. From it stretched a number of suspension bridges. One led to the upper plateaus at the center of the valley, where royal estates perched. These lofty aeries were joined to each other by rope footpaths, looking like cobwebs. Another bridge led to the wide lower plateaus with their marketplaces and guilds: the city proper. There, all of Aphetto's conventional trades had their homes. A third bridge led in switchback steps to the fighting pits: the city improper. Kamahl would head down that path.

His sister was there, in the pits of Aphetto.

All during his march across the desert, he had known where Jeska was. The forest's power, its stillness, dwelt within him. In his hand, the century stalk became a divining rod. He need merely sweep the staff through the arcs of the compass, and it dragged him toward Jeska. Even now, the staff trembled toward the cliff's edge and eagerly pounded the ground. Jeska was below.

"Patience," he told the staff. It was a word unknown to him before that morning at the tumulus. Its meaning had only deepened during his long trek across the desert.

Ahead, the gates of Aphetto towered atop the cliff. Horns jutted from the archway, and spikes lined both portcullises below. A full garrison of soldiers manned it. Along the main road stretched a line of folk seeking entry.

Kamahl got in line with the others. He did not wear his armor, nor did he carry his sword. Even his wolfskin cloak was in tatters. Still, with tawny skin and massive physique, his profession seemed clear.

"Another jack," muttered an elderly woman to her mule. They seemed long-time companions. Their hair was the same gray-brown, bristly and bunched, and their shoulders had a similar stoop. They snorted simultaneously.

Kamahl did not respond to them, though his staff pounded impatiently on the ground.

The woman sighed and hung her head. She waved Kamahl forward. "If you're so impatient, go on."

With stony seriousness, Kamahl replied, "I am not impatient. My staff is."

The old woman brayed a laugh. "So say all men."

Kamahl was about to disagree but instead chuckled. "Yes. So we do." He tightened his grip on the overeager pole. "Still, I will wait."

"Suit yourself," replied the woman as her mule dutifully

plodded up before the archway. A guard captain waited at a podium there.

The man wore Cabal black, and his face had the rumpled look of a dirty pillow. He glanced up from the ledger he kept. "Name?"

"Zagorka."

The man's eyes narrowed to steely slits. "Not the mule's name, yours."

"That *is* my name. The mule is Chester."

Through tight lips, the man murmured, "Chester and Zagorka. Business?"

"Zagorka and Chester," she corrected. "And our only business is being an old woman and an old mule."

The captain's nostrils flared. "You can't bring a pet mule into the city."

"All right, it's a pack mule, in the business of moving my stuff."

"There's a ten silver toll on all pack mules."

Zagorka shook her head and laughed despairingly. "What if he's not my mule but my brother?"

"You must pay the toll."

"Can't an old woman make her way in the world without every young man trying to tax her ass?"

"Pay the toll, or go back."

Zagorka's hands trembled before her as if she was about to grab the Cabal officer by the throat. "Don't you understand? I can't pay the toll, and I can't go back."

"Then there is only one option," the captain said, stepping forward.

His knife flashed, and blood sprayed from Chester's throat. The mule tried one last bray, but air gurgled in the wound. His legs seized up, and he dropped to the path.

"Its meat will be sufficient payment," the officer said.

Kamahl had watched all this, certain Zagorka was a match for anything—but not this. She knelt and wailed over her fallen mule. Kamahl knelt too, and his size made it an ominous motion.

The guard captain drew back and barked orders. Cabal soldiers surged up, swords raking out.

Kamahl ignored them. He wrapped one arm around Zagorka and the other around her mule. His staff cast a long black shadow over the creature. It shuddered its life away, blood forming a red pool across the stones. The rusty hue of other spots told that this was an approved remedy for those who refused the toll. Kamahl had his own remedies.

His hand tightened on the century staff, and he lowered it atop the fallen beast. One corner of his mind dipped down to drink from the myriad trickling pools at the core of his being. The waters of the perfect forest welled up in him. Another corner of his consciousness reached out to this wreck of a creature. Kamahl dipped his fingers in the pool of blood and touched the ragged wound.

"Wake again, noble beast. Wake," he whispered.

Kamahl opened his being, becoming a conduit for the waters of life. They flowed up through him and coursed down his arm and into the beast. Water and blood mingled. The wound ran afresh, but the red flow poured in rather than out. Flesh knit to flesh, and skin closed over meat. The mule's lungs convulsed, pumping blood out its nose and mouth and sucking air in.

Chester bellowed. He struggled up from the dust and blood and shook his ragged pelt to get rid of both.

Despite the foulness, Zagorka wrapped the beast in a glad embrace. "You saw what he did. He raised my beast from the dead!"

"No," Kamahl said quietly. "I am no necromancer. Life lingered, or I would not have been able to awaken him."

The Cabal soldiers had withdrawn to a wary distance, their swords still leveled. The captain managed, "What of the toll?"

"Yes," Kamahl responded. "What of the toll? Aphetto will be richer to have Zagorka within, and me as well. I stake my life on it. Send report to the First that Kamahl, slayer of Chainer, has returned. If the First wishes to exact a toll, he may do so."

The captain's face rumpled uncertainly. "We are to charge our tolls without exception."

Kamahl lifted the century staff in bloody fingers. "Would you like to see my other powers?"

The soldiers backed up again, and the captain shouted at them to clear the way.

Kamahl gestured to Zagorka and Chester, who straightened their necks and walked proudly through the gauntlet of soldiers. Kamahl followed. As they passed into the echoing archway, Zagorka nudged the barbarian's hip.

"You're not just a healer."

"I did not raise him from the dead," Kamahl replied.

"You raised him from something. He's two hands taller than he used to be.

Kamahl stared wonderingly. Indeed, the mule had grown, nearly a foot in height and perhaps a hundred pounds in weight.

* * * * *

Together, Kamahl, Zagorka, and Chester navigated the switchback path from the cliff down to the pits. Each step brought them into a darker, wetter place. They watched the grand noble estates rise on their pinnacles. They saw the marketplaces and guildhalls grow across the wide plateaus below. All was swallowed as they entered a subterranean passage of stalactites and rocky rivers. They spoke little within those passages, the unsteady clomp of

Chester's hooves making racket enough. No one passed them on the way down, though glimpses through the murk showed other folk walking far ahead and far behind.

In time, the way widened into a cold grotto. Stony arches opened to either side. These niches held lighted scenes of great pit fights of the past. The figures looked so real they seemed to be the fighters themselves, preserved by the taxidermist's art.

Ahead came voices, laughter, cheers—the true fights. Kamahl's staff did not draw him that way. It tugged toward a small door on one side of the passage.

"We must part company here," Kamahl said. He lifted an eyebrow. "Surely you don't have business in the pits?"

"Surely I do. What business is there outside the pits, in Aphetto? You don't think I'd come to a pesthole like this just on a lark."

Kamahl crossed his arms over his chest. "What business?"

"The First has put out a call for mule teams," she said, whapping Chester on the side. "That's us. A mule team."

"Why would he possibly want mule teams?" Kamahl wondered aloud.

"Don't know. Don't care. Thanks to you, I got a giant mule team." She nodded. "Take care of yourself, Kamahl. This place eats up nice folks."

"You take care of yourself as well, Zagorka."

She waved off the comment. "Oh, I ain't nice folk." With that, she and Chester clomped toward the sound of cheers and laughter.

Kamahl turned toward the door and the labyrinth beyond. Once he had pursued his friend Chainer through such a tortuous maze. In the end, just before devolving into madness, Chainer had granted Kamahl the Mirari—an act of altruism. Still, many in the Cabal thought Kamahl a murderer. That belief granted him a fearful respect, which proved useful. Kamahl tried the door, but it was bolted.

A slim panel drew back, revealing a pair of yellow-glowing eyes beyond.

"I am Kamahl, slayer of Chainer."

A tremor moved through those eyes. "You are not Kamahl. Kamahl could not have raised a beast from death."

Grimly, Kamahl realized that word of his deed had traveled faster than he. "I am Kamahl, slayer of Chainer and raiser of mules. Let me pass."

"What business have you in the pits?"

"You have my sister, Jeska."

Something like humor played in those lemon eyes. "There is no one here by that name, but you are welcome, slayer of Chainer and raiser of mules, to come see for yourself." Multiple bolts slid back, and the door creaked open to a black passage. "Forgive the darkness. Those who know these ways need no light, and those who do not know them will never need light again."

Kamahl pushed through the doorway. His century staff tugged him eagerly forward, its butt rapping the ground like the cane of a blind man. "She is here," Kamahl said to the door guard. "Send word ahead that I am coming. Anyone who seeks to deter me can expect the fate of Chainer." Kamahl did not wait for a response but strode down the darksome passage behind his pounding staff.

Word *did* precede him. Along the ever-winding, ever-descending way were checkpoints, all of which let him through. Kamahl's threat had not won him passage: The Cabal would not be threatened. They let him believe he bullied his way along because they had some grinning plan underway. They wanted him to go below and find what he would find.

Unerring, the century staff led him past the quarters of dementia summoners, below the practice chambers, beyond the beast pens, and to the slave grotto. It was a long, low cavern segmented into cells. Each held a fighter-slave.

Kamahl reached the grotto's black iron gates, bristling with spikes. There he halted. His staff jittered excitedly, straining toward the cells. "Open, in the name of the slayer of Chainer."

Something arrived. It came with a rush of hair. It landed on the stony ground before him, and Kamahl realized he didn't know where it had come from.

"Braids," he said by way of greeting.

In the dim light of that place, the dementia summoner's scarred face glowed with enthusiasm. "Kamahl. What happened to you?" She sniffed. "You smell like compost."

"Where is Jeska?"

She shrugged, wiry shoulders shoving back her braids. "Dead."

The word made his heart flail. If not for the staff, he might have believed it. "No. She is here. I've walked across forest and desert and into the pit to find her. She is here."

Braids shook her head slowly. "No, I remember quite clearly. Jeska died in the Krosan Forest. She died from your sword. You were too busy killing a merman to save her."

Kamahl tried to step past her and grab the gate.

Braids was too quick. With preternatural power, the little woman spun him aside. "Jeska died in the forest. Someone else was born from her corpse. I took her away and called her Phage. I changed her, retrained her. She is unbeaten and unbeatable."

The facts piled up in Kamahl's mind. Braids had taken Jeska from the forest to the pits and had made her a champion of the Cabal. "I want to speak to . . . this Phage."

Braids laughed. "She's not a talker. She's a fighter. I can't take bets on talk."

"Let me in to see her, or I'll tear down these gates," Kamahl growled.

"You'd die trying," Braids responded. Her black eyes seemed tidal pools, filled with beasts. At a whim, she could call them forth. "You've been allowed this far, Kamahl, but no farther. You're being watched by everyone. Press your luck, and you'll be dead. You can't speak with her."

"Then I will fight her," Kamahl replied. "If she is a fighter, let her fight me. You cannot keep her from me in the pits."

Braids gave a frightening smile. "So clever. I'm glad I didn't have to spell it out for you. We've billed the bout as 'Sibling Rivalry' and scheduled it for the last slot today. Be in the prep pen by midnight, and you'll get to face Phage. You should know that she prefers to fight to the death."

Kamahl turned, heading back up the corridor. "I prefer to fight to the life. Tell Phage I will meet her there."

* * * * *

Kamahl strode through the gates of the prep pen. He entered the sandy arena and looked up at the stands, curving overhead like the inside of an egg. Spectators packed every tier and balcony, and they cheered the return of the barbarian champion. Kamahl was a living legend, a victor who gave a good show. The folk had endured countless lesser matches in anticipation of this grudge match, this blood feud. The ovation pounded him like a downpour. He made his way through the shouts to stand in the center of the pit.

Kamahl carried only his century staff and willow whip as weapons. He wore only his travel armor, with tattered wolf skin from shoulder to waist and light plate from waist to knees. His truest defense would be the place of stillness in his soul. His truest weapon would be questions for his sister: What has happened to you? Who has done this? Will you come away with me?

The crowd noise became a veritable gale.

Jeska's gate had swung open. She emerged—a coagulation of darkness. Black silk covered her from knuckles to toes. A crimson lightning bolt sketched across her belly. On some level, Kamahl knew he ought to recognize that emblem, but he did recognize her—spiked black hair standing above a pallid face.

It was Jeska.

The pit shook with the screams of the crowd. Through the deafening roar, Jeska walked, as poised as a cat.

Kamahl watched her with outward eyes. Inwardly he sought his core of calm. It had saved him from jackals in the desert and had allowed him to heal the mule. It would empower him to save his sister. He breathed from that inward place, and the breath of the perfect forest spread through him.

The start bell tolled.

The woman in black made no move. She neither lifted her hands to cast spells nor crouched in a ready stance.

Kamahl mirrored her quiet posture. He only stood, clutching the century staff. A few derisive hoots twisted down from above, but otherwise all was still.

"It is I, Kamahl. Your brother."

She hurled herself at him, hands lashing.

Without shifting his stance, Kamahl raised the staff. Grasping it in both fists, he sent the verdant power of the forest into the wood. The staff moved with the lissome grace of a dragonfly, there one moment and gone the next. Too fast to see, one end caught and bashed Jeska's first strike. The other whirled inward to strike her in the gut and shove her back.

Jeska took a great bound away. Never before had an opponent

been able to avoid her attack, let alone throw her off. She landed lightly on her feet and circled like a leopard.

The two ends of the staff moldered, blackened to rot by the mere touch of her skin. Kamahl eyed the corruption. The staff's aura told him of the corruption that lay deep within her, a well of despair.

While she circled, Kamahl pivoted calmly, keeping her before him. He took another breath of the perfect air. "Jeska. Don't you know me?"

Mention of her name made her snarl. Phage vaulted across the arena, throwing sand in her wake. Where she crossed an old blotch of blood, black footprints remained. Phage leaped toward him, hands and feet foremost.

Kamahl swung the staff. It seemed as light as a reed, as quick as light. It struck her side and thrust her away.

Jeska came down in a roll. She crossed half the arena before jumping to her feet.

Jeers resonated through the pit. This wasn't blood sport. Only one combatant sought to kill. This was a boy setting his hand on his little sister's forehead while she swung at him.

Even Braids was angry, howling on the sidelines. Dark figures streamed from the dementia summoner's eyes. They crossed the sands and sank into her champion.

Kamahl ignored all the noise. While he fought his sister in this hell, his feet were grounded in paradise. "I don't want to harm you," he said soothingly. "I came to bring you back. Come with me, Sister."

She charged him. Black enchantments trailed her as she went. Her legs were fast on the sand, snapping like the blades of shears.

Kamahl drew upon the inner quiet and planted the butt of his staff.

Jeska bounded toward him.

He flung his feet into the air. Instead of hitting him, she hit the staff. Any other polearm would have snapped under the impact and rotted away a moment later, but the power of the wilderness filled the century stalk. It hurled Jeska back on her hands and haunches.

Kamahl came down beside her, staff yet in hand and robes unruffled. He extended a hand to his sister.

She panted on the ground nearby. No longer was she circling, no longer prowling. Her dark eyes fixed on him. Perhaps she would listen at last

"What happened to you? Why do you fight this way? Who did this to you?"

Each question seemed a blow to her belly, but her eyes never left her brother's. She rose slowly. Sand fell from the silks. She absently brushed the red thunderbolt on her stomach. Her muscles were calm, her pallid face impassive.

"Just answer me," he said.

Jeska took a step toward him, well within his guard.

It didn't matter. The forest had given him sufficient strength and speed to deflect any blow.

Very deliberately, Jeska took her forefinger and sketched it across the lightning bolt on her midriff. Raising her hand, she extended it toward Kamahl's stomach. With the gentlest touch, she drew her fingertip in a jag across his flesh.

A slim black line followed her touch. It clove through his skin and spread out foul tendrils. The wound opened and oozed. It ate inward with indescribable pain.

Jeska stepped back, her face still dispassionate.

Kamahl could not stand. He doubled over around the gangrenous wound. It would have killed any other man. Kamahl survived only by marshaling the woodland power within him. Still, he could only stop the advance of the corruption. He could not heal the wound.

As he fell to his knees, Kamahl understood. The jagged red line on her suit represented the unhealing wound on her belly. He had cut her there, and now she had cut him. She had answered all his questions: What happened to you? Why do you fight this way? Who did this to you?

You! You! You!

He had done this to her. He had driven her to this.

Her shadow lengthened across the sand. She approached to finish him off.

Kamahl was never sure whether it was mercy or torment that the death bell tolled for him. The match was done.

The crowd responded with cheers and jeers in equal measure, disappointed with the bland show.

Kamahl could not even look up at her. She was right. He had done this to her. He lay on his face as her shadow retreated across the bloody sand.

"I will return for you, Jeska," he vowed quietly. "I will return to save you."

CHAPTER FIVE

HER TOUCH

*P*hage sat in her cell, her home.

The violence of the day was gone. Only this sweet stillness remained. Her muscles ached from the bout with Kamahl, but her skin remained ever ready to corrupt. She was at her most virulent now, bare but for the black silk robe given her by the Cabal patriarch.

She could not wear most fabrics. Her skin simply rotted cotton or flax or wool. Leather putrefied instantaneously. Anything that lived or once had lived could not withstand her touch. She had to sit on iron, to sleep on stone. Of all fabrics, only silk could survive, for life had never been in it. It was comfortable and beautiful, stronger than steel but thin enough to let her deadliness sieve through.

Phage was a weapon, the First's weapon, and these silks were her sheaths.

Phage's fighting suit hung from hooks worked directly into the bars. Some prisoners killed themselves on those hooks. It was the reason they were part of every cell. A suicidal fighter made for bad shows, and occasionally for costly upsets. The First wanted only warriors with fight in them. Besides, Phage was not his prisoner.

This cell was all she could want. The cool of the cave walls salved her burning skin. The shuffling of fighters nearby provided all the entertainment she needed. These bars were walls enough. Phage decorated them with her memories.

Kamahl lay on his face. His burly shoulders, which once had borne the weight of a nation, were grounded in sand. His hands clutched the suppurating black wound across his belly.

She lay facedown not in sand but gravel and gripped a red wound across her own stomach. She bled and wept into the craggy face of the Pardic Mountains. Her assailant held high his sword and shrieked in triumph.

Her brother.

The visions drained through the black bars like sewage through a grate.

Jeska clutched the wound, and the wound clutched her, and Kamahl clutched her, and the sword clutched him. He carried her across half the continent. From mountain to forest he carried her. It was his penance. Perhaps it healed him, but it did not heal her. She was dying slowly. Why had he struck her the coward's blow, in the belly? Why had he hurt but not slain? Did he hate her so much?

Betrayal. He had left her with beastmen—centaurs and mantis folk—had claimed another victim with his sword while she had died.

She had died.

Sewage down a drain.

Phage breathed deeply and watched the gray curl of her breath roll out in the black air. She was home. Silk and iron, stone and memory, she was home.

There came a glimmer of gold among the black bars. Braids was on her way. Savior, master, friend—Braids was always welcome, no more obtrusive than dream. A dementia summoner, she was half dream herself.

Braids passed along the bars. She seemed to skip, but how could a killer skip? How could she carry the tray of food? Braids always seemed that way to Phage, a stark ambivalence—two conflicting truths overlaid. Old and young. Scarred and beautiful. Evil and good. Idiotic and brilliant. Killer and savior.

Jeska lay on her belly in the forest, dying. Seton could do nothing for her. He bent above her, his simian face rumpled in concern, his fingers feeling her life flee away. Braids came skipping. Her feet poked down like knives. She did something that killed Seton and saved Jeska. Just as she died, he died. Just as her soul fled, his soul shifted into her. Braids did something that killed and saved.

The bars swung open, and Phage lay on her face on the stone.

"Oh, sweet girl," said Braids, delight in her girlish voice, "you know you don't have to bow."

"I know," Phage murmured to the stony floor, though she knew she would bow every time.

"We're girlfriends. Remember that."

Phage nodded.

"You can get up now, little sister."

Phage rose. The cold moisture of the stone floor lingered in the silk. Steam coiled up from her robe.

Braids smiled a smile that had been crooked even before knives has split it twice. She lifted a platter that held a plate of raw meat. "I brought your supper." Braids believed in raw meat for all her fighters—to whet the appetite.

Phage stared at the gleaming pile of meat and slowly shook her head.

"Don't worry," Braids said comfortingly. She lifted a complex silver utensil from beside the plate. "I've made more modifications. The retractors are wider and more curved. They'll hold your lips back while the fork slides the meat in." Braids's last design had been insufficient, and the meat had rotted before it reached

her teeth. Only Phage's internal membranes did not bring putrefaction. Braids squeezed the utensil, causing the retractors to
widen and the tines to plunge through. "Feel game?" She speared
a bit of meat.

Phage settled resignedly into her iron seat.

Braids swooped forward, setting the platter on the floor and
kneeling before her champion. Eyes sparking avidly, Braids
relaxed her grip. The red gobbet withdrew between closing retractors. She set the device to Phage's lips and gently squeezed. Her
lips were forced outward. The meat jabbed between her teeth. It
settled, still warm, on her tongue. The fork withdrew. The retractors closed.

Braids smiled. "I think we've worked it out. No more rot."

Chewing quietly, Phage nodded.

"You fought well today, little sister," said Braids as she
absently skewered another hunk of meat. She twirled it to keep a
drip from falling away. "Aggressively. Like never before."

"I fought my brother—"

Braids's utensil interrupted the words, forcing Phage's lips
back. "He's not your brother. He was Jeska's brother, not yours."

"Jeska is dead," answered Phage as she had been taught. *Her
corpse lay there amid the weeds, dead hands clutching her dead
belly. She had been taught to remember standing outside her
corpse and looking down at it.*

"Why are you holding your stomach?" Braids asked.

Phage released her grip. "I'm not hungry—"

"It's not that," Braids said as she inserted another morsel.
"Open your robe."

Phage did, revealing the jagged scar sewn closed with black
stitches.

"Jeska had a wound there. A killing wound. You have a scar.
It's completely different."

"I'm completely different." Phage pulled the silk back around her waist.

Braids intently watched her. One eye glowed with love, the other with hate. "You are different. Completely." She blinked, and only compassion remained. "The First has plans for you, little sister."

He stood there beneath the oil painting of himself, and Jeska was unsure which looked more alive. The First's skin was as gray and smooth as stone. He wore robes of black hide, gleaming with oil to keep them supple, and a tall black miter. Eight attendants accompanied him, wearing the Cabal's livery of hand and skull. He touched no one, for his touch could kill. Only his hand servants touched for him, and his skull servants did the bidding of his mind. She had known she would be sick in his presence, and she was, and the hand servants cleaned it up. She had not known he would invite her into his killing embrace. It stung. It blistered. It burned, but she did not die. She was different. Completely.

"He has plans for me?" Phage asked, feeling still that stunning, killing touch.

"Yes. He wants to see you."

"When?"

Braids positioned the utensil between her lips and squeezed. A too-large hunk of meat shoved between the widening retractors. Though most of it cleared her teeth, the juices that dribbled from it turned rancid on her lips. "As soon as you are done eating."

Chewing, swallowing, Phage pushed the plate away with her toe. Immediately, the meat turned gray and then mottled white and black, with maggots crawling through it. "I am done."

"You've always been different, little sister," Braids said, "since before I made you."

Phage marched across the desert, feeling the occasional goad of a stick in her side. Braids drove her like a skinner driving a mule. "You didn't make me," she said absently. *Phage was else-where, feeling the jab of a worse goad, an iron bar tipped in jagged glass, and she fell in the arena sands beneath the gloating smile of Braids.* "*He* made me."

Braids's face hardened. "Kamahl did not make you. He killed you."

"No, not *him.*" *Those killing arms wrapped around her.* "The First made me." At last, Phage had caught Braids short, with nothing to say. "Did he think I would die when he embraced me? Was it an execution? Or did he think I would become . . . what I am?"

"You have always been different."

* * * * *

Phage and Braids stood side by side in the dark antechamber. The walls were soot-black, papered in black vellum and hung with gold-gilded portraits. Fat candles on silver sticks glowed solemnly beside glass doors. The women had come straightaway. They had been waiting for more than an hour.

Phage stood unmoving in her black silk suit—tall, straight, and imperturbable. She was not confined to the present time and space but wandered the whole of her life. Whether surrounded by iron bars or silver candlesticks, she conversed with memories.

Braids was fit to be tied. Short, crooked, irate, she clutched arms across her chest to keep from cracking her knuckles. One leg jittered impatiently, and her teeth skirled slowly across each other. Still, her composure was admirable, given that her mind was turning back flips.

The glass doors parted and swung inward. Two glaze-eyed attendants appeared in the space, stooping just slightly as they conveyed the doors to rest against the antechamber's walls. The emblem of a yellow hand showed on their chests. The First had many hands—all those in the Cabal were his hands—but these servants physically touched and grasped for him. One stood to either side, bowed, and motioned the two women into the inner sanctum.

Level-eyed, Phage strode forward.

Braids snorted and took a hitch step to catch up to her.

They passed between the attendants, who swung the doors closed behind them. Braids eyed them suspiciously. In the fall of Cabal City, the First had lost his hand servants and had lived for a time as a social amputee. Eventually, he had gained new hands, this time making sure they were hands that could kill.

The servants followed Braids and Phage into a room that was cavernous, though it felt small. Black walls, deep carpet, dark portraits like cave mouths to either side, polished mahogany tables, thick-embroidered seats, and candles that seemed to rob the room of light and warmth—all shrank the space. The presence of the man on the other side made it claustrophobic.

The First stood staring at them. His eyes were like obsidian, and his face was like limestone. He did not move beneath the portrait of himself. His black robes were utterly still. To either side stood more attendants, eyes downcast.

Braids clenched her fists, warring with the nauseous aura that surrounded the man. Her eyes streamed. She trembled and repeatedly swallowed. A brief lurch in her stomach ended with a gulp.

Phage had felt it too the first time she had entered his presence. Not now. She was accustomed to his dread aura. Her own skin emitted it.

The First moved, spreading his arms. Two of his hand attendants stepped toward the two women, but he stopped them with a simple "no." During any other audience, the hand attendants performed every manual task for the First, but not when Phage came calling.

She understood. Like called to like. She walked steadily toward him. A small smile came to his lips and to hers. She opened her arms as well. They two, who could not touch any whom they would not kill—they could touch one another. It was an extravagant intimacy in their utterly solitary lives. They embraced. Death battled death. Skin poisoned skin. They felt the physical press of another being and were in that moment as father and daughter. Still, they were not the same. Phage's body burned with inner fire while the First's was unutterably cold.

The embrace ended. The small smiles that had begun it were lost in soured expressions.

Phage wasn't sure whether she regretted the hug or regretted its ending. She stepped back but lingered near the man.

"Phage," he said simply. He shook his head. "Phage, whose secret name is Jeska. Welcome."

"The Cabal is here," she replied ritually.

"The Cabal is everywhere," the First answered. Without moving his eyes from Phage, he said, "Braids, whose secret name is Garra, welcome."

"The Cabal is here," Braids said, bowing.

"Yes, we know, little daughter," was the unusual reply. The First took a step forward, and his attendants moved with him as if they were a living robe. "Oh, do not look chagrined, Garra. I owe you a great debt for finding and healing this one. At first I was displeased to see the sister of Kamahl in my chambers." He flicked a glance at Phage. "Yes, I had meant to kill you in these arms. Sometimes death holds a delightful surprise." He took another step, bringing his retinue along. "An execution became a birthing. An enemy became a daughter."

He lifted his hands upward—gray and stony, like the hands of a statue. "Here is the power of the Cabal, the embrace of death. None can kill death. None can kill us, yet our power limits us." He stopped before Phage and seemed to consider. "Tell me, little daughter, why do we run these games in the pits?"

Phage ran her finger along Kamahl's stomach, bringing corruption. "It is the embrace of death. None can kill death. None can kill us."

Fondly, the First patted her cheek. "You have listened well, but you're too dogmatic. This is a pragmatic question. Garra still has something to teach you."

Braids simultaneously smiled and flushed. She blurted, "We run the pits for money."

"Precisely, little daughter," the First said. "Blood sport is for money. Money is for power. Power is the currency of hearts. The more blood sports we arrange, the more money we make. The more money we make, the more power we wield. The more power we wield, the more hearts we rule. We run the games for dominion—nothing less."

Phage nodded, memorizing that utterance as if it were a holy credo.

"We rule hearts, Jeska, not rot. How can we rule a heart that we rot away to nothing?"

"We cannot," she answered.

The First smiled. "I have plans for you."

He turned his back to them for the first time. Bringing hands up, he gestured toward his portrait on the far wall—a full-length, larger-than-life oil painting. Two of his hand servants retrieved a set of stairs that had waited in one dark corner and positioned them in front of the portrait. The First glided slowly toward the stairs, all the while seeming to grow smaller as the painting expanded.

"We have grown too poisonous here in our trickling pit. What hearts can we gather in a place so dark and deadly? Only dark and deadly hearts. Cutthroats, cutpurses, and guttersnipes; barbarians, beasts, and bastards. They bring precious little money with them, and each has an elaborate scheme for doubling or trebling it. It is hard to deprive them of their coin and harder to reap hearts among folk who have none. Fruitless. Pointless. We have become too poisonous.

"No. We need a new vision. I want to draw in everyone, not just the dregs. I want the purest hearts, the youngest and sweetest. I want the least guarded purses. I want the world to come to our blood sports, to be entertained, to be trained and taught, to be rectified and transformed. I want arena combat to become the center of every community, the ground of all being."

Phage had not felt nausea at the man's presence, but she felt it now as she glimpsed his vision. A suffocating terror took hold of her at the first inkling of what he had planned and the fact that she was to bring it into being.

"We need a new vision," he repeated, hands lifted as if in praise of his portrait. He took a step up the stairs, and another, and a third. His raised hands pierced the black canvas before him and jutted through. A fourth step, and the First pressed his face through the portrait. What had seemed oil paint shifted around him, allowing him to pass. He disappeared into the enchanted portrait.

His servants startled. The two skull attendants leaped for the stairs and bounded up after their master. They ran headlong into a solid painting on a solid wall. Eyes spun in their faces as they staggered back.

From beyond the portrait came a dry laugh, and the voice of the First. "Only one may pass." A hand servitor climbed the steps and gingerly prodded the canvas, but it did not give. The First spoke again. "I have been waiting a long while for one such as you, little daughter. Come."

Trembling, Phage approached the stairs.

His arms had meant to kill her, so tightly they held her. When she didn't die, they held her tighter still.

Phage ascended toward the looming image of the First. Her hands rose as if in praise. Her fingertips clove through the fabric. Oil and canvas parted from her killing touch. She stepped again, and her face buried itself in his painted stomach. She pressed through to a place of deep darkness and great cold.

This was not a room sketched out in crude physical dimensions. The height, width, and depth of this space were magic functions. Time was a vector of sorcery. Phage did not exist here within her poisonous form but rather as a focused intentionality. She felt like a will-o'-the-wisp, a drifting point of light above primordial waters. The First occupied a similar aspect, and for a time the two lights only spun in orbits about each other.

Then, the peaty waters beneath them gathered and coalesced. Something formed. A low archipelago of islands emerged from the swamp, with a wide, low parkland at its center.

You will bring a new arena into being. You will build it in the swamps at the center of the world. On the large island, a great coliseum took shape. Across the smaller islands, roads and bridges converged in a vast web on that central place. *It will be clean, bright, and safe, and best of all—cheap. So too will be the matches you schedule—bloodless duels, battle reenactments, ocean combats, gladiatorial games, animal races. With them, you will draw all the world into our web, you will draw their open purses and untarnished hearts. Once we have them, we will have it all.*

It was never wise to speak to the First without invitation, but she and he were the same, motes of light streaming about each other above a vaporous vision. *You would conquer the world with entertainments?*

The First paused, as if startled by her umbrage. In a moment, he answered gladly, *We will draw them in with entertainment, but the fights must become more. You will schedule battles to the death, yes, but only between condemned killers, and they will be offered not as entertainment, but as object lessons in morality. The people will slowly come to see the arena as the place where ultimate justice is meted out.*

This time, she did not question, but only said, *Yes.*

It will be a simple thing to schedule grudge matches between folk who have a common grievance. The level of violence, of lethality, will be commensurate with the gravity of the offense. Border disputes will be to first blood. Cuckolds will be to maiming. Wrongful death will be to death. You will encourage all folk to settle their conflicts in the arena, not in the streets like dogs. You will allow them to hire gladiators to represent them. Once again, such matches will not be called entertainment, but trials of justice.

Yes.

You will teach the people to come to us for entertainment, for morality, for justice, for community, for meaning, for purpose, for life. You will train them in this great coliseum, and you will build arenas at the heart of every city and town. You will move us from the pits to the center of civilization.

Even without a body, she could still tremble. *Yes.*

The vision was complete. The future had been laid indelibly into the lines of her soul. She would bring this new world into being.

While you build this new spectacle, I shall destroy an old one.

In the primordial waters, Phage thought she glimpsed her brother, struggling away across a sandy waste. *He must die?*

Only one man in the world could take you from me, Phage. Soon, no man can.

The motes twined about each other in one final swift dance before they parted, retreated, solidified into clumsy bodies staggering out through the larger-than-life portrait of the First.

* * * * *

They followed him from his private chambers, they who knew his mind about most things and they who were his hands. The servants of the First had packed a bag for him—armor, weapons, rations—and had cleaned the sword he had not wielded since he was a fighting mage. It was as if the First were marching to war, but he did not reveal his mind to them.

The First strode to the glass doors, and his servants followed, holding pack and weapon belt ready. The First paused. Servants gingerly cinched the weapon belt on his waist and positioned the pack on his back. They all wished to ask him where he went, but none dared. With a silent nod, the master of the Cabal strode alone out the glass doors. He left his servants behind.

What terrible business would require the First to use his own hands?

CHAPTER SIX

VISION'S FUGITIVE

Sun struck the sand like a mallet on a drum, continuous and thundering. Wind roamed the dunes, tearing apart anything it found.

It found Ixidor. As he trudged, grit gnawed his sandals to strips and heat blistered his feet until the water within boiled. His burnt brow was scaled with salt, and his muscles were so dry they rasped in his skin. Instead of eyes, he had dead hunks of glass in his skull.

He had lost the one thing worth looking at: Nivea.

She appeared as she had throughout a day and a night and a day—white and gleaming, with arms wide open. She was not in that burning desert. Nivea stood beyond the sands, her feet grounded amid grass. She stood in a beautiful place, and she invited him to join her.

Ixidor clambered toward the vision, but she retreated, her eyes clouding.

Don't weep, my sweet, he said, though his breath made no sound in his dry throat. Don't weep for me. I will join you. I will run across this desert and catch you and join you.

There was only one way to join her. His body could not pass that shimmering portal. Only when it was torn away could he be with her. Sand and sun were his allies, picking at his flesh with small hands, the fingers of Phage.

Phage. She stalked the corners of Ixidor's mind, pursuing his visions. She closed in on her quarry and leapt. Her hands took hold of Nivea. Light turned to darkness and life to rot. Once again, Nivea dissolved to nothing.

She had died a thousand times during the day and night and day. Each time, grief ripped into Ixidor anew. He watched his only hope dissolve into blinding tan below and blinding blue above.

Eyes of glass reflected the razor horizon.

Ixidor trudged. He would die; it was a certainty. The Cabal was very efficient. He would die and join Nivea, but only after every tissue flaked away and every hope fled into the killing sky. He would die by degrees, a penance for letting Nivea die in an instant.

In truth, he would die slowly because he could not give up life. The survival instinct was stronger than the blazing sun and the winnowing grit. Even without hope, he walked on.

And then, hope: a green spot in all that gray. Water, plants, life.

It was a mirage, of course, like the others. Still, false hope was better than no hope. It drew Ixidor, and he strode toward it.

If this oasis were a mirage, why need it be a small, mean place? Why not something grand? Ixidor squinted. Why not date palms and coconut trees? Those slender slips of tan along the edge—why shouldn't they be gazelles? What about a wide pool—pure, clean, and charged with fish?

Ixidor tried to take a deep breath, though his lungs felt fused. He walked faster. His legs crackled like stilts. Closing his eyes, he imagined the oasis, willing it on the world.

Why not paradise? Why not life?

He opened his eyes. It was gone—not only his vision of palms and pools, but even the green wedge. It all had been but a fold in the air, a trick of the heat.

Ixidor shuffled to a halt. There was no reason to go on. He wondered how far he had come and looked back across the ridges of sand. His footprints stretched away over two dunes. A breeze had followed him, erasing his steps as he made them. Even now, a dozen tracks drifted in a brown ghost on the wind. It was as if he had gone no distance at all. The desert was an endless scroll, rolling out before him and rolling up behind.

Ixidor dropped down to sit on the sand. It burned his backside. He didn't care, waiting for the pain to ease. He needn't march himself to death. He could simply sit himself to death.

How long he remained there, he wasn't sure. He might have slept. Orange sand and blue sky began to tumble over each other. Shapes appeared in the heavens—leviathans swimming amid faint stars. They dived toward Ixidor. He did not cower away. A pod of kraken flew past his ears. Their tentacles spread and closed to propel them over the sand. They left snaking trails of dust in their wakes but were not fast enough. The leviathans jabbed down. They bit, caught, killed, ate, and swam back to the stars. Only thin red trails told of their passing.

When Ixidor awoke, one side of the world had turned dark. A wall of black cloud boiled up out of thin air: a desert thunderstorm. It held the promise of rain and shade and cool. It would wash him, slake his thirst, would fill hidden wadis and lead him where the water went. Salvation was coming from the brutal skies.

Ixidor sat and waited. He smiled, knowing it would all be over soon.

The storm galloped across the desert, darkening as it ate ground. In its heights, leviathans sported and swam. Kraken and jellyfish twirled their helpless tentacles in the eddies while schools of silvery fish churned the squall nearer to Ixidor. It was very close. He heard it—moaning wind and rumbling thunder—though sound only barely outpaced the racing thing. Droplets came down with dry, crackling reports.

Then Ixidor knew: This was no rain cloud but a dust storm. The only promise it held was death.

Still, he sat. It would be over soon.

The storm billowed like a brown curtain across the dunes. It rushed upon him. The last of his footprints were snuffed out. The wall struck him.

He could not keep his eyes open. Lids and lips clenched. Head curled down. Even though he knew he would die and meant to die, the survival instinct was strong. He lifted his collar up over the bridge of his nose, and his breath felt cold against his chest.

The storm roared until it filled his ears with sand. The wind battered him numb. He tried to shift, but already his legs were buried. It wouldn't be long now. He was dying by the slow murder of particles.

Nivea, you came to me while I fought to live. Come to me now as I fight to die. Bring your brilliant vision and wide-open arms. Ixidor's voice made no sound in the sandy space between his shirt and his chest. Still, she should hear. He spoke the words beside his very heart. *The dust eats me as Phage ate you, and we will be together.*

She did not come. No light pierced the dust. No voice came except the roaring wind. The only hand that clasped his was a hand of sand.

He was buried to the waist.

I don't want to die. Why not live?

Ixidor struggled to rise. The sand held him down. He dragged his arms from the entombing ground and dug around his sides. Each handful he scooped only slid back. His legs trembled to escape. The sky poured more grains atop him, inches piling up every moment. He desperately fought to break free, but the storm was equally desperate to kill him. His collar slipped down off his nose, and the breath he took clawed through his lungs.

That was it. He had to stop digging to pull his shirt up, and then coughed blood while the sand filled in around him. From chest downward, it clutched him in a giant hand. Sand rose like flood waters and swallowed him to the shoulders. It poured down until only the crown of his head remained, then that too was gone.

All grew strangely quiet except for the fast panting of his breath. The air in his shirt was stale. How deeply would he be buried?

Nivea, listen. I will join you, yes, but not now, not yet. Save me. Dig me free. Come, my angel, and save me.

He willed light into darkness, life into death. He willed Nivea into being and made her come and save him. If it was all a dream, it might as well be a grand one.

Nivea came to him with angel wings that sang as she flew.

She glowed last in his mind before nothing glowed there again.

* * * * *

Ixidor awoke beneath a sky riddled with stars. The air was cold, but the sand breathed heat all around him. He sighed. He could breathe. The sand was gone from lips, ears, and eyes. He lay cradled in the lap of the desert.

What had happened? What of the storm? He had been buried alive.

Ixidor sat up. By starlight, he could see dunes undulating to a distant horizon. He also could make out, near his leg, the deep well in which he had been entombed. The sand retained the shape of his body.

Someone had dug him out.

"Hello!" He could speak—even shout. "Hello!" There came no answer from the dark desert. Who would have dug him out, cleaned him up, and left him lying here?

"Nivea!" Ixidor stood, a smile spreading across cracked lips. "Where are you? I know you're here." He laughed, holding his hands up. "I know you're here. Nivea, come to me. You've given me life. You could have taken my life and brought me to be where you are but instead you saved me." He laughed again.

The sound was eaten by the vast darkness.

Ixidor quieted. He wasn't saved yet. If Nivea had dug him from the sand, she had only brought him from a swift death to a slow one. "Lead me. Lead me from this place to somewhere I can live."

A light flitted nearby, on the periphery of his vision.

Ixidor spun just in time to see the gray form disappear across the sand. Was it Nivea or a phantasm of his tormented mind? "That way. Yes, I will go that way." He walked toward the spot where the ghost had disappeared. The sand beneath his feet felt silken, cool on the surface but as warm as a balm beneath. He could walk this way a long while.

"Show me where to go. Show me where the water is."

The gray figure appeared again, gossamer like a woman swathed in veils. The form shrank, not so much retreating but dissolving inward. His own voice echoed back to him: Show me where to go. Show me where the water is.

The request was ardent. Where was water? He was done with date palms and gazelles. Where there was water, he would find all the rest.

"Where?" His ghost guide was gone. "Where?"

Ixidor pivoted slowly, eyes scanning the desert. Beneath a billion stars, the sands were not so forbidding. The heat-folds were gone from the air. He saw dimly but saw true.

In the gentle weave of sandy hills, there was a single irregularity—a place where the warp and weft of wind had laid bare a long narrow ribbon. Shadows clung strangely to that spot, perhaps only the crouching shoulders of nearby dunes, but perhaps something solid. A long, narrow ribbon—

"There. The water is there," Ixidor said, his finger jabbing before him. His eyes marked the spot. "Water."

The apparition appeared again before him. She flitted across the hills toward the distant oasis. She seemed almost to dance now, glad he neared.

Ixidor suddenly understood. It didn't matter whether the figure was real or phantasm, savior or muse, as long as it inspired him to save himself.

Come, my love, come to our undreamed land.

Ixidor walked. His eyes were trained on that jumble of shadows and his heart on that dancing ghost.

She smiled and laughed. Her arms opened to receive him and closed to spin atop the sands. Her feet marked out his path.

I needed Nivea and brought her back from death. If I can do that, I can bring water into being.

It grew nearer, the undreamed land. He kept to the ridgelines so that he would not lose sight of the spot. His mind shaped the shadows into a palm forest. His thoughts dug out a wadi of wet clay.

"Just there is a cool curve where the water rushes, and that is a pool, deep and clean. Palms lean there and there, and off on that side is a cave into rock, where the river runs." He stared them into being.

Reality is unkind to dream. As Ixidor approached, the shadows told a different tale. The curve where the water should have rushed was just a dark bank of sand hollowed out by the caprice of wind. The jangle that should have been a palm forest was only the tangled shadow of a descending dune. The cave mouth was nothing at all.

Ixidor did not stop like last time. He kept striding, driven not by desperation but by anger. How dare the world deny him? How dare this desert resist? It had presented him with death after unacceptable death. Ixidor was furious. He glared at the landscape, eyes reconfiguring it.

That *is* a stream. That *is* a palm. That *is* a cave.

The ghost glided through the scene. In an aura around her, the place was transformed. She brought daylight beauty to the nighttime desert, but the changes did not remain. All of it devolved back into dust.

At last, Ixidor stood in the midst of the illusory spot. It was desolate. No stream, no trees, no pool: Even his muse had given up the ghost. He was alone in nothingness. Only cruel sand and killing wind surrounded him. Still, Ixidor did not sit. Rage stiffened his spine.

He closed his eyes. He imagined individual ripples on the water, touched the damp banks, smelled the waves, and heard their manifold muttering.

Ixidor knelt. He reached out and slid his fingers into the water. Cupping his hands, he drew up a dripping mouthful.

His eyes cracked a moment, and he saw sand filling his grip.

He didn't care. Closing his eyes again, he lifted his hands and poured the drink down his throat. It was cool and clear. It filled his mouth and rolled down his chin. He swallowed. The water sent joy through him. Either he was dying in an ecstasy of delusion, or he was drinking, truly drinking.

Letting fall the last of the water, he sat back on his heels and slowly opened his eyes.

There before him spread the oasis, just as he had imagined it. A stream wove, wide and patient, across a bed of clay. It rushed around a smooth curve. Farther along, palms reached roots down into the water and stretched fronds out above. At the end of a plush palm forest, a cave opened its mouth to swallow the spring.

It was real, all of it—and not just as he hoped it might be. It was real as he knew it must be.

Either that, or he was insane, drinking handfuls of sand.

Did it matter? Live or die, but do it happily.

As he stooped to drink, his muse danced in a circle around him. Together, they were glad in their undreamed land.

CHAPTER SEVEN

ARMIES FOR KAMAHL

*B*attered and bleary, Kamahl left the desert behind. He climbed from sand to the root network of the forest. His boots were in tatters, held together only by the remains of his willow whip. With sandy fingers he gripped the green wood and with trembling arms hauled himself upward. Handprints of fine dust tracked his progress up the forest's head wall. Kamahl clambered to a natural nook in the tangled boles, and there he collapsed.

The onetime barbarian lay on his back and panted. His staff jabbed beneath him, but he didn't care. He would lie here awhile, die here if he needed to, in the womb of the green Mother. At least he would not die in the desolate desert. It was a killing place, endless and empty.

Empty except for the One Who Followed.

Kamahl had glimpsed it only once but constantly sensed the dark presence that tracked him. By day, the follower skulked just beneath the dune crests. By night, the thing had had greater power, spreading its darkling soul through cold black heavens to harry Kamahl. No armor could guard against that presence. It nipped at him like a murder of crows. Kamahl could only clutch his century staff, draw upon its power and his own, and walk until dawn. Some rotten thing had followed him up from the Cabal pits and sought to kill him or drive him mad.

No more. The dark creature would be impotent before the power of the forest. That power now surrounded and suffused Kamahl. Every fatigued muscle relaxed. Surely the follower could not stalk him here, where growth was omnipotent. Flora and fauna advanced upon the very desert. Aerial roots sank into sand and then widened into new boles. Leaves and blossoms proliferated while boughs extended the shadow of the wood. Since Kamahl had last seen the forest, it had gobbled up half a mile of sand. Eventually it would eat it all.

Kamahl was glad. Such places as that desert should not be.

Shaky fingers drew aside the ragged bandage that wrapped his stomach. Beneath lay an unhealing wound, jagged counterpart to the cut on his sister. The wound, the desert, and the follower had conspired to kill him. They had failed.

The Krosan Forest had its own conspirators. Even now, creatures approached. They quietly converged in a wide ring.

How ironic to survive desolation only to be devoured by a crowd.

Kamahl clutched a gnarl of wood, and through galvanic impulse, conveyed his fears. The prayer, if that was what it was, was heard.

The creatures that approached slowed. Their leader stalked silently around to the mouth of the niche. A wicked-headed lance jabbed in, two bulbous eyes hovering above. The spear withdrew, and the mantis-man bowed his head. He spoke the common tongue, but with an uncommon clack.

"Kamahl. You have returned. We had been watching but did not recognize you. You seemed . . . someone else."

A rueful smile spread across Kamahl's face. "It is no wonder." He nodded down toward the wound across his stomach. "You must have sensed this."

The nantuko captain peered down. Above his weird green eyes, antennae moved slowly, tasting the air. He laid down his spear. As lithe as a spider, he ambled into the niche. On rodlike legs, he hovered, studying the cut. "A fresh wound, then?"

"No," Kamahl replied, "not fresh. Ever bleeding, unhealing."

The creature nodded his triangular head. His mouth parts shifted, and he emitted a low whistle. It was a patrol signal—quiet enough to be mistaken for birdsong.

From the tangle of brush, another nantuko emerged. This one bore the pods and blooms of a healer. Medicinal leaves hung in bunches across her thorax. She arrived with the same rapid grace as her captain, eyes studying the wound. All the while, her arms worked at a poultice—cutting, mashing, mixing.

"Take no offense, healer," Kamahl said, "but this wound will not heal. Druidic medicine could not heal my sister, and it will not heal me. Jeska gave me this in repayment of what I did to her. This wound will not be healed until I have brought her back."

The mantis healer nodded. She heard his words, but the chunky poultice she loaded into the wound told that she didn't believe him. "You are a champion of the forest. You cannot succumb."

"I will not succumb." Kamahl's eyes gleamed brightly in his dusty face. " I have crossed the desert with this ever-fresh wound and fought off a fell presence that lurks there even now. I will champion the forest, even with this wound in me."

"Lie still," the healer cautioned. Her claws poked at the leaf pack. "Even if it cannot heal the wound, it will strengthen you. The vital essences of the leaves are seeping into your flesh."

Kamahl stiffened at the bite of the leaves. "Yes. I will lie here awhile; then you will bind this wound again, so that I may march once more."

The healer tilted her angular head. "You only just returned. Where will you head now?"

"To the heart of the forest," Kamahl replied. "Something evil follows, and it will brings greater evils. All of this is of a piece. If I am to slay this thing, I must heal my wound. To heal my wound, I must save my sister. To save her, I must have an army. I go to the heart of the forest to heal, slay, and save . . . to gain my army."

* * * * *

The First stood on a sand ridge and peered toward the Krosan Forest. He waited for dark, when his powers would be greatest. For three nights in succession, he had nearly slain Kamahl. Veiled in death-scent, the First had crept up beside the man, behind him, before him, and jabbed. That touch would have killed any other, but not Kamahl.

Even wounded, he had proven powerful. Perhaps it was the staff he clung to, brimming with the life-force of the wood. Perhaps his blood had saved him, as it had saved his sister. Twice now, the kin of Auror had survived the First's death touch, and even he could not guess why.

That power had made Phage the ultimate ally. It had made her brother the ultimate foe.

"Kamahl will die," the First told himself.

Swollen, the sun sank toward the sea of sand. The First's shadow lengthened, crossing the desolation. It grew until it stood like a titan on the Krosan head wall. Soon the whole world would be swallowed in shadow, and the First would stalk the Krosan. Soon Kamahl would die.

The First stood and waited, dark magic tingling on his fingers.

* * * * *

It could no longer be called simply a mound—the swollen ground where Kamahl had stabbed Laquatus. Rampant growth had changed it. It was now a veritable mount. Some called it the Gorgon Mount for the snaky growths across its emerging head. The tumulus rose a hundred feet from the forest floor. Dreadlocks of wood and vine draped its sides. The cycles of fecundity, sprout to blossom to fruit to seed to sprout, ran in daily loops. The forest wove flesh out of air, soil, water, and sun and blanketed the ground in a foot of new humus each day. Among the burgeoning boughs trundled beasts like swollen ticks. They ate and rutted, dropping their vasty broods amid the roots.

Kamahl stood in the literal shadow of the Gorgon Mount. He squinted against the sun, which brought its fiery bulk down upon the rioting branches. A similar sunburst covered the bandage across his waist. The poultice had been unable to heal him, and the milkweed packing was unable to stop the bleeding.

The druid healer and the honor guard of mantis warriors stood around him. Suspicious, they watched Kamahl. "No one ventures onto the Gorgon Mount except the druid elders," said the captain. "It is a place of wild spirits, sacred and vicious."

"That's what I need. Wild spirits," Kamahl said, "a whole army of them."

"You see what that place does to the creatures on it," the captain said. "They are grotesque. The same will happen to you, my friend."

Kamahl smiled, his face red with the setting sun. "No. I'm already grotesque. You can't parody a parody." With that, he left them and strode up the mount.

Kamahl forged forward like a man against the tide. His staff split the currents of growth that poured past him. Fecundity made the air curdle and boil. It hurt to breathe. Vitality burned Kamahl's lungs and tingled through his bloodstream.

"Move aside," he calmly told a roiling thicket.

Its thorns ground against each other as if a pair of giant, invisible hands dug into the patch and parted it. Kamahl stepped within. He marched up the passage. Thorns on all sides proliferated. If the wood so chose, he could be trapped and picked apart. The forest spared him. He emerged from the hedge of briars, but the forest ahead had braided itself into an impenetrable jungle.

Kamahl did not bother asking the branches to part. Instead, he hung his staff from his belt and climbed. Hand over hand and foot over foot, he ascended the wall of boughs. Near their summit, the way flattened, and the branches thickened. He walked atop their twisted backs. As the tentacles of a sea monster lead inevitably toward the thing's mouth, the tree boughs led toward the spot where Laquatus lay pinned. While the mount had risen, its heart had sunk. This was no simple hole but the vertical mouth of a twisting cave.

"The spirit well," supplied a stump sitting by the edge of it.

Kamahl glanced in surprise at the stump, noticing only then that it was a nantuko woman. She hunched beneath a gray cloak and stared down into the black pit. Her eyes reflected the darkness—wide, empty, and unblinking.

"It holds a wicked spirit. Its blood transforms the wood."

Kamahl's hand strayed to his own bleeding wound. He then reached for a fat vine at the edge of the pit and set his foot on a ledge within. "I'm going."

"You're gone," said the sentinel. She breathed once and grew as still as a stump.

Kamahl descended. At first, he found footholds down the slick side. Soon, though, the cliff sucked in its belly, and Kamahl had to climb down with hands only. The vine ended before the drop did. He let go and fell through the swirling cold. His feet struck ground in a shallow creek, and Kamahl rolled and rose.

Before him, the creek wended downhill into darkness, seeking the lowest level. It would find Laquatus and the Mirari sword. Kamahl followed it.

Darkness deepened, and cold reached to his bones. Occasional fists of stone struck his head. Kamahl would reel, wait, and let the waters lead him on.

At last, in the deep heart of the ground, a cavern opened. Its lowest reaches were filled with a lake, which centered around an island. There the corpse of Laquatus lay. Even it had grown. Pallid and swollen, the merman seemed a skewered manatee. The Mirari sword cast a steely glow across the scene.

Kamahl waded through shoulder-deep water to reach the island. He arose, streaming water. Waves of energy bled from the bluish corpse, and Kamahl trudged through them. He stared at the wound that pierced Laquatus—the same one that pierced him, his sister, and the forest. All the wounds were one.

"To save them all, I must save myself," Kamahl said even as he placed his hand on the Mirari sword.

Power surged into him. He recoiled, but the energy held him fast. A voice came with it. *This wound will kill us, but until it does, it empowers us. Do not draw it.*

Kamahl shuddered. He still clutched the sword, an envious hand against a jealous world. *An evil one is coming.*

Yes. He enters Krosan on the flood of night.

Kamahl could sense the follower's fell presence. *How can I fight without this sword?*

I will form new beasts through you. They will be your foot soldiers and your command corps. Build an army from the abundance within me and shape them from the abundance within you. Make your army and march them to war. Heal yourself and heal the land. . . .

The contact broke. Kamahl staggered away. The darkness around him was profound. Though the revelatory moment was fleeting, it had changed all. Kamahl brimmed so full of power that it poured from his eyes and nose and mouth.

"I will gather my army," he said, flames standing on his tongue. "I will make new warriors. I will heal the land."

* * * * *

Swathed in night, the First sat beyond the Gorgon Mound. Around him spread a riot of dead boughs. Kamahl had descended into the pit and communed with a very god. He was its champion, just as his sister was the champion of the First.

A bleak smile cracked the man's face. He would soon descend to commune with that same god, but not yet. The forest was still too vital, but a great evil ate into its heart. The evil gave the Krosan power for the moment, but it stole power for eternity. Once the forest was weak enough, the First would touch its heart.

He withdrew into deeper shadows. He would test the forest's champion, and when the man was found wanting, he would strike to kill.

* * * * *

Kamahl emerged into a benighted forest. He was its only light. His face beamed with power, and he stood—lantern-bearer and lantern both—atop the spirit well.

Beside him hunched the druid sentry. In her gray robes, the nantuko woman seemed a stump, but her eyes glistened with hope. Prior to this moment, she had seen only darkness in that cave-tomb, but now she saw light incarnate.

Kamahl descended the hill. He was not truly light incarnate but only a vessel that held the inestimable power of the forest. The perfect place within him had grown until it verged on his very skin and would flow out at a single touch. His tattered boots left glowing footprints, and in them rose the tender shoots of new life.

He walked, refulgent, focus of this once-chaotic power. The fecund force that had lashed mindlessly, warping plant and beast into grotesqueries, now would emerge mindfully.

Before him, the great thicket spread. It had trebled in size since he had passed it. Thorns interlaced in an impenetrable wall.

Kamahl reached it and stopped, power oozing from his pores. In places, the green energy gathered and leaped outward. Tracers bounded down his legs and onto the ground, and flowers bloomed there.

Clenching his jaw, Kamahl stared at the thistles. His eyes traced out the slender stalk, the tripartite thorns, the way in which—branch added upon branch—the whole bush formed a round mass. He raised his index finger and touched a single thorn. Verdant energy leaped from the nail onto the stem. At first, the green power danced like lightning along the hard-edged thorn. It found a ring of pores beneath the cluster and pierced to the core of the stalk. Down sap channels it ran, enlivening the branch, adjacent stalks, and finally the whole bush. It glowed with green flame. Energy spread into the roots, lighting up the dirt. The bush rocked and pulled itself loose from the ground. It tumbled, its thorns walking like a million legs.

"Away," Kamahl quietly commanded, gesturing up over the mound.

The spiny creature rolled, climbing the thicket. Where its thorns touched, power bled into other bushes. Each transformed. One plant at a time, the briars came to life and spun away. The thicket broke into countless green-glowing tumbleweeds, which made room for Kamahl to pass.

He wanted more than room. "Go, defenders of the forest. Patrol her borders. Protect her from any who would do her harm."

All the thicket bounded outward now, the deployment of an army.

Kamahl watched them go. They would be vigilant defenders of the forest. Still if he would march an army, some would have to be aggressors.

Kamahl remembered the Pardic Mountains; he remembered heaps of his own folk, slain in his anger. It was a potent memory, and he mixed it with the life-force that raged through him.

His fingers flung red radiance onto another thistle. Anger burned the plant away, but a ball of scarlet power remained. It whirled, spreading its fire to other such bushes. These would be his shock troops, living fiery tumbleweeds rolling before his army.

"Go to the desert's edge and patrol and wait. I will come for you." Kamahl watched with satisfaction as the burning spheres bounded out through the woods. He was pleased with these first creations but not satisfied. More potential lay latent in his skin.

He had transformed plants. Now, he strode out to change beasts.

The denizens of the forest watched: Mantis-folk peered from dark hollows; centaurs lingered like statues; druids turned gleaming eyes to the glowing man.

Kamahl could not begin with them, not sentient folk. Let him start with something simple—a primeval creature that kept its breast on the breast of the world.

Two snakes entwined nearby. Whether they writhed in battle or mating, Kamahl did not know. They were his primordial beasts, though. He hung his staff at his belt, reached down, and gingerly plucked the snakes apart. He lifted them, one in either hand. They coiled around his wrists and strained toward each other.

Kamahl raised his left hand. Power ran in green rivulets from his fingertips and twined about the snake. Every scale glowed, and the flesh beneath swelled. Sinews grew broader, longer. Ribs widened to make room for enlarging organs, and the riling spine lengthened.

In moments, the snake had doubled in size. It grew as large around as Kamahl's leg. He set the serpent on the ground. The beast's scales lengthened to feathery tips. Its mouth broadened to the size of a crocodile's, to the size of a giant shark's. It grew as wide around as a horse, an elephant—as long as a centennial tree.

"Remain," Kamahl said simply. His hand touched the beast, fingers barely spanning one scale. A spark leaped from human flesh to serpentine, reminding the giant beast who its creator was. "You are Verda, and you will remain here in Krosan to guard it from any invaders."

The serpent coiled slowly. Its body rose, loop on loop, as it listened. Verda's eyes met Kamahl's, and the man read the hunger there.

"You may not eat me. Nor may you eat mantis folk or druids or centaurs or any other thinking thing." The question remained, what might Verda eat? A hiss in Kamahl's right hand reminded him of a more pressing task. He glanced from the small snake to the hungry giant. "Wait, and do not eat."

Kamahl lifted high the other snake. "For you, I have even greater plans."

Power erupted from his palm, and flame mantled the snake. Scales burned and twisted, and flesh flared. Ribs exploded, sending gray smoke up through the air. While the first snake had swelled, this beast burst. Kamahl tried to drop the incendiary creature, but its flames expanded and took form, extending into a massive head. Rolling billows of orange grew into a huge body and tail. Heat and light solidified as scales of black and red. The crimson beast moved with volatile, darting motions.

"You are Roth. You will be my war steed," Kamahl said. He swung his hand out, and flame splashed over the fiery beast.

Roth hissed and recoiled, eyes burning in its skull.

"You must come with me—" Kamahl began, but before he could finish, Roth leaped upon Verda.

Jaws spread and clamped down on the great green snake. Teeth grated against feathery scales. Verda responded in kind, wrapping its powerful body in a constricting grip. The reptiles wrestled as before, though now each creature weighed a hundred tons. The massive boles of the Gorgon Mount shuddered. A tail crashed to ground beside Kamahl and left a trough as wide as he was.

Kamahl stepped back. He should have foreseen this. Verda was hungry, and Roth was angry or perhaps amorous. They would tear each other apart unless they found another focus.

Roth's fiery head darted in for another bite, but Verda reared back. Massive red jaws clamped on a rotten bough and shattered it. Roth hurled itself after its mate. From its gaping mouth tumbled wood and softer things—furry things.

A colony of squirrels had lived in the hollow bow, and they pattered one by one to the ground. They had been feasting on huge hunks of nut and scrambled to recover their spilled hoard.

Kamahl smiled and walked slowly toward the scolding squirrels. He grasped a large nut and lifted it, raising also the squirrel who had claimed it. The creature chattered furiously, attracting the attention of its comrades. Squirrels leaped for the stolen nut and clambered up Kamahl's arm. Vital power jagged into them.

In moments, they had grown to the size of badgers. Kamahl shook them off. Still they grew, clawing despondently at nuts that seemed to shrink in their midst. Squirrels as large as ponies, then as horses . . .

Even Kamahl backed away.

The serpents had gone ominously silent. Roth and Verda, necks entwined, stared at the brood of giant squirrels. Forked tongues darted out to taste the air. As one, the green and red creatures slithered toward their prey.

"You are to eat, and cavort, and flee," Kamahl said to the squirrels. They had noticed the serpents' attention and had gone still.

"You are to reproduce and to feed my guardians, but only when they deserve it."

One squirrel let out a tearing shriek. It hopped away, shaking the ground. Others did likewise. For a moment, there was no sky, but only furry bellies.

Snake heads darted in behind. Razor teeth snapped down on nothing. Had the giant serpents not been intertwined, each would have gotten a meal. As it was, they tumbled petulantly across each other while giant squirrels hurdled away. Roth and Verda slithered afterward.

"Eat," commanded Kamahl, "then return to your duty. Verda, you will begin to patrol. Roth, you will find me wherever I roam."

The hisses that replied were sullen but affirmative.

Kamahl's face shone with power as his creations pursued each other across the Gorgon Mount. He turned and walked through the wood. New creatures waited eagerly within his fingers.

* * * * *

What power he holds over beasts!

The First watched Verda and Roth slither into the distance. He would have to avoid them. Snakes could taste the very air, and they would sense him unless he masked his scent among rotting things. Luckily, there were plenty of rotting things in this rampant forest.

The First slid from his hideout and followed Kamahl at a distance. The man might have been raising an army, but the First would turn that army to his own purposes. As he stalked, his smile was like a dagger across his face.

CHAPTER EIGHT

BUYING THE SWAMP

*H*uge black shapes moved across the vaporous swamp. They seemed giant water striders, their long abdomens dragging over the surface and their rodlike legs patiently plying the muck. The shapes weren't spiders but barges, loaded gunwale to gunwale with murmurous beasts. Long poles rhythmically reached down, found the bottom, shoved along slowly, and rose dripping. Hundreds of barges wove among low islets, down crocodile channels, and toward a broad central island.

Phage stood at the prow of the first vessel, her command ship. The barge was loaded with cut stone for the new colony—no livestock or slaves, who might die from her touch. Wary of their mistress, the five pole men gave her a wide berth. They remembered what had happened to the sixth.

Eyes narrowing, Phage peered through the mist. It was as thick and white as milk, curdling along still channels. Ahead lay open water, and beyond it appeared a low, grassy headland.

She pointed, her black silk sleeve cutting a stark silhouette against the fog. "There." The word was spoken quietly, but it was undoubtedly a command.

The pole men responded, hauling, positioning, pushing. The barge turned slightly and drove toward the shore.

Phage knew that land. She had seen it in the vapor of the First's dream. It looked no different here and now. Before her lay the island primeval, as it had looked since it arose from the swamp. In her mind, though, she saw the island transformed: the grounds of a new coliseum. It would draw the whole world. These waterways would throng with pleasure craft. Those archipelagos would bear a string of bridges, which would in turn bear wagons and carriages and foot traffic. The very skies would throng with griffons and winged steeds.

Phage saw it all. Her mind traded equally in memories and visions. The coliseum already existed, for the First willed it. While Phage lived, the dream coliseum was real.

As the barge approached the shore, a veil of mist slid gently back. It revealed, at the height of the island, a small, stockaded village. This had not been part of the dream. The land had been virginal, ready for exploitation. Phage stared at the stockade of woven boughs, the low huts beyond, the sod roofs, the fire holes that trickled smoke, the small figures in the crude watchtowers.

She drew a breath. The village did not exist. As far as the First was concerned, it was not there. It was no more impediment than the tender grass.

The barge landed. To stern, men leaned on their poles. To fore, men dropped anchor and slid the gangplank.

With her eyes fixed on the village, Phage descended the gangplank. She set foot on spongy ground—mud covered in long grass. The touch of her feet blackened the blades. She would leave burned-out footprints all the way up the hill. It didn't matter. Soon this would be a beach of white sand above a clear-water lagoon. The First had sent a whole arsenal of flesh eaters to scour the muck and cleanse the waters. That was work for another day. Today Phage would be the flesh eater.

As more barges bumped ashore, Phage strode up the muddy swale. Behind her, grass curled and dissolved.

Ahead lay long gray logs. One shifted, eyes rolling open and gazing gravely at her. Crocodiles—a dozen of them.

She did not slow her pace.

With a series of snorts, the crocodiles shifted. Sinking their claws into mud, the beasts dragged scaly bellies across the grass. Most of the reptiles scuttled toward the water. One snapper, though, larger and meaner, stood its ground. It raised itself on lizard legs and lifted a head full of wicked teeth. It lay directly in Phage's path, between barge and village.

Phage strode on.

The crocodile took a step back. It snapped massive jaws.

Phage walked on as if to climb down its throat.

The crocodile obliged, opening wide.

Phage stomped down on its lower jaw and drove her knee into its pallet. The beast bit, four teeth piercing her thigh just above the knee. Flesh tore loose and fell away, but not Phage's flesh.

The reptile's pallet had rotted to bone. Its gums blackened and dissolved, and its teeth dropped from their sockets. The crocodile tried to bite, but the jaw muscles were gone. It flapped in agony. The line of rot moved up the creature's head and consumed its vitals.

Phage kicked with her free leg, shattering the jawbones. She pulled free and plucked the teeth from her thigh. They were as brittle as chalk. Casting them aside, she stepped onto the convulsing back of the creature. Darkness spread in rings from her feet, and the little life that remained in the corpse quivered to nothing.

Phage climbed, her first few steps trembling from the tooth wounds, but they quickly closed and healed. She advanced on the village.

Behind its stockade, warriors gathered. They had seen what she did to the crocodile. They saw too the hundreds of barges converging, the work crews offloading, and the black-armored Cabal enforcers that followed Phage. There was no mistaking the intent of these arrivals.

Phage halted a stone's throw from the gates. In her slim black bodysuit, she was only one quarter the size of the brutes that sidled up behind her. They wore dark suits under dark capes, with hoods pulled up over jutting brows. Though no weapons showed in their meaty hands, these were warriors.

The villagers did not look at the thugs but only at Phage.

She called to them. "In the name of the patriarch of the Cabal, I command all who dwell within this village to come forth."

They did not. They muttered behind their stockade of twisted boughs.

Quietly, Phage said, "How many of you drink?"

It took a moment for the Cabal enforcers to answer. One coughed into his hand. "Never on duty, ma'am."

"How many of you have a flask?" she pressed, adding, "Don't lie."

"All of us, ma'am. Standard issue. We've got to study up for barrel raids." The whole time he spoke, the man kept his eyes on the stockade ahead. "You want a drink?"

"It has to be more than whiskey. A hundred proof or above."

The thug smiled. "I've got a hundred fifty-one proof. Karl has his own brew, near two hundred. The other two, I don't know."

One of the others offered, "It'll put hair on your chest." He reached into his waistcoat. As if by habit, he drew out a hand crossbow, loaded and cocked. Returning it to its holster, he produced a large glass flask, three-quarters full of a clear liquid.

"It's not for putting hair on my chest," replied Phage, "but for burning hair off others'." She took the flask and uncorked it.

Ripping the cuff from one of her sleeves, she stuffed it down, wicklike, through the mouth of the flask. "The rest of you, pull out yours too. Get them ready."

They did, some producing multiple flasks.

All the while, the villagers watched. At last, they answered Phage's summons. "What happens to us if we come out?"

Phage hefted the incendiary in her hand. "If you come out now, you will live to join this building effort."

"What building effort?"

"Your village stands on the site of the new coliseum, which will be the new center of the world. You may join us in building the coliseum, or you may join the foundation stones of the coliseum."

Silence answered at first. Then came a voice of outrage. "You want us to leave our village to be destroyed by you, and become your slaves and build your coliseum?"

"Or die," said Phage. "That is the other option."

Voices debated beyond the stockade.

Phage said to the thugs. "Do any of you smoke?"

While the brutes searched their coat pockets, the village speaker called out. "Our families have lived on this island for two centuries. Not even monsters could drive us—"

With a powerful overhand swing, Phage hurled a flaming flask over the gates. It came down perfectly, smashing atop the ridgepole of the largest shack. Glass sprayed out, and alcohol with it, and fire thereafter. Thatch and twig and timber burst to sudden flame. It was as if a fireball had smashed into the building and tore the heart of it out.

The village speaker yammered, but no one listened.

Ten more burning flasks vaulted up through the skies, striking hovels and walls, towers, and even the gates themselves. All burst into flame. The dry wood gave itself eagerly to oblivion. Fire burned white-hot and smokeless. Heat dragged in swamp gasses that fueled the blaze, turning the flames blue. In a moment, the village was an oven. No one could survived that inferno.

The fiery gates opened, and figures ran out. They did not run as if to attack but staggered, burned and blinded. Some were on fire. All screamed and clutched their faces.

Phage strode toward them. She had given them an ultimatum, and an ultimatum had to be ultimate.

In wide-open arms, she caught a staggering young man. He came to pieces in her grip. An old woman nearby struggled with her burning dress. Phage wrapped her in killing arms, extinguishing the soul within. The next man burned too much to be embraced. Phage merely tripped him. While he rolled to put out the flames, he dissolved from the foot upward.

Male and female, old and young, screaming and silent, they died in her arms. While fire turned the village to ash, Phage did the same to the villagers.

The Cabal thugs stood and watched their mistress work.

In less than an hour, nothing remained—no hovels, no walls, no villagers. The spot was virginal, ready for exploitation.

Phage walked back toward the enforcers. She didn't pause as she passed them, expecting them to turn and follow. They did.

"Tell the survey crews to plot the site. Tell everyone else to make camp. Tonight, we sleep beside the new center of the world."

* * * * *

While her workers labored, Phage sat upon an iron throne. She could not sit in camp chairs, nor could she reside in a tent of canvas and wood. The masons and mages had fashioned her a stone house. It stood on high ground along the natural path toward the northern peninsula. With pillars of limestone, slab roofs, and even rock doors, the house was cold, powerful, and forbidding. It suited her.

Phage sat on a stone portico and took her breakfast. She watched slaves and taskmasters march in gangs from the tent city to the work site. None came near. She had forbidden her underlings from approaching while she ate, for the retractor fork distorted her face gruesomely.

Again she lifted the device to her lips and squeezed. Metal curves forced her lips back, and the fork jutted a warm gobbet between her teeth. Gingerly, Phage bit down. One tine dragged briefly across her lower lip, and the juice on the implement immediately went rancid, emitting a nauseous vapor. Phage flicked the device and dipped it into a cup of alcohol on her tray. Lifting the sterile thing, she speared more meat.

Phage's gaze roamed the work site. The teams had made much progress in the last month. Already, the foundations were laid, a circle a thousand feet in diameter, sinking fifty feet into the ground. Footings for massive buttresses jutted all around the perimeter. Paths radiated to the ports and bridge footings. At dawn, the foundation seemed a giant sun inscribed on the ground. In a way it was. Whole nations would orient themselves on the great coliseum. At noon, the foundations seemed the mouth of a drawstring bag. It was another pleasant resemblance. This one building would cinch up the whole continent. At night, the footings seemed a toothy pit. That was its best aspect. It was the Pit, let loose to roam the world.

The final morsel settled on her tongue. Phage withdrew the retractor. She set the tray aside on a small iron table. It was the signal that she was ready to receive her underlings.

The slave queues continued to march. The taskmasters kept their heads bent. The masons and mages remained busy.

That was her greatest difficulty. Her officers rarely reported in person and never consulted with her. They received her written orders—set down by a scribe—followed her directions without question, and sent back reports. When she toured the work sites, every last worker fell prostrate. Phage could see their ardent, fearful labors. Each team exceeded its daily assignments. Never did unforeseen obstacles impede progress. No one would report problems or deficits to Phage.

Today that would end. She had summoned her chief taskmaster and would make it clear that he must report in person every morning. Already he was late—a grave offense. Phage's wrath was known to be absolute. Gerth had better be dead, or soon he would be.

Phage stood, her eyes narrow with anger. She studied the workers, some marching wearily to work, others slogging more wearily away. Dwarf stonecutters, human joiners, centaur haulers, merfolk longshoremen, lich taskmasters . . . Gerth was not among them. He was not even among the slave apes or the shorn rhinos.

Phage stepped from the portico. The moment of grace was ended. Had he been in the crowd, she would have spared him, but now, even if she met him en route, he was a dead man.

She strode down the hill. The workers in the slave queue seemed to notice her approach and recoiled just slightly—all except a little old woman leading a mule.

The woman was not a slave like so many others. She was one of a handful of free folk who had answered the First's summons and hired on to work on the coliseum. Though bent and craggy-faced, the skinner had a sharp gleam in her eye. She peered fearlessly at Phage. Only as she approached did Phage realize the woman wasn't so small; her mule was monstrously big. It was the size of a horse, though with all the hardy sturdiness of its species. It clumped along beside its owner, ears back as the woman poured out a torrent of complaint. "—think your hooves had been turned to glue already, with how slow you're walking. You'd be better company in a pot." The woman strode straight toward Phage.

Some slaves lingered to witness the apparent suicide.

Reaching Phage, the crone bowed her white head and executed a crusty curtsey. "Hello, Mistress Phage. I've been sent by Gerth to report."

Phage stopped in her tracks, standing within hand's reach of the skinner. Black corruption spread from her feet through the grass. She looked the old woman up and down. "Gerth *sent* someone?"

"Yes, if I qualify," the skinner replied with a wink. "He said he was real sorry not to come himself. Just this morning, he impaled his foot on a sculptor's chisel, so he can't come. He sent me instead."

"You? A mule skinner?"

"I'm the only one who's not afraid of you."

Phage stared at her levelly. She wasn't sure whether to be angry or impressed. Still, she knew what she felt about Gerth. "You will take me to him." She walked on toward the cringing crowd of slaves.

The skinner gaped, then hauled on the reins and muscled her beast around. She growled at the animal and urged it along. They ran side by side, crone and mule, until they reached Phage.

The women, young and old, strode like sisters down the bank. Before them, the stream of slaves parted. All watched, goggle-eyed.

Phage said to the old woman, "Your duty to Gerth is discharged. Your duty is now to me. Gerth claims to have wounded his foot on a chisel. What is the truth?"

"He has . . . Mistress," panted the skinner.

"Intentionally?"

The crone smiled beneath her white mop of hair. "They say you can see through things to the truth. I guess they're right."

Phage chewed on that. The man would rather maim himself than report to her. He would have to die. She had no jobs for cowards. This crone, though, showed not the slightest fear. "Why aren't you afraid of me?"

The woman shrugged, struggling to keep pace. "I'm too old to worry about dying."

"Perhaps I'll kill you now."

"No, you won't," said the skinner. She seemed to note the anger in Phage's eyes. "Not that you couldn't, but that you won't."

"I won't?" asked Phage.

"You kill traitors, laggards, spies—folks who might destroy what you're building. You won't kill me. I'm on your side." The old woman paused. "I'm not afraid of you because I understand you."

"You presume to understand me?"

The crone laughed. "I'm an old, wrinkled woman. Folks recoil from me. Yes, I understand you."

A smile tugged at Phage's lips. "You do not know how it feels to be full of horrors."

"Did you ever play dead while a raider found uses for you? Terrible to experience. Even worse to survive. I'm full of horrors. I know what it is to keep them locked away in my skin."

Phage looked with new eyes on this old creature. Behind the crow's feet and the sagging jowls lurked a deep sadness. Here was a fearless woman—honest and hard working. "What is your name?"

"I'm Zagorka. This here's Chester."

"How would you like to be a taskmaster, Zagorka?"

Chester snorted, and Zagorka agreed. "Wouldn't. Just 'cause I can wrangle this one thick-headed ass don't mean I want to be in charge of a hundred of them. Besides, they'd not listen to me."

"Then you will be my messenger. They'll listen to you then. You'll tell them not just what I say, but what I mean. You'll tell me not just what they say, but what they mean."

Zagorka hobbled along. "I'm a little gimped up for all that running."

"Ride Chester."

The skinner and her mule traded dubious glances.

"Or I'll kill you both."

"She will," Zagorka warned her mule. "She's at the end of her patience."

"You *do* know me."

"We'll do it," Zagorka decided.

It was done. The gulf was bridged. Here was a woman who understood Phage without hours of fruitless discussion. Zagorka would speak honestly about all aspects of the job. The taskmasters would not fear to talk with her, and Zagorka would not fear to talk with Phage. With this new mouthpiece and earpiece among her taskmasters, Phage would know everything.

Phage and Zagorka strode down among fields of cut stone. There, masons labored with hammers and chisels. The steady ring of steel on stone faltered and hushed. Dwarves and men lifted their heads and stared at the two woman.

They paid no heed, striding on toward the taskmaster.

Gerth sat in a camp chair at the edge of the field. One foot, wrapped in white gauze, rested on a log. Fresh blood spotted the top and bottom of the foot. When he noticed his commander, Gerth gaped stupidly and pushed himself to his feet.

"He drove the chisel right through?" asked Phage quietly.

"Right through," affirmed Zagorka.

Phage pursed her lips. She strode to where the man stood and ignored his deep bow. "I summoned you."

"Forgive me, Commander. I wounded myself."

"Who is your next-in-command?"

Gerth went to his knees. His voice trembled. "The lich Terabith, my lady."

Phage stared angrily at the man's bowed head. She lifted her hand and imagined setting it on his shoulder and rotting him to nothing.

Without looking up, Gerth said, "Are you going to kill me?"

That was the question. He was a worm, kneeling there. Somehow, though, Phage could not set her hand down. It was his fear that made him disobey.

Zagorka blurted, "Will he be a better lesson dead or enslaved?"

At last, Gerth lifted his eyes. Hope was there, but also terror. The other slaves would not be kind to a former taskmaster. Still, it was better than death. Phage's hand cast a black shadow across his face. Gerth said, "I will be your slave and work hard for you and be ever faithful. I will go to the other taskmasters and warn them against my fate."

"If they disobey," Zagorka said, "she'll kill them and you too. You live only as long as you're a lesson."

Phage could not have put it better. "Your death sentence is commuted but not canceled."

Zagorka said, "First warn Terabith not to fall to your fate. Then tell the others. Last, report to the slave pens."

Gerth bowed his head in thanks. "Yes. I will tell them. It will not happen again."

Phage looked to her new mouthpiece. "I think you are right."

CHAPTER NINE

IMAGE MAGIC

The delusions of night cleared away, and the sun rose upon Ixidor in his undreamed land. Doubt had proven false. The mirage had proven true.

Ixidor dived. It was deep enough here. The sandy shore gave way to tan contours in clay, and they in turn to green depths. Water enveloped him—cool, clean, bracing. It washed away dirt and salt scales. The water was life. Ixidor opened his mouth and drank as he swam. Water poured through and around him. Life filled him.

He had almost missed it. Three days of tortures in the desert, mirage after mirage, rainstorms that turned to sandstorms, dunes that turned to graves—all of it had taught him to distrust hope. A man who distrusts hope is a dead man. When he had found his paradise, he had nearly been unable to recognize it. He had to drink sand before he knew.

Ixidor rose. A cry of joy began in his throat and burst up through struggling bubbles toward the surface. His shout erupted from the water just as he did. Amid leaping waves, Ixidor roared the defiant cry of survival. He had wrestled death and pinned it.

Ixidor's feet dug into the clay. Small curls of mud streamed away from his toes as he climbed the bank. His hair rained water down around his shoulders, and he laughed in the midst of it. He sat on the bank. The river tugged insistently at his feet as if it were eager to bear him to the dark cave where the waters were swallowed.

Drips ran like tears down his face. Ixidor had not truly defeated death. It had defeated him.

Nivea was gone.

Rolling over into the shadow of a palm, Ixidor cried until he slept.

The waters tugged at him. The dark cave growled like a hungry stomach.

Nivea haunted his dreams. She had brought him here to live. He had brought her to the pits to die.

Bleakly, Ixidor woke. The sun had reached midday, driving away palm shadows, and burning him. His feet were numb and cold. His heart was too. It would have been unbearable except that hunger eclipsed all else.

Ixidor sat up and peered into the blue-green stream. There should have been fish darting through its verdant waters. He saw none. He had not seen any as he swam either. How could there be fish? The spring rose from killing sand only to descend into a voracious cave.

What of animals? The oasis should have swarmed with creatures. Ixidor stood and stalked among the curving boles of the palms. He followed the sandy shores, looking for footprints, droppings, any sign that other creatures had come to this spot. Only his own tracks marked the sand. He saw not so much as a bird flitting among the trees or a line of ants rising up a palm. More telling still was the profound silence. Only the murmur of water, wind, and his own breath disturbed the quiet.

Surely the palms would hold something—dates, coconuts, fruits. . . . He walked among them, his head craned back. There were at least three separate species of palm but no fruit on any of them.

Ixidor seated himself beside the stream. He would die in paradise after all. It was another mirage, promising life but offering death. Waters flowed, deep and cool, away to the yawning cave mouth. Ixidor had been a fool to hope. All the while that he jeered death, it only tightened its grip.

Absently, Ixidor dragged his fingers through the clay. It curled up in little rolls that looked almost like prawns. Ixidor stared at them. His stomach rumbled. In trembling fingers, he lifted a single curl of mud. The outside of the clump was smooth and round while the inside was jagged like the jutting legs of a crayfish. Ixidor lifted the thing to his mouth and bit. Sand crunched, clay clung to his tongue, and mud dissolved and spread. Ixidor spat the clod from his mouth. Angrily, he backhanded the other curls of mud.

They struck the stream and sank. The clods left ribbons of mud as they spun slowly through the water. Halfway down, currents grabbed the clay and flung it in circles. Ixidor watched, fascinated. There was something familiar about that churning motion. Ixidor crouched on his knees above the stream and stared down. The clods were swimming. They weren't just hunks of clay, but actual prawns. They had transformed.

Ixidor glanced back at the mud curl he had spat out. It was undoubtedly clay. It had never been alive. He stared into the flood again. The other clods had become living things.

It all was beginning to make sense—the sand that became water, the shadows that became trees, the clay that became crayfish . . . a new power.

Nivea's death had given it birth. Ixidor's desperation had nursed it. He had been buried alive, but someone had dug him out. He had been lost in desolation, but someone had led him to water. Nivea had become his muse, inspiring him to create.

Image magic. Instead of making images into illusions, he was making them into realities.

Ixidor stooped at the stream bank and dipped his hands into the water. The crayfish shied from his touch. He swiped down to catch them. They darted and spun away. He was their creator, true, but he would also be their killer, and they evaded him.

Ixidor dived into the water. He rushed down among them, hair streaming and hands lashing. He caught one of the creatures in a tight fist. Not even waiting to surface, he rammed the thing into his mouth and bit. It was not clay anymore but a creature—flesh, fins, scales, head. It crunched between his teeth. The last of its life fled as he swallowed. It was real. The thing tumbled uneasily in his stomach, the first food it had held in three days. Ixidor reached out to snatch another of the creatures, but they were gone. They had escaped downstream.

There would be easier prey. Stroking to the bank, Ixidor climbed. He sat, water streaming down the clay. The blood of the prawn lingered on his tongue, but it was time for better fare.

Kneeling, Ixidor murmured, "Nivea." He closed his eyes.

She hovered there, gleaming and beautiful, within his mind. She seemed an angel, with white pinions glowing fiercely.

Opening his eyes, Ixidor dug his hands into the clay bank. Two great scoops of mud came up in his grip. He pressed the hunks together and began to shape the mass. Fingers traced lines into the clay. He narrowed one end and twisted it into a conic shape. The other end flattened to a tapered edge. A small avian head took form. Mud smoothed into a downy body, and wings tucked up tightly. At first, it was only the approximation of a bird. Ixidor added scales to the feet, an idiosyncratic tuft behind the head, and deep slanting nostrils. To be real, it had to be individual. Creators moved from general forms to specific actualities.

Every medium struggles against the artist, but this clay began to struggle in earnest. No sooner was it a specific bird than it had a will. Will made mud into feather, skin, muscle, and bone. The bird—the gull, for Ixidor had grown up beside the water—squawked loudly. Hollow bones flapped and bent like a fan struggling to open.

Ixidor dug his fingers in. This was to be his meal.

The creation had other ideas. It fought free. Downy feathers whirled in the air and pasted themselves to Ixidor's hands. The gull's wings stroked once, twice. It leaped into the palm-cluttered sky and rose to a high roost. In utter rejection of its maker, it shat a great white stream onto the undergrowth below. The bird laughed raucously.

Covered in feathers, Ixidor glared after it. His eyes were mad with hunger but also with discovery. He had made a bird, a rebellious bird whose insides apparently included a gastrointestinal tract. The prawns had been one thing—cold blooded and imbecilic. This bird was a higher life form. It lived and wanted to go on living, just like Ixidor himself.

Gleeful, Ixidor stood and applauded the raucous gull. Feathers flew in a gray flurry.

"Go on, you glorious horrible meal!" he shouted. "Go on and live! Far be it from me to create a creature who wants to live and then make it die." The gladness went out of his face. His own creator had done the same to him.

Ixidor turned and dived back into the water. It would cleanse him of feathers and mud. As he swam, he thought. His next creation would be different. He would not make something in slavish imitation of nature, for no beast wished to die. He would make something simple and new, perfectly suited to be a meal.

With one strong stroke of his hands, Ixidor rose to the surface of the stream. He swam to the bank, surprised how far the current had carried him toward the dark cave. Working his way back upstream, Ixidor reached a likely spot with smooth, tan clay. He scooped up a batch of it and set to work.

The creature would be delectable, yes, but also practical. It would provide meat for immediate consumption, organs for stewing, and even its own crude pot for cooking them. Ixidor's hands worked quickly, forming the smooth sweep of the thing's back. If he was careful, he could get three meals from the creature, and thus not have to kill as often. Of course, it wouldn't matter that much: This turtle would want to be eaten.

He finished it—a deep shell holding plenty of muscle and organ meat, a small head with only a pliable and toothless mouth, stubby little legs devoid of claws, and best of all, no shell across the creature's belly. Ixidor could eat the first bits raw and then build a fire to stew the rest.

He set the creature down and completed the last polygons across its shell. With these final lines, the thing went from artificiality to reality. The turtle trembled to life. It lifted its too-small head beneath the massive, pot-shaped shell. Querulous eyes stared at its creator. Then, struggling on stumpy legs, it advanced toward Ixidor. It climbed slowly up his foot until it reached an awkward angle and toppled on its back. There, it waited, head tucked submissively on its pink belly.

Ixidor wouldn't even need a knife. The skin was as tender as wet paper. He need only dig in with hungry fingers. The turtle even wanted him to; it existed only to be his meal. Ixidor ran his hand across the creature's belly. A snagged nail drew a dotted line along it. Blood welled up from the seam. The turtle trembled, as if steeling itself for the inevitable.

Ixidor spread his hand atop the turtle's stomach. The skin there hardened to a tough shell. He tweaked each leg until it was larger, more capable of bearing the weight. A touch on the mouth gave the beast teeth with which to feed. Last of all, Ixidor brushed its head, giving it a will to live.

The turtle flailed, flipped over, and rushed into the stream. It left a turbid cloud of sand in its wake.

It was bad to kill a creature that wanted to live but worse to create a creature that wanted to die. Perhaps natural forms were safer. In them the complex dynamic of predator and prey were long established.

The creator was hungry. He knelt by the riverside, and his hands dug deep into the clay. He had made one turtle, and another would be easy. It took quick shape. Its shell was flat on top like a cooking pot, but its belly was guarded. The turtle had real legs with real claws and great snapping jaws. Put simply, it had a chance. If it eluded its creator, it could live a long, long while. Ixidor stooped over it, adding knobs of flesh beneath one knee.

The snapper whirled. Its mud-flesh became true, and its impressive jaws spread and clamped. It caught Ixidor's right hand and bit.

The pain was blinding. He shrieked and yanked. With a sick crackle, his hand came away, missing the ring and little fingers. The carpal bones were shorn halfway up his palm. Blood poured from the severed spot.

Howling, Ixidor leaped after the fleeing turtle. He landed on its back, forcing it to ground, the shell slick with blood. Though the turtle withdrew legs and tail, its head still lashed out, snapping at his heel.

Ixidor struck back. His heel smashed down atop the turtle's head. The creature shook. Ixidor struck again. The brain-pan caved. Ixidor continued to kick, feeling the skull crack. He kicked for revenge. In moments, the turtle stopped moving, but still, Ixidor kept up his attack until nothing but pulp remained beneath his heel.

He climbed off the carcass and limped to the stream. Some jags of bone had stuck in his foot. He dipped it in the water, and his hand beside.

Ixidor felt dizzy but triumphant. The battle played in his head. There was no denying it now: He created realities. Not only did he create them, but he lived with them and suffered the consequence of their being. They could wound him. They could kill him. . . .

They could feed him. . . .

Compressing his wounded hand beneath the opposite armpit, Ixidor stood up. He was covered with blood, mud, and water. Though he had pulled the skull shards out of his ravaged heel, it deeply protested. He limped back toward the carcass, set his toes under one edge, and flipped it over.

The turtle was dead. Ixidor kicked hard, his foot landing flat on the belly plate. The shell split, and blood swelled the seam. Ixidor knelt. He gripped one edge of the cracked shell, braced a foot on the creature's leg, and yanked. The shell did not give. Ixidor set his bleeding hand on the other side of the crack and yanked again. After four vigorous pulls, tissues began to pop. Still, the shell held.

Roaring in frustration, Ixidor stood and stomped on the creature. The carapace caved. He stomped again. A red paste gushed from the edges of the shell. Voracious, Ixidor knelt and ate. The stuff was still warm from the life of the creature. Another stomp produced more of the substance. It was not the way he had planned on eating the turtle, but he was desperate, and had no time, no tools.

Survival was a messy business. Creation too. It was a business of mud, blood, and water, of shattered shells and shards of bone. Ixidor had tapped a primordial power, and was becoming a primordial creator. Even with his own bleeding hand, he greedily scooped up the flesh of the turtle and sucked it from his fingers.

It was not merely messy. It was madness—divine madness.

Capering about the fallen beast, Ixidor began to hum and chant. The words were a mystery even to him. He crouched to snatch up more of the paste and shove it into his mouth. He smeared red lines across his face—war paint from his first kill.

Ixidor danced, sang, and ate.

* * * * *

He lay within a shallow well of sand, dug out by his own hands. Beside him rested the turtle shell, empty and clean. Reptilian flesh wormed its way through his intestines. Reptilian blood covered him from nose to knees, and gnawed bones lay nearby, bleaching in the sun.

The sun was forsaking Ixidor and his strange paradise. Palm fronds glowed iridescent green against the darkening sky. Boles draped long shadows across sand and stream, and breezes moved among the leaves without rattling them. It was the time for night birds to begin their weird songs, but Ixidor had not yet made such birds. All was silent. The desert's desolation seeped slowly into the oasis.

Ixidor was tired. His stomach was full and his mind empty. The madness was gone. Only gore and mud remained. He was done creating. Tomorrow he would fashion more beasts. His image magic would impose new things upon the world, but for now, he was done—exhausted.

Lying there in a delirium of fatigue and satiety, he saw her.

White and pure, shimmering in the midst of the darkling oasis, his muse appeared. It was unfair to call her Nivea, for Nivea had never had white wings and glowing robes. It was equally unfair to call her anything else, for the face of that glorious creature was Nivea's. She hovered above the waters, her wings unmoving in flight. She stared at him.

Ixidor crawled up from the sandy hole and knelt before her.

He could not have felt more unworthy—crusted in filth and

missing two fingers and part of his mind. If she were truly his muse, she would be horrified by what he had made. Crayfish, a raucous gull, and two turtles. Worse than these creatures was their creator.

"Forgive me, beautiful lady. I was hungry, and I ate."

She did not respond, but only floated before him.

Ixidor lifted his face. "Nivea, is it you?" he asked. Sand sifted from his face and made small sounds on the ground. "How I mourn you. You are my heart, absent from my chest. You are my mind, absent from my head. You are my soul absent from my body. Look at me." He spread his arms, revealing a ravaged figure. "You were all that was good in me. I am what remains."

She faded. Black boles showed through her gossamer form.

"I will create nobler things tomorrow. I will create not just beasts but ecologies. I will create marvels worthy of you."

The muse was gone. Only shadows lingered above the stream.

Ixidor bowed his head again to the sand. He clawed the ground with his three-fingered hand.

Weeping, he crawled toward the stream. Like a wounded rat, he slithered into the water. It embraced him. Currents cleansed the day's filth. The waters enlivened him, and he swam and felt new.

The stream hid his bitter tears.

CHAPTER TEN

STONEBROW

The First crouched in a wet hole and clung to a tangle of roots. His death-touch had killed them, and now they were his. Touching here, touching there, he could take control of whole stands of trees. The First was delighted to discover that a kindred darkness lurked in their heartwood. The corruption at the forest's heart had already reached its dark tendrils this far. Soon, the metastasis would be complete, and the First would go to the Gorgon Mount and take hold of that cancerous heart.

Just now, though, he had a trap to set. "Let's see how the champion fares against a forest turned to darkness."

With a twitch of his hands and a twist of his mind, the First hurled trees down upon a cringing village of centaurs. They screamed, some dying instantly, others bolting, and a blessed few lingered in broken agony. Their wails would draw Kamahl, and then these boughs would slay him.

* * * * *

It was a time of terrors. Trees lay on the ground and grew like hair. Their trunks were as thick as hillsides. Their branches reached for miles. In violent surges, the forest overran itself.

Many of its creatures perished beneath the crushing boughs.

A few fought.

Sixteen centaurs crouched, a bulwark of muscle before the advancing tide of wood. Their ancient home lay buried beneath ravenous foliage. Encroaching limbs lashed with a will. The centaurs had retreated twice, but here they dug in to stand or fall. If the forest would make eternal war, the centaurs would be its eternal foes.

A great bough plunged down from the top of the snarl. It struck ground like a pummeling arm. Its impact shook the glade and sent dust spinning. The bough twitched, growing rampantly even where it lay.

The centaurs roared. Their simian faces split in fury, and their fangs gnashed. Sixteen stags leaped over the rock embankment, hooves sparking on stone. Arms as brawny as oak boughs swung axes, though they were sacrilege to the forest folk. The blades rose and fell. Sixteen steel teeth bit deep into the bough. Their impact reverberated through the glade. Axes reached the quick, canted to widen the wounds, and then chucked loose for more blows.

The bough recoiled. It screamed through twisting fibers and lashed slender shoots across its tormenters.

Welts striped the centaurs' backs. Their steel stormed into the wood. They cut crosswise, hurling great chunks into the air. Two blades sank into heartwood, rotten and rank. A third followed and chopped straight through.

The bough riled like a severed serpent, lashing violently and jagging across the glade. It would take a long while for the branch to die. Other such boughs still convulsed their lives away on the far side of the clearing.

The stump wouldn't die, though. It spewed sap onto its attackers. They retreated. Bark crawled across the wounded end, closing it off. New tendrils jutted with green defiance and swept toward the centaurs.

The beast men had retreated to their wall, but the shoots had followed them. Axes were no good against tendrils. Green scourges whipped them.

"Fall back!" shouted Bron, the centaur leader.

He and his warriors did, but they all knew what it meant. If they lost the wall, they would return with fire. If axes were sacrilege, fire was abomination—no weapon at all but a hateful god, the anti-forest. Still, the centaurs were desperate.

Two more boughs surged down from the height of the forest tangle and crashed before the centaurs.

"Back!" called Bron again. Though he and his warriors were massive, they seemed mere ants before the onslaught.

Turning, they galloped away, heading for a pile of deadfall and dry straw. At its base lay sixteen fist-sized stones—flint. Reaching the spot, the centaurs dropped to their knees and lifted the stones. They struck the flint obliquely upon their steel axes. Sparks showered away like meteors and lighted upon straw. The centaurs blew to awaken flame, but the straw would not even smolder.

Sudden illumination drew their eyes up from the tiny sparks. Golden light poured through the glade and cast shadows on the deadfall. Fire did not provide the glow. Something had arrived, something brilliant.

The centaurs shielded their eyes. It seemed as if a star stood at the edge of the glade.

The star was a man. He emerged from folds of rampant growth, his face and hands beaming brightly.

Boughs coiled and recoiled around him. One great tree bent and rushed down to crush him. The man reached up. The tree struck with purpose, but as soon as the man's hands touched the wood, it shuddered to stillness. Green power bled from his fingertips and bounded down the gnarled bark. Where it struck, the dead bark came to life. Steam hissed from the bole, and fibers wrestled against each other, black against green.

The man, seeming to hold aloft that massive tree, tilted his head back and roared. Power fountained from him into the tormented trees. The black tide ebbed away before a surging green wave. It poured down the trunk and rushed through to the root tips. Sparks and smoke leaped from a wet hole at the tree's base.

The bole rose and stood upright again, and the rampant glade grew suddenly silent.

All eyes turned to the man, who stood inviolate in the midst of the trees. He was cloaked in verdant leaves over gleaming armor, booted in vines atop metal soles. In one hand he lifted a gleaming staff, which burned a slanted line in the centaurs' minds. *Come. Come.*

Bron dropped the flint. He stood and stowed his axe at his waist. His hooves shifted as if following channels in the air, and allowed himself to be inexorably drawn toward the man.

The other centaurs shouted. Their fingers clawed at his pelt, but they could not keep him back.

Bron walked across the glade. There was no simpler thing to do.

He knew the man, the barbarian Kamahl who had brought these horrors, but Kamahl had been changed by the divinity within him.

Bron wished to be so changed. He approached to within a few strides and knelt. He bowed his head, power streaming around him.

You once defended this forest, sent the man by way of mind.

"Yes," Bron replied simply.

Now you fight against it.

"Yes."

I need such a fighter as you. Others will remain to defend the forest, but you will be my general, to come with me and fight in distant lands.

Bron exhaled. "I would gladly fight anything if I did not have to fight my own home."

The light changed. For a moment, its radiance seemed reflected inward, casting long shadows through the man's soul. *It is a terrible thing to fight one's own home.* The luminosity returned. *What is your name?*

"I am Bron, leader of the Cailgreth centaurs."

The staff sparked on the ground as if it were lightning touching down. The man reached out and touched Bron's forehead. *Henceforth, you will be called Stonebrow.*

Bron hadn't time to approve or disapprove. With that touch, he had ceased to be. He was Stonebrow now, and he grew.

Though the centaur still knelt, his eyes rose even with those of the man. Next moment, they were above him. Beamy shoulders widened, stout bones lengthened, and iron muscles strengthened. Ribs became the size of an ox's. Arms grew until they could shatter boulders, legs until they could topple trees. Fur thickened into a pelt that would turn arrows. Even belt and axe had grown.

Stonebrow climbed to his feet and towered above his creator. He was a giant among centaurs. He roared. The forest paused its tumult to listen to that sound. He pounded a hoof on the ground, and the glade trembled. Snatching the axe from his belt, he hoisted it high. It caught the sun and threw a violent wedge of light across the ground. He was not just huge but filled with fury. As if blood welled up through every follicle, his pelt took on a red cast.

There is new fire in you—too much for you to defend the forest. You will do more to slay than to save. With me, you will go. Together we will take the fight to the forest's foes.

"Yes. I will go, Master—"

Kamahl. You will call me simply Kamahl.

"Kamahl."

Kamahl turned his gaze away from General Stonebrow. Oh, it ached to go from the heat of that gaze to the chill of its shadow!

Kamahl looked to the other centaurs. They stood wonderingly on the opposite side of the glade. Their hooves churned the soil as if preparing to flee. Their eyes, though, were locked on Kamahl. Invisible cords drew them forward.

These will be the forest's defenders. These will fight to protect the wood.

Stonebrow shifted to stand alongside his master. "How can they defend the forest when it is fighting itself?"

Kamahl did not answer at first. He only watched the fifteen beast men stride slowly nearer. *The forest does not fight itself. It grows. Forests grow. It will continue until all the world is forest.*

Even transformed, Stonebrow sensed the lie. This rampant growth was not good for the forest. Kamahl was deceiving his new general. Was Kamahl also deceiving himself?

Who will succeed you as leader of this village?

Stonebrow considered the folk. "Boderah was my lieutenant. Let him be leader."

The named centaur stepped forward. He seemed only a colt beside Stonebrow. They no longer belonged to the same species, but soon that would change.

Boderah, you will be called Granite, for you will be bedrock for this wood. Kamahl touched the beastman's forehead. The transformation began again.

Stonebrow watched. It had been a glorious thing to transform, but it was a hideous thing to witness. Every tissue, every sinew warped out of all natural proportion. The skin bulged as if inflated with air. The bones crackled in their rush to outgrow each other. Granite thrashed and screamed. Stonebrow realized he must have screamed as well. Years worth of growth were crammed into breathless seconds.

Stonebrow looked away while sockets popped and muscles split. When he looked back, the transformation was complete. Beside him stood a similar creature—a giant centaur whose flesh bore a greenish cast.

Granite gave a rueful smile, and his teeth were like wooden stakes.

Stonebrow looked away again, this time to the trees. His own twisted sinews were brother-flesh to the twisted boughs. He had become grotesque. Of course he would no longer fight the rampant growth of the forest. Now he embodied it.

There was no going back. He could not regain the creature he once had been. Nor could Granite. Nor could any of them.

Kamahl walked among them and touched their brows and gave them new names.

*   *   *   *   *

What power he wields! the First thought as he clung, within the smoking hole. Though the forest is riddled with rot, this Kamahl is a channel of pure green power.

The First's hands still stung from the life-force that had lashed at him. He would not attack Kamahl directly again. Instead, the First lurked in the wet hole, waiting for Kamahl and his new warriors to move on. When finally darkness settled, the First climbed out.

Kamahl was already too powerful to be slain in his homeland. Luckily, his homeland was weak enough to succumb.

The First crept toward the Gorgon Mount. Under cover of night, he would slip in, and his death touch would turn the forest's power into his own.

* * * * *

In their plethora, he made them—giant serpents, great centaurs, fire panthers, forest goblins, spine folk. . . . Wherever Kamahl's hand came to rest, new life came to being. Those creatures who would defend the forest grew larger, imbued with its vitality. Those creatures who would march with Kamahl grew fiercer, tempered by fire. He had done what he had come to do. He had awakened an army.

At their head, Kamahl strode solemnly, and beside him marched General Stonebrow. From the desert's edge, they carved a highway toward the center of the wood. Huge squirrels leaped from bough to bough, surefooted on warping branches. Emerald-eyed elves climbed across gnarled shoulders of wood. Enormous slugs slithered along the ground, and toad men scampered among roots, gathering bugs. To all sides rolled spinefolk—tumbleweeds replete with thorns and will. It would be a terrifying army to face, but tonight Kamahl did not march them for war. Tonight they were an army of peace.

"There, do you see?" Kamahl asked, gesturing with his staff toward the Gorgon Mount. "It is the source of power." His eyes shone as he gazed at the rumpled mass. It was tenfold the peak it had been before and grew even still. Soon it would be like the mountains of his homeland, and here in the midst of the forest. "We go there."

Stonebrow marked out the site. His eyes were flinty. "Where is the ziggurat?"

"What ziggurat?"

"The sacred ziggurat. The druid temple, palace of the mantis lord," answered Stonebrow matter-of-factly. "Where is it?"

Kamahl's eyes roamed the tortured ground. Where was the ziggurat? Built of the entwined branches of four majestic trees, the ziggurat should have stood here, on the near slope of the great mound. It was nowhere. Only an endless twist of vast boughs covered the ground. "I don't know."

The giant centaur stomped a few steps farther. "There it is," he said, gesturing to one side.

The ziggurat lay there. Its trees had grown like all the rest and become too tall, too massive to stand. They had bent over. The walkways were twisted wreckage, the parapets shattered.

It was a grim sight, that ruined tower. Mangled bits of dead wood were clutched in coils of living. The old glory of the forest had been ruined by the new.

"All things change," said Kamahl. "It is the way of Nature."

Stonebrow gave a noncommittal grunt and strode onward.

"I embody the very power of the forest—this new, voracious life," Kamahl continued as though to justify himself. "Never before has it lived as it does now."

"Never before," echoed Stonebrow, though the centaur's rumbling voice left doubt as to whether he approved.

Kamahl's own brow turned stony. "It seems wrong only now, for the mantis folk have not yet felt the transforming power. I will touch them. I will change them so that they match the new sacredness."

To that, Stonebrow offered no comment.

Kamahl bristled at the silence. Had he not transformed this ingrate? Had he not given a new, more powerful aspect to this whole army? His eyes swept back over the creatures. They followed him dutifully. A moment before, it had seemed enough. Now he wondered why they didn't follow joyfully.

No looking back. Kamahl turned his attention to the mount, a thicket gone mad. Each thorn stood the height of a man, each twig the width of a tree. The forest moaned. It grew so quickly that wood ground against wood. Trees plowed deep furrows as they shoved along, and giant things loped in the midst. They grew visibly and preyed upon each other—rutted, birthed, hunted, and ate in fast cycles of want. It was an ugly place, caught in transformation.

Ah, but when the changes were complete, how glorious it would be!

Kamahl and Stonebrow approached the thicket. It was impassable. No creature, not even an ant, could penetrate its thick nap. Only one path gave entry—an archway hewn by stone blades and retained by poison. The space was guarded even now by the creatures that had cut it.

Nantuko warriors stood before the gate, their stone-bladed polearms held across their chests. They stared at Kamahl, and their podlike eyes showed no sign of fear.

Kamahl signaled his army to cease their march. He and General Stonebrow approached the guard. "Allow us through."

Unblinking eyes studied the man and the centaur. "It is forbidden."

Kamahl said, "Forbidden by whom? To whom?

"Forbidden by Thriss, Nantuko Master. Forbidden to all those beneath his sway."

"I am not beneath his sway," Kamahl said.

"We know. If you enter, you will be defying him."

Kamahl took a long breath. "I contain the power of the land. The mount is not too sacred for my feet."

The mantis shook his head slowly. "No. It is too profane."

"Profane?"

"Those who venture within become monsters. They stalk it even now. Any who pass this wall are killed by them or become monsters themselves."

Kamahl peered up through the passage. The shorn ends of dead stalks formed a weeping cave, unhealing. Kamahl could not keep his hand from straying to the wound in his belly. "I will go there. I will change these monsters into new forms. They will become defenders of the wood."

Even those merciless bug eyes showed surprise. "Defenders such as these?"

Kamahl did not look behind him. He didn't need to. Giant serpents, huge squirrels, toad men—of course his creatures would seem monstrous to this simple warrior, but these would be the saviors of the forest.

Kamahl said simply, "I must go."

"I cannot follow," rumbled Stonebrow.

His master shot him an angry look. "You agree with him?"

The centaur lifted one weighty eyebrow and gestured into the small passage. "No. Physically. I cannot follow."

"That's fine," Kamahl replied. "I go in alone and return with an army twofold." He ducked his head, gently brushed the mantis men aside, and stepped into the long passage. His century staff angled like a lance beside him.

It was a strange tunnel, a dead place in the midst of endless growth. The dry stalks were the color of sun-baked rocks, and they echoed Kamahl's footsteps. No breeze moved through the gap. Decay permeated the air.

At the far end of the passage, a gray and thorny light shone. Things moved there, massive, horrid things. A scaly leg flashed past, and then another—as if a giant lizard ran by. No sooner had its lashing tail disappeared than enormous bug legs pounded the ground. An abdomen with hissing spiracles eclipsed the light, and then the bug was gone. A reptilian wail told that it had caught its prey.

Kamahl neared the end of the tunnel, seeking the perfect forest within himself and its boundless power. He gripped the staff tightly in both hands, and motes of power scintillated along his arms. Three more steps, and Kamahl emerged.

A terrible beast crouched there—a monstrous mantis. It was the size of Stonebrow. Gone was the elegant slenderness of the insect folk. Bulky and brutal, the monster gorged on the lizard it had slain. While its mandibles ripped off scaly flesh, its haunches shuddered with violent transformation. A split began in its carapace, and fibers stretched and broke. All across its grotesque body, the outer skin failed. A worse beast, rumpled and wet, was emerging.

"Turn!" shouted Kamahl, his staff lifted high. "Turn, and be transformed."

The mantis lifted its triangular head from the gory corpse. Gore dripped from its mandibles. It seemed to consider its opponent. Rodlike legs shifted, and within splitting sheaths, muscles gathered. The creature leapt.

Kamahl stomped his foot, sending a jag of green energy down from his skull through his spine and legs and into the ground. It rooted him solidly. He swung his staff. It swept the legs of the charging mantis.

It stumbled but did not fall. The creature rammed him. Claws tore into his arms, and mouth plates bit into his head.

The wounds gushed not blood but power. It arced in a crown from Kamahl's head and jabbed into the monster's mouth. It rattled out of his pierced arms and into the creature's legs. Green transformation swept through the beast.

The splitting shell gave out entirely and sloughed to the ground. A slick and steaming creature emerged. Its head warped into a long, wolflike snout. The hairy thorax of the monster grew as deep as a barrel and blackened beneath thick carapace. The spiracles all down its abdomen widened into toothy mouths.

No, railed Kamahl, struggling to shape the magic he poured into the beast. *No. Something pure . . . something good . . .*

It was neither pure nor good. The creature's legs became barbed stalks with razor edges. Its antenna drooped and widened into a pair of lashing tongues. Its face began to boil.

No! You will be conformed to the new way of the forest. You will not be a monstrosity, but a noble beast.

Kamahl sent a new impulse surging into the creature. The glare of energy became blinding. In each violent flash, he saw a greater atrocity. The thing's eyes burst, its mouth drooled maggots to the ground, and its new shell split, oozing pink material.

No! You will be transformed.

The beast exploded. Its innards spewed until every plate shot free and spun in the air. The cracked exoskeleton slumped to the ground.

Kamahl fell back. Mouth parts still formed a coronet around his head. Little more remained of the creature. Gelatinous hunks shuddered across the thicket.

What had happened? Why had the transforming power failed?

"It did not fail," he muttered breathlessly. "It succeeded all too well."

In grief, Kamahl closed his eyes, and over the image of the monster he glimpsed the creature as it must have looked before becoming a monster.

The sentinel. This nantuko had been the druid sentinel beside the spirit well. She who had looked on his ascension with eyes of hope had been transformed horribly by the power he had awakened.

Kamahl lay there panting. He reached down to the perfect forest within him but found only a tangle that matched the Gorgon Mount. At last, the glory was gone from his eyes, and he saw this rampant growth truly. It was simply a cancer. What worse foe could a forest have?

Even as he knelt there, breathing raggedly, Kamahl knew he must withdraw and regain his strength. He could not advance farther this evil night—perhaps not even in a fortnight. To recover, he would have to steal power from a dying forest, but in time he would return, whole and hale, to do what he must do.

Kamahl would descend to the Mirari sword, destroy it, and kill the cancer.

* * * * *

He will come soon. The First sent his thoughts down through the Mirari sword and into the heart of the wood. *He has defeated your watcher, and once he has had time to heal, he will descend. He wishes to draw the sword. Do not allow it. Tell him what I have commanded of you. Convince him of what he must do. . . .*

Night lay deep on the Gorgon Mount as the First rose from the spirit well. Swathed in his death aura, the man was invisible. He floated upward and glimpsed Kamahl, sitting to one side and panting as if almost slain.

For a moment, the First considered killing him. No. That would only end all his best-laid schemes.

Setting his feet to ground beyond the mount, the First picked his way easily among the boughs. He had become a coconspirator with the cancerous wood. It opened a trail for him out of Krosan and toward distant Aphetto.

Soon Kamahl would be acting out the First's plans. A smile of glee lit the patriarch's face. Now he need only enlist one other barbarian. The First would fly upon the wings of darkness, across the desert and to the swamps. There he would acquire a barge crew, and pay a visit to Kamahl's other half.

Phage.

CHAPTER ELEVEN

TO THE DEATH

From malarial mists, a grand arena rose. Its curving wall lifted uneven battlements above the fog. Sunlight splashed across the dwarf masons who set stones atop it, and murky fog shrouded the crews that toiled below.

Shorn rhinos strained against leather traces, pulling massive blocks across rolling logs. Gigantipithicus apes hoisted cement sacks up long stairs. Goblin grunts worked the pumps or stirred the mortar or scrambled up ladders or sat in stocks. Taskmasters watched them all, their whips of black magic driving the whole machine forward.

Pain was the coin of the realm—pain and no little fear. Like it or not, Zagorka had become the usurer of that coin.

She and Chester made their plodding way among the work teams. Sight of that old woman and her doughty ass put fear into the hearts of even the most brutal taskmasters. The woman's disapproval meant Phage's disapproval, and Phage's disapproval meant pain or death. Zagorka preferred fear. If she could make the crews fear the consequences of failure, they would not have to suffer those consequences.

Chester snorted irritably as another mule, smaller and younger than he, bustled by beneath a crushing load of gravel. Despite his size, Chester's main use now was as a ride for Zagorka.

"Not much farther," she murmured to the beast.

He brayed in response, and nearby goblins shied as if from a blow. Chester's other role was enforcer, for he could kick over a rhino.

Zagorka and her comrade approached a particularly ominous taskmaster. Yokels would have called it a demon: a goat-headed, bat-winged, lizard-bodied thing that once had hid in a cave. It was a leftover from the War—but then again, so were they all. This beast had been hunted and snared by the Cabal, brainwashed and forced to fight in the pits, and eventually commissioned as a taskmaster. So far, it was not a very good one.

Zagorka dismounted and tugged the leathery wing of the thing. " 'Scuse me. You're Gorgoth?"

"What's it to—" he began, spinning around with teeth notching each other. As soon as he saw Zagorka, though, the red fire in his eyes turned greenish. His talon fell, dispersing the scourge-spell it had conjured, and his knees folded to the ground. "Zagorka! My humblest apologies." He bowed his curved horns and touched a furry forehead to the dust. "I am indeed Gorgoth."

Zagorka smiled absently, a look she knew inspired terror. "How does your work progress?"

"Well. Very well," Gorgoth replied. "We have met every quota for two weeks and are right on schedule according to the timetable."

Zagorka scowled. "That's too bad."

The demon's rectangular pupils closed to slits. "Too bad?"

"All the other crews are running three days ahead—"

"But we are meeting our quotas—"

"—and whenever their work overlaps yours, they have to wait."

"But the schedule—"

"You're dragging down the whole project."

"But—"

"Why not be first rather than last? Alive rather than . . . ?"

Gorgoth offered no more objections. He had sunk lower with each reply and now lay prostrate before the old woman.

Zagorka stroked Chester's mane. "You've survived since the War. It's clear you want to keep on, but the old way of surviving—hiding and skulking—won't work anymore. You cannot hide from Phage."

The demon released a whimper.

"You have to drive these workers."

"I'll beat them to a pulp—"

"No, you won't. Maimed workers don't work. Dead workers don't work. You cannot beat them to a pulp, but you must make them think you will."

The beast lifted his horned head, and a cocky glint showed in his eyes. "Is that what you are doing? Threatening with no thought of following through?"

"No," Zagorka replied. "I don't threaten. I advise. I don't follow through. Phage does. She plans for all of you to die, whether in building this coliseum or fighting in it. I advise you how to avoid death." She took up Chester's reins and pivoted him slowly away. "Listen to me and live. Ignore me and die. It is as simple as that."

"Yes," Gorgoth replied, forehead once again pressed to the ground. He remained that way as the woman mounted her mule and rode off.

*   *   *   *   *

Though outwardly the demon was utterly still, inwardly his mind churned. Zagorka's words were more than a warning.

They were an object lesson. She gained the ear of the taskmasters by acting as their advocate. Phage would punish, yes, eternally—unless one listened to the advocate. Gorgoth would work the way Zagorka did.

He rose from the ground and roared into the mists, the signal for his workers to assemble. They answered immediately—dwarves and goblins from the cutting fields.

"There is a new decree," Gorgoth said. "The slowest team will be flogged each night. We are the slowest."

"But we're meeting our quotas—"

"We are the slowest."

"But already we work twelve hours—"

"We are the slowest."

"But—"

"Silence!" he growled. "You will work faster and harder. Every night, I will flog the slowest among you, whoever is dragging the rest of us down. Now, work!"

* * * * *

The fog burned off by midafternoon but rose again at sunset. In the raking light, the mist looked like spun gold. It was a fitting metaphor. Phage was turning this fetid swamp into gold: gold for the Cabal, gold for the First.

Phage stood atop the coliseum wall. Through rags of fog, she glimpsed the workers below. Many labored on, despite the dark hour. Some slept beside their work, having fallen unconscious. Phage let them sleep in the shadow of half-hewn stone or the heat of smoldering forges. Even in their dreams, they would work. Only the bridge crews were allowed true camps on the nearby islets. They had lost too many workers already to alligators and panthers. Now archers and swordsmen guarded them against such large-scale onslaughts, but nothing could defeat the clouds of mosquitoes.

Nothing but Phage's skin.

The stars above the desert were fiery. Jeska lay in chains and stared at them. Braids crouched nearby, doing something. She was always doing something. She had healed Jeska's wound and was carrying her away in chains to the Cabal. Jeska had submitted. This was her life. The alternative was death.

Phage shook off the reverie. Above a far shore, a line of torches slid out and slowly headed across the swamp. A barge, lit by brands on either gunwale, poled toward the main island. Barges were not to land after sunset, due to daily changes in mooring points. Nor were they to waste wood on torches. What load would need such a late and grand arrival?

Silhouetted against desert stars, Braids worked at Jeska's chains. "The First is eager to see you."

A chill swept through Phage. She pivoted on her heel and descended the stair. She touched every third step, nearly running. At each landing, guards startled, whirled, and recoiled from their dread lady. Phage paid them no heed. She rushed down the main entry and out into the fog.

A huge figure loomed up and brayed.

Phage withdrew her hand. She had almost killed her second's mule. Still her pace didn't slacken.

Zagorka ambled after her mistress. "Forgive us. We were just waiting around to see if you needed something." She coughed. "You seem to need something."

"Go to my quarters. Double the guard. Tell them to clean everything. They must find the thickest, cleanest pallet and put it on the iron cot. Enlist the cooks to make a feast. Then report to me at the barge below." The commands leaped from her lips like bolts from a crossbow.

"What is happening?"

"The First is coming." It was all Phage said before she outpaced her second.

It was all she had to say.

Zagorka gave a strangled yelp and mounted Chester. The mule clottered off through the mist toward Phage's quarters.

Phage didn't spare them a glance. If Zagorka went to arrange quarters and food for the First, they would be arranged. Phage only hoped the docks would meet with his approval—only hoped the island, the workers, the coliseum, the progress, that all of it would please him. She would live or die at his hand.

"Rouse yourselves!" she called into the misty camp. "Prepare for grand inspection!" Her voice, though rarely used, was known to every last taskmaster and worker.

The word went out. Whips cracked to punctuate the commands. The troops would be ready—awake, straightened, and marshaled in rows. Anyone who failed inspection would not survive to morning.

Phage swallowed. Ahead of her, through the parting mists, she saw the torches of the approaching barge. They were not simple torches but burning skeletons. The First had perfected this execution technique—anesthetizing traitors, wrapping them in a gauze wick, dousing them with an accelerant, and lighting them aflame. They produced a hot, slow fire, and they lit the First's way. It was a well-known aphorism that the tallow of traitors was the light of the Cabal.

No light, though, penetrated the black pavilion at the center of the vessel.

Phage reached the shoreline and waited. The foremost of the skulls leered at her, its mouth and eyes trailing fire. Was it mocking her faithfulness or hailing her as a fellow traitor?

Black waters rippled before the barge. It eased forward, and poles stabbed into the muck to slow it down. With a gentle bump, the craft struck ground. Men leaned on their poles, and the anchor splashed in. Workers lifted a broad gangplank from the bow and slid it into place.

Phage waited for the curtains to part, for the man to disembark.

A voice called from within, "Phage, whose true name is Jeska, come forward."

Phage slowly ascended the plank. Wood sizzled beneath the balls of her feet, forever marking her passage. As she advanced among smoldering skeletons, the smell of burning fat gave way to the aura of the First. Most folk were nauseated by his presence, but Phage was renewed by it. Like called to like. Her skin trembled to touch cousin flesh. She approached the pavilion, curtained in black silk like her own body suit. She was home.

"Enter, Jeska," came a voice from within. The First's stare reached through the cloth that separated them.

Hands parted the curtains from within. The First's servants drew back the folds. Air spilled out over Phage—cold and dry, death smelling. She walked into it, and the fabric dropped behind her. Darkness filled the place, and the drapes showed only dim columns of gray where the corpses burned.

Phage went to her knee and then to her face. She lay prostrate. Beneath her, the woolen rug withered and rotted.

"Rise," said the First. He sat in a large chair at the end of the space, only just visible in the gloom. "The Cabal is here."

"The Cabal is everywhere," Phage answered as she came to her knees.

Eyes studied her. "I said rise. To your feet."

She stood up. Her black silhouette remained on the ruined rug. "Forgive me, Lord."

"You need no forgiveness, Jeska," he whispered. "I am well pleased with the reports you have sent—running ahead of schedule and behind budget, raising bridges and deepening canals, paving the way for the world. You say you have even found a way to render the swamps sterile?"

She nodded. "Lime will poison every plant and beast and will settle thickly on the bottom and harden. Within a mile radius of the coliseum, all waterways will be sky-blue and lined with cement."

A dry chuckle came from the First. "It is, of course, perfect."

"Also, I've commanded the dementia summoners to devise some amazing beasts. They are swamp creatures that eat sand and disgorge water. Even now, they extend the reach of the swamp into the trackless desert. Only when we reach the Corian Escarpment will we have to cease."

"You are a credit."

Beyond the barge came a small commotion. Someone had arrived, and the First's guards were barking questions. Amid the replies came a familiar bray.

"Even now, my quarters are being cleaned and converted for your own use, and a feast is prepared," Phage said.

Zagorka's protest could be clearly heard in the pause. "She ordered me to report to her."

The First continued as if oblivious. "It is not your progress or your preparations that concern me. It is my reception."

Phage felt a flutter of panic in her chest. She strode to one of the First's hand servant, knelt, and kissed his fingers. The touch of her lips brought a bubbling necrosis to the servant's knuckles. "I honor you with my life."

"Yes, you do," responded the First as he wrung his own hands. He waved his servant back from Phage. "But do your people? They treat you as a goddess—with fear, reverence, and admiration."

"They do?" she echoed, incredulous.

"They swear by you, Phage," he replied. "They are to swear by me, not by you."

"I w-will tell them."

"You will tell them tonight."

"With your leave, I will tell them now."

"Go."

Phage rose and headed for the curtains. Hand servants drew them back. Phage emerged from cold dryness into the wet heat of the swamp. She strode down the gangplank.

At its base clustered the First's personal guard, arguing with an old woman and a very large ass. Zagorka's voice rose above the din. ". . . Not here, he ain't. Phage is the law here, and she said to meet her—"

"And here you are," interrupted Phage as she strode into their midst. All those gathered recoiled instinctively from her rotting touch. "What is my best work team?"

"This week, Gorgoth and his masons."

"Bring them. Command all the rest to watch what happens here."

"Yes," said Zagorka, once again scrambling onto the back of her mule. She kicked her heels into the flanks of the beast. It bounded forward whickering.

The woman and the creature rushed amid mustered troops. They stood like rows of corn across Coliseum Island. Zagorka would find Gorgoth and his team quickly and bring them. Phage planned a demonstration of fealty. The workers would know soon their true master. The First would know it, too.

Jeska vomited on the floor when she entered the First's presence. He stood there, arms open wide. There was no escape. She stepped into the killing embrace.

An algid breeze tapped Phage's shoulder, and she knew the First had emerged. With hand servants on either side and skull servants behind, the First descended the gangplank. Out beneath the sickle moon, the man's multiple robes and towering miter made him seem huge.

He *was* huge. He was the black sun around which they all revolved, whether they knew it or not. Shortly, they would know.

As the First made his way past rot holes in the plank, Phage went to her knees. None of her folk had seen her that way before.

Zagorka returned. She bounced on Chester's back and poured out a harangue. "Watch Phage! Turn your eyes upon the shore. Watch Phage or die!"

In her wake came a motley collection of dwarves and goblins, gigantipithicus and shorn rhino, all driven forward by the lashing scourge of the demon Gorgoth. They winced away from their taskmaster and hurried toward their kneeling mistress.

None of this helped Phage. It only proved the First's suspicions.

Zagorka rode to one side, clearing the way for the work crew to spread out before Phage. They did, and went to their knees, and to their faces. Gorgoth lashed them until they were facedown and still. Then he, too, knelt—

To Phage. Every last one bowed to her.

"Tell them they are not to kneel to me," Phage growled, "but to the First."

Zagorka cupped an old hand to her lips and shouted. "Kneel to the First!"

Unsure what to do, the dwarves and goblins squinted where they lay.

"All of them must bow to the First. The whole camp."

"Bow! All of you! Bow to the First!"

With a rumble like thunder, hundreds of creatures knelt.

"We serve him unto death," Phage said.

"Serve him to the death!" shouted Zagorka.

They bowed their heads, but Phage could feel their hot glares on her back, as surely as the cold glare of the First on her face. She rose. It was time to prove her loyalties and those of her workers. She strode before the work crew. All lay prostrate. None had shifted toward the First.

Phage shouted, "Not to me! To the First!"

Looks of terror filled their features. Dwarfs and goblins shuffled on their faces, reorienting. They touched their foreheads to the ground and clenched their eyes.

"You are my best work team. Quickest. Most efficient. Most skilled. You are *my* best. You must be the First's best." She strode on, stopping to stand on the back of the first dwarf.

Cotton burned away. Skin peeled back, muscle sloughed to rot, and bone went to chalk. Vital power rose ghostlike from the corpse and twined around Phage. She drew her hands to one side. Webs of life force rolled from her fingertips to stretch across the darkness and wrap the First. He seemed to breathe in the power. Soon his figure glowed, and Phage stood in the burned-out midst of the body.

With a shriek, the goblin lying beside the dwarf tried to scuttle up and away.

Phage stepped again, pinning the creature to the ground.

While the goblin died, the other workers tried to rise, but Gorgoth dutifully lashed them. Black coils of magic struck and stung, enervating them.

Phage's words lashed them as well. "I am faithful to the First unto death. Now so are you."

Despite the barbed thongs that opened wounds just ahead of her, she advanced. The scourge brought agony. Phage brought death. One by one, she slew the workers of her best team.

Every eye on the island watched these summary executions, and every mind understood. Pay homage to the First or die. Phage was not their ultimate leader. She was only a knife in the hand of the First.

Gorgoth watch more closely than any other. Though the demon's scourge roared mercilessly, his eyes held sick pity. He had turned these workers around, and now they all were dying. Still, Gorgoth knew about survival. This was what he must do to survive.

"Man . . . woman . . . child . . . beast . . ." called Phage. She grappled the rhino's head and rotted it away to a skull. The vacated body gave a groan and crumpled. "All must serve the First unto death." Almost tenderly, she wrapped her arms around the gigantipithicus. It tried to fight back but dissolved to gray slime wherever she touched. In her embrace, it ceased to be. The gang's most powerful workers lay in heaps. Phage shifted to stand before the taskmaster.

Gorgoth went to its knees. "I-I have whipped them. I-I have been faithful to you to the death."

"Faithful to *me*," Phage said, shaking her head sadly. She grasped his goat head and kissed it—the kiss of death. Her hand slid to his neck and squeezed. The skull came off in her grip. While wings shivered, the body fell over. Phage carried the fragile bones to the First. She laid them at his feet, and laid herself there as well.

The First stared down at her, then at the skull, then at the whole island, covered with prostrate figures. Even the crone knelt deeply, her mule beside her. "You have done well, my servants." He spoke quietly, but magic carried his words to all those who knelt. "The Cabal is here."

From thousands of throats, the answer came. "The Cabal is everywhere."

"I am especially pleased with my daughter Phage. She wisely builds my coliseum. She wisely speaks through the old crone there. She will speak also through another." The First's smile glimmered in the darkness. "Phage, I have brought the one who gave birth to you, who once ruled you. Now you will rule her. As this crone is your voice to the workers, this one will be your voice to the world." He gestured behind him.

The curtains on the barge parted. From them emerged Braids, a smile stitching across her face. "Hello, big sister!"

"I am honored," Phage said, still in her deep bow.

"Stand, Phage, Zagorka, and Braids. Approach."

While Phage rose, Braids skipped down the gangplank and came up alongside her. Zagorka left her mule, hobbling up with the others.

The First's smile deepened, and he lifted his hands to the starry heavens. "You three will make this coliseum into the center of Otaria, the center of Dominaria."

In that killing embrace, Jeska lived. In trembling agony, she became Phage.

CHAPTER TWELVE

THE GODS LOOKED UP

*I*n the midst of endless sands lay a tiny spot of green. Were any gods looking down, they might not have noticed that solitary acre of brush amid millions of millions of acres of nothing. No gods looked down, though.

It was left to Ixidor to look up.

He knelt on a little sandbar in the midst of the stream. Sand caked his arms and legs. Mud hung in dry scales from his face. Blood painted his three-fingered hand. He was creating. Feverishly. Already, his oasis teemed with life.

While fingers scooped and shaped clay, fish schooled to either side of the sandbar. With unblinking eyes, they watched Ixidor work. He paused and stared back, and the fish flitted away to wavering depths. Something else flitted, and Ixidor's focus shifted to the gleaming surface. It reflected his birds, flocking through an eggshell sky. Bright plumes and brighter calls filled the oasis.

Ixidor had set them there—birds in the heavens and fish in the stream—before he had thought of feeding them. At first he had made fish-eating birds—cranes, kingfishers, gulls—and bird-eating fish—creatures that had never been before. Some fish flew. Some birds swam. It was impractical, though, an endless solipsism. At last, Ixidor had relented, created harmless but prolific bugs—water striders, bottle flies, mayflies, gnats. Even now, they swarmed, plaguing their creator.

Growling, he turned his mind back toward the thing in his hands. Water had eaten at it. He rose, working the resistant material. This glob of nothing was soon to be a monkey. He had already created mice, moles, bats, hares, foxes, goats, and pigs. He only half understood what any of them ate and suspected some would eat each other. Such practical matters would work themselves out. After all, he was only their creator—an artist, not a husbandman. As long as he kept creating, there would always be abundance, and in their abundance, the creatures would work it all out. How more responsible could a creator be?

Ixidor paused again. Animals eating animals . . . people eating people . . . creators abdicating all . . . Behind this creative fury lay a different fury, the mania of loss. Every body he formed was an apology in flesh to the one body he would never touch again. Every mind he made was a vain search for the one mind that was irretrievable. He could hardly breathe. He had to focus, to think about something other than her, anything other than her.

The mud hung heavily in his hands. Cradling what would become the creature's head, Ixidor ran his thumb in to form an eye socket. Beside it, he formed a second. With his pinky, he created nostrils and began to carve out a mouth. The head lulled free of the shoulders. Ixidor scowled. He pinched clay together, trying to get the thin neck to reform. The head was too heavy. Grabbing a stick, Ixidor rammed it into the narrow body and up through the neck. The stick cracked the torso of the beast, though, and it crumbled into two clods. Ixidor tried to shove them together, but the mud would not bond. Angry, he hurled away the half-formed creature. It spattered against the river bank.

He stood there in the midst of the stream, clumps of clay falling from his hands. Fish snapped stupidly at the little clots.

Bugs swarmed him, their mad buzz in his ears. The trees thrashed with warring birds, and the undergrowth with tiny predations.

"Not enough room," Ixidor said to himself. "Not enough room."

Maybe he should make smaller creatures. Maybe he should make creatures that didn't eat, that didn't reproduce. Aside from those things, though, why live? What was the point of life except to eat and reproduce?

Ixidor stood, abstracted. There had to be more to life than that. If there wasn't, Ixidor would make more—he would create not just life but also meaning.

Before he could create either, though, he had to create room.

Ixidor slogged out of the stream and strode toward a desert agave. It was a light green plant with broad, sawtoothed leaves that jutted up all around it. Ixidor studied the configuration. He chose the widest frond at the base of the agave. Setting one foot beneath the foliage and the other on the flat of the blade, he bent it down and cracked it. He yanked back and forth until the fat leaf came off in his hand.

He was bleeding again. It was fine. He kept the blood off the leaf and walked along the bank. His feet knew the way. Ahead stood a burl of rocks, gushing water—the headwaters of the stream—and beyond those rocks, desert sand stretched like an empty canvas. Ixidor settle down on a shaded spot near the burbling spring. He laid the agave leaf beside him and stared out into the blinding desert.

Light flooded his eyes, blinding him. Overwhelming light and overwhelming darkness were the same—the unknown emptiness, begging to be made into something. In that blankness, figures moved. They were made of the same ethereal stuff that made up his spirit guide, his muse.

Ixidor reached for the agave leaf. In mud and blood, he drew a long, waving line up it. He widened the line and gave it depth, so it seemed to be a river with broad banks running through the trackless sand. He glanced up from the leaf to the desert and saw his vision imprinting on the world. At first, the curving line was only a retinal afterimage. He blinked, and it became real.

The stream reached its slender, intrepid way out across the desert. The rocky gnarl had become a bubbling prominence in the midst of rolling water. What had once been but a brief stretch of water had become a long stream.

"A river. I want a river."

His bloody finger widened the line, and a sudden roar told of the widened waterway. Without looking away from the agave, Ixidor created a distant lake—large and deep. Quick strokes raised a forest along the banks of the water.

At last, Ixidor looked up and saw the wide river, the thick stands of tree, and the deep and distant lake. He had created them out of his own mind, his own blood.

Ixidor trembled. This was new power, unbelievable power. Image magic could do more than raise mud pigeons to life. It could create whole landscapes.

He had created the oasis. The realization struck Ixidor with the pithy weight of fact. The oasis had come into being out of his own desperate desire for it to be. He had seen it in his mind and had made it.

A pit opened in the sand before Ixidor. A second and third formed in a curving line. They were deep pits, black, with no visible sides or bottom. Three more took shape. It was as if some great beast burrowed quickly below, causing cave-ins. Ixidor staggered back. He goggled at the agave leaf, only then seeing the blood spots that had dripped from his finger onto it. Those droplets had formed the pits.

Power indeed. His very blood could carve bottomless holes in the world.

With his uninjured hand, Ixidor wiped the spots away. Sands smoothed over the pits as if they had never been.

He had never created on such scale. He had to think of water flow, habitat, heat, and light. "The land needs shade."

Ixidor mixed mud and blood on his hand and sketched a tall mountain just beyond the lake. He made the peaks impossibly tall and curved so that they seemed like claws. One summit even reached up to pierce the sun. The jagged range of peaks cast deep shadows across the lake and much of the sandy desert.

It was time to transform that sand. Ixidor rubbed his hands together, forming a wet paste. Opening his palm, he smeared it across the agave frond, turning bright sand to brown topsoil. The light before Ixidor dimmed, and he looked up to behold his labors.

Where once the dunes had beamed, now rich, brown earth extended. Ixidor reached out beside him, plucking up fern fronds and grass. He scattered them across the paste. Jabbing and prodding, he righted each of the segments to make them seem trees in a forest. The effect was less than perfect. Ixidor focused his will upon them, imagining how he wanted them to look.

The trees came, not rumbling up from the earth or striding out across it but simply appearing where they would reside. Trees became glades, and glades became forests, and forests joined the already-verdant oasis. It was a rough-and-tumble wood, the best that could be expected from finger-painting in mud and blood on agave. He needed true brushes and paints and a real canvas if he were to make this place look the way he wished it to.

He would make one final thing out of his own blood. Lifting a sanguine fingertip, he sketched a small, leaning rectangle. Its two sides extended down into a pair of legs that rested in the grassy ground. Ixidor drew two more legs behind the first, reaching from the top of the rectangle. A slender dribble of blood formed a chain that would keep the front and back legs in a peaked frame.

Beneath the rectangle, Ixidor formed a small shelf. He set upon it round jars with wide mouths and lids. In a cylindrical tube at one end of the shelf, Ixidor created narrow stalks, tipped in horsehair. A shapeless board hung there too, with a hole just the right size for a thumb.

Ixidor stared at his painting one moment longer, closed his eyes, and said, "Pow!"

Opening his eyes, Ixidor looked out at his proudest creation—an easel with paints and brushes, water and oils, and the almighty palette. Tenderly, he set down the agave leaf, for fear its destruction would mean the dissolution of the land he had made. Ixidor smiled. That easel would give him astonishing new power. He took a step toward it.

A clod of mud fell from his forehead to smack upon the ground. No, he was not yet worthy.

Ixidor turned and descended into the fast-running river. It carried perhaps ten times the water that it had before. The currents dragged at the filth that covered him. Dirt turned to mud and washed away, the red stains across his flesh lifted, salt dissolved, and sand sloughed. Ixidor dipped his head beneath the water and let it cleanse every pore. He stripped off the rag that did so little to protect him and was created new in cleanliness.

Ixidor emerged, dripping, from the river he had created. It would be called the Purity River, and the palm forest would be Greenglades, and the claw-topped mountain would be Shadow Mountain.

The arid air gulped water off his flesh. He was dry even as he stepped up to the easel. Naked and clean, the creator stood before a blank canvas. Below it, the pigments gleamed in their jars—ochre, saffron, woad, kobold, beet, reseda, calcimine, koal—absolute potentiality. With these pigments, these brushes, and this canvas, he could make anything.

Already he had filled this corner of the compass. A new canvas needed a new desert. He hoisted the easel, and naked and unashamed, strode through Greenglades. In furtive groups, rabbits followed him out into the new forest. The bugs in their ubiquity went too, and the birds after the bugs. All seemed to sigh, glad for the new lands.

Greenglades was a jungle of giants. Trees as wide around as villages rose to unthinkable heights. Vines draped from them crosswise, forming a network of elevated highways. It was a hot place, hot and wet, and brought sweat out across its creator's skin as he struggled through it.

He was glad to have so savage a place. He would have to make jaguars and anacondas, once he had the chance, but he needn't live in its monstrous heat, among its primeval foliage. He needed a cooler place, a place of sky and water, fluidity and potentiality. Already his palace formed in his mind, and he smiled. In a castle like that, with infinite rooms and recursive stairs, he could hide forever from his grief.

Ixidor reached the edge of his creation. The forest ended abruptly, its flora seeming almost crimped off by the edge of a frame. This had been the limit of his vision. In a rumpled line, the jungle gave way to wide-open desert.

Ixidor planted his easel in the sand and stared out across the blinding emptiness. While his eyes drank in that desolation, his hands worked. He opened the woad, mixed oil with it, and deposited some of the deep blue pigment on his palette. Opening the calcimine, he dipped in his fattest brush and mixed the white with the blue. When he had acquired the right color, he painted with broad strokes from the top of the canvas to the bottom. The horizon line, near the top of the canvas was the lightest blue, with the color deepening above and below it. White formed high clouds in the firmament. Thicker pigments in mottled tint and shade formed waves on the waters beneath the firmament. With a different brush and tones of light ochre, he created the dry ground, sands descending in the foreground to the beautiful waters.

Pausing and stepping back, Ixidor sighed. He had brought it into being. Before him to the blue horizon lay a scintillating freshwater lake. It seemed like a vast slice of sky laid down within the dunes. Ixidor felt as though he stood at the edge of the world and stared off into infinite possibility. He closed his eyes, letting his spirit roam over the face of the deep.

His mind traced out lines there—vast drums delving down through the flood to sit upon the foundations of the world. Above the drums and just above the water, he imagined a single massive slab of stone, two fathoms thick and a mile square. He cut out its center so that every chamber of his palace would hover above deep waters. On this slab, a rock below the sky and above the sea, he would form his world.

Ixidor opened his eyes. Already he was mixing the stony pigments. Gray slate and white granite, marble in red and black, tan limestone and jewels throughout the spectrum. He mixed and dabbed. Brush strokes scrambled over the canvas, coalescing into a glorious palace.

At its center rose a huge onion dome covered in gleaming mosaic. Its peak poked holes in the ragged clouds. At nine points around the dome's perimeter, ornate fountains clung and shot water up the tiled roof. The liquid gleamed as it ran back down, sluiced into channels, and poured from nine waterfalls into floating pools below. The streams descended nine flying buttresses to nine twisting minarets. From there, the waters followed the spiral grooves down to join the lake.

Just as water draped the palace in finery from top to bottom, so did foliage. Hanging gardens filled the castle, brimming with fruit and verdant with life. Enormous balconies held whole glades, palms flourishing amid fields of orchid. Vines trailed down to dip their tips in the flood. Everywhere, curtains of moss veiled the lower reaches.

Ixidor stepped back from the canvas and stared beyond it. He smiled, seeing his palace stand there, glorious amid the waters. The high lancets, the golden pilasters, the magnificent courses: It was a place of impossible beauty.

Ixidor's eye caught on one detail, and he frowned. He had miscalculated one of his vanishing lines, so that the palace's easternmost wall became a floor halfway down its length. In disgust, Ixidor stared at the offending lines. His brush angrily mixed the paint that would eliminate the error. He lifted the brush, filled with the colors of stone.

His hand paused above the canvas. His fingers trembled. The color was wrong—the gray of rotting flesh, the last color of Nivea before she was gone. Ixidor withdrew his hand. He would not eradicate this error, any error. They would help him hide. His palace would be perfect in its imperfection.

With a steady hand, Ixidor reached in with his stony pigments and modified another wall so that it too would flip to floor somewhere along its length. He repainted the flying buttresses so that they tangled with each other, the farthest arches overlapping the nearest. As each new line took form on the canvas, the reality beyond conformed. If it was possible in art, it was possible in truth.

Ixidor jabbed new colors on the brush and modified the front archway. The passageway became a solid slab and the stone arch above it dissolved into a space. Figure-ground relationships. He reworked stairways so that they never rose but only ran in recursive circles or ascended to the foundations or descended to the heavens. Every optical illusion that he knew, and some he discovered along the way, he incorporated. Solids turned liquid, and liquid turned to air, and air turned to solid. It was a building in the literal sense of the gerund, for it was always building itself out of impossibility.

Ixidor breathed. He could lose himself in this creation. It was exactly what he wished to do. Glorious, absurdly huge, gleaming and perfect, diverting, infinitely diverting, but he needed more than a shell. He clutched the edges of the painting, bent his head toward the canvas, and imagined each room. He hung drapes from the windows and paper from the walls. He furnished each chamber, put clothes in the wardrobes and food in the pantries. Bed linens, table linens, place settings and flower settings, supplies for art and supplies for life—everything he could imagine needing. He would live here the rest of his life. It was his undreamed land.

Those had been her words. Words held such peril. Even in this place of utter impossibility, Nivea intruded. He could not bear the pain of having her ghost instead of her.

Most men lived out their days surrounded by their memories. Ixidor would live out his hiding from them.

He touched his brush to the kohl and added a small detail to the shore. A boat, a barge, really—wide and flat, with low walls and a single long pole to drive it across the waters. It would take him to his home. He would not propel himself across, no. He needed a barge man.

Here was the great conundrum: He had not yet needed to make another thinking thing and didn't wish to do so now. Perhaps a huge ape could send him along, but what would be more dangerous than a gigantipithicus crouched upon his landing? He didn't want a creature with free will, with thoughts, hopes, and aspirations. He wanted a husk of a man, an unman.

Ixidor mixed kohl and calcimine. They formed a silvery hue, like mercury, shot through with light and shadow. He dabbed it onto the ferry, a simple glob in the relative shape of a man. He gave him arms and legs, hands and feet—but no mouth, no eyes, voice, or will. The man was simply an outline, a hole in reality. This was the sort of man Ixidor was prepared to live with.

Looking away from the canvas, he stared down the long beach. The barge waited below, its mercurial attendant leaning on the long pole.

Ixidor stowed the brushes and capped the paint pots, ready to descend to his creation. He lifted the easel and strode down the sandy slope. Only sweat and paint garbed him. It didn't matter. In skin, he was more fully garbed than the unman who waited below. The sands burned Ixidor's feet, a good sensation—purifying and purgative. He strode down to the barge and set up his easel on its floor. Then, before alighting himself, he immersed himself in the cool waters. They washed away sweat and paint.

Wet and naked, he stepped into the barge and stood beside his finished canvas. Only then did he look to that amorphous shadow, the unman who waited.

"Care much for art?" Ixidor asked, indicating the painting.

The unman did not move and made no reply.

Ixidor nodded. "Take me to my palace."

The barge man set his pole and pushed away from shore. The boat glided out on the glimmering flood. With each thrust of the pole, they moved nearer to the glorious palace. Its true proportions resolved themselves, with walkways large enough for elephants and halls huge enough for dragons. It was a maze in three dimensions—or more, for all its warping of height, width, and depth—a labyrinth of mind.

The unman poled for two miles across the waters to a stone landing. Ixidor would have to walk two more miles of curved stairways and deceptive corridors to a room where he might sleep. He enlisted the unman to carry his easel, though he was unnerved by the thing's inscrutable silence.

They climbed. Thrice they arrived back at the same landing. Only when Ixidor gave in and slumped against a wall did he find himself suddenly outside this grand private chambers.

Tall double doors gilt in gold swung inward to a high hall. Red velvet and ornate tapestries adorned the walls, and thick rugs covered floors of white marble. An enormous canopy bed stood to one side, and to the other stood a wardrobe that was infinitely deep and brimming with clothes all his size. Another cabinet held all his art supplies. From it, he drew new brushes, a new palette, and a new canvas. The best feature of the room, though, was the broad bank of windows that opened onto a huge balcony.

Ixidor walked out onto it. The stony space hung between sky and water as if it floated. Views through two hundred seventy degrees of arc showed only endless sky and endless water. There Ixidor set up his easel.

"You may go," he said over his shoulder to the unman.

The creature retreated among the shadows.

Ixidor opened the kobold blue and the calcimine and mixed up a whole new palette. Soon there would be fresh-water dolphins and manatees swimming below, with lake bass to feed them. The sky was his palette, too, and he would fill it with aerial jellyfish and coiling sea monsters, flying mantas and schools of cerulean cetaceans. His world would teem with things, all of them under his control.

No longer need he limit his mind to possibilities. No longer need he lurk among memories he could not change, for before him lay futures he could change forever.

CHAPTER THIRTEEN

THE MAGNIFICENT ADDICTION

Staff in hand and hale at last, Kamahl ascended the Gorgon Mount. No beasts confronted him this day. They had seen him kill the mantis druid a month ago. The monsters cringed away, as well they should, for Kamahl would have slain any of them. He planned to destroy even the source of their power, the thing that had made them: the Mirari sword. The beasts knew it.

So did the forest. It had no intention of allowing him to succeed.

From the top of the green canopy, a great bough crashed down toward him. Kamahl couldn't leap aside in time, but he planted his century stalk. It was like a lightning rod, channeling the power of the forest against the forest. The bough struck the staff and split. Massive halves fell to either side of Kamahl.

He stared down at the cross-section. The heartwood of the bough was slender and rotten, but the quick was a single thick ring—all that growth in one year. The Mirari had perverted the singular power of the forest, turning growth to cancer. It had seduced an entire land.

Why do you persecute me? The voice of the wood rose through the staff and shook Kamahl's hand. *You, who swore to defend me.*

Kamahl climbed up the riven bole and strode toward the spirit well. "I do defend you. I defend you against yourself."

Since last he had departed this cave mouth, it had grown, like all else. Now it seemed the throat of a volcano. Steep sides of mud, shot through with roots, descended to a deep black pit. It would seem an easy enough descent, but when Kamahl's boot dislodged a stone, it rolled down to be snatched up and crushed by the root tangle.

The forest again spoke through his staff. *I do not wish you to descend. I wish to keep the sword.*

Kamahl nodded gravely. "With the Mirari, what you wish is what will kill you."

No. What I wish is what will kill you.

Kamahl lifted the staff, tucked it to his waist, and hurled himself out over the root network. The white tendrils came alive. They rose and reached. Kamahl flipped over and fell, slipping just past the snapping roots. He plunged. A tip snagged his armor and yanked him back, but he whirled the century stalk and broke its hold. Planting the butt of the staff in the steep wall, Kamahl vaulted down into the blackness.

He passed the hoary lip of the hole and dropped for ten pounding pulses until his feet struck stone. He rolled along a smooth pathway, a wall rising to one side and a sheer drop falling away to the other. Kamahl came to a stop in a small alcove. Sitting there, he panted and waited for his balance to return.

The bright heat of the forest had given way to the dark chill of the underworld. Mutating magic clawed at his flesh and would have twisted or destroyed Kamahl if not for the century staff.

He rose, his eyes adjusting to the light. Staff in hand, he strode out of the alcove and down the tortuous path. Ahead, the trail ended. Wide-spaced peaks jutted above a sheer drop. Kamahl jumped to one, then another, then a third. He bounded to a narrow lip of stone on the far side and ran down a slope of loose scree. At its base, he entered a deep, twisting cavern.

While the rocks above had been jagged and broken, shattered by the traumas of growth, these passages were smooth, as if they had been melted. As Kamahl took a few more steps, he realized why. The stone itself was waxy, not hot but *quick*—growing, changing, moving.

He stood within the cancer itself, and the cancer knew him.

The stone beneath his feet shifted. It withdrew into shallow wells, the edges of which formed claws that clutched Kamahl's feet. He leaped and barely got free, his left foot trailing blood. It would pay to be quick now. He ran. The passage was morphing around him, struggling to close.

Ahead, a narrow section pulled in like a drawstring pouch. Kamahl leapt, leading with his century staff. It rammed through the opening. Kamahl followed. Arms, head, waist—the rock closed over his knees. Growling, Kamahl wrenched himself and his staff through the valve, which slammed shut behind him. He rose quickly, planting the pole for balance.

Through it, the forest spoke. *If you think it is hard to get in, imagine how hard it will be to get out.*

Kamahl marched on, snarling, "You will let me out. If I succeed, you will be different than you are, and you will let me out."

The chamber before him would have been utterly dark except for its inhabitants: numinous orbs and luminous ectoplasm—the ghosts of the wood. Millions of ghosts. On its own, nature was ravenous. The law of the forest was kill or be killed. When that law was sped up exponentially, the result was genocide. Not just individuals but entire species had ended up in these caves. Spirit hares leaped and dived through the air. Ghostly wolves lurked among archways. Spectral elves sat around a remembered brook and poured their laments to the sky. Every spirit made a keening wail.

The sound tore at Kamahl. Shreds of creatures twisted around his staff. He strode on like a man through sleet.

You will not pass these caves, Kamahl. Though your body advances, your soul is winnowed away.

"These are your aborted children, Krosan. Don't you hear their cries?"

Don't you hear their cries? Their maddening cries?

"I hear them, and I will end them. I will stop this mad growth and the killing it brings."

Growth is growth. Growth is the be-all and end-all. There is no such thing as mad growth or bad growth.

"When growth brings death, when it destroys, it is mad."

The forest grows more in a month than in a century. It has brought more creatures into being than in a millennium.

"And it has ushered out a hundred millennia of species. If this growth continues, the whole forest will be destroyed before winter."

You have given me six months to live. I give you six seconds.

With sudden fury, the spirits in the cave rushed upon him. Ectoplasmic hands grasped the staff and struggled to rip it free. Kamahl held all the tighter, whirling the pole in an arc before him. From its powerful pith flowed the true energy of the wood. It gathered the tormented spirits: In its simple strength, they sensed the old forest, the home they longed for. Like cobwebs wrapping around a stick, the ghosts mantled the staff. They roared and spun in hopes of returning to the way things were. In a scintillating white mass, they covered the head of the staff.

Kamahl advanced into utter blackness, his way lit by the pulsing souls. Their howls were maddening. Still he bore them. As potent as they were to the ears of an outlander, they would be doubly so to the heart of the forest.

Ahead the passage opened into a huge cavern whose ceiling and walls were lost in blackness. The floor was slick and utterly flat, and it gave off wisps of mist. A rotten stench filled the air.

Kamahl had reached the bottom of the labyrinth. He knew what lay at the bottom—or more rightly, who.

There, half sunk in the glassy floor, lay the corpse of Laquatus. Like all else in the rampant forest, this dead thing had grown horrifically. The body was huge. Its feet were as tall as Kamahl. Its legs were as wide around as ancient trees. All across its flesh, scales had turned to leaves, veins to vines, flesh to humus. The corpse had become a forest giant composed of compost. Worse yet, the giant moved. It possessed life but not true life. Its belly quivered with maggots. Its fingers trembled with the shouldering hunger of rats. The gasses of decay filled its chest and came hissing from its lips. In eye sockets, things swam.

Kamahl had the strong impression that if not for the Mirari sword through the thing's heart, it would rise.

It would, Kamahl. Draw that sword, and you will have a giant to fight.

Kamahl did not respond. He had come to stop the rampant growth. He would do so, whatever the cost. He stepped out upon the smooth floor and found it to be unutterably cold. It was ice. The natural fluids of this deep place had been frozen by the unnatural chill of that corpse. Kamahl's boots cut shallow marks into the ice as he went. He walked cautiously, fearing to break through into the black waters below.

The spirits atop the staff moaned all the louder.

"You threaten me with a corpse. I threaten you with spirits," Kamahl said, edging his way along the giant's legs. "The corpse is the creature I killed." He lifted his staff. "The spirits are the creatures you have killed."

Not even the Mirari sword, not even your spirit staff, will stand against this giant. You will never escape this cave with the sword in hand.

Kamahl gritted his teeth. "You have invested me with the

power of transformation," he said as he approached the giant's fuming chest, "and now I use my gift upon you."

Holding the spirit staff high in one hand, he reached the other to the Mirari sword. It dragged at his hand, as of old, and begged him to take hold. The sword's seduction had only grown, bedded here in the heart of the wood.

Kamahl had also grown, but inwardly. He would not be so easily enticed again. Grinning with determination, he eased his fingers around that so-familiar hilt. His hand tightened. Flesh touched metal, and mind touched mind.

The forest mind was enormous. Every branch was an axon and every leaf a dendrite, each species an axiom and each creature a thought. Even Kamahl was but a favorite fancy of that great mind. He was a wandering hope that touched other thoughts and changed them, a rubric that freshened the corners of that fetid brain.

Do you see now how small you are? You are only a notion, a thing to entertain or dismiss. What umbrage for an itinerant idea to think it could change the organ that had made it! Do you see how inconsequential your soul is, how meaningless these souls are? They are only old thoughts, forgotten. This growth is not genocide; it is learning. I have not slain all these creatures but only outgrown them. I am thinking thoughts a thousand years beyond you.

Kamahl did not answer aloud. He needn't. His mind was part of the greater mind. He needed only think to remind the forest of those memories it had forgotten. His body became a conduit between the Mirari sword and the spirit staff. Souls raced from wood through flesh and into steel. They took with them their wailing dread, their hopes and desires.

Remember, thought Kamahl, *remember these dismembered parts of you. Thoughts are alive. They are creatures who wish and*

hope, grow and change. Even I am a multitude. You, then, are a
multitude of multitudes. To so callously kill these children of yours
is to callously kill yourself. Remember. You are more dead than
alive, more scar tissue than new flesh. Regain what you have lost.
Become again what you once were.

All the while that he spoke, the ghosts of the forest coursed
through its forgetful mind. Their piteous wailing brought forth
other emotions—recognition, fondness, sadness.

The forest remembered. Once again it saw the bright macaws
and heard their sweet cries in its upper branches—pale ghosts
returned to life. It glimpsed tigers amid bamboo stalks where
tigers no longer survived. It remembered the ticklish touch of bush
babies, the patient nibbles of ground squirrels, the savage cries of
howler monkeys. All were gone, now and forever.

Worst of all were the millions of vanished insects. Their drone
had been the pulse of life. While the insects thrived, all that ate
them thrived. They were the foundation of the food pyramid.
Now, they were gone. The foundation had cracked and crumbled,
and the apex even now was falling in on the rest. The extinction
of the smallest thoughts in that great mind foretold the death of
the mind itself.

The mourning of the lost spirits had infested the forest. It too
began to mourn. While it did so, Kamahl rooted out his true foe,
the mind of the Mirari.

Abruptly, it was all around—curious, insatiable, ceaseless. It
was a mirror, yes, but liquid. It not only reflected but also conformed to what it encountered. That was why it was so destructive. It became the apotheosis of what it beheld. Among the
barbarians, it had become Bloodlust. Among the Northern
Order, it had become Tyranny, and among the merfolk, Deception. The Cabal had made it Corruption. The forest made it
Cancer.

The Mirari had traveled Otaria and manifested itself as five pure, evil gods.

Still, Kamahl did not sense a mind that was fundamentally evil—only insatiable. It was a mighty intellect, not human or elf or dwarf, but deeply interested in all of them, otherworldly but somehow Dominarian. It wanted to know and grow, and therein lay its magnificent addiction.

Kamahl would teach it. He had sparked the forest's memories to demonstrate its evil. He would spark the Mirari's memories to do the same.

Do you remember when you came to the Northern Order?

It did. It remembered shining in their midst, embodying all that they wished to be. It remembered transforming them into images of perfection. It remembered their worshiping eyes as everything soft and corruptible in them turned to stone. There was no recollection, though, of the misery, of the death.

Kamahl had plenty of recollections. He poured them into the Mirari. Folk froze in place as their legs calcified. Hands shuddered in panic as death crept over them. Screams ceased only when ribs no longer could squeeze out air. The Mirari had given them their hearts' desire and removed the last of doubt. It had killed them.

The insatiable mind darkened a bit. Before, it had merely reflected evil, showing it on its outward skin. Now, true darkness entered the Mirari. Still, it needed more.

Do you remember the young man who first had found you?

The Mirari filled with images of a burned out ruin and a slender young explorer—intent of eye and sure of hand. It recalled the sensation of riding at that young man's side, bouncing against the warmth of his hip, listening to his complex negotiations. There was fondness in the great mind for that young man.

Kamahl showed his own memories of Chainer—when he had lost his innocence and his mind. His shoulders were still young despite the crushing burden they had borne. His eyes were old, though, and his mind older still. His head was coming apart like an onion losing its skin. Layer upon layer of his mind split and sloughed, forming into monsters. Soon there was nothing left of Chainer except monstrosity. Just before that final, horrid divide, the young man had granted Kamahl the Mirari, had beseeched him to carry it away from the Cabal forever.

Again the mirror darkened. It was losing its infinite reflection. Atrocity kills curiosity; virtuous minds cease to want to know. The Mirari was a virtuous mind, and the darkness troubled it. One more memory would bring this rampant growth to an end.

Do you remember what you did for me?

Reluctant, suspicious, the Mirari brought to mind what it had done. It showed Kamahl mantled in power, invincible in battle, surrounded by his admiring people. It showed him overcoming any foes that came against him and ruling more surely than any of his folk ever had.

Kamahl turned his thoughts toward one of those foes—his sister. He remembered the look of horror and betrayal that Jeska wore as his sword sliced into her. He dredged up his deep self-loathing for having struck the blow. He tasted again the bitter gall of fighting her in the arena. Kamahl poured out his terror, all the darkness that clouded his soul. Let it cloud the Mirari. Let it darken the mirror and kill the cancer.

That mind blackened. It had seen enough. No longer would it reflect the world around. Its eye had turned inward to darkness, and it ceased wishing and wanting. It only ached. The Mirari went inert, a benign and inactive tumor in the brain of the forest.

Kamahl had taught it something new—compassion. He had shown it the way past reflections and to the heart.

Do not be so arrogant, Kamahl. You are, after all, but a thought in our mind. We have many more thoughts, ones that could teach you a few things.

Suddenly, Kamahl saw. In its fever, the forest had grown across hundreds of miles of desert. It stopped near the Corian Escarpment, a great spine of granite that thrust up from the sands. On the other side of the stone wall, another realm rampantly expanded—a vast swampland. Just as Kamahl had become the avatar of the wood, his sister—his nearly slain sister—had become the avatar of the swamp.

"I know. She is my own great wrong, which I must right. There are evils that consume me as well. I know."

Not all. You do not know all.

Through the eyes of eagles, the forest saw. It soared above black swamps and found avenues laid there. It followed lines dredged through water and lines laid upon land. Roads, bridges, canals thronged with folk. They rode and walked and sailed along convergences, drawn to the center of a vast web.

And what a center—a great circle in stone. Kamahl had never seen so stately a stadium. Though thousands flocked toward it, a whole nation already sat in its seats. On the sands below, elephants raced fifty abreast. Their feet churned up clouds of dust, and their blade-barded shoulders brought blood from each other. Red lines followed them as they went. Cheers roared out with each pachyderm that fell, and great lizards ran across the sands to tear into the beasts.

The Cabal pits had been recreated for a vaster audience.

Stands, luxury boxes, vendors, waiting pens, the sands, the elephants, the speaker's pinnacle—all of it centered on a single figure. Jeska. The unhealing wound on her belly had festered into a wound on the world.

Leave the Mirari sword here. It can do me no more harm and can do you no more good. Leave the sword, and leave the forest giant that it pins.

I will let you go from the cave, from the forest. You have set right the evil within me. Now, you must set right the evil within you.

Go, Kamahl. Take your army. Bring back Jeska.

CHAPTER FOURTEEN

OPENING DAY

From the top of the central pillar, Phage watched the elephants race. They really were magnificent beasts—so powerful, so fast, so full of blood. They were down to twenty now. The ones that remained had to dodge the ones that had fallen. Phage had planned on the corpses providing obstacles, but she hadn't realized that every time the beasts came in sight of their slain kin, they would trumpet and charge the giant lizard scavengers and set in for a ferocious melee. It was all the handlers could do to drive off the remaining beasts and resume the race.

Down to thirteen.

The crowd loved it. Most of them had never seen an elephant. Now, they saw fifty of them and watched forty-nine die. It was merely the opening act, the diversion that kept everyone happy while they got seated.

Half the world was getting seated. Twenty thousand filled the lower reaches, and twenty thousand more flocked across the bridges and rode the courtesy barges. Once they had seen today's entertainments, there would be fifty thousand tomorrow, and then eighty thousand, and then a capacity crowd of one hundred thousand.

Braids had brought all these people. She had traveled the

whole continent of Otaria, taking with her a taste of the coliseum's splendors. To yokels, she presented a freak show. To families, she showed a menagerie of exotic creatures. To magistrates, she offered an arena for the resolution of disputes.

The coliseum was everything to everyone. The rich enjoyed luxury boxes replete with every pleasure both legal and illegal. The poor crowded on dusty benches and screamed their lungs out. Braids had proven herself a human Mirari, knowing just what each person wanted and providing it—for a price. She had arranged walk-in one-day passes and boat-in week-long excursions with full accommodations.

By the end of the week, the coliseum would have paid for itself. By the end of the month, its revenues would have outstripped those of the pits.

Only one elephant remained—bloodied but unbowed. The crowds cheered it with almost vicious approval. The animal meanwhile stomped stupidly beside the bone piles of its kin. It bobbed its head in manic distress. Its handlers jabbed it with short hooks, leading it toward the animal paddock.

At the arena's edge, Braids announced the next spectacle. She opened her throat to two worlds—reality and dementia space—and wove the sound together into a bellow that reached for miles: "Come one, come all to the newest, truest wonder of the world! Come see beasts you have only heard of. Come see beasts that have never been! Leave behind your weary world. In the Grand Coliseum, every man is a king. Every woman is a queen. Every child is heir to the riches of the world!"

Braids was both the coliseum's promoter and one of its star attractions. Even as elephants died below, many folk watched Braids capering above.

"Behold the brutality of beasts. View the vendettas of warring clans. Witness the wonders of history.

"Get ready now for the battle of the centuries—the War!" crowed Braids. "Look here to the south and behold the heroes of Dominaria!"

A thick wooden door swung wide, and from it emerged two great gladiators.

The first, a seven-foot-tall giant of a man, wore a tan and maroon jumpsuit and bore a huge polearm.

The crowd responded with a furor of cheers and boos in equal measure.

Beside him stood a very different figure—tall and gaunt, with ash-blond hair and goggles that looked like gemstones. The fidgety light that played at his fingers promised impressive combat spells. The mage raised a hand to a violent ovation . . . and a pelting rain of rubbish.

The crowds didn't care who won or lost, but only that the men fought.

A fight there would be, though in keeping with the century-old tradition, these two gladiators would begin on the same side. They strode from the doorway, leading a continent of humans, elves, dwarves, minotaurs, and Keldons. This team— the Dominarians—would square off against the Invaders.

"Every last one of them is a condemned murderer, but fear not! They all are well controlled by our handlers. You will see them pay their debt to society and reenact a critical battle in the history of our world. Now, behold to the north, the Invaders!"

Another door swung wide, and from it emerged a horrid host. A scaly demon led his team out upon the sands. Demons were rare in the extreme, ancient creatures that had evaded a century of hunters, but they had not evaded Phage's folk. This one had a head like a sack of skin stretched across a skull. Horns jutted up all along its shoulders. Its torso was an amalgam of cable-taut muscle and metal framework. Its legs and arms were living mechanisms as well. The thing trudged forward, lifting its minuscule eyes to the crowd and raising clenched claws at them.

They cheered as much for it as they had for the defenders.

Behind the demon came a horde of beasts—huge serpents, enormous crabs, scaled wurms, rhinos with metal horns, giant ground sloths fitted with claws and spikes, and a host of gibbering dementia creatures only dreamed in ruined minds.

A roar went up from the Invaders, and an answering roar came from the Dominarians. The crowd itself took up the shout. The two sides charged together, and their cries shook the coliseum. The sound spun through concentric rings and flew out the parabolic arena as if a single great beast had awakened upon the world.

Atop the central pillar, Phage stood in the black throat of that hungry beast. She had created it out of swamps and stone, out of the throng and its darkest desires. Now she need merely feed it and watch it grow.

The warriors converged. Horns and blades rushed in to meet steel and spell. Minotaurs crashed head on with rhinos. Already bodies fell to the sand.

Feed it and watch it grow.

Something flashed in the stands. Phage looked toward the light—a mirror in the hand of Zagorka. She was signaling for Phage to come down to the grandest luxury box of all—the royal box of the Cabal.

Phage nodded. Braids was her voice to the world outside the coliseum, and Zagorka was her voice to the world within. The old woman would not have called unless the summons was urgent.

Following the rails atop the pillar platform, Phage came to a narrow set of stairs. She descended around the capital to an iron band that wrapped the column. The band was as wide around as a man. In each of the cardinal directions, it sported a massive cable that stretched to the coliseum's wall. These lateral supports for the column provided quick access from it down to the stands.

Phage lifted a metal hook from a holder full of them, looped the thing onto the cable, and pushed free.

She dangled high above the epic battle, gaining speed on her way toward the stands. Hook and cable began to spark, a bright tail behind Phage. Folk below pointed. An avid cheer rolled up for the slender, black-garbed woman. She was the architect of this new spectacle, and they loved her for it.

Hurtling like a comet, Phage soared toward the wall. She raised one foot and set it on the cable to slow her descent. Even so, as she came down she leaped free and rolled. The hook clanged brutally against the wall. Phage could have broken her own fall, except that a fat man carrying drinks ducked under her. She landed, smashing him to the ground. For a moment, her outline formed a rotten well on his body, but then he was gone.

Phage rose and descended the stairs. She headed toward the royal box. Why would the First have summoned her during the opening ceremonies? Was he pleased or displeased? Did he wish to share this victory or to shame her in defeat?

It didn't matter to Phage. Her labors were done. Her creation would live or die apart from her.

"Mistress," called Zagorka, ambling up the stairs without her ever-present mule. "The First summons. It is urgent."

"Tell the attendants to rope off the landing platforms," she gestured over her shoulder. "Give the family our condolences and a thousand gold to make up for the death." Phage continued past the old woman.

Zagorka stood and gaped. "What if they still aren't satisfied?"

"Then they can challenge me in the arena," Phage said simply. She left the woman behind, knowing the matter would be resolved.

Ahead the stands gave way to a long ring of luxury boxes, the largest of which was draped in black and guarded at either door. In the midst of the populace, the First had a space that was all his own—ten rooms, including an exact replica of his inner sanctum in Aphetto. The only difference was that his full-size portrait had been replaced by a wide view of the arena floor. After all, it was in that portrait that Phage had first glimpsed the coliseum.

Phage stopped before the door to the First's box, but she needn't have. The guard had swung it wide and had dropped to his knee, head bowed.

Impassively, Phage said, "The Cabal is here."

Without looking up, the guard muttered the reply, "The Cabal is everywhere."

Phage edged around him, lightly brushing past his tousled head. The hair withered and dissolved away. He gave a little whimper.

The way was clear through antechamber and chamber to the Inner Sanctum. She was expected.

He waited within, seeming almost an avatar of the black-walled room. He wore his full robes of stiff leather, the joints oiled to keep them supple, and a black miter on his head. Within all that fabric, his face was a pallid hunk of stone, and his eyes were steel bearings. Just now, his attention was focused on the match. Despite his impassive face, the hand servants that stood to either side occasionally clapped for him.

Phage bowed low. The First was her creator. He had made her what she was, and he was the only other creature in the world like her.

Without looking away from the battle, he began to speak. "There is much blood. Perhaps too much, Daughter."

So this was to be a reprimand. Phage pressed her head into the thick carpet. "They are convicted murderers. All matches to the death feature those who would be executed anyway. They are offered as object lessons—testimony to the horrible end that awaits wrongdoers."

One of the hand servants waved away Phage's defense. "It is not the killing, but the blood. There is too much blood for families. It is merely an aesthetic concern."

"I will charge the mages to use magic skin spells to keep the blood in."

"Precisely," said the First, turning at last. A servant motioned Phage to stand. "There has to be some, or the deaths will not seem real, but not gallons this way."

"Not gallons," she echoed as she rose.

The First approached, his own hands spread wide. He embraced no one unless he planned to slay—no one except Phage. His killing aura surrounded her, and hers surrounded him. He crushed her to him.

"You have done well, Daughter. I am more pleased than I can express."

She sighed. Those were the words she had longed to hear.

He broke the embrace almost too soon and turned his eyes back to the match. All the Invaders, including the demon, lay dead. Most of the Dominarians also had been destroyed. Just now, the two Dominarian gladiators fought each other. The crowd screamed its approval, and the First's hand servants clapped.

"How will you top today's offerings?" the First asked quietly.

Phage began to respond, but a rattling clamor came behind her. Someone arrived, a very certain someone.

Braids bounded in. No sooner had she arrived than she bowed, not in reverence but nausea. She vomited unceremoniously on the floor but lifted a grinning face. "Like the show?"

"Very much," the First responded regally. He did not look to the vomit, seeming to consider it an offering of obeisance.

"The rug will be replaced, of course," Phage said.

"Of course."

As if she had heard the First's question, Braids said, "You should see what we have planned for the future! Grudge matches!"

The First still did not turn toward her, but an eyebrow lifted, a sign of intense interest. "Grudge matches?"

Braids draped herself over a nearby chair and said, "Yeah. What's more entertaining than watching a fight between people who hate each other? When we can, we'll get famous feuds, but it'll also work to have theme days—cuckold fights, cat fights, holy wars, vendettas, revenge. We'll offer the combatants their choice of weapons, staging, and lethality."

"Good," said the First. "Very good."

Braids fiddled idly with her hair. "It's the first step toward your vision, making the arena a judicial system." She cupped her hands, using her barker's voice. "Don't fight in the streets like dogs! Come to the arena. You'll get justice, fame, and valuable prizes!" Dropping her hands, she said, "The fights will teach morality. When there is a draw, the citizens themselves can decide who wins and who loses, who lives and who dies. We can even make people feel it is their civic duty to attend such matches, to make certain justice is done."

The First nodded very slowly. "Let's not use the word 'duty' in conjunction with the coliseum. We want folk to think of pleasure and fun, not of duty. We want to lure them, not drag them in."

Braids was suddenly out of the chair, kneeling low in sick worship. "Forgive me."

The First watched the distant fight, seeing the Dominarian warrior decapitate the mage. "There is nothing to forgive." While the crowd roared, the First glanced toward Phage. "I have the perfect such match in mind for you. I have spent the last few months arranging it."

"Only say the word, and it is done," Phage said.

The First smiled. "You will fight your brother Kamahl. He is on his way. You will fight in a month."

Phage bowed. "Eagerly, Master."

"Forgive me," Braids snickered, bounding away. "I must announce the next match." Her voice faded as she withdrew through chamber and antechamber. By the time she got outside, the sound rose again. "Behold, young and old," she barked, leaping up the stands, "the miracle coliseum brings you none other than the miracle workers who built it. Behold!"

While giant lizards dragged away the remains of the armies, doors swung wide. A trudging platoon of dwarves emerged. Behind them came gigantipithicus apes and shorn rhinos, goblins and mule men. They were armed with the tools of their trades—hammers, chisels, ropes, wedges, chains. All had the sweat and grit of months of labor on them. Their faces were grim despite the glad shouts of the crowd.

The First watched in amazement. "Who could they possibly fight?"

From beyond the luxury box, the voice of Braids belted out. "A thousand slaves, kept in line by a hundred whips. Behold their foes, the taskmasters!"

More doors opened, disgorging a motley group of creatures in black leather suits and spiked helms. Magic scourges cracked in their hands. Hisses and boos greeted the taskmasters, but they only whirled their whips more viciously.

The First smiled.

"They've been at war all this time," commented Phage quietly. "The wreckage of their war is this new coliseum. While they built, I forbade them to kill each other. Now they have permission, and all have agreed to it. It is a sort of prelude to the grudge matches."

Braids' voice intruded, ringing throughout the stands: "And at the head of the taskmasters will fight their own masters—Braids and Phage of the Cabal!"

The resultant ovation was deafening.

"I must go," Phage said, gesturing toward the door.

"Win, Daughter," the First said. "I will place a hundred thousand gold on you."

Phage bowed her head. "That is too dear a price."

"If you lose," the First said, "I will have paid a far dearer one."

* * * * *

Phage and Braids walked side by side across the sand. The roar of the crowd heaped on their shoulders. It was a perfect moment: blue sky above, red sands below, taskmasters behind, and slaves before.

The two sides rushed into battle. Oh, so many scores would be settled today. Best of all, though, the world was watching.

The First was watching too.

"They've strength, but no magic and little speed," Braids said, bouncing gladly as the lines neared. "I say we strike with speed and magic—"

Kicking up her feet, she hurtled across the sandy no-man's land. Braids flashed into and out of being, running half the distance in dementia space. It was as if she ran through an invisible forest. In a heartbeat, she reached the slave contingent, leapt, and darted across their heads. Spike heels dropped dwarves and goblins in their ranks. Braids ran up the chest of a gigantipithicus, kicked its massive chin, and flipped over backward as it fell. She gave a ululating cry and cartwheeled away over the heads of the goblins. In mere moments, she bounded back to her army.

"Sounds fine," Phage answered.

Braids grinned avidly and fell in step. "That was the quick bit. Here's the magic."

Her face blanched. She gripped her stomach and wretched. Her mouth stretched violently wide, and from between ragged teeth, she spat a huge creature. The thing was all sliding triangles of black carapace and claws. It squeezed past distended jaws and thumped down on the ground.

As it rose, the hulking beast dripped saliva. A pair of bug eyes lolled in its bristly forehead. Teeth splayed in a false smile, and it galloped out across the sand.

"A brotal," explained Braid. "Saw it in dementia space and swallowed it to bring it here."

"Very nice," Phage said quietly as the monster tore into the front ranks of the slaves. Its claws were the length of sling blades, and they cut apart the dwarf vanguard. It seemed to be hungry for goblin.

Still more slaves came on, their weapons clutched tightly.

Impassive, Phage raised her hand and signaled her forces to launch their ranged attacks.

Grinning eagerly, the taskmasters complied. They brought their scourges hissing and snapping before them. From each metal-tipped thong spun vicious magic, the sorceries they had used on the slaves all along.

A torrent of spells whipped the dwarfish vanguard. The blackest bolts killed outright. Husks of skin and bone tumbled to the ground. Other strands, laced with blue radiance, were even more pernicious. They lashed the arms and legs of the slaves and attached themselves like the strings of a marionette. Dwarves and goblins turned, screaming resistance even as their limbs attacked their comrades.

A hundred slaves had fallen in those first moments. Nine hundred more remained. Each taskmaster would have to kill ten even to survive.

"Attack!" shouted Phage, hand held high.

They did. Taskmasters with whips and swords laid into slaves. Slaves with mauls and spikes fought back.

Braids ran atop them all, belching beasts into the fray.

Phage meanwhile strode in the midst of the fight. No one wished to attack her, whether because of her brutal reputation or because she was in some ways the great ruler they all revered. Slave and taskmaster both recoiled. They would rather ram into each other than confront their mistress. Phage walked, queerly calm in the midst of the horrors. Wherever she stepped, bodies rotted rapidly to nothing. Most had not been dead but only maimed, writhing until she touched them.

The crowd chanted something. Over the wild roar of the melee, it sounded merely like a great heartbeat—*lub-dub, lub-dub, lub-dub*. Phage lifted herself on tiptoes to listen. At last, the sound came clear:

"Death-touch. Death-touch. Death-touch. . . ."

That's what she would do. Her taskmasters were only butchers. She was the one who brought quietus. These had been good workers, and they deserved a rapid death. The crowd deserved it too.

After all, the world was watching, and so was the First.

Phage began the dance of death. Her hands floated out in gentle, flashing flourishes. She grazed the neck of a goblin. . . . A step, a leap, and she caressed the cheek of a bloodied dwarf. . . . She pirouetted, brushing a gigantipithicus. . . .

"DEATH-TOUCH! DEATH TOUCH! DEATH-TOUCH!"—a staccato accompaniment to staccato death.

Phage swept forward, trailing her hands along the flanks of folk who parted before her. . . . On she danced, death untouched in the midst of battle.

CHAPTER FIFTEEN

STRONG RIGHT ARM

Amid a forest of easels, Ixidor sat upon his broadest balcony. Its white sweep of stone jutted above a lake where dolphins sported and leviathans sang. The platform hung beneath a sky draped in giant jellyfish and teeming with flying fish.

This was his world, Topos. It had been born from his mind through his hand, borne on canvas into truth. This was his palace, Locus, huge in dimension and infinite in recursion. He should have been in ecstacy here, but instead he was fretted, rattled, panicked.

"I'm tired," he said to no one—in fact, six no ones.

They surrounded him, six shadows cast upright in the air. He had created these guardians in his own image. They remained always around him, only a leap away. Each unman was a living portal to somewhere in the palace. Should a threat arise, Ixidor need merely dive through one of the unmen as through a doorway. The other unmen would follow, and then the portal man would close forever. Ixidor could elude six separate assassination attempts before running out of unmen. He should have felt safe, but he felt fear instead.

Ixidor stared critically at the living portals. They kept him safe, yes, but their lurking silence was unnerving. They were like animate pits gaping around him always. Any moment, he might fall through one. His own creations terrified him.

"I'm tired."

A caravan had happened upon Topos. They had drunk its waters and hunted its game, thinking themselves saved from death by sun. They had been welcome until they approached the palace. They called out, promising a grand show. Ixidor had not responded, but aerial jellyfish had. They swarmed, their tentacles long and lethal. They had only been following their instinct: Defend Locus. It was an unfortunate encounter.

Afterward, Ixidor posted warnings in the sand: STAY OUT OR DIE.

Yes, the needless deaths distressed Ixidor. He was done with death, dealing it and being dealt it. Sadly, it wasn't done with him. Someone would come looking for the caravan. It waited, intact but for the drivers. Ixidor had left more warnings, which would of course be ignored. Where words failed, jellyfish, griffons, and air sharks would not. It was inevitable: All kingdoms had border disputes.

Topos's borders separated fantasy from reality.

Was that the reason for this gnawing dread? Armies would come to Topos and try to take it . . . and die trying. Ixidor was confident his defenses would stand.

No, his discontent lay within the creation itself. Locus was as haunting as it was huge. Its grand vistas were so immense that peering into them was like peering into the Void. Infinite rooms held mute furniture and blind portraits and brooding tapestries, most of which would never be seen by their creator. The thought of all those dark corners in his home made him shiver.

Ixidor rose. He turned his back on the easels and strode into his palace. The unmen went with him—one before, one behind, and two to either side. He didn't know where he was going. It didn't matter.

All of Topos was fearsome. The lake was fed by a cascade that appeared in midair a mile above the ground. The waters emptied into a grotto that plunged, cavern by cavern, to hot magma a hundred miles below. Sand dunes formed spirals in space that turned one's feet ever inward. Forests reached roots down to become branches in underworld groves. Ixidor had populated these terrible places with terrible creatures: mayfly men who were born at dawn and died by dusk; plants that wept and pled not to be eaten; stones that thought great thoughts but had no mouths with which to speak them; dirt that ached with implacable desire.

He could have created anything. Why had he created terrors?

He reached a garden, one of hundreds. He had had to walk across air to get there. The bridge that led to the garden was a transparent fold in time, impenetrable. It led to a hovering disk of stone that held hundreds of tons of topsoil. Fruit trees thrived above berms of flowers, and paths led among green shrubs and white statues. Ixidor shambled along one such route, his living shadows accompanying him. He approached a stone bench and sat.

Before him stood three statues—a girl kneeling to feed a bird; a berobed woman summoning magic from the grass; and an angel leaping with sudden power out of the jealous ground. They were three statues but one likeness: Each had the face of Nivea.

She was the reason for this haunted place. All of Topos was meant for her, yet she would never see it. He had plumbed the depths of the world and set sentinels in the sky, looking for a creature who was in neither. He had made empty shells for companions because no companion could be her.

"You haunt me," he said to the staring face of the angel. "You have given me this power but have forbidden me yourself."

The unmen leaned toward him, their empty heads cocked, listening.

Ixidor ignored them. He stared at the angel statue, her limestone robes rippling in resurrection. Up from the grave she surged, throwing aside the black ground in her quest for white skies. She was perfect, incorruptible. No grave could hold her.

Ixidor's heart flailed, as if packed in mud.

The truth was that Nivea was not the incorruptible angel, but rather the corrupted dirt. She had fallen apart in the arms of Phage.

The best Ixidor could do was surround himself with everything that was not her and then stare unseeing at it all, hoping to glimpse her in absence.

* * * * *

"The Cabal!" Ixidor startled awake, clutching his chest.

Someone was there beside the bed.

Ixidor yanked back the silken veils.

A figure stood there, dark against the nighttime wall. It was no one, an unman. Panting, Ixidor tore back the rest of the curtains. Six unmen stared at him, their heads bent in worry.

Ixidor hurled off the covers and stood. He tried to shove away the unmen, but they shadowed him. Flinging open the glass doors, Ixidor strode out onto the balcony and stopped at its balustrade.

The midnight sky held only a handful of tepid stars, which gave off a sickly glow. Ixidor peered beyond the shimmering waters and the dark tangle of Greenglades. He could not see the edge of the wood let alone the desert's first dunes or the caravan waiting there.

"How could I have been so stupid?" Ixidor growled. He whistled loudly between his fingers. The shrill sound leaped away across the waters. "They promised a show. Who promises a show but the Cabal?"

In the deep distance, a shadow struggled free of the palm fronds. It stroked huge wings once, twice, and soared on the wind toward Locus.

"They'll come for more than wagons and wares. They'll come for revenge."

The shadow shot out over the lake and shrieked, its eagle beak gaping above a leonine body. The griffon fought through clouds, pulled up above the rail, and lighted there beside its creator. In the tepid light, its pallid coat seemed deep blue.

Ixidor climbed onto the beast, grabbed a fistful of mane, and dug in his heels. With a squawk, the creature launched itself from the balustrade. Its wings caught hold of the air, and a second and third surge lifted it away from the stony bulk of Locus. Amid whirling vortices, Ixidor sensed a stripping of power. He glanced back to see his unmen, stranded on the balcony. He had made them out of his own shadow, and so they could not ride on clear air.

It felt liberating at last to be without them. Not until that moment did he realize how much he hated the unmen.

Powerful wings stroked above the pitching treetops. Beneath the wan stars, palms moved like monstrous heads. The griffon's wings stripped back the forest. In merciless minutes, it neared the desert's edge. Five box wagons waited there, lined up across the sands.

"What kind of show would the Cabal bring to the middle of the desert?"

Spreading its wings to glide, the griffon passed over the last the trees. It slid slowly down to touch ground at a run. Padding up beside the caravan, the bird-lion sat. Ixidor dismounted.

The sand was cold. He walked quietly toward the first wagon, wishing the stars were brighter. He wished many things—that his unmen were here, that he had brought a weapon, that he wore armor.

The wagon was ornately painted, with large-spoked wheels and many doors. Panels were meant to slide back or fold out into various bits of scenery. It was a moving theater, and the now-dead folk had been its troop. Even despite the dimness of the stars, Ixidor could easily read the inscription: "THE GRANDE COLISEUM ROAD SHOW."

Ixidor blinked stupidly. He grasped the hasp of one of the scene pieces and drew it slowly out. It showed a minotaur gladiator, striped with wounds. Ixidor positioned it on the sand and one by one pulled out the rest.

To the right opened a wide panel, within which was painted a gray set of stands filled with cheering folk. A similar panel opened to the left. The wagon's awning, when laid down across the door, completed the picture of the inside of a great coliseum.

"Why?" Ixidor wondered aloud.

A voice came from within, a weary voice at the edge of survival. "For the amusement . . . of Phage."

Ixidor took a step back. "What?"

"For the glory of the Cabal . . . and the amusement of Phage."

"Who are you! What are you doing here?"

"I'm dying. . . . Without food or water . . ."

"No, what are you doing in my lands?"

"The taskmasters . . . promote the coliseum. We fight . . . an exhibition."

Ixidor's eyes narrowed as he approached the wagon. He discerned bars in the windows. "You are slaves?"

"Gladiators, or I am. . . . My partner is dead."

Gritting his teeth, Ixidor said, "All for the amusement of Phage." He patted his pockets, hoping to find something he might use on the lock. "Don't worry. I'll get you out. I have a score to settle with Phage."

From behind the wagon came a terrible shriek—the griffon. Its wings thrashed, and its claws raked the sand. A sudden silence followed.

Ixidor rushed around the wagon.

Phage stood there, blacker than the black night. She clutched the griffon in a headlock. The thing's flesh rotted away, just as Nivea had. Phage hoisted the skeletal griffon and waggled its ribs, so that the great feathery wings seemed to sprout from her own shoulders.

"I knew I would find you," she said. "I killed Nivea, and now I kill you."

Ixidor did not know what to say. How could he fight her with no tools, no weapons, not even a paint brush?

Virulence ate through the griffon's skeleton, and bones tumbled like white sticks from Phage's fingers. She advanced.

Ixidor took a step back, keeping the distance between them. He would not run. He would bluff and bargain until he had reached Greenglades, where his own beasts could rise to protect him. "Why do you hunt me?"

Phage crept forward, keeping eyes locked on her prey.

"For sheer spite?" Ixidor asked, nearing the edge of the wood.

"Yes," Phage replied in a hiss.

Ixidor shook his head. "Vengeful beast." He hurled himself up a tree bole, scrabbling to climb aloft.

With a shriek of animal rage, Phage leaped after him. Her hand swiped just behind his retreating foot. Instead of climbing, Phage merely wrapped her arms around the tree. Bark split and peeled; quick blackened and sloughed; heartwood burned right through. With a sudden lurch, the tree and its occupant began to fall.

Ixidor flung himself across the emptiness, toward a high crotch nearby. His hands snagged the bark, but it ripped away. He fell. Fronds slapped his back as he tumbled. He struggled to get his feet under him but could not. Vines snared his legs, and he crashed down on his back amid undergrowth. There he lay, beneath a thin layer of flapping leaves. He could not breathe, the air knocked from his lungs.

Phage loped froward through the forest, looking for him.

"You cannot hide, Ixidor. Darkness is no ally of yours. I am darkness," Phage said quietly. All around her, undergrowth rotted, and soon, Ixidor's cover would be gone.

He stared up beseechingly toward the branch of a tree, where a pair of red eyes watched.

"There you are," Phage said. Even in the gloom, her teeth glinted. "Don't make me walk on you. I would rather wrap you in my arms and cradle you to death as I did to Nivea. Rise."

Fall.

The black panther plunged from the branch.

Phage glanced up too late.

All teeth and claws, the cat impacted her. Its jaws clamped down, crushing her face. Fore claws ripped open her throat and hind claws her belly. Next moment, the cat was slain by rot, but its corpse smashed Phage to the ground. Ribs and putrid meat pinned her.

Ixidor gasped a breath, struggled free of the vines, and cracked a branch from a nearby tree. The broken end came away in a long spike, just as he had wished. He charged, holding the bough lance-like, and rammed it into Phage. He felt the jagged point pierce her chest, punch through muscle, and crack bone. He thought he even sensed the spongy lung beneath. Yanking the branch out, he plunged it into another spot.

Already, the sharp point was gone from the branch. It struck this time like a blunt pole. Worse, as the last of the panther fell away, Ixidor could see that the claw marks down her belly were knitting closed, and her throat had ceased bleeding. Phage shuddered, throwing off the remains of the panther's skull. Even her face had healed.

Ixidor rammed the stick at her again, but she grabbed it and yanked herself to her feet.

Dropping the branch, Ixidor turned and ran. He had nearly killed her. The panther was, after all, just another weapon in his hand, and he had a whole forest of them. If only he could get far enough ahead—

She was too quick. Phage thrashed through the forest, closing on him.

Ixidor half-turned, raising his arm to ward back the blow.

She grabbed his arm, and contagion spread from her fingers. Her touch was agony—cold, numbing, killing. It turned his flesh black and made his muscles into gray jelly. Fingertips to shoulder, his arm rotted. Phage closed her hand around the bone and twisted. Sinews snapped, the joint popped, and like a wing pull from a long-roasted bird, Ixidor's arm ripped entirely loose.

Screaming, he clutched the bloody stump.

"If you had let me, I would have held you. You would have been gone completely by now. Will you make me take you one piece at a time?" Phage asked. She tossed the rotten bones aside and stalked toward him.

Ixidor staggered away. He stumbled backward over a root and fell, staring up into the canopy. "Nivea!"

Phage reached for him. Her arms opened in the all-accepting embrace of death.

"Nivea!"

Something flashed like lightning in the forest. A wide, white blade swept down and struck Phage's shoulder. Her right arm fell cleanly away. It thumped in the weeds beside Ixidor, and he had the crazy thought of grabbing it and placing it on his own stump.

A figure came between Ixidor and Phage. It was a woman—an angel. Her flesh was alabaster, the color of the statue in the garden. She was no statue, though. Her feet hovered above the ground, unblemished by dirt or grass. Her hair streamed, and her huge wings drove back Phage. She advanced, the lightning sword beaming above her shoulder.

Ixidor stared, dumbfounded.

Phage hadn't a chance. She stumbled helplessly.

The angel lifted her blade high and turned its point downward, and rammed the sword into a scabbard across her back. She was not going to kill Phage—or at least not that way.

The angel opened her arms and wrapped Phage in an embrace. Snow-white fabric enfolded black silk, purity warring with corruption. Smoke poured from their flesh. Skin peeled like burning paper and muscles caught fire. Bones split and organs drooled from ruptured cavities.

Phage crumpled. She slid like a greasy bag out of the arms of the angel. Whatever remained of her on the robes of the angel burst into flame and were gone.

The angel turned. She did not step or flap, but only swung slowly about, her wings gathered at her back.

Ixidor fell to his knees and then to his face. He clutched the ground with the fingers of his remaining hand. "Nivea."

She hovered above him, staring down.

"Forgive me, Nivea," he muttered into the ground. "Forgive me."

"I am not Nivea."

Ixidor raised his eyes. It was like staring into the sun—blinding and painful. "You are Nivea."

"I am not. I am your new creation. I am the Protector."

Ixidor blinked. "New creation?"

"Your dream was the medium."

He shook his head. "My dream?"

"All of this is a dream. It began when you thought you had startled awake. It ends now. . . ."

Ixidor sat bolt upright in bed, breath raking into and out of him. He was covered with sweat. He dragged back the silk curtains and swung his legs down, seeing the unmen crowd nervously up around his bed.

A dream. The whole thing had been a dream.

Except that something beamed brightly—powerful, feminine, floating above the floor. The angel drifted beyond the circle of unmen, who cast watery shadows across their master.

"You are real," Ixidor said breathlessly.

"You created me out of your dream. I am your Protector. I will keep you safe from all foes."

Ixidor averted his eyes to the marble floor. "You will avenge Nivea. You will kill Phage."

The angel nodded with Nivea's own likeness. "I will kill Phage."

Ixidor smiled for the first time in days. At last, he had created something beautiful. He stood and held out his hands toward the angel.

Only one arm rose. His right arm was gone.

He gasped, prodding the stump of his shoulder. It was not gory as it had been in the dream, but still the limb had vanished.

"I am your Protector, your strong right arm," said the angel. "You made me out of dream and out of your own body. I am bone of your bone and flesh of your flesh. I will defend you."

Unbelieving, Ixidor probed the stump of his shoulder.

The angel held her arms open. "Come, my master. I will protect you."

Tears streamed down his face. Could he refuse? What would she do if he spurned her?

Ixidor staggered into those brutally pure robes. Radiance scorched his skin and prickled his hair. He was unworthy, yet he was her creator. "You are pure of every stain, and so I shall call you Akroma."

CHAPTER SIXTEEN

DEATH MATCH

*C*ommander Kamahl rode his red battle snake Roth out of the forest. The wood had spread across hundreds of miles of sand and stopped in sight of the Corian Escarpment. Beside the commander, General Stonebrow trudged toward the granite ridge. In time, commander and general reached the height of the escarpment and signaled a halt. Behind them, with fist or claw or bough, the vast army of forest folk passed on the signal. They shuffled to stillness.

Standing there, they did not seem so much an army—two miles long and half a mile wide. They seemed the forest itself. Dryads had come in marching groves; spinefolk like fiery tumbleweeds formed ubiquitous hedges; brownies herded thistle stalks; and these were only the flora. Among them slithered giant serpents and enormous slugs. Toad men stood with legs akimbo beside elves in watchful rows. Giant centaurs and giant squirrels, bear warriors and mantis warriors—the great army of Krosan was, in fact, Krosan.

Sitting astride Roth, Kamahl got his first glimpse of enemy territory.

"It is like a great spider web," rumbled General Stonebrow beside him. The huge centaur's eyes flitted in their deep sockets.

Kamahl took a fortifying breath. "It is. My sister spun it."

Below their rocky vantage, the ground fell away to a wide black swamp. Brackish water reached to the horizons. Small islets rose here and there from the muck, piles of offal in a latrine, and from peak to peak ran a network of bridges. Here was a pestilent land with its borders wide open. It beckoned visitors as any snare beckons prey.

"There is her lair," Kamahl said, pointing to a huge ring of stone far away. Even from this distance, the coliseum was impressive. Tall, broad, perfectly proportioned, it was the only solid thing in that place of mud. More amazing still were the throngs that filled the distant roadways and bridges and the folk who blackened the stands. "She has already caught tens of thousands."

Stonebrow brooded a moment, his gaze shifting to the bridge that descended nearby. "Tens of thousands in the stands, and tens of thousands in the swamps. Look." The islets below were not empty, each garrisoned with a small contingent. Other things patrolled the waters. Thousands of eyes peered up at the army. There would be no way to bypass Jeska's minions.

One minion particularly promised great difficulties. Kamahl growled low as he recognized a manic figure that bounded up the nearest bridge. "Braids."

Though the suspension bridge was sharply pitched from the swamp to the escarpment, Braids climbed as if racing across flat ground. Her feet made hollow sounds on the planks, a counterpoint to her giggles. This woman was lethal. She was not so much small but stunted, not so much capricious but chaotic, and her giggles were utterly mad.

With a final cartwheel, Braids planted her feet on the ground and her hands on her hips. She smiled toothily at Kamahl, her skin like sun-stretched leather.

"Welcome, Kamahl, to the lands of the Great Coliseum."

Kamahl's hand tightened on his staff. "I have come for Jeska."

"Same old Kamahl." Braids flicked a hand in annoyance. "She's dead. You killed her. Don't you remember?" She yawned and turned back toward the bridge. "This conversation bored me the first time. No sense even mentioning the proposition. . . ."

"I have a proposition for you. Turn her over, or I march my army to take her."

Peering back over her shoulder, Braids nodded disinterestedly and yawned again. "Your army. Yeah. Gator food."

Only then did Kamahl recognize the huge, swimming forms beneath the waters.

General Stonebrow clutched his great axe. "Some of us will reach the coliseum. Some will be enough!"

"Suit yourself," Braids said, starting back down the bridge. "We don't mind a bit of carnage. More carnage, more coinage."

"Wait," called Kamahl. "You know my proposition. What about yours?"

Braids paused, gripping the rope rail and lifting her nose into the air. She sniffed dramatically. "What is that wonderful smell? Is it desperation I smell? Surely not. It smells like desperation, but why would a man with an army be desperate?" Shaking her head, she continued down the bridge.

"I will fight her! That's what you want, isn't it?" Kamahl roared.

Braids stopped. Without looking back, she asked, "To the death?"

"To *my* death. If she wins, she can kill me. If I win, she comes back with me—she submits, and all the folk of the Cabal let her go."

Sniffing again, Braids pivoted slowly. "It wasn't desperation I smelled. It was the sweet smell of a deal."

"Part of the deal is that my army accompanies me. They will

cause no trouble, even at my death, if the terms of this deal are kept. I need them for security, in case you plan a double-cross."

Braids shook her head, climbing slowly. "Not in the arena. We don't have seats for trees."

Kamahl snorted. "All right, but any creatures that can sit comes into the coliseum."

"Your command team—no more than fifty—will be admitted free. The rest can enter for a gold piece each." Braids stopped at the top of the bridge. She smiled and shrugged. "It's the standard entry fee."

"Since when do forest creatures carry gold?" Kamahl said.

Braids lifted her hands. "All right. Deal's off. Phage stays with us. Feel free to attack if you'd like to be decimated. Otherwise, go back and hold a bake sale. Once you gather a few thousand gold, we'll talk."

Kamahl barked. "You let them on the coliseum island, and they wait outside, but my command team gets to come in. Then I'll fight my sister."

"What are you doing—?" Stonebrow began.

Braids panted, sniffing eagerly. She reached up the flank of Roth, grasped Kamahl's hand, and shook. "Yes. I smell a deal."

* * * * *

Kamahl had wanted this to be a triumphal entry—he and his armies sweeping in to save his sister. It was not to be. Kamahl was no conquering hero but a lamb led to the slaughter.

As they crossed the final bridge, Braids walked beside him. Roth, Stonebrow, and the command corps followed. After them came the army in a long and vulnerable line. No gator, no guard rose to oppose them. At each garrison, Braids smiled and nodded knowingly. She had planned all this.

Not she, but Jeska.

Banners hung from the height of the coliseum and proclaimed: "Today's Death Match: Kamahl of Krosan vs. Phage of the Cabal!"

She had even known it would be today. They had sold tickets for weeks, knowing brother and sister would fight to the death today.

Kamahl and Braids left the bridge and wended their way among hawker's carts and stalls. One sold mandrake roots dyed red and dressed in miniatures of Kamahl's armor. The seller lifted an effigy and shouted, "Guaranteed to create virility and drive women wild. Whether you want to conquer your sister or get conquered by her, you can't miss with a Kamahl mandrake."

Gritting his teeth, Kamahl hissed to Braids, "Why do you do this? Why do you create misfortune and sell tickets?"

"That's our trade," said Braids easily.

"You are scavengers, watching creatures kill each other and swooping in to feast."

Braids laughed easily. "As long as there are killers like you, there will be scavengers like us."

They passed the marketplace and a ring of Cabal thugs who surrounded the coliseum. The line of muscle split to allow Kamahl, Braids, and the fifty commanders through, including Stonebrow. Afterward they closed, barring the way to the rest of Kamahl's army.

He shook his head. "You even knew the particulars of our deal before we struck it."

Braids simply repeated, "It's our trade." She nodded toward the great gates of the coliseum, and they swung wide. The arched tunnel was filled with warriors. They formed a wall to the inner coliseum. To either side rose wide stairways to the stands. "Here's where we part company. Spectators go up the stairs. Gladiators go through the tunnel."

Kamahl nodded. He turned aside to Stonebrow and spoke in hushed tones. "Be ready. You're the one to sound the signal, if need be."

The giant centaur tightened his hairy fist on the horn that hung from his belt. He stared down grimly. "Treachery will be answered in blood."

Braids patted the centaur's flank. "Glad to hear it. Now get a move on. You'll miss the match of the century." Though she was one tenth his size, her shove on his side sent him moving.

The Cabal warriors parted, opening a pathway. Kamahl peered past the crowded darkness to the bright and desolate sands beyond. His sister would be waiting for him there.

Kamahl stepped among the warriors. In the darkness, his staff sparked with green fire and his eyes with red. This would be the final confrontation. The day he had struck Jeska and nearly killed her prefigured the day she had struck and nearly kill him. Now the odds were even. Both bore an unhealing wound. Both had been transformed into power. Kamahl had come to drag Jeska up to life, and Jeska had come to drag him down to death. Whatever happened today, they would never fight again.

Kamahl emerged from the tunnel. He went from a place of crowded blackness into a place of blazing light. The sun was omnipresent. So was the roaring crowd. It swept away all thought.

At the center of the sands was a circle, and in its midst stood a woman. Jeska.

* * * * *

They loved him. "Ka-mahl! Ka-mahl! Ka-mahl!" The crowd had only just laid eyes on this man, this legend—warrior of the pits, warlord of the Auror tribe, slayer of Laquatus, brother of Phage—but already they loved him. Perhaps Braids had done her promotions too well, casting Kamahl as the quintessential hero.

Phage stood at the center of the coliseum and listened as the crowd cheered him and jeered her. She was unfazed, watching the furious work at the betting counters. Money flowed in an absolute cascade from the pockets of the patrons to those of the Cabal. That's what this sound meant, more money for the First.

The First was her true brother. He was the one creature in all the world who understood what it was to have demons in his skin.

Phage lifted her hand clawlike toward Kamahl. The crowd went wild. She squeezed her fingers into a fist, literally wringing more money from the pockets of the spectators. She watched it flow.

The people were living vicariously—fighting, killing, dying, and yet remaining unharmed. They felt like gods peering down upon the plight of mortals, making their bets, lending their minds and souls to those below. What they did not realize was that this spiritual usury made Phage a true god. She could inspire them to fight, could whip them to riot, could lead them to war.

Today, everyone would be a gladiator.

Phage lowered her arm and stared at Kamahl.

He stood a hundred paces away, his staff grounded in the sand. Druidic robes ruffled in the wind. Beneath gleamed his barbaric armor. If anything, his new devotions had made him more muscular. He would be a formidable foe, except that he hoped not to kill but to save. That was his weakness.

Phage shrieked and ran toward him. She glanced into the stands and saw bars descend across the betting windows. It was time to fight. Some fans would rage. Let them. It would only deepen their desire.

Feet were not fast enough. Phage launched herself in a series of forward flips. The world spun end over end. Blue sky tumbled with tan sand.

Kamahl rammed his staff into the ground, and it drew mana. Power surged through the wood, crackled up Kamahl's arms, and filled his frame. He lifted the staff horizontally above his head.

Flipping toward him, Phage smiled. No matter how he blocked her—head, hands, waist, chest—he could not block all. Whatever won through would strike him and rot him to nothing.

"Good-bye."

Rounding out her last flip, she launched herself into the air and hurtled down upon Kamahl.

His arms were locked on his upraised staff.

Phage reached around it to kill.

Kamahl was not there. With an easy sidestep, he had moved out of the way.

Shrieking in anger, Phage raked one hand out to catch his shoulder. His tattered robes disintegrated. It was all she could do.

It was not all he could do. He whirled around, swinging his staff toward her back. She had not even struck ground yet when the stout pole whacked her spine. Air rushed from her lungs and blood from burst vessels. The strike left a welt, but it would take a better hit than that to break her spine.

Phage crashed down in the dust. It caked her face and hands and pasted itself across her sewn-up gut. She scrambled up and spun to face him.

He was already a stone's throw back and still retreating.

The wild ovation of the crowd devolved into hisses and moans. These folk had come to see attacks, not retreats.

Kamahl shouted, "I do not wish to harm you, Sister."

"It is too late for that," she spat and hurled herself toward him again. Sand flew. The welt from his staff was already healing. It had not weakened her body but only strengthened her hatred.

Kamahl would die today. Phage had no brother but the First.

She didn't flip this time, keeping her eyes on him. He would not escape.

Kamahl merely stood, staff in hand to one side. He didn't even brace for attack. Only his robes moved, and the green magic that climbed across his staff. The power peeled away the first of the stalk's hundred rings. It was as though the staff were a tight scroll that unrolled before Kamahl. It eclipsed him for a moment.

No thin shield would stop Phage. She barged toward it like a bull toward a sheet of paper.

Spinning suddenly, the staff rolled itself back together. It spun and snapped, and Kamahl was gone.

Phage dived through empty air, somersaulted once, and came to her feet. She spun, searching for her foe. He was gone utterly. Only his staff remained, standing in the sand as if rooted there. Power mantled it, buzzing menacingly, but otherwise the arena floor was empty.

Cheers gave way to nervous laughter, then to expectant silence.

In that hush, Phage heard Kamahl's voice.

"I will take you with me." The sound jangled with energy.

"You will not!" she snarled.

"If I must maim you, I will take you." He was near that staff—perhaps within it. Had the scroll rolled him in with it?

Phage cautiously approached. "You are skilled at maiming me."

"I mean only to save."

"You'll have to kill me," Phage said, reaching her hand toward the staff.

"We shall see." Suddenly he emerged, boot first.

The metal sole shoved from a fissure in the wood, caught her jaw, cracked it, and flung her sideways in the sand.

The crowd roared. They were on their feet.

Phage was off hers. She spun and fell on her face.

The rest of Kamahl followed his boot. He stepped onto the sands and stood there above her, glowering. "I did not want to do that."

She didn't respond. She couldn't. Her jaw was in two pieces. Though the power of the Cabal raced through her veins, working to realign bone and heal flesh, Phage had momentarily become Jeska again, struck down by her brother.

"You will not speak," he said. "Then I will."

The crowd's noise died away as one of Braids's spells took hold. She had known there would be great speeches given before the killing blow, and she had made provisions to let those words be heard throughout the stands.

"Forgive me, Jeska. Though you are the one whose skin has turned to poison, though you are the tool of the Cabal, I committed the evils that brought about your doom. I should bear this curse, not you. Forgive me, Sister."

Many folk began to boo, especially those who had betted on Phage.

"Come with me," Kamahl pleaded. "Let death be drawn out of you. Let life flow back in. Come with me."

The catcalls grew louder. Phage listened to them, to her brother, to her own secret heart.

"You needn't even rise. Just remain there. The bell man is beginning his count. Let the bell toll, and come back with me to be healed."

She turned her head upon the sand to see the great cylindrical bell and the bellman with mallet in hand. She looked along the stands to the royal box. Somewhere within that darkness sat the First, watching her.

"Only a moment more, sweet Jeska. Let the death bell toll and return to life."

* * * * *

Kamahl stared down at his sister. She knelt before him, not the all-powerful death dealer that she had become, but his little sister. He had struck her down again. This time, though, he would heal her. He would not rest until she was healed.

Kamahl dropped to his knees before Jeska. "Forgive me," he muttered one final time. Looking up from her hunched figure, he saw the bell-man lift the mallet and swing.

It never struck. Phage struck instead.

From a full crouch, she hurled herself like a ram at his chest. Hands, head, shoulders, all butted him backward. Her touch dissolved the last of his leafy cloak. It made his metal breastplate steam.

Kamahl tumbled backward, Phage landing like a hellcat on his chest. His armor cracked and shattered. He rolled again to throw her off. In the spin, he lost his staff, but if he hadn't spun, he would have lost his life.

Phage was hurled one direction and Kamahl the other. He clambered to his feet. Her handprints showed in black on his chest, and the wound in his belly suppurated. Kamahl stared at Phage.

She crouched low and stalked him, a predator waiting for him to run.

Kamahl backed away instead.

The crowd hissed him and cheered her. Kamahl had suddenly become the villain and she the hero.

What had happened? A moment before, Jeska lay there, ready to be healed. Now she was utterly gone, and only this incarnation of death remained. He could see the print of his boot on her jaw, healing even as she approached, but her eyes would never heal. In them, the imprint of his evil was profound.

Kamahl's hands closed to fists. The power of the perfect forest was depleted in him. He needed his staff. It could heal the rot on his chest and cleanse the unhealing wound on his gut, but it lay behind Phage. It might as well have lain in the afterlife. Perhaps, if he could circle around . . .

"Now that I can speak, I will," Phage said, rubbing her jaw as she patiently pursued him. "You think I am doomed and cursed. I am not. You think your wounded sister lies hidden in my black heart. I have no heart in which to hide her."

Hoots and applause came from the stands.

"I am not damned, Kamahl; I am Damnation. I am not diseased; I am Disease. You cannot bring me back to life, for I am Death."

Let the bloodthirsty masses cheer her words. It distracted her, gave him time. Already, he had managed to circle around so that he was closer to the staff than she. He needed only a little more time.

"There are two ways to defeat death," Kamahl said as the crowd sounds died. He edged nearer to the staff.

Obsidian-eyed, Phage stalked him. "How?"

"The first is to bow to it," Kamahl said. "That's how I defeated you last time, by surrendering. If I fall to my face—"

"I'll kill you anyway!"

"And queer the match, so all bets are off? I don't think so," Kamahl replied, his feet still shuffling.

Avarice gleamed in Phage's eyes as she glanced toward the booking windows. "What is the second way to defeat death?"

A few more steps, and he smiled. "It is quite simple. Defeat death by living!" He leaped for the staff. His hands reached across trammeled sand, and he descended, his fingers closing.

She struck him in the belly—a hard blow that knocked the wind from him and sent him tumbling away from the staff. Kamahl rolled in agony, clutching his torso. Beneath the rotting hand prints on his chest, rotting knuckle marks showed. On his stomach, Phage's face had made a ghastly silhouette—brow, nose, and empty eyes. The unhealing wound formed a crooked mouth. Phage had struck his chest with fists, and his belly with her skull, and hurled him away from the one thing that could save him. Now, her contagion slowly ate him away. He convulsed.

Everyone cheered. This bout was proving to be well worth the entrance fee: fierce fighting and fiercer words, high drama and low blows, a sibling rivalry with teeth in it.

While Kamahl thrashed his life away, Phage strolled slowly up to stand above him. She pursed her lips. "Forgive me. Though I am the tool of the Cabal, you are the one who bears the doom." The spectators cheered the mockery of Kamahl's words. "Let death be drawn into you. Let life flow out. Come with me." She reached out her hand. "Just take my hand, and all the pain and guilt will be gone forever. I will heal you so that you will never ache again. Just a moment more, sweet Kamahl. Let the death bell toll, and be done."

He stilled his thrashing and stared at her. Something showed in his eyes—terror or pity. "Jeska. . . ."

"I am Phage."

"Look out!"

She laughed, shaking her head incredulously, and reached down to wrap her hands around his neck.

* * * * *

The impact was horrific. It felt like a rhino bashed her in the back. White-hot pain burst through her spine, and Phage hurtled through the air. She lost her putrefying hold on Kamahl. Curling into a ball, she struck the sand and rolled. Her back clenched, dying tissue by tissue.

Is this how my death-touch feels?

Biting back the agony, Phage scrambled to her feet and glared at her attacker.

It was an angel, bright-beaming in the midst of blood and bets. She was beautiful, her face somehow familiar. At her belt hung a magna-sword, which she could have used to cut Phage in half. She had not, for this was no doubt a creature who fought fair.

The beaming warrior drew the sword and pointed it at Phage. "I am Akroma. I have come to kill you."

CHAPTER SEVENTEEN

GRAND MELEE

Kamahl lay gasping in ecstatic pain.

Before him hovered a creature of light, glorious and beckoning. It was the death vision. Many barbarian warriors reported seeing this creature as they lay dying—a light so intense as to cast all else in a tunnel of darkness. Kamahl was dying, coming to pieces at throat, chest, and belly. The angel of death called him, her face so beautiful and yet so stark. She reached toward him.

If he took her hand, he would die.

Kamahl clawed away from her. He was a barbarian warrior, and all barbarian warriors clawed away from the angel of death. Kamahl rolled onto his face on the sand, and suddenly he could breathe. His throat was in ribbons, air sucking into and out of an open windpipe. Breathing, he averted his eyes from the beckoning angel.

She turned her eyes away as well. She moved with savage surges around the coliseum. It was as though she pursued another soul. Let her.

Kamahl crawled. If he knew anything in that moment of exquisite pain, he knew he needed his staff. The power of life was gone from him but not from that staff. It sparkled with green lightning where it lay in the sand. If only he could grip it, power would flow into him and knit him together.

Everything else fell away. He forgot who he had been, how he had become so wounded, what he fought for. Caught between the angel and the staff, Kamahl became a tabula rasa, a soul upon which nothing has been written.

White and black, figures flitted by. They shrieked, two raptors swooping, slashing, tangling, breaking. Their battle verged near to the crawling man. For a moment, he feared they would catch him in their lashing midst and tear him to pieces. He dug in and clung to the sand, throat rasping rotten breaths. The two creatures tumbled past.

The man scuttled forward, a lizard sliding on his scaly belly. Sand packed the gangrenous spots. One more surge, hands before him, and he gripped the sparking pole.

Life leaped in green bolts into his fingers. It hissed and cackled, sinking into his flesh. Putrid skin and muscle dribbled away. Power burst in bright loops from the wound at his throat, and lines of force wove themselves into new flesh. The surge of power plunged through his chest, healing it as well. Only when it reached his belly and the wound carved there did it stop.

The wound. "Jeska!"

It was the first word he had spoken since his throat had been eaten away. With that word, all his long life scrawled itself across him—a feverish and violent graffiti. How good it had felt to be white and unmarked, the crawling man instead of Kamahl. He had reentered the scarred carcass of his life. He was Kamahl again, and Kamahl had a sister.

He clung to the staff and turned over. "Jeska."

There, before him, she fought. The angel of death pursued her, a moth battling a roach. Her magna sword, as wide as an axe and as long as a sword, roared down to slice Jeska in two.

"No!" shrieked Kamahl. "No!"

* * * * *

Phage could not escape that blow. She had dodged every other, had flipped backward and dived low and performed every possible evasion, but Akroma learned with each leap. No evasion remained. Phage lay on her back, and the magna sword descended.

It struck. Metal that was stronger and keener than steel cut through her shoulder, cleaving silk, skin, flesh, and bone. It hung up halfway through her third rib, only inches from her heart. Gritting her teeth, the angel shoved downward. It would kill her, its eyes as white as ice.

Phage grabbed the blade. It was a thing of pure light and she of pure darkness. Her fingers clamped tightly around the metal. It hissed under her touch, and metal ran like wax. Her nails jabbed through. Phage ripped away a hunk of the sword and hurled it across the coliseum, where it struck stone. Her hand fastened again, and another slab came away. The angel struggled to withdraw the blade, but Phage was tearing it apart. Molten metal poured from her riven shoulder.

The black sorceries that filled her joined bone to bone and flesh to flesh. Even as the cleft closed, Phage hurled the last of the sword away.

She leaped to her feet, hands shoving the chest of the angel and leaving black prints.

Akroma recoiled in agony, her incorruptible flesh bearing marks of rot. Her face twisted in horror. It was the first time Phage had gotten a good look at her. This angel had the face of Nivea, but not just Nivea. She seemed the incarnation of all Phage's victims.

Unafraid, Phage stalked toward her. "You would kill me, but you know nothing of death. I am Death. I will take you to my lands."

Someone approached—Kamahl. Phage had almost forgotten. The druid-barbarian walked with staff in hand, verdant lighting jagging around him. His chest and throat had healed to puckers of pink flesh, and his eyes were violent and grim. He dug footholds in the sand.

Phage glared narrowly at him. "I suppose I will have to fight you as well."

Kamahl shook his head. "I came here to save you." He flicked his eyes toward the angel. "Anyone who would kill you is my foe."

"All right." Growling in irritation, Phage edged nearer to the angel. "Together, we kill her, and then we fight each other."

"If we must," replied Kamahl.

Side by side, brother and sister strode into battle.

* * * * *

Braids bounded along the rim of the coliseum, braying her excitement. "Behold! Brother and sister, sister and brother—mortal foes, this Phage, this Kamahl—and yet they ally together against an immortal enemy! New wagers for the next five minutes. Bet upon the angel. Bet upon the siblings! Prizes and purses collected first. Then the winners fight to the death."

Beneath her, the stands boiled. Folk flooded toward the betting counters. Others filled the air with their fists and shouts.

Never on Otaria had such din arisen. Never before had war been so profitable or entertainment so deadly.

* * * * *

Once again, Kamahl was caught between life and death. Akroma hovered brutally above, just out of reach of his whirling staff. Phage stood ready beside, seeming a cobra rising to strike. They were life and death.

The question was, which was which?

Akroma darted in, angry and white, a lightning bolt unfolding toward Phage.

For her part, Phage leaped in to catch that lightning bolt and ground it.

They clenched. Their power, black and white, battled for dominance. On contact, decay spread across Akroma body, and sterile welts rose on Phage. Where hands locked on arms, the skin peeled back from both women. Where eyes locked on eyes, the very air crackled with antipathy. They would consume each other.

Kamahl rammed his staff between the two. The butt struck Akroma and pried her away. He followed up the strike with the power of his shoulders. The angel jerked farther back. Kamahl swung the head of the staff before Phage, stopping another lunge.

Both women stared furiously at Kamahl and his scintillating staff. They were ravaged—black gouges across Akroma's arms and torso and white necrosis across Phage's. Even as Kamahl watched, the wounds closed. These creatures danced on the strings of puppet masters. Some unknown mind drove Akroma, but Kamahl knew too well who drove Phage.

He lifted one hand from his staff and raised it high in a signal.

He should not have released the staff.

From opposite sides, Akroma and Phage grasped the glimmering pole. Green magic rolled each direction. When the power reached Phage's hands, spores of energy showered around her fingers. Wherever those green motes landed, Phage's flesh pitted and burned. Black and green magic were ancient enemies. Black and white, though. . . . At the other end of the shaft, Akroma drew off the power. It mingled with her own energies, strengthening her, healing her.

"No!" Kamahl shouted, but it was too late.

Akroma yanked the century stalk from both of them. It gleamed in her hands. Her eyes glowed green with power. She whirled the staff expertly, and energy ambled across her knuckles. On hovering wing, she surged toward Phage and Kamahl. Side by side, they backed away.

"Nice work."

Kamahl could only grunt. He wasn't use to fighting this way, caught between two foes. How could he slay one, save the other, and not die in the process?

He raised his fist in that same, insistent signal.

* * * * *

Stonebrow snorted. He thought he had seen the signal, but Kamahl had been surrounded by the other two and his own bright staff, and the general had not been certain. Its import was too grave to proceed until he was entirely sure. Now, Kamahl's upraised fist could mean nothing else:

Storm the coliseum and kill the First.

Stonebrow gazed down toward the luxury box of the First. Between Kamahl and it stood rows of cheering spectators, fists pumping the air. They would be an army, once roused, and would protect the Cabal patriarch. The Krosan warriors would have no hope of reaching the luxury box. Let them save Kamahl. Stonebrow himself would kill the First.

He stood, shoved his way through the crowd, and strode down the stairs. His hooves hardly fit on those steps, and each stride shook the stone floor. He reached for the horn that rode on his side. He lifted the great thing, set it to his lips, and blew.

The sound pealed out even above the cacophony of the crowd. It was joined by the call of a second horn and a third. From every stairway around the coliseum, the horns of the commanders rang. They called the people of Krosan, the people of Kamahl—called them to attack.

Many of the fans cheered, expecting some new wonder from the proprietors of blood sport. It would be a new wonder, but not from the Cabal.

A second roar arose, this one outside the coliseum. From the throats of centaurs and mantis warriors, elves and goblins, giant serpents and great jaguars came that violent sound. The green forces charged. Fiery spine folk led the vanguard, burning anyone or anything that stood in the way. Already, the great doors burst into flames.

A living forest rushed to invade the coliseum.

*   *   *   *   *

Braids clapped as they came. She could hardly smile more deeply, more sincerely. Things were going wonderfully.

Of course, she and Phage had planned on the storming of the coliseum. They had expected the attack to come when Kamahl lay dying beneath his sister's grip, but Akroma had ended all that. She was a surprise, though a diverting one. This attack by the forces of green only brought things back on schedule.

Leaping from prominence to prominence, Braids cupped her hands and shouted, "Behold, the armies of Krosan! Behold, the Grand Melee! Place your bets! Krosan vs. Cabal. Who will win? It's ten to one odds on Krosan! Win tenfold if the beasts conquer!"

A shout of delight and avarice swept through the stands even as the green beasts began to emerge on the sands below.

Braids applauded. Oh, what a diversion, to run the wars of the world! How wonderful to pit folk against folk, and all for sweet, sweet cash.

* * * * *

The air rang so loudly that the sky seemed solid.

Kamahl labored beneath it. He had lost his staff to the angel, and now she used it against his sister.

Akroma vaulted through the air above Kamahl's grasping hands. She flipped over and came down on Jeska like a stooping eagle. Instead of talons, though, she attacked with the staff. The butt struck Jeska's chest. Green and white power crackled down its length and ripped through her. Jeska shook, a living conduit. Wounds burst open, and verdant force followed, filling each injury with moss. Jeska's necromantic power was proof against a single mana assault, but not against two simultaneously.

Wailing, she hurled herself back, flipped twice, and landed on her arms and hands. Her stomach was a garden in red and green, blood and moss. Her eyes rolled beneath pools of tears. She collapsed to her back, the air rushing out of her.

Akroma surged in for the kill.

"No!" Kamahl shouted.

He leaped toward the angel, and the crowd shrieked its delight. Kamahl climbed up the fury-frozen air. His hands filled with angel pinions. He clawed them free and dragged himself higher. Fingers closed around stony flesh—ankles and then knees. He scaled her wings, his weight forcing them flat and flinging her down to the sands. Akroma struggled beneath him, a dove beneath a devil.

The crowd overtopped its ovation. Bets flew across the counters.

Akroma surged suddenly upward, hurling Kamahl from her shoulders.

He too landed on his back in the sand.

The angel lunged upon him. She brought the shocking staff down to kill.

Kamahl grasped it. The power grasped him. Green and white mana dived into his flesh. It did not destroy him but strengthened him. Veins swelled with magic; muscles bulged with force. Though the angel wrenched the staff, trying to rip it from his hands, Kamahl's strength was greater. He broke Akroma's grip, dragged the staff back, and swung it. The end cracked against the angel's head.

She whirled in the air, plunging. Stunned wings fought to hold her aloft, and sand spun in wide vortices beneath her.

Kamahl rose. He snarled, gripping his staff, and stalked toward his sister.

Jeska lay nearby, supine and panting. Her native magic worked to drive back the wounds and the infestations, but she would not fight again—not soon.

"You've done it again," she rasped quietly.

He lifted the staff. "Yes. I've gotten it back."

"No, you've killed me again."

Kamahl's jaw clenched, and his eyes grew as hard as ivory. "You'll not die today, Sister." He held the staff out before them, ready to ward away Akroma.

Even then, the angel landed and approached.

"You've killed me again, and you'll kill yourself too."

* * * * *

Stonebrow blew the last, long call into rioting heavens. They were coming, every last elf and goblin in Kamahl's vast army.

They would pour into the arena and turn its sands into a sudden forest. Stonebrow stowed the horn at his hip and descended the final flight to the First's luxury box.

He had some of his own killing to do.

"Stand back, in the name of the Cabal," growled one of the two black-garbed guards at the door. It was iron-banded oak with a viewing slot. Long switchblades flicked out in the hands of the two guards.

Stonebrow lowered his massive head and snorted, his breath gusting hot. "I have business with the First."

"No one sees the First without an invitation," sneered the guard, yellowish skin tight across his cadaverous face. "If I were you, I'd step back."

"All right," agreed the giant centaur with a shrug, "step back."

The shrug flowed down his arm in a wave that broke at his fist. Backhanded, it pounded the guard's midsection and flung him, kicking, over the crowd. The switchblade had cut a long line down Stonebrow's arm but missed veins and tendons.

With a yelp of surprise, the other guard stabbed his switchblade into the centaur's shoulder. The blade struck bone and snapped off, leaving the man with a stumpy handle in hand. He dropped it and reached for a black-bladed short sword at his waist.

Stonebrow grasped the man's arm, pursed his lips, and shook his head.

The man, jowly and gray, gabbled, "I'll step back."

"Yes, you will," Stonebrow agreed.

He tossed the fellow away. This guard didn't thrash, seeming resigned to his fate. He crashed down atop the luxury box's roof, skidded, and dropped into the stands.

Stonebrow picked the broken blade out of his shoulder and dropped it to the stone. Balling his hand into a fist, Stonebrow stooped and knocked on the door.

The spy slot slid open, and a pair of feverish eyes stared out. "What?"

Stonebrow jabbed two fingers through the gap. It was all that would fit. They hit the man's forehead with sufficient force to knock him unconscious.

Wrapping his fingers around the door, Stonebrow yanked. Iron shrieked and crackled. The oaken door bulged. Setting a fore hoof on the doorpost, Stonebrow hauled hard. The hinges exploded, and the door came away in one piece in his hand. Seeing a contingent of Cabal enforcers rush up the stairs toward him, Stonebrow flung the door at them. It rattled down the stairs and felled them like kegel pins.

Stonebrow nodded in satisfaction. Eventually, he would be overrun by Cabal guards, but it wouldn't matter as long as the First was already dead.

Ducking his massive shoulders, Stonebrow surged through the gap.

Within lay a velvet antechamber where cloaks and shoes were left—and the slumbering figure of one guard. Careful not to crush him, Stonebrow cantered through the far doorway.

In the next room—a gallery of gladiatorial memorabilia—stood another Cabal thug. She was as scarred and scabrous as the guards outside, but the mad tumble of her eyes told of her profession: dementia summoner.

The woman smiled a dagger grin. From the brutal gaps between her teeth emerged creatures. They were gaunt men the color of yellow ivory, their limbs razor-edged.

With a sound like horn on slate, the things scrambled toward Stonebrow.

* * * * *

The tunnels beneath the stands roared like storm sewers in a flood. Instead of water, though, the corridors ran with wood—and all the creatures of the wood.

Roth led the way. The serpent's mouth gaped, snatching up Cabal guards. Lumps struggled in his red-scaled bulk as he reached the forbidding doors. Hissing and biting, Roth could do no more than splinter the bar.

Up bounded more ferocious creatures. They seemed like giant badgers, but were in fact ground squirrels the size of hippos. The things leaped eagerly through the darkness, passed Roth, and stopped at the barred doors. Whiskered snouts worked over the obstacle, sensing fresh air beneath. The squirrels hunkered down to dig. Claws hurled sand from the hole, and columns of grit showered out behind.

Roth withdrew his fangs from the bar, studied the situation, and ate one giant squirrel. He would have eaten the other one too, but he was distracted by new arrivals.

Goblins rushed up panting. They got lungfuls of kicked sand. The green fellows doubled over, grabbing their bellies and coughing viciously. Unsure what else to do, the goblins headed for high ground-up Roth's flank.

The great snake knew the difference between creatures clawing deliciously within and those clawing impiously without. Roth's head lifted, and he eyed his next meal. Fangs darted down.

The first goblin saw them coming and shrieked. His warning was literally swallowed by the serpent's mouth. A second goblin heard the muffled cry and gave his own, which had the benefit of echoing from the snake's gaping mouth. He fell amid teeth. A peristaltic wave grabbed him and yanked them down through the cool tube of muscle. A third and fourth goblin turned to run but found themselves treading on a slippery tongue. It slid steadily back into the serpent's mouth. Jaws snapped up a final goblin, and the serpent swallowed. Five knobs wriggled wonderfully in its gullet, and Roth gave a big smile.

He suddenly gagged. He had never eaten such dusty creatures in all his life. With a convulsive retching motion, he spewed them out, one by one. They held to each other in a long, slimy chain. The filthy beasts piled atop his back, mewling like newborn kittens. Giving a reptilian shudder, the serpent sloughed them off onto the ground.

They struggled to their feet only to be struck by tons of airborne sand. The grit sank into the digestive slime that covered the goblins. It amalgamated with the stuff, thickening to cement.

Moments later, the sand ceased. A ululating cry rose from the giant ground squirrel. Its head dipped into the hole it had dug, and its shoulders slid easily through. Hind legs shoved the massive beast beneath the doors and out onto the arena's sands.

Seeing daylight, Roth went as well. Soon, he slithered rapidly across the coliseum.

Behind him in the tunnel, thousands of Krosan troops marched to war. A contingent of elves raised their short swords and their voices in an ancient battle cry. Their eyes were fixed on the hole ahead, though they all took a moment to admire the statue of dancing goblins there in the midst of the tunnel.

* * * * *

Akroma soared down. Her wings flashed blindingly in the sunlight. She stared with wasp eyes, unblinking and merciless, at her foes.

Phage lay helpless on the sand, nearly slain. She would have been dead already if not for Kamahl. He stood above her, his sorcerous staff held horizontally.

What obsession drove him? Why did he care whether she lived or died?

The angel growled, "Stand aside. I have no quarrel with you, barbarian."

"If you would kill my sister, you have quarrel with me."

The angel canted her head slightly, considering. She tucked her wings and dropped from the sky.

Kamahl stood resolute, staff lifted crosswise.

The angel's feet struck the shaft and broke it in two. An explosion of green fire roared out of the shattered stalk. For a moment, it eclipsed Akroma, Kamahl, and Phage. When the initial blaze diminished, green force remained, clinging in viney lines to Akroma's legs. It emerged from the riven ends of Kamahl's staff and dragged her down.

Growling, Kamahl hauled the halves toward the sand.

Akroma struggled against the green force. "Release me! I have no quarrel with you!"

"Swear off your vengeance against my sister!" he shouted.

"Never."

"Then you will die." He muscled the two halves of the staff together. The bolts of green energy fused. She would never escape now.

With a great surge of her wings, Akroma lifted her eyes to the skies and cried, "Ixidor, Creator! I return to you." One more surge, and she pulled free—

Not entirely free. Her legs were yanked off her body, and they fell, wrapped in green magic. Those perfect, severed things dropped in the dirt.

Wailing, Akroma flew away.

* * * * *

Kamahl stood gaping after the maimed angel.

With a horrid roar, his armies converged in a great ring around him. Spine folk and woody dryads mounded in a protective dome of bough and branch, blocking out the sky and the last, fleeting glimpse of Akroma.

CHAPTER EIGHTEEN

SIBLING ALLIANCES

The world devolved into madness.

Zagorka crouched at the head of the slave pits, clutching Chester's huge neck. Before them, the sands of the arena were full of ferocious wood folk—elves, goblins, centaurs, serpents, and strange plant creatures she had never before seen. They held the sands as though they were declaring a new nation. In their center, a huge mound of animate wood had formed over Phage and Kamahl.

Crazier still, the fans had become fighters. They boiled down out of the stands, attacking the edges of the green army. Most hurled only fists or food, but some few had real weapons and laid in with them. Spectators and soldiers died in the tumult.

The literal height of lunacy was Braids. She leaped merrily along the coliseum rim and called out in a brazen voice, "Join the fun! Place a bet or place a kick! It doesn't matter which. The losers will be dead! The winners will be rich!" Her words broke into cackling. The sound echoed throughout the coliseum, as if the hungry stones laughed.

"It's all right, Chester," said Zagorka, her hand trembling as she patted his neck. "I'll take care of you."

The giant mule gusted a dubious reply as Zagorka wedged herself in a corner behind him.

* * * * *

Kamahl lowered his eyes from the cage of wood and stared bleakly at the sand.

His staff was broken. The last of its green magic sputtered away. Lines of force dissolved from the dismembered legs of the angel, which lay in the sand beside him. There was no blood, no torn tissue. Bereft of the spirit that had given them life, those white legs had simply turned to stone.

Not so his sister. Jeska rolled in the agony of her wounds.

Kamahl went to his knees at her side. He reached for her, but she shook her head violently.

"Get your hands away." She gulped a breath. A wound in her chest sucked air. Clamping her fingers over it, she hissed, "You couldn't heal me before. You won't heal me now. I will heal myself. . . . If you touch me, you'll die."

Kamahl nodded. "Heal yourself, Sister, then come with me."

Her eyes flared. "Never."

"I have won. You cannot deny it. I saved you from the angel. I ended the match standing and could have slain you. You must come with me . . . or does the mighty Cabal renege on its wagers?"

She gritted her teeth and spat. "Yes, you have won. Take me, but I go as a hostage."

"Listen, Jeska—"

"I am not Jeska! I am Phage!"

"Yes, I see you, Phage, your poisonous skin, your bitter mouth and vicious eyes. I see the husk that you are, a leather shell stiff with scars, but I know who lies within that egg. She is the one I speak to. Jeska, fight your way out of this foul shell. Puncture it, tear it, slough it, step free. I know you are alive in there, Jeska. Fight your way out and return to me."

Phage's angry eyes softened, and her lips spread in a smile—an ironic smile. "Tear this shell, Kamahl, and all you will find within is hungry darkness. This shell is what keeps you and all of Otaria alive."

"We shall see," he replied levelly. It wasn't working. He had won and yet lost. He had to show her that he truly was on her side. "In the meantime, we have work to do."

"Yes, getting out—"

"No," Kamahl said. "We have an angel to kill."

"What are you talking about?"

Kamahl swept his hand out. "She is sworn to kill you. As long as Akroma lives, you are in danger. We need to go find her."

Phage stared, unbelieving, at the man. "If we couldn't kill her here in the coliseum, how will we ever kill her in her own homeland?"

"I have an army," Kamahl said, idly scanning the dome of wood for some means of escape. He walked to the boughs, set his hands on them, and tried to awaken the power of the wood. The fibers felt dead within his fingers. He was drained, tapped out. Without his staff, the power of wood had deserted him. "You have a few thousand under your command."

"I command no one. Only the First commands the Cabal."

Removing his fingers from the branches, Kamahl said heavily, "It's a good thing Akroma fled when she did. I'm drained."

Phage was suddenly behind him, standing, healed. "Weak, are you? I feel suddenly strong."

* * * * *

Stonebrow faced down a platoon of ivory warriors. Tall and thin, with tapered limbs that ended in spikes, the white warriors strode toward him. They made a screeching sound as they came. Their flesh was as hard as tooth, as sharp-edged and merciless.

Stonebrow turned around, but not to run. His hind legs lashed out. Hooves hit the foremost ivory man, cracking it in half. As the shattered chunks fell, Stonebrow took a bounding step backward and kicked again. The next creature exploded like glass. Its razor shards cascaded around Stonebrow's legs, cutting them.

He could not kill all these monsters that way; they would tear him to pieces.

Stonebrow bounded back once more and kicked. His hooves swept among the ivory men, missing them but striking the marble pillar that held up the center of the chamber. With a shot like lightning, it cracked. Stone ground on stone, and the column caved.

Stonebrow dropped his hooves amid the clawing soldiers. He leaped away. There was time for one more bound before the pillar failed entirely. The stone ceiling cracked and fell. Stonebrow shot out over the threshold. He was still gathering his haunches beneath him when the great slab smashed down on all those white warriors. Stonebrow glimpsed them and their dementia creator in the moment before they were rubble.

With a crackling boom, the slab smashed to the floor. Dust rose in huge, curling walls on each side.

Brushing off his hands, the centaur stomped over the fallen stone, heading toward the First's private chambers. They remained intact, jutting out above the stands and giving the best views. Stonebrow clomped across the slab and hurled himself through the doorway.

The space within was cavelike, with black walls and dark portraits. At the center of the chamber sat an unmistakable chair carved of obsidian. From that spot, the First would watch the games, flanked by his hand servants and skull servants. No one remained though.

Stonebrow looked for other exits but found none. He

approached the throne. Across the seat lay a black cloak, which Stonebrow gingerly lifted. He dropped it again, shaking his fingers.

The First must have slipped out of it only moments before, for the fabric was still cold. Deathly cold.

* * * * *

Braids enjoyed madness, but even it could go too far.

All the bets—millions in gold—hung in the balance if there wasn't a clear winner. Worse yet, if all the fans killed each other, who would bet tomorrow?

"Hey! One on one!" Braids shouted as she vaulted down the steps.

Her fist cracked solidly atop the head of a man, one of five who had been pummeling a lone elf. Braids dropped the man and caused the other four to fall back. She leaped onward, and so did the elf.

Braids took the stairs ten at a jump. Whenever a spectator strayed into the way, she merely turned a shoulder and barreled past. Another spring brought her down atop a pile of rubble—the royal box of the First. Someone had done a great wrong. The First did not lie beneath—somehow Braids sensed that—but wherever he was, he would not be happy. Assassination attempts always infuriated him, almost as much as lost revenue. The First had foiled countless assassins but had not suffered a single day in the red.

Today will not be the first, Braids vowed.

As she flung herself farther down the stands, she let out a new cry. "Return to your seats! You have one minute. Brute squads will circulate. Return to your seats!"

She punctuated the command by bounding off the horned head

of a goat man. He instinctively added his own thrust to the jump, propelling her up over the crowd. Braids turned a slow flip, arcing above the front row and the green troops.

A clutch of goblins waited below. They had been hurling insults at the crowd, waggling their swords and tongues and backsides. One goblin pointed toward her, and two dozen eyes came about to see a shadow with snaking hair descend from heaven. Two dozen legs bent to run, but too late.

Braids squashed two goblins outright, innards spraying on the others.

The green beasts shrieked and reached for the attacker. Their claws came away empty.

Trailing goo, Braids leaped over a brake of thistles. A crowd of elves milled beyond. She chose an empty square of ground to land in, bounced up, and slipped through their hands.

No one would have guessed she could leap like that. In fact, she couldn't, not in reality. She built each jump out of multiple jumps in dementia space, selecting only the highest part of the arc to bleed into the real world. It was why, for her, leaping was almost flying.

Coming down on the spine of a giant serpent, she ran. The snake provided a highway toward the mound of wood—an unwilling highway. The reptile lifted its massive head, scaly flanges spreading angrily. In its huge golden eyes, Braid saw hunger and her own reflection.

She saw something else—two feline forms closing quickly behind her.

The snake opened its gaping mouth.

The huge jaguars launched themselves.

Braids did likewise.

She slipped out of reality and into dementia space and plunged again into the flood of time and space. Out she went, and in, weaving for herself a precise trajectory that bore her beyond the translucent fangs. While Braids flew just wide of the snapping mouth, the great cats hurtled within its jaws. One might have been a reasonable meal. Both, though, jammed the throat of the creature.

Braid's leap carried her over the heads of more green monsters. They stared at her in bald incomprehension.

It seemed all the coliseum stared at her. Most had clambered into their seats. Brute squads patrolled the stairs, enforcing her edict. Fights had ceased, and fighters looked to see what the crazy woman would do.

"We will have a winner!" Braids shouted as she closed upon the mound of wood at the center of the arena. How she would penetrate that hill, she didn't know, but one thing was certain—Kamahl and Phage were there. "Hold all tickets. In a moment, we will have a winner!"

A ragged cheer went up from the crowd, malice turned to avarice.

Braids smiled, scrambling up the mound. "Who survives within? Emerge! Let us know who is victorious?"

No movement came, no sound. It was as if the boughs had eaten them up. The last murmurs of the crowd ceased as everyone listened.

"Who lives? Who triumphs?" called Braids, her voice ringing through the coliseum. "Phage, the world demands to know! Kamahl, do you live?"

Something smoldered on the nearby boughs.

Braids leaped toward it. "We have movement. Someone comes."

It wasn't smoke but steam, water liberated from wood as it decayed. A narrow cave opened, a tunnel in the shape of a person—a woman. She walked slowly through the boughs, dissolving them as she went. In triangles of space, Braids glimpsed her and fairly danced.

"It is Phage! She lives!"

A thrilled roar erupted from the stands. Phage was the odds-on-favorite. Half the folk thrust winning stubs into the air, while the other half tossed their tickets to the wind.

From beneath a veil of crumbling wood, the woman emerged. Though her silken suit was shredded, the flesh beneath had closed again, solid and whole. She lifted her head and climbed steadily out of the tunnel. Her hand rose, and the ovation deepened. Phage was not giving a signal of triumph, though, but a call for silence.

"She wants to speak!" shouted Braids, even then adjusting her speaking sorcery so that it would sweep out around Phage. "Silence to hear the victor speak!"

Phage lowered her arm and said, "I am not the victor. The Cabal does not renege on its wagers. The victor is my opponent." She gestured down toward the rotten passageway, where another figure crawled. "Kamahl!"

The crowd shrieked—those who had lost and those who had thrown away winning tickets. Even as Kamahl pulled himself from the wooden mound, folk scrambled for discarded paper, and fights broke out.

"I am the true victor," announced Kamahl. Braids's spell carried his words loudly to the throng. They quieted to listen. "I have defeated my sister and driven off our common foe. Yes, our *common* foe. Jes—Phage and I will march together at the head of two armies. We will go to slay Akroma."

* * * * *

A month later, night lay thick across the swamps.

Kamahl stood at the height of the torchlit coliseum and gazed down toward the sands. On either side of the arena sat his two armies. War loomed. Kamahl was nominally in charge of these antithetical forces—forest and swamp, growth and decay. He needed both if he were to invade the land of Akroma and slay her.

It was time to join these broken armies into a new and powerful whole.

Kamahl looked toward the northern stands. There the Krosan Legion waited. Serpent and cat, elf and goblin, centaur and dryad, they had captured this grand structure. To do so, the green force had defeated Cabal guards and a vicious angel. In their minds, theirs was total victory. They wished to climb all over the coliseum and pull it down, stone by stone.

Kamahl had forbidden it. He had even allowed the games to continue while the armies mustered. They had not come to destroy the Cabal but to save Jeska, and to do so, Kamahl needed to ally with the First.

The mysterious leader of the Cabal had been all too willing to comply.

On the south side of the coliseum waited the newly formed Legion of Phage. Gigantipithicus apes and shorn rhinos, dwarves and goblins, slaves and undead things of every description gathered beneath the banner of their mistress. They would fight for her against Akroma the Anathema. They had sworn allegiance to Kamahl while he battled the Foe.

The First himself had promised there would be no treachery.

Besides, it would be profitable. Braids had arranged observation caravans to witness the war. Not only would the Legion of Phage put up a great fight, it would also put on a great show. Hundreds of rich patrons had paid handsomely to accompany the troops and watch the war. Even now, brightly painted barges waited on the black waters.

The war tourists weren't in them yet, instead filling the

coliseum's luxury boxes. They sat along tables spread with white linens and lit with citronella, and before them steamed delicacies. On this, the eve of the march, they feasted like kings. Tomorrow the show would begin.

Kamahl was appalled at this war profiteering, but he needed the Legion of Phage. Despite hard bargaining, he had to allow the pleasure safaris.

Of course, all of this had been the First's plan from the beginning. Had Phage won their battle, Kamahl would have been slain and his forces scattered. Instead, Kamahl had won, and the Legion of Phage was simply Plan B.

"The Cabal does not renege on its deals," Kamahl reminded himself grimly.

He stood a moment more, gathering all their eyes, then, with stately tread, descended the stairs.

The sand was empty. Gone were the bodies and blood, and gone too was the tangled hill of branches. It had been a miniature Gorgon Mount, a pile of boughs that grew up over someone Kamahl had killed. A riddle lay there, something about festering wounds and martyrs made monsters. . . .

Shaking his bedeviled head, Kamahl strode down the stairs. There was no time for riddles. He had a war to wage. His armies were watching. Unless he amalgamated his forces tonight, he never would.

He needed a symbol of this new alliance—a symbol and a weapon.

Reaching the first row, Kamahl leaped down to the sand. From his belt, he drew the broken halves of his staff and held them high. The green army let out a great cheer, even though these riven stalks no longer held the power of the woodlands. Soon they would hold new power. Gripping the portions of the staff in one hand, Kamahl headed toward the center column of the coliseum.

From the opposite side of the arena approached another creature. Within manifold black robes and a tall miter, the First was unmistakable. He too clutched a ruined weapon—the stone head of an ancient axe. He lifted it high. Its razor edges stood in stark silhouette against the inner wall of the coliseum.

The Legion of Phage shrieked its delight to see this ancient blade—the First's own weapon when he had established the pit fights. His strides were the equal of Kamahl's as the First strode toward the center pillar.

There, they met, druid and patriarch, allies against a common enemy.

The night was too solemn for Braids and her antics. She sat silently in the stands beside Zagorka and her asinine friend. Still, Braids had prepared a spell that would bear the words of these men out to all listening ears.

Kamahl spoke: "We come together tonight to forge a new alliance, what might seem a strange alliance, but it is not so strange. That which joins us all is Jeska, is Phage. In every outward way, she belongs to the Cabal. In every inward way, she belongs to Krosan. She is yet one person and as such unites us. We fight for her and against her sworn foe."

Though nothing else Kamahl had said had moved the crowd, the single word *foe* brought a roar from both sides. They could never be united in love but in hatred—yes.

"Behold!" cried Kamahl, lifting the two halves of the century stalk. "This shattered staff, locus of green mana, was broken by Akroma, but it will be remade tonight. It will unmake her."

Roars turned to cheers.

"Behold!" shouted the First, holding aloft the ancient axe head. "This blade, locus of black mana, was riven from its haft by my greatest enemy. Tonight it will be remade to unmake the greatest foe of Phage."

The crowd's ovation was nearly deafening.

Kamahl and the First shouted in unison, "Power of sand, arise!"

From the ground leaped twin bolts of gray lightning. It jagged into their legs and pulsed up their arms. The strikes continued, rattling in thousands of discharges. Both men began to glow.

Even while pinioned on that terrible force, Kamahl pivoted his broken staff toward the Krosan Legion. "Power of forest, to me!"

Lines of green plasma rose from the foreheads of all seated there and stretched toward Kamahl. From his own hand, tendrils of power reached out hungrily. In midair, the channels met. Energy arced down into Kamahl's fingers and joined the radiance that lit him. The combined force made Kamahl shine.

The First extended the axe head toward the Legion of Phage. "Power of swamp, to me!"

Black mana, darker than the darkest corners of night, streamed in a clotted web from the monsters. The First was a power vacuum, and mana fled into him. It mixed with the energy in his chest, and he burst into flames.

Without seeming to move at all, the druid and the patriarch pivoted. The riven shaft and the haftless blade met. They touched. A second sun arose between them.

North and south, the armies shied from that blazing power. Green and black, they were one in their fear of the blinding presence.

As quickly as the light was birthed into being, it faded and died. In its final flare, a shape shone: a great axe. It was not the blade of the First or the haft of Kamahl, but a new weapon recreated out of them. The head was huge and curved. Barbed along its edges, it was made of a stuff denser than stone and smoother than glass. Its handle was broad and metallic, inset with gleaming gems like Thran crystals of old.

Though none had ever seen that axe before, all who saw it then knew it was destined to slay Akroma.

Kamahl lifted the blade high and gave an inarticulate shout of triumph. It echoed from the stands and came back from the throats of every beast.

He had forged two weapons into one. He had forged two legions into a great army.

* * * * *

Kamahl had won the devotion of every heart in that black swamp—every heart except one.

Phage sat alone in her headquarters. She might as well have been in her cell. She was once again a captive—this time to her erstwhile brother. She had lost and was his slave. There was no escape without breaking the bond of the Cabal. Phage had to submit. She hadn't a single ally against Kamahl—not Braids, not Zagorka, not even the First.

A shadow disconnected itself from one dark wall. It had been no more than a shadow before, but now it was a man—*the* man.

As if he could hear her thoughts, the First had arrived.

Phage did not turn toward him. She only breathed slowly.

The First walked along the bars, watching her. He was like a man at a zoo, lingering near his favorite beast. "You are troubled."

Phage shook her head. "I am not troubled. I am resigned."

Another step, and the First paused beside the door. "You think I have sold you out. You think I do not care."

Of course he was right. The First was always right.

"Kamahl wants to get beneath your skin and find his sister, find your true soul." The First approached her. He laid his hands on her shoulders. His touch, brutal as it was, brought extraordinary bliss to her solitary universe. "I allow him to take you because he will not stop until he does. He will find your true soul and show it to you. When you see it, you will be rid of him at last, and you will know that you and I are one."

Phage rose. She wrapped him in an embrace. Poison tears rolled from her cheek and fell on his shoulder.

At least tonight, she would not be alone.

CHAPTER NINETEEN

THE MARK OF IMPERFECTION

*I*xidor sat on the highest balcony of Locus, deep in the blue sky. Here, the air was sweet and cool, and the sun was biting. The gentlest breeze, the brightest light, the best food, the safest company—solitude. Yes, his unmen were here, watchful around him, but Ixidor had come to think of them as absences rather than presences. Surrounded by his creation, Ixidor was alone.

He ate a piece of toast. The jam came from a purple fruit he had created. The tea was good too, stimulating but soporific. It excited the mind but calmed the nerves.

Ixidor suffered terribly. Even here, at the heart of his world, he was shot through with terrors. Normal men walked through an utterly alien world without fear, their minds too small to glimpse every peril. Creators dwelt in their own universes in utter terror. They knew the best and worst that awaited them, and the worst was nightmare.

Akroma was returning. She had been returning for a month—maimed, nearly killed. Ixidor's perfect protector was no longer perfect. Phage had done this. Ixidor had sensed when it had happened, for he was connected to both women—the slayer of Nivea and the bearer of Nivea's face. He had felt Akroma's defeat as phantom pain in the arm he no longer had.

Once again, Phage had marred the perfect beauty of Nivea.

In the distant sky, there came a wounded flapping, like a dove struggling for life. It labored awhile through thick blue air, then dropped down to pant on the treetops. Its weakness naturally drew the aerial jellyfish. They drifted like storm clouds toward the creature, their translucent tentacles dragging the ground. The white being saw them and knew it must fly or die. It flew. It worked toward Ixidor in his balcony.

The jam was a little too sweet. Ixidor would have to make a different fruit.

One of the jellyfish closed in. Its tentacles reached toward the fluttering figure. Stingers slapped and wrapped. They convulsed, dragging the wounded creature up toward its transparent belly.

The dove could little fly, but she could fight. Hands lashed out and grasped the tentacles. Twisting, she ripped two of the legs in half. Another followed, and a forth. The little bird tore out the legs of the giant beast, which recoiled from her, dragging its watery limbs away.

Akroma fluttered free. Yes, it was she—scarred and diminished. Her wings beat with much force but little effect. Still, she had sent the great jellyfish reeling across the sky. Akroma climbed toward the balcony.

Ixidor flung away the too-sweet toast. He left the tea to turn tepid in its cup and stood. It was only right that a creator stand to receive his greatest creation.

She wasn't great anymore. Her wings were battered and bore bald spots like those of a molting hen. Jellyfish slime covered her, and her flesh showed the hand-shaped scars of Phage's putrid touch. Worst of all, as the broken angel surged up over the balcony rail, Ixidor saw that her legs were gone. Only stumps hung down where once they had been.

On those stumps, the pathetic creature settled. She fell

forward—there was no way to prevent it—into a prostrate bow before her creator. Her wings folded and shoulders shuddered. She was weeping.

Ixidor gazed at her, and tears rolled down his cheeks as well. He did not know what to feel, and so felt everything—pity and love, yes, but also revulsion, sympathy but also dread. His greatest creation was insufficient to stop an inevitable foe. Ixidor wished to take her into his arms as he would have taken Nivea, but Akroma was not she. Here was the face of Nivea without the soul of her. He wished to fling her away as he had the toast.

She spoke. "I have failed you."

Shaking his head sadly, Ixidor approached her. "No, I have failed you."

Akroma raised tearful eyes. "I have failed in the task you set me."

"No," the creator said again, cupping her jaw in his remaining hand. "I sent you to attack, but you were never to attack. You were to defend. You were my Protector—"

"*Were*," she echoed miserably.

"*Are* my Protector. How could you protect me in the faraway coliseum? Only here, in the midst of my creation, of which you are the culmination—only here can you protect me."

She lowered her face again. "How? How am I to fight for you when I am . . . incomplete?"

Ixidor walked toward the rail and stared out at his bright-beaming world. His eyes idly wandered the treetops. "Incomplete?" he echoed. "Surely you mock me."

"Mock you? No, Master."

"You know the stories of the war—of the monsters and how they were compleated?"

"No," she replied. "I do not know those stories."

"It doesn't matter. I will compleat you just the same." Averting his eyes, Ixidor muttered feverishly, "Could the old demon have done what he did as innocently as I?"

Akroma spoke behind him, "Already, you have sacrificed one arm to make me. Do not sacrifice another."

Ixidor did not respond, his eyes fixed on the distant trees. Something moved beneath them, something fleet and tawny. It came at his silent summons. A feline form burst from the edge of the jungle, dashed down the sandy banks, and plunged into the flood. It swam. It would take ages for the jaguar to swim the whole way.

Ixidor searched beneath the waves. He found a darting pod of dolphins and brought them to rise under the swimming cat. Amid froth and foam, they bore the beast toward Locus.

"You will have legs again, twofold," Ixidor said placidly. "And I will heal every scar on your body. New plumes, new flesh, new sword. You will be complete."

At the base of the palace, the jaguar leapt. It bounded up the round, white shoulders of stone. Tireless, the beast approached its creator. It was larger than a natural jaguar, a creature of imagination. Up five hundred feet, up a thousand it came—and two thousand and three. Its pelt gleamed with water as it leaped over the balustrade. It shook itself once, stalked slowly along the rail, and knelt dutifully at its creator's feet.

Ixidor stroked the creature's head.

Akroma watched keenly. "This great cat will bring me legs?"

"It *has* brought you legs," Ixidor said. "Its own. You must come and take them." The jaguar released a worried growl. "Don't fear," Ixidor purred to it. "The pain will be brief, and you will be part of a greater creature."

The angel's eyes were troubled. She stared at the docile creature, its head laid down and ears folded back. "You want me to take its legs?"

"Its legs, its body—all but neck and head."

"Why?"

Ixidor blinked. Why? It seemed almost blasphemy for her to ask.

"You lack something, and not just legs. You are an ideal creature, born of pure thought. Of course you could not battle one such as Phage, who is all flesh and flesh eating. You need a baser self, a bestial self. Here are legs for you, and a savage heart. You need them both." He drew a deep breath. "I offer them to you. Will you take them?"

Akroma rose to her hands, wings folded behind her. She crawled toward the jaguar, dragging her own severed parts behind. Reaching the beast, she set her elbows on the ground and peered at the creature. Into its backward-slanting ear, she whispered, "Forgive me."

The merciful words faded before merciless fingers. They stabbed through the creature's beautiful pelt, eight knives slicing deep. Muscles severed, and tendons snapped. White hands turned red. The creature tried to cry, but those nails sliced its larynx on their way to its spine. Her nails found a disk within and jabbed, severing the all-powerful cord. Fingertips met.

Again, the angel was weeping. Beneath her, the creature had gone limp, its life pouring across the white stone balcony.

"Off," Ixidor said quietly. "Entirely off."

Akroma twisted her hands. The head and neck of the great cat came free. She laid it reverently aside and sank down upon the red pool. "What now? How will you join us?"

Ixidor did not answer. He reached his hand down, dipping fingertips in the red. Drops jiggled as he walked away. "Creation is messy. It is painful and maddening."

He approached a wall of white stone and stood staring at it. Suddenly, he understood the old demon Yawgmoth. Whether or not he was evil to start with, the pain and madness of creation—the limitless power and limitless responsibility–had made him evil.

Idly, Ixidor lifted a finger and dragged a vertical smudge down the wall. "These things are inevitable. Every creature cries out to be saved, but who can save a creator?" He broadened the base of the line and sketched one feline leg, and another. Smearing his thumb sideways, he formed a powerful body, ending in a tail and hind legs. "Even love cannot save a creator." Two canted lines to either side made for wings, and individual drips of blood traced out the plumes–coverts, primaries, and secondaries.

Ixidor stepped back, squinting at the image before him. He raised his hand and watched the blood trace out his fingerprints and soak into his nail beds. He rubbed the red stuff across his thumb. "The more powerful the creator, the more certainly he will be trapped inside a world of his own devising."

Stepping forward, Ixidor pressed his thumb against the stone, creating a blob that would be the angel's head. It was the right size and shape, yes, but he could never capture the face of Nivea. "To create is perilous. In the end, it will kill the creator." He leaned forward to the wall and pressed his lips to the bloody head of the angel. Closing his eyes, he drew the image into himself and projected it outward onto reality.

She was there. He sensed it in his missing arm—health, strength, wholeness. He had completed her.

"Master," Akroma said behind him. "You have done it. I am once again your Protector."

Ixidor leaned against the wall, panting. He was kitten weak. He couldn't hold himself up but slid down the cold stone. His lips and face smeared the image he had drawn. It didn't matter. It had transcended its materials and taken on a life of its own. As Ixidor slumped, he turned slowly around and sat in a disheveled heap.

Before him hovered a vision—his vision made real. No scars remained on Akroma's body. She was stronger, smoother, more powerful than before. Her lower torso fused with the body of a great cat—four massive legs, a flashing tail, and wide wings. The plumes reached twice their previous span and jutted from the shoulders of the cat. In one strong arm, she bore a staff like a jagged lightning bolt, energy made solid.

Ixidor glimpsed these transformations only briefly. His eyes were drawn away instead to the angel's glorious face—the face of Nivea.

No, she was Nivea no longer. Surrounded in a mantle of flesh—part mane and part halo—Akroma's visage was more beautiful than Ixidor could have imagined. She had transcended his memories of Nivea, as every lost love grows greater in time. Her glory was almost unbearable, and the look of sadness in her eyes nearly slew him.

"What is it?" she asked, magnificent before her disheveled creator.

He could only shake his head. "You have eclipsed her. Now, as long as you live, I can never see her again."

* * * * *

Ixidor waited until midnight. The Protector slept, and darkness ruled every corner of paradise. He needed darkness and solitude for what he was about to do.

Phage and Kamahl were on their way. They were bringing a conglomerate army bent on slaying the Protector. Once she was gone, they would ravage his creation and kill him as well.

In solemn silence, Ixidor stepped from the white-marble pier onto the dark barge. It lay low in inky waters. Like avatars of night, the unmen followed. They spread in a circle around him and stood, nervous sentinels. Stars sent streaks of white across the black face of the deep. The barge man's pole stirred those lines, like a stick gathering cobwebs, and the barge shoved out over the blackness.

Ixidor needed other protectors and defenders—armies of them. He needed as many as the stars in the sky.

While the craft glided before rhythmic strokes of the pole, Ixidor watched those stars. Brightly they beamed, gregarious. Even here in the midst of his creation, those patient eyes followed him—soothing, healing, sending news from distant worlds. The stars were Ixidor's peers. He could not change them, but he could fashion something beautiful from their light.

He would make disciples from their reflections.

Stepping to the edge of the barge, Ixidor knelt and peered down at the crazings of light. It was primordial energy, ready to be shaped. But how? What medium could he use to craft beams of light? He had not brought canvas or paint, clay or wood. He trailed his hand in the water, shaping the light into whorls and eddies, but the barge itself was more powerful, sending waves before and behind.

Ixidor scooped up a handful of water, the stars momentarily trapped within. Before he could transform them, they dribbled away between his fingers.

The thrust of the pole made an insistent rhythm. It entered Ixidor's knees and dragged at his whole body. It shaped the water too.

What were waves but sound? If he could shape sound, he could shape waves and the lights that lay upon them.

Ixidor lay prostrate, his hand spread across the planks. He hummed in time to the pole man. Music would be his medium. He wanted to make disciples of these points of light, so he sang a song of discipleship.

Come with me, my children.
Ride within my eyes, upon my brow.
Learn what I have known, and then
I'll learn all that you know.

Heal the heart that's broken.
Salve the flesh that dies, that's fainting now.
Drink the cup I drink, my children.
Together we will grow.

He rose and stood, chanting all the while. His voice droned, regularlizing the waves. The peaks rose into a matrix of mounds; the valleys sank into cup-shapes among them. Starlight gathered on each prominence. Ixidor needed only to bring them to final focus. Stomping his foot in time with the pole strokes, he sang the final stanza.

Come with me, my children.
Come to life, my thought, my heart's desire.
Light eternal, sweet companion,
I'll be your living pyre.

With the final note, the waves around the barge achieved perfect form. Hundreds of points of light coalesced. They rose from the water. No longer were they simply reflections, but living radiance. Like will-o'-the-wisps, the newborn creatures whirled up into the air. Sparking blue-white, they curled in a scintillating cloud of orbs and orbited their creator. The sky danced with a choir of creatures—changeable stars beneath changeless ones.

Laughing, Ixidor lifted his hand and stirred the cloud of them. The sound of his gladness made the stars rejoice. "You will know what I know," he said, touching his forehead.

The creatures curled in a cyclone around Ixidor. One by one, they descended and struck his head between the eyes. The creatures sparked through his mind, learning what lay there, and issued in a laughing stream from his mouth. They flowed through him and emerged with reverent joy.

"You will read the mind of any I wish and bring their thoughts back to me. We will teach each other."

The disciples swarmed across his flesh, learning his form. They gathered around his shoulder stump and coursed along the scars there.

Ixidor watched them. His voice was heavy. "Yes, you sense the old wound, one you cannot heal, but you will heal any new wounds. You will stitch me together when I have come apart."

The barge neared shore. Three more shoves from the pole man and sand hissed on the hull. The craft ground to a halt. In a cloud of worshipers, Ixidor stepped from the gunwales. Darting lights and lurking shadows went with him. The creator walked through the cool of his world, heading for the cold desert beyond.

He had hundreds of new defenders, but Topos itself would need armies. They would arise from the clay shoulders of the ground and the choking desert sands. Ixidor smiled as he marched.

His disciples lit the caliginous wood. They seemed fairies illuminating leaf spaces and mushroom rings. They knew where he was going, for they knew his every thought. A gleaming line of the creatures stretched away through the jungle, making a highway of light.

Following it, Ixidor at last emerged on the mud flats east of Topos. There, he stopped. He crouched, breaking loose a hunk of dried clay. He considered it, turning it over in his hand. The disciples considered it as well. They spun and jittered wonderingly around its curled edges. This was something new. Ixidor had not known how he would make his next creatures—what he would make—until now.

He spit upon the shard and rubbed his thumb across it, creating mud. It was a minuscule portion, a fingerprint or two, nothing more. It would be enough.

Ixidor raised his thumb, like an artist judging dimension. Instead of squinting his eyes, though, he held them wide open and smeared the mud across first his left cornea and then his right. It was painful, of course, but creation was not true unless it was painful. Keeping his eyes open, Ixidor stared out across the mud flats. He hadn't enough spittle to turn all of it to mud, but he had enough vision to. As far as he could see, it all seemed mud.

As tears traced minute tracks down his eyes, the brown curtain rippled and folded. Columns washed clear. Other columns formed into twisted figures of clay.

Ixidor wished desperately to blink, but if he did, his new creatures would be washed away before they could take full form. Gritty tears streamed down his cheeks.

They were solidifying, these clay men—with long arms and legs, round heads and hairless bodies, attenuated figures, and faces that looked as if they had been drawn in mud by a child. They showed no muscular definition, none of the angles that told of a skeleton. Still, they were solid now, as much as they would become. He wanted them to remain somewhat amorphous. They were creations in progress, pupae that could transform instantly into new forms.

"My putty people," Ixidor breathed reverently, his face dark with tears. He blinked at last, clearing away every lingering stain on his vision. There they stood in their thousands, like identical and featureless statues, stretching away to the horizon. "My putty people."

Ixidor opened his arm and walked into a forest of gray folk, expressionless and unmoving but undeniably alive. They watched him with eyes like holes eroded through mud. Approaching the first of the putty people, Ixidor wrapped his arm around the thing.

Stiffly, it returned the gesture, keeping one hand at its side while circling the other in an awkward embrace. As soon as it touched Ixidor's skin and his silk robe, colors bled onto its gray skin. With color came texture, contour and shadow. Sleeves grew out of the arm and a robe out of the body. The arm that had remained at the creature's side fused with it, leaving a gray outline for a moment. Hair jagged from the thing's head. Its face clenched and rippled, as if molded by some unseen hand and formed a jutting jaw, ravaged cheeks, and haunted eyes. The transformation was complete.

Ixidor released his hold and stepped back. It was as though he stared into a looking glass. "Come see," Ixidor said to his disciples.

They rioted down around the simulacrum and probed it. Outwardly the beast was identical to its creator, but when the disciples tried to sink through its forehead and read its thoughts, they found only dead clay beneath.

Ixidor smiled. "These new creatures are flesh wandering free of thought. You, my disciples, are thought free of flesh. Together, you will serve me, body and mind. Just as you can duplicate the minds of those who come against me, these folk will duplicate the bodies. Our foes will fight themselves." Staring fixedly at the creature, Ixidor said, "Return."

Color melted away. Line eroded. The figure resumed its smooth shapelessness.

Ixidor strode through the forest of putty people. "Remain here." Rank on rank, the men of clay stood. To Ixidor's glowing disciples, he said "Onward."

The disciples followed. They bobbed in his wake, washing the army in an eerie blue light. Lit that way, the putty people seemed gaunt headstones in a graveyard. Soon enough, they would stand above the dead of Krosan and the Cabal.

Ixidor walked in nervous silence. He was making monsters. It wasn't that such terrors were new to his mind. It was only that he had never before created something simply to kill.

In their monotonous thousands, the army of putty people at last gave way to true desert—endless sands. His next creatures would be craggy like sand crystals.

Ixidor stomped. Dust rolled up in a coiling ring around his foot. It seemed a jellyfish bubbling up through the air. Ixidor needed no more jellyfish, but the forms of the sea gave him inspiration.

Ixidor leaped out on the sand, grabbing a handful of it. He spun and hurled it high. From a dense dust cloud, long lines trailed down. Not pausing, Ixidor whirled and grasped more grit. He flung it up beside the first cloud and moved onward. It was a dance, yes—a dance of exorcism. He was casting horrors out of his mind onto thin air.

Not so thin anymore. Each cloud of dust formed into a body of thick carapace. Each trailing wisp became a chitinous leg. Tall and gangly, twice the height of a man, the things seemed huge spiders. They were, in fact, leggy crabs. Each limb—and some of the beasts had ten or twenty—ended in a deadly spike. Those legs alone could skewer countless invaders. The claws beneath the body, though—long and sharp like shears—would literally cut the foes to pieces.

Ixidor danced, throwing sand and bringing horrors to life. Disciples spun about him in a blue-white cloak. He would make as many crab folk as he had putty people. He would go on dancing his terror until dawn. Sand was getting in his eyes, blinding him, but it didn't matter. His breath moaned in a hoarse half-music. That was fine too.

Let dance and music and vision bring into being a whole host of nightmares.

When Phage came, and Kamahl, and their armies, they would pay in blood for invading Topos.

There is no more dangerous being than a creator hiding in his own mind.

CHAPTER TWENTY

WHO'S WHO

*B*raids loved her job. It was like playing with toys.

Across the wetlands poled festival barges, their particolored flags snapping in the wind. A few had reached shore and offloaded their patrons onto fringe-covered palanquins. They stood on a path that led up the escarpment to brightly painted caravans. All were toys. So too were the slaves who bore them forward and the rich folk who rode within. Fun, fanciful, expendable toys.

"Welcome, all," Braids shouted to them from atop the Corian Escarpment. "Journey from the wonders of the wetlands to the delights of the desert. You've seen crocodiles and piranhas, now prepare for jackals and buzzards. Beyond lie unimaginable nightmares!"

Barge crews served drinks and shrimp pastries while litter bearers struggled to keep palanquins upright on the switchback path. Before the waiting caravans, escorts danced, promising to help weary patrons "settle in." All of it delighted Braids. She loved to listen to the rich folk complain, sheep bleating among dogs. How they would bleat when only wolves remained!

"Avail yourselves of every amenity! Where else can you lie at ease, alone or in company, and watch warriors fight and die? Who else can lounge like a god and witness mortal wars? Feast upon red meat and blood wine, upon sweetbreads and marrow! The finest beasts have been slain for your bellies, and the finest warriors will be slain for your eyes."

Braids glanced out toward the army. It rode on grim barges and marched on dusty feet and bore blades instead of flags. How dull—until the killing started, of course. But all this travel . . . well, it would have been just plain dull if not for the entertainments. It was Braids's job to make the trip fun, and she was very good at her job.

A couple of slaves caused trouble below. Not really. All they did was struggle under a weighty dowager as they climbed the hills. Their motion, though, drew Braids's eye, and she could use them. It was time for a little show starring those fun, fanciful, expendable toys.

"Watch this now, folks!" she shouted as she leaped down the escarpment toward the troublesome slaves. "Where else do you get to witness a summary execution?" Even as she said the words, her mouth was beginning to distend. Something was forcing its way out, being birthed from her teeth, something that would eat the slaves alive. As she vaulted down, Braids smiled, and the thing came into being.

Braids loved her job.

* * * * *

Side by side, Kamahl and Phage rode across the wasteland. They were not brother and sister, not even comrades, but only commanders. To one side, General Stonebrow stomped stolidly, and to the other, Zagorka rode aback Chester. The allied army, twelve thousand strong, followed.

The commanders straddled a pair of gigantic serpents. Kamahl rode Roth, whose rubious scales had been scratched to a dull gray by ever-present sand. Phage's beast had no such difficulty. Its belly had long since worn away, and it wriggled along on rib tips like the white legs of an enormous millipede. Only an undead beast could bear Phage's corrupting touch.

"We'll destroy Akroma," Kamahl blurted, his thoughts suddenly spilling forth, "and the external threat to you will be gone. Then we'll deal with the internal threat."

Phage did not look at him. She only stared toward the gray hills on the extreme horizon. "What internal threat?"

Kamahl barked a laugh and threw her an incredulous grin. When he saw the flat line of her mouth, he grew serious. "This . . . infection, for lack of a better word. The poison in you that bleeds out of your skin. If it can kill anyone you touch, imagine what it is doing to your insides—"

"The poison *is* my insides," she growled. "There's nothing but poison."

"I don't believe that—"

"Obviously." At last, she turned to look at him. "Your sister is gone, Kamahl. I am the wolf who ate her."

He fixed her with a level stare. "If you ate her, she is inside you."

Phage's face was dispassionate. "I bit through her neck, crunched her skull, chewed her flesh, and worried her bones. My teeth murdered her, my gullet swallowed her, my gut digested her. She's gone. You look at me and see her, but you don't know who I am."

Turning his face back toward the trackless waste, Kamahl said, "We shall see."

Shaking her head, Phage said, "For all your transformations, you're still the same smug bastard."

Kamahl laughed again. "You see? I knew my sister was alive in you."

That ended the exchange. They were utter opposites, bound together only by a wager. Even so, when Phage's hate grew too strong or Kamahl's love grew too deep, they seemed somehow to feel the same thing.

In silence, they rode. Behind them marched a strange menagerie. Zombies shuffled mindlessly beside ranks of elf infantry. Goblins dodged among fiery tumbleweeds. Gigantipithicus apes knuckle-walked amid dryads. Shorn rhinos, giant squirrels, dementia horrors, great cats, doughty dwarfs, and enormous serpents all made their way toward a distant foe.

Strangest of all, though, were the fat merchants and indolent princes who rode in the sightseeing caravan nearby. Their feet were brushed with water and their lips with wine.

Soon the armies would be killing and the spectators applauding.

"Beware!" Stonebrow barked. "Something comes."

A light appeared above the gray rill on the horizon. It seemed a star, but no star could outshine that desert sky. It came toward them, not moving, but only growing larger and more intense.

"Full halt!" Kamahl called, lifting his hand to stop the army.

Something was wrong with that blazing figure. It was lopsided. Its radiance beamed to the right but not to the left. As it neared, the reason was clear. It was a man, with one arm sticking out and the other missing entirely. The man's eyes shone like mirrors, and his hair stood in flames from his head. He jutted his jaw toward Phage.

Out of the corner of his mouth, Kamahl asked, "A friend of yours?"

"I don't know his name," Phage replied flatly, "but I know who he was. He was the partner of a woman I killed, a woman who looked like Akroma."

The glowing man arrived. He hovered above that great

company, casting their twisted shadows across the sands. Hundreds of glowing motes spun in a nimbus around him. Orbs occasionally peeled from the cyclone of energy and circled Phage and Kamahl.

The man in their midst said simply, "Turn back. Enter here and you will die."

Ignoring the motes that probed his armor, Kamahl sat up straight aback the great red wurm. "We wish you no harm. We seek only Akroma, the vengeful angel."

The man's face pivoted toward Kamahl, and his fiery eyes were terrible to behold. "If you wish her harm, you wish me harm."

"Who are you?" Kamahl asked.

"I am Ixidor. This is my land. You are not welcome here."

One of the motes struck Kamahl between the eyes. A spark flashed through his mind. Kamahl tried to shake away the sensation. "What connection have you to Akroma Anathema?" As he spoke, the spark tumbled away between his lips.

"I created her," said the floating man, and he swung his arm to point at Phage. "I created her to destroy this one."

Growling, Kamahl reached to his belt and drew the axe that glinted eagerly there. He lifted it and said in a low voice, "If you made Akroma, you can unmake her. Do so, and we will turn back this army. Your land and you will be spared."

"I cannot," said Ixidor, a spark striking him in the forehead.

Kamahl's brows knitted. "You would sacrifice your land and all your people to protect one monstrous creature?"

"I am my land," Ixidor said placidly. "I am my people. I am every monstrous creature. Yes, I would sacrifice all of these for Akroma. You and I are the same, Kamahl. You cling to this thing that is not your sister in hopes of having her back. I cling to a thing that isn't my beloved for the same reason."

Gaping, Kamahl said, "How did you know—?"

"I cannot slay Akroma anymore than you can slay Phage."

Steely-eyed, Kamahl stared at Ixidor. They *were* the same. Somehow he sensed it. Neither was a villain, but both were poised to commit villainous acts. Neither could give up the woman he championed; neither could back down from defending her to the death. War was inevitable. Perhaps it was always so when two men were the same.

"What is this?" asked a new voice. Kamahl had been so entranced by the eyes of Ixidor that he had not seen Braids charge up the line. She stood with a hand on her hip, her scarred face squinting impatiently. "The audience is getting restless. They've paid for a war. Let's get to it."

Kamahl ground his teeth. Of course he could not fight this man. The madness of it was only too obvious in Braids's face. Without intending to, she had saved them all. "Yes, Ixidor. You and I are the same. That is why—"

"Why we will destroy Akroma," interrupted Phage, "and pursue you to the ends of your land and kill you as I should have done in the pits."

Astonished, Kamahl tried to gabble out a rebuke. He was too late.

A fading star, Ixidor retreated across the wastelands. Beneath him, the ground riled like the belly of a giant awakening from sleep.

Braids clapped madly and grinned. "Great speech, Phage. They heard it all!" She went from clapping to rubbing her hands. "Let's get to it then. The war must go on!" She skipped away, leaving tan ghosts of sand in a line behind her.

"What did you do?" Kamahl asked Phage.

"He was twisting your mind. That's what that spark was. It read your mind and planted thoughts in you. He made you pliant. He almost made you surrender."

Kamahl blinked, unsure what to think. "Why didn't he send a spark to you?"

"He did," she replied, "and it died in me."

Shaking his head to clear it, Kamahl said, "If it's going to be war, then let's fight it." He glanced to General Stonebrow, who gave a brooding nod. Signaling over his shoulder, Kamahl shouted. "Ahead at double-time!" He dug his heels into the sides of the great red serpent, and Roth slithered forward.

Phage did not deign to convey the command to her own troops. She let Zagorka clamber atop Chester and give the order. Already Phage advanced. Her undead snake ambled forward on its rib tips. Rags of flesh dragged across the sand. Phage rode easily, her eyes on the wasteland ahead.

General Stonebrow rumbled, "That isn't a ridge." He pointed to the gray rill on the horizon. "It's moving. It's coming toward us."

Regaining her seat on Chester, Zagorka stared at the wall. "What is it?"

"I don't know," Kamahl said. He squinted. "What are those? Those folds in the air?"

Kamahl hadn't noticed them a moment before—definite contours, as if the air had turned to warped glass. Some spots gathered and folded. Others formed tubes, or walls, or valleys. Kamahl was struggling to make out the patterns when Roth's jowl struck one slanting portion. He continued forward, channeled by transparent forces toward a whirling tube in the air ahead.

"Do we dare continue?" asked General Stonebrow. His hooves struggled against a strange slope in the air.

Phage's face was set, though her serpent also followed a groove. "We will not turn back."

Invisible walls closed in. They clamped around Roth's sides

and tightened their hold. Though he could still slither forward, his skin grew taut around him. It was as if the wurm swelled within.

Kamahl said, "What's happening?"

"The space is bent," Stonebrow growled, "the dimensions distorted. Your serpent is too big for its own skin."

Already, Roth's scales were beginning to pop loose. They shot from stretched follicles, the skin beneath as tight as the casing of a sausage. A terrible and manifold ripping sound began. Roth shrieked in agony.

The invisible force tighten around Kamahl's legs. He clambered up the serpent's back and leaped away, tumbling over a rift in space. Kamahl sprawled in the dust.

The serpent lashed his head, eyes rolling in their sockets. His skin split open, and muscle spurted out. Another hernia appeared, gushing meat, and a third and fourth. All the while, the wurm's skin shrank in upon his body, ever tightening as if crushed in a giant fist. Soon ribs cascaded in a gory fountain.

Kamahl staggered up and stared, disbelieving. He took an unsteady step but felt a wall of magic hold him back. "He's twisting space itself!" he shouted. His words were lost in the explosion of the serpent's body. Only the spine remained, with ribs cracked away and meat in a red well around it. The vacant spine settled down upon the gore.

Just beyond the carnage, Phage yet rode her undead mount. Without skin and flesh, the creature seemed immune to the compression of space.

The folds in air relented. Ixidor was shifting his assault, warping a different vector. Energies coalesced in front of the undead serpent and formed into a looming wall.

Kamahl scrambled to his feet and shouted, "No!"

He was too late. The undead serpent lurched into that scintillating wall. Its head broke through, and it slithered on. Just beyond the disturbance, flesh and bone dissolved. Still, the body of the snake wound forward, as if its head remained.

"A temporal wall," Kamahl muttered in realization. Ixidor could fold not just space but also time. The temporal loop had rotted the snake's head in moments. Its body crawled on because the temporal wall still conveyed the signals from its missing head.

Kamahl rushed up beside the serpent. There was no time for delicacy. With the flat of his axe, Kamahl struck Phage and knocked her from the creature's scabrous back.

Phage rolled in the sand, came to a halt, and looked back.

The snake slithered on through the wall and dissolved to nothing at all.

The commanders stared, amazed.

They weren't the only ones who had witnessed the power of Ixidor's nightmare lands. The army shuffled to a stop.

The safari patrons let out a surreal cheer.

"Idiots," Phage growled, spitting into the dust. "They'll be reamed as well."

Kamahl shook his head. "This is his worst. He wants us to stay out and so throws his worst at us first. I doubt he can sustain such powerful effects for long." He gestured toward the scintillating wall, which was already fading. Kamahl rose and dusted off his clothes. "You are right about one thing."

Phage climbed to her feet and snapped. "What?"

"The safari patrons are idiots."

Kamahl and his sister shared a rare smile. Together, they bowed low, both mocking the spectators and heartening their own armies. The roar of the caravan doubled, and the army shouted in cocky fury.

Between gritted teeth, Kamahl said, "There isn't only darkness in you."

"Or lightness in you."

Together, they raised their hands in the gesture for march. Turning, they strode deeper into the nightmare lands. The armies shoved up toward their commanders. They were ready to fight. Dwarves, goblins, dryads, centaurs, rhinos, and spinefolk all spread out in a wide line of advance that reached from the caravan on one side to the horizon on the other.

Still Kamahl and Phage were ten strides ahead of them.

Phage eyed the gray ridge. It seemed a great worm, rolling across the hills. "You think he has thrown his worst at us?"

Kamahl nodded, his axe gripped tightly in both hands.

"We're about to find out."

No longer a worm, the roiling line ahead resolved into an army. The soldiers were gray skinned and naked, human in shape but hairless and half-formed, like hunks of clay. They strode with staring eyes toward Kamahl, Phage, and their army.

"What do you think they are?" Kamahl wondered aloud. "Zombies?"

Phage shook her head. "He wouldn't dare throw undead at the Cabal."

Kamahl scowled. "Whatever they are, they have no weapons."

"Maybe they themselves are the weapons."

The commanders grew silent as the land between them and the gray men vanished. An anticipatory cheer arose from the spectators. It goaded the army to raise its own battle cry. Only the gray men marched in silence.

Kamahl raised his axe overhead, ready to split one of these beasts from brow to belly. It seemed almost slaughter, and something in him quailed at the thought. He glanced to Phage, whose hands were at the ready. She had no such reservations.

With a roar, the lines converged. The hairless creatures reached toward Kamahl, almost like beseeching children. His axe descended but then caught short. They laid hands on him—as gentle and soft as putty.

How could he slay such helpless things?

Those fingers hardened and strengthened. Kamahl stared down to where a dozen gray men grappled him. Their hands became callused replicas of his own. In a rapid wave, transformation swept up the arms of the beasts, making them brawny and tan. Shoulders bulked and neck muscles snapped, chests grew broad, and armor and clothes took shape. Strangest of all, though, the crowd of heads around him transformed to bear his own face.

In a moment, every last bit of gray was gone, and Kamahl was surrounded by duplicates of himself. From their hands jutted axes like his own.

He took a staggering step back, but his doubles advanced. He glanced sideways, seeing a score of Phages battling each other. Another step back, and Kamahl ran into the tide of his own warriors. As each creature crashed against the gray men, more transformations took place. Dozens of Stonebrows took shape. Multiples of Zagorka and her mule came into being. In moments, none of them would be able to tell friend from foe.

With a furious roar, Kamahl brought his axe shrieking down upon one of his doubles. It was caught unawares, its own axe half raised. Kamahl chopped the thing's arm off.

It fell, turning gray before it hit ground. Black blood oozed from the severed limb. From the thing's shoulder, though, the blood was as red as wine.

Kamahl swung the axe again, this time cleaving the monster's brain. Its false image bled away from the blade, and the beast was gray again as it struck the ground.

Even as one of the gray men fell, two more hands reached in to trigger the transformation.

Kamahl lopped them off and whirled his axe in a path around

him to keep them at bay. At all cost, he must avoid being touched, then he must kill until every last one was dead. His axe chucked into the forehead of another simulacrum. When metal met brain, the visage peeled away.

At least fighting his own semblance, he knew which one to kill. The only way he could know a true Phage from a false one was to sever a limb and watch for red blood.

With a growl of frustration, Kamahl bashed back another axe and sliced open the guts of its wielder. It felt strangely satisfying to kill himself again and again and again.

* * * * *

Phage was laughing. She never laughed, especially not when she fought, but to fight herself and find herself so weak was laughable.

She slapped one of her assailants, leaving an indentation on the creature's cheek. The impression quickly turned black and ate away the face. These gray men could withstand a fleeting contact, flesh to clothes, but anything more made them fall apart like old cheese.

Phage's laughter turned to a shout as she grabbed the necks of two nearby simulacra. Squeezing, she removed her likeness from their shoulders forever.

These monsters couldn't stand before her. They bore no weapons and did not wield the power of rot. They weren't even convincing actors, for all crowded together to attack her.

Kamahl also was surrounded by lookalikes, all swinging their axes at him.

Phage plunged toward him, dragging the gray men down with her fists. She dismantled flesh and strode full-out toward Kamahl. "You were right about these. They aren't Ixidor's worst." Tightening a fist, she smashed another of her doubles in the face, cracking her nose and making all turn to black.

She had run through most of her own duplicates and now came upon the back of a Kamahl—a rather inferior Kamahl. She grabbed the arm of the hulking barbarian, twisted it off, and hurled it away. The gray man spun in surprise and got a face full of fingers. He fell like a bag of bones.

Phage kicked out, clearing her way through the crowd of barbarians. They fell easily, mud to mud. Soon only one more remained between her and Kamahl. His back was turned, his axe lifted overhead to fall upon the true Kamahl. Phage merely reached up, grasped the shaft of the axe, and yanked backward. The imposter—nowhere near the mass of the barbarian—toppled back. Phage leaped onto his chest.

As rot spread through the simulacrum, Phage grinned at Kamahl. "A few more of these monsters, and we'll see what else Ixidor has."

Kamahl nodded his thanks and then kicked her hard in the stomach.

Air rushed from Phage's lungs, and she tumbled backward. It had not been Kamahl, but one of his doubles. Phage cursed herself as she rolled to a stop.

The towering simulacrum raised its axe and advanced to finish her off. Its foot, though, had turned to putrescence. A jagged end of bone rammed into the ground, and the thing toppled.

Phage rolled out from under the falling man, but not in time to avoid the bite of his blade. It sank into her leg, laying it open to the bone.

The simulacrum crashed down nearby, gangrene racing up his body.

Phage was in no better shape. Yes, her inner power would heal the wound, if she lasted long enough. Perhaps the true Kamahl would fight off the others.

Again Phage laughed, this time bitterly. It was the old story. How could Kamahl save her when he didn't even know who she was?

* * * * *

Kamahl had killed all his own replicas, but now he faced a dozen Phages. They all fought each other, all fought without weapons. How could he find his sister in this?

The whole army was beset. Not a single gray man remained untransformed. All seemed to be part of the great army. Only the blood told the difference, and by then it was too late.

"Help me!" called Phage, grasping his free hand.

Kamahl clutched the woman's hand and swung his axe. It struck her waist, just where he had struck before, and sliced her in two. The pieces fell away, turning gray of flesh and black of blood.

This was agony. He could not touch the hand of his true sister, but he could the hands of all these, and to win, he had to slay Phage over and over.

"Jeska!" he called out, desperately reaching to one of the many Phages, "come here!"

A nearby creature took his hand. He yanked it forward onto his broad blade.

Twelve times he called them, twelve times they touched him, twelve times he slew them. Here was the penance for an old, old sin. When the final Phage grasped his hand and awoke no rot, Kamahl had to strike her twice, so blurred was his vision with tears.

Where is she? This is all for her. If she is dead now, all of this was in vain. . . .

The last body he had slain shifted on the ground. Kamahl looked down to see the pieces of gray flesh decay. Beneath them lay his sister—wounded but alive.

"Jeska! Come to me!" he called extending his hand.

She did not take it and shook her head ruefully. "Quite a test you developed. The only Phage who would not come to you is the true Phage."

"Can you stand?"

"In a few more moments, yes," she replied heavily.

He wiped his sweaty brow. "I hope that was Ixidor's worst."

"I'm sure the worst is yet to come."

CHAPTER TWENTY-ONE

READING MINDS

To Ixidor, this was not so much war but nightmare, for the battlefield lay within his own mind.

The creator's body sat cross-legged on the highest balcony of Topos, but his spirit rushed in fury among clashing armies. He imposed the geometry of his subconscious onto reality and thereby folded space and strangled time. For weapons, he wielded his most twisted dreams. For warriors, he sent pieces of himself. Ixidor's army of gray men rose from his gray matter, and as they touched his foes and took on their forms, Ixidor learned.

Only a hhundred putty people remained alive, many hiding amid the sightseeing safari. Through their ears, he heard applause and laughter, gurgling wine and steaming food. War should not sound like this.

Ixidor needed time to think about what he had learned, so he prepared his scaly warriors—aggression incarnate. They could fight with only minimal attention.

Ixidor closed his eyes and let a sense of irritation well up within him. Anger prickled on every nerve ending. The emotion reached to the fringe of Greenglades and awakened an army of knob-shouldered and gaunt-legged beasts.

Carapace shuddered, and legs untangled themselves. Shelled

bodies rose among the tree boles, pincers plucking at the bark. An army of gigantic crabs suddenly strode among the fronds, heading toward the nightmare lands. Little red lights shown in their searching eyes, and the beams jagged across the wastes toward the invaders.

Tracers swarmed up the legs of the creatures—equine, elfin, reptilian, goblin—found the eyes that waited above, and locked on. Crab warriors surged from the jungle's edge. Claws clacked, mouth parts scissored, legs rasped—a clattering roar as the things descended.

Ixidor smiled. It always felt good to go from fear to fury.

They ran on four legs, lifting the rest in a set of deadly lances. Barbed claws snapped excitedly above.

The first of the crab folk—a long-legged beast that had pulled into the lead—struck the invaders. Vicious feet speared through heads, chests, and bellies of elves, then flung the flailing folk away. Claws snapped around necks and severed them. The crab ate its way rapidly into the line.

The elf contingent split, and a rhino charged through their midst. The ram affixed to its head crashed through the forest of chitinous legs. It struck the crab's belly, cracked the carapace, and shattered it.

The crab fell back, clawing at its broken body. It would die, yes, but it had killed six foes first. More scaly comrades struck the lines a moment later and ripped in with equal brutality.

Ixidor opened his eyes and stared, abstracted, at a blue sky cluttered with giant jellyfish.

Why would his foes do this? Why would Krosan and Cabal, ancient enemies, come together to slay him? Could it be true that this was all for Phage?

Those questions pressed on a fragile part of Ixidor's psyche. To kill Nivea had been madness. To march two armies to kill him too . . .

The jellyfish hung there, languid in the steamy sky.

Ixidor closed his eyes. He shooed away the questions and let anger rise.

Those beautiful, glowing beasts should not simply hang there. Let them fight. In his mind's eye, Ixidor gathered them into a brooding storm cloud. They formed an enormous squall line of plasmic bodies and drifted toward the battlefield. Beneath them, tentacles descended in a stinging rain. Whatever beasts would not fall to carapace would fall to it.

Through the ears of his putty people, Ixidor heard thrilled cheers from the safari folk. They had just glimpsed the jellyfish. Some even clapped excitedly as the beasts bore down on the battle.

Tentacles dragged across soldiers' upraised faces. Goblins curled up and died while elves shrieked and clutched at blinded eyes. Centaurs grappled the tentacles, struggling to rip them loose but only losing control of their own limbs.

Spectators giggled, placing and taking bets.

Ixidor could bear those incongruous sounds no longer. *Kill them,* he commanded his putty people.

They did. Disguised in the finery of nobles, the gray folk rose from their caravans and killed and killed. Cruel laughter turned into shrieks of terror, and instead of wine gurgling, it was blood. Such noises befit a battle. The putty people slew a few dozen of the royal patrons before they themselves were destroyed. Laughter and screams both died to nothing.

Finally, Ixidor could think.

He opened his eyes. The blue skies were clear again. Where once there had been giant jellyfish, now only Ixidor's own disciples remained, daytime stars around him.

Could this all be for Phage? What if she were as much a victim as Nivea?

Ixidor shivered. If that were the case, no one fought for what was right. All were wrong. All was madness. If the battlefield was Ixidor's own mind, then he himself was mad. The more violent the battle, the madder he became.

Already Ixidor had used his worst nightmares, but the invaders did not relent. It was time for them to face their own worst nightmares.

Lifting his hands to the heavens, Ixidor said, "To me."

The sparking disciples swirled down his upraised arms. They poured into his brow, and energy cascaded through him. Minds touched upon his mind, knew what he knew, wished what he wished. Opening his mouth, Ixidor sent them pouring forth.

Between cerulean sky and azure lake, the darting blue sparks went. Though silent and small, these were the most vicious of all Ixidor's warriors. They would plow the minds of the foe and uproot their deepest fears.

As Ixidor watched his disciples spread through the world, he wondered if any creature would survive this battle and if those survivors could be anything but insane.

* * * * *

What sort of monster would make such monsters?

Kamahl slashed a groping tentacle. It fell, smearing its stinging poison down his side. Were it not for the axe he gripped, power of growth and power of death, he would be dead already. Still, this was hell—to suffer agony and not die.

Scrambling away from the jellyfish, Kamahl sought cover. The giant beast followed him, and his only escape was blocked by a crab warrior.

Ah, a solid foe for a change.

Growling, Kamahl hurled himself to the attack. His axe

cracked through one leg of the crab. He swung the axe in another arc beneath it, and a second leg severed, and a third. Kamahl ducked under the crab's body as if it were an umbrella.

The jellyfish caught up to them, and a rain venom poured down atop the crab. Under the convulsing creature, Kamahl was safe—sort of.

What sort of monster is Ixidor?

He was the partner of a woman I killed, a woman who looked like Akroma, Phage had said. She had killed Ixidor's beloved. No doubt that murder had something to do with all these horrors.

I bit through her neck, crunched her skull, chewed her flesh, and worried her bones. My teeth murdered her, my gullet swallowed her, my gut digested her. She's gone.

Phage had killed Kamahl's sister and Ixidor's beloved too.

"She has destroyed us both."

Dying in the rain of poison, the crab constricted its remaining legs around Kamahl. He was suddenly caught in a cage of carapace, his axe trapped outside. Worse, the jellyfish's feeding tube descended. Sinewy lips slid down around the crab and sucked it up. Kamahl went with it.

The clangor of battle was muffled inside that translucent tube. Membranes slapped and organs pumped. A huge stomach gurgled above, one already filled with half-digested warriors. It would be more than full when Kamahl reached it.

There was no room. Kamahl struggled to shift his axe so that the blade would rub against the peristaltic muscles. The rubbery stuff only stretched instead of cutting. Down around the tube flowed digestive juices that lubricated and suffocated. Already, they had eaten away enough of the crab's shell to kill the thing. Once Kamahl reached that bulbous stomach, even his regenerative axe would not save him.

A spasm gripped the tube, and the crab bolus ground to a halt.

Kamahl merely hung there as another constriction tightened around him. The dead crab pinched his sides, spikes digging in. It didn't matter whether he reached the stomach or not. He would die here.

Something darkened the tube that held him. It was as though black mold grew rapidly across it, mold in the shape of a hand. The fingers of decay widened, lengthened. The translucent flesh of the mouth-tube trembled. Tissues tore, and through a hole that smelled of rot, air came to Kamahl.

He gulped a breath. Struggling against the might of the esophagus, Kamahl reached out to drag more of the foul flesh away. Air gushed in. He inhaled gratefully.

Phage's severe face appeared in the opening. Another black spot spread where her other hand clung. She must have shimmied all the way up the outside of the mouth tube, killing it as she climbed.

Kamahl could only pant and gape.

"I thought I saw your axe," she said, nodding toward the blade, which glinted despite the oozy flesh around it.

Kamahl's voice was raspy. "You came for me."

She shook her head. "I came for the axe—the blade enchanted to kill Akroma."

Grimacing tightly, Kamahl nodded. "Just get me out of here."

A regretful light shone in Phage's eyes as she glanced down. "All too easy. From here to the ground, it's all rot. Get ready to drop."

Kamahl glimpsed lines of putrefaction striping the feeding tube. Chunks tumbled away, and his legs hung in clear air. Soon, the muscles would lose their hold altogether, and Kamahl and Phage would plummet.

They lurched downward. "Good-bye, Sister."

"Only keep hold of the axe," she replied flatly.

Then both were falling. They tumbled beside each other in midair, accompanied by an unwholesome cascade.

Kamahl tumbled backward and saw that the skies were nearly cleared of jellyfish. He flipping toward the ground and saw that half his army had been decimated by crab warriors, but none of the gangly monsters remained.

Kamahl tucked himself into a ball, ready to hit ground. He struck a mound of bodies, the fleshy hill taking much of the impact, and rolled to one side. Remembering his sister's words, Kamahl clutched his axe, allowing its power to scintillate through him.

The rotting jellyfish fell. It whirred down and splattered. Its guts rolled out in waves, one of which caught Kamahl and hurled him farther.

At last, the slimy and bruised barbarian tumbled to a halt. He lay there for a time, coughing. The axe remained in his hand, tight against his chest. Its healing strength was a salve to his body.

All around, the battle lulled to silence. The jellyfish and crabs were gone, and the allied army paused to climb from the slime and breathe.

What horrors would come next?

A constellation drifted in the heavens—a swarm of blue stars. Kamahl recognized those darting points of light—the aura of Ixidor. He had used them once to read Kamahl's mind. How would he use them now?

Struggling out of the mire, Kamahl tried futilely to leap aside.

A blue star arced down and struck him in the forehead. His mind flashed, alight with alien intelligence. It held him paralyzed as it searched among memories. Into the deepest corners it probed, and at last, it found what it sought.

Something was in his mouth, something that scuttled. Kamahl spat. A black beetle fell from his lips and struck the ground. It landed on its back, legs flapping. The bug was big, the size of his thumb—no, his palm, his fist.

Squinting, Kamahl leaned down to stare at it. It was getting bigger.

Kamahl staggered back.

Plates shifted across the creature's back. Flesh bulged between. The blackness faded to brown and then to tan. Rear legs broadened and thickened until they were as large as Kamahl's own. Front legs fused into arms, and thorax plates became hardened muscle. Armor formed at shoulder and waist, and a buckler at wrist. Worse of all, though, the head of the bug became his own head—not as it was now, but as it had been in those mad days when he wielded the Mirari sword.

Ixidor had not dreamed up this horror. Kamahl had. This was his own nightmare made manifest.

The monster smiled a sanguine smile, reached over his shoulder, and drew forth the massive Mirari sword. He lowered it in front of him, challenging Kamahl to a duel.

He would have to fight his worst nightmare—the bloodthirsty man he once had been.

* * * * *

Phage had lost sight of Kamahl when they both struck ground. She had rolled one way, and he had rolled the other.

Rising, she climbed atop a fallen gigantipithicus and looked back. She barely had time to dive away again as the jellyfish plunged and splattered. Landing on her face atop a pile of dead, Phage waited as jellyfish parts smacked juicily all around.

She stood and surveyed. The crab warriors were dead, the jellyfish were fleeing, and half the army remained. In the distance, Stonebrow lifted his gory figure above the charnel grounds, a sword flashing in his hand. Nearby, Zagorka sat astride Chester. The old woman and her mule seemed both a counterpart to and a mockery of the great centaur. Those two commanders could marshal the living troops and lead them in a march over the dead ones.

Of course, it would be easier to regroup if Kamahl waved his blessed axe.

Where was Kamahl?

Something danced in the sky, blue-white stars spinning. They reached down to the battlefield and spread above the heads of the gathered throng.

Phage remembered these stars. They were Ixidor's probes.

One whirled nearby to strike an elf archer. It sank into his head and disappeared. A moment later, the man dropped his bow and doubled over to retch. From his mouth emerged a buzzing bug. It flopped out onto the ground and then swelled to take hideous form. It was a demon soldier—pallid skin stretched over spiky bone and violent mechanism.

The elf shrieked and backed away. He tried to snatch up his bow, but the demon stormed in. Shoulder spikes impaled the elf's belly. The demon stood, and the agonized elf flailed across its back. He lived only a moment more. The demon dragged his riddled form from the spikes, threw him to the ground, and stalked on to kill again.

It was a living nightmare.

All along the line, the blue-white probes struck. From the mouths of each creature issued those bugs, which swelled into more monsters.

Phage's eyes narrowed. Only she would be immune, for she already was a living nightmare. The last time a spark such as this struck her, it had sunk into the ravenous darkness within and not emerged again.

She made little effort to avoid the blue light that jagged down toward her.

It hit and burrowed into the skin between her eyes. It did not extiguish itself as had the last spark but sank through to her brain. This spark was different. The last had sought light in her mind and perished from lack of it. This spark sought darkness and found it.

Either Phage was the only one who was immune, or she was the most vulnerable one of all.

A chunk of something scuttled out from between her teeth. Clacking wings beat, and the thing jagged free. It was a roach, blacker than any beast Phage had ever seen. In disgust, she spat, and felt another such creature heavy on her tongue. She spewed it out, and there were two, and another, and more. The bugs gagged her. They scrabbled to get free, clawing at her lips. She vomited them, five at a time, then ten. She could barely breathe as the black torrent of them poured out.

They didn't fall to the ground but rose on saliva-shining wings. The roaches gathered in a churning swarm that spread like ink in water. Still more emerged.

That single spark had discovered the mother lode of nightmares. It was bleeding them away from Phage.

Already the sky darkened with the swarm, no less than an insect plague. As yet, the roaches were only gathering, but once they swept down in hunger, they would consume everything.

Phage fell to her knees. She tried to clamp her mouth shut, but barbed legs jutted between her teeth. Pincers gnawed her gums, and leathery shells pressed against the back of her throat. She began to gag. Let them kill her. Better to die than to let this evil plague out on the world.

The thought stunned her. It was not her own. When would Phage had ever died to save the world?

Still, she couldn't hold the bugs within. They burst out in a slick column.

All joined the cloud. It was huge, spreading above the whole battlefield. Many of the warriors paused to stare up into that boiling cloud—a horror worse than any they had ever conceived. It did not look like separate insects, but like one great darkness eating away the blue sky. Planetary gangrene, it turned all it touched to nothingness, and it grew greater by the moment.

Tears rolled down Phage's face. She had not wept since that horrible day in Krosan, when her brother had left her to die.

Phage shook her head, tears flying from her cheeks. Kamahl wasn't her brother. She wasn't Jeska, but with each new roach that tumbled from her mouth, she felt less and less like Phage and more and more like Jeska.

He had been right; Kamahl had been right. Jeska had survived within that cloud of horrors. The sister he sought had been imprisoned in pollution.

Still, the foulness gushed from her as if it would never cease.

"Jeska!" said a husky voice, and a powerful hand grasped her arm.

"Ka-mahl!" she gagged, turning toward him even as the plague poured out.

It wasn't Kamahl. General Stonebrow knelt beside her. He had apparently slain his own greatest nightmare and come to help slay hers. Strangest of all, he touched her without rotting away.

"Jeska! What is happening to you?"

She tried to answer but could not for all the roaches.

* * * * *

Even for Ixidor, high in his glimmering palace above the sapphire sea, the battle had turned deadly. Outwardly, he was at peace, surrounded by his unmen and the finery of his bedchamber. Inwardly, he was dying.

Ixidor trembled. His jaws clenched, teeth grinding upon each other until grit covered his tongue. Rot spread in his mind. It ate away will and thought. Ixidor wanted to rise, but he could barely breathe.

This Phage's skin had held a nightmare that could destroy the world. No wonder her very touch killed. No wonder to her the death of a single woman was nothing. She held within her the death of everyone.

Shuddering, Ixidor managed to scoot forward on the seat. It was a seizure, yes, but it was movement. If only he could break through this rigidity that held him. If only he could . . . but the part of his mind that contained the answer no longer remained.

Ixidor fell from the chair. An unman swooped as if to catch him, though Ixidor would have simply fallen through to another part of the castle. Instead, the creator's own instinctual mind took hold. His hands broke the fall. Ixidor crumpled to the floor.

Instinct. It would save him. Panting, he cried out the first word that came to his tongue. "Nivea!"

The unmen heard. In voices like bleeding air, they repeated the name.

Ixidor growled, convulsed, crawled. "Nivea!" It was not the right name, but it was the only name he could speak. "Nivea!"

She came, not Nivea but the creature who had once had her face.

On majestic wing, Akroma dropped down to the balcony. Her feline claws scratched the marble floor. When her face cleared the archway, its faint color fled away entirely.

"Creator!"

Akroma hurried toward him. Once she would have drifted above the floor, but now her claws scrabbled like a beast's. She had been soaring the skies above Topos, guarding her creator against any approach, but this attack had come from within.

Ixidor wished he could comfort her, but he could hardly join thought to thought.

Akroma knelt above him. "What has happened? Who has done this?"

If only he had the words. It was not Phage who had done this. Phage had kept this monstrosity imprisoned in her skin. To kill the woman now would be to destroy the one vessel that could contain all this evil. It was not Phage whom Akroma must fight. It was the blackness.

"Blackness . . ." he muttered. "Blackness . . ."

Akroma's face was quizzical. "Blackness?" She lifted her eyes, glaring at the unmen. "What blackness? Speak a name, Master, and that creature will no longer be."

He could speak the name of Phage, but it would mean the end of all. No, Akroma must not kill Phage, but the blackness.

The contagion changed in his mind. No longer was it a great amorphous shape, no longer a swarm. Now, it was a tangle—a mass of glistening tubes. They were eating and eating.

"Eating," gasped Ixidor. He struggled, managing to shove himself upright and sit. He was regaining his mind, his strength, but not quickly enough. "Eating."

"What is eating?" Akroma asked.

"Wurms," blurted Ixidor. He grasped her hand, stared into her piercing eyes, and squeezed the words out. "Kill the wurms."

CHAPTER TWENTY-TWO

THE TRUEST FOE

*H*ave a look, all of you!" Braids shouted ecstatically. She gripped the sides of her head and yelled, "Clay warriors, crab men, jellyfish, and now living nightmares!" Shrieking her delight, Braids leaped from roof to roof atop the long curve of the caravan.

The wagons formed a broad semicircle on one flank of the battlefield. Nobles within watched avidly, feasting on appetizers and atrocities, drinking wine and drinking in blood. Their appetites had been only whetted by the sudden appearance of monsters among them. Though a few nobles had been killed, the beasts were quickly dispatched, and the other nobles considered it all a thrilling show. Why worry about death when it was someone else's—and when the amenities were so stellar? Attendants saw to their every want.

Braids saw to their entertainment. "The death toll stands near to six thousand in our armies alone. Ten thousand of the foe have died! For those who have placed bets on individual deaths, hold your tickets. The lucky winners will be toted up when every body is tagged!"

Braids paused, staring at the battlefield. Something big was on its way, something boiling out of Phage. It gathered above her, churning in a black cloud, and ate away the air wherever it spread. Already, Braids had made mention of it, but until the horror was fully formed, she needed a more immediate attraction.

"All eyes, turn to Kamahl! He's easy to spot. There are two of him. Many of you will recognize the old Kamahl, tawny of skin and bloody of eye, a barbarian in the Pardic tradition—killer of thousands, of Chainer, of Jeska!"

An impromptu ovation answered her call, and Braids turned an eager flip.

"Others know Kamahl of Krosan, druid in the forest tradition—creator of thousands, of giant serpents and Stonebrow."

More applause answered.

"Place your bets. Who is the more powerful? The old Kamahl or the new? We all wish to escape our past, but now Kamahl will kill it or be killed by it. Place your bets!"

*   *   *   *   *

Kamahl circled warily, keeping the stone axe before him. His truest foe—he, himself—crouched on the other side of that blade.

It had been one thing to slay dozens of false selves. It was quite another to face down this one true one.

The man was tall and muscular, with not an inch of fat anywhere and skin that gleamed like polished bronze. His shaved head seemed a battering ram and his red armor the carapace of a rangy spider. Never had Kamahl faced so brutal and bloodthirsty an opponent. Never before had he faced the man he once had been.

Kamahl breathed. His soul sought the perfect forest within.

With a ferocious growl, the red barbarian hurled himself forward and brought his huge sword roaring down. He drew power from that blade. No weapon in the world could stop the blow, no armor could turn it.

Kamahl sidestepped. He had learned much finesse since he had been this rangy bastard.

The Mirari sword flashed past and embedded its end in the ground. The weight of it dragged its bearer forward.

Kamahl's axe was in the wrong position to strike but not his boot. Lifting it, he kicked the barbarian brutally in the belly. The warrior reeled back, yanking his sword with him. Kamahl merely set his foot again on the ground and stood ready.

A blood-swollen scowl filled his former face. "I am ashamed of you, of what I became. I would never have received an attack with my own blade in the wrong position to defend."

Kamahl's brow lifted. "I am ashamed of you, of what I once was. I would never invest all in a single, terrible attack."

"Isn't that what you have done with your army?" goaded the red man. He charged suddenly. His enormous sword swung up in a wide stroke, too low to duck, too high to jump.

Kamahl used his boot again, smashing it on the flat of the blade and shoving it ground-ward. The arm of the barbarian was too strong, though. The blade swept on. Putting all his weight on the boot, Kamahl stepped up into the air. Even as the sword swung where his body had been, Kamahl stood on it and kicked his other foot into the barbarian's throat. He continued the motion, flipping backward and landing out of reach, among piles of the dead.

Staggering, the red barbarian hawked and spat. Blood and spittle smacked the face of a dead elf. "I am your worst nightmare."

"Every evil thing I once was," agreed Kamahl.

"No, I am every good thing you once were. I am your worst nightmare not because I am less than you but because I am greater."

The words had the sting of truth. Had Kamahl transcended his former depravity or descended from his former glory? In uncertainty, he lost his center. He winced too late.

The sword—that massive, vicious sword—carved the air and bit into Kamahl's shield arm. It cut to the bone and would have taken the whole limb had Kamahl not leaped back. He did so again, tumbling over a rhino carcass. His shoulder crashed on the ground, and blood streamed from the wound. His arm would be useless until the axe could work its healing.

There was no time for healing in the midst of battle. Kamahl rolled to his good side and scrabbled backward on elbow and foot.

The barbarian towered on the other side of the dead rhino. Gore crazed his broad blade, and the Mirari below looked like a bloodshot eye. The man laughed. "Look at you. You haven't landed a single blow, and there you lie, cut open by me and—" his eye shifted to the gangrenous wound across Kamahl's belly "—the one given you by little sister."

Kamahl struggled to sit. He cradled his axe in his wounded arm.

The red warrior climbed atop the rhino and laughed again. "Only a fool tries to right old wrongs. Only a madman takes responsibility in an irresponsible world. Nature has pitted mouth against mouth to see who eats whom. Predators have no time to weep."

Kamahl climbed to his feet. He was hemmed in by more bodies. In his good hand, he held the axe propped on the wound, hoping against hope for healing. There was no escape. Still, he stalled.

"Look at you. You stand tall on your victims."

"Yes," said his former self, lifting the Mirari sword overhead for the killing stroke. "And you will be a poor podium." He swung the sword toward Kamahl's head.

Kamahl jabbed with his axe. It was a weak blow. It could never have pierced the man's armor, but it did pierce the rhino's hide. Blood gushed beneath the feet of his foe.

The man slipped. The Mirari sword sliced just shy of Kamahl's brow and buried itself in the broad belly of the rhino. Sliding on gore, the red warrior fell back. He lost his grip on the sword.

Kamahl dropped his axe and lurched forward. His good hand grabbed the hilt of the Mirari sword and used it to lever himself over the impaled beast. Feet came sloppily to the ground, and he yanked on the blade. It slid free in a red arc. Kamahl roared, and the Mirari sword surged down toward his former heart.

The blade stove armor, bit through body, and plunged into the ground. The nightmare lay pinned.

In a sudden flash, Kamahl was back in the Krosan Forest, standing above Laquatus. That moment was tied to this. Ever since Kamahl had chosen to kill Laquatus instead of saving Jeska, he had struggled to revoke that single, lethal moment. Now, standing above his own slain self, hand on the Mirari sword, Kamahl at last had done so.

The Mirari sword trembled and disintegrated, returning to the dream that had spawned it. So too the corpse vanished, but the wound it had struck remained.

Clamping his hand on the spot, Kamahl looked beyond himself and saw a horrible sight.

Jeska knelt beneath a plague of black beetles.

He had almost let her die again. Clutching his wounded arm in a bloody fist, Kamahl strode toward her. "Jeska!"

She lifted her eyes—haunted eyes—and saw him. It was the first time since Krosan that she had really seen him. Jeska was herself once more. "Kama—" she pleaded, but the name was cut off by a black lump that forced its way out of her mouth and flew into the churning cloud.

Trudging through a labyrinth of the dead and dying, Kamahl reached his sister. She was on her knees, vomiting forth the blackness of her soul. With each beast that scuttled from her teeth and took wing, Jeska's face lost some of its deathly pallor. Unsure how to help or what to do, Kamahl fell to his knees beside her and wrapped his good arm around her.

"You're back," he said heavily. "I knew you were in there, alive despite all the death."

She nodded wretchedly and, between the bugs, blurted, "It has been . . . a prison. . . . Phage is the worst part of me . . . holding the best part captive."

Kamahl watched the swarm emerge, insect by insect. "Where did all this come from, all this blackness?"

She couldn't answer, so choked on roaches. The awful cascade eventually slowed and ceased. The last of the evil scuttled from Jeska's mouth, and she hunched on the ground like a sick dog.

"Sister . . ." Shaking his head, Kamahl lifted Jeska in a gentle embrace.

"Stonebrow was here . . . He went to find you. . . ." She began to sob. "My stomach . . . The old wound."

Drawing back, Kamahl saw it—the jagged laceration. Though once stitched together by Braids's dark magic, the wound had broken open again. Jeska was as near death now as on the day that Kamahl had abandoned her. "We have to find a healer." Kamahl scanned his troops, hoping to see a druid. "Perhaps my axe. . . ." His hand strayed to his belt, but then he remembered dropping the axe to pick up the Mirari sword.

"Where is your axe?" Jeska asked wearily.

"I don't know," Kamahl muttered. He glanced around the battlefield. A rebel impulse cried out for him to go find it. "It doesn't matter. I'm not leaving you."

"We need your axe," Jeska said. "Not just to heal me. To fight those." She pointed toward the spinning cloud.

"Fight beetles with an axe?"

"Not beetles. Not any longer."

From the convulsing swarm, individual bugs were dropping. They thwacked the ground, one after another, like hunks of meat. Their shells split and oozed, and the flesh within expanded. Beetles stretched into long pills of muscle. They riled, becoming pupae, as if the adult beasts were reverting to more primitive forms. Pupae in turn elongated into black worms, and they too grew. The length of a man, then a sapling, then a tree, soon they were not just worms, but wurms, dwarfing even the giant serpents.

Each of those black things became as wide around as a house and a league long. Their heads were masses of fleshy spikes, and their mouths were wide, fangy things for eating away the world. Already two score such creatures filled the nightmare lands, and every moment, more beetles crashed to the ground and began to transform.

"What are they?" cried Kamahl in astonishment.

Jeska's eyes, so briefly bright with hope, reflected the dark tangle of monsters. "They are my worst nightmare. They are the folk that Phage—that I—have killed: one wurm for each murder. Deathwurms."

The first such beast lifted its head above the fields of the dead. The green army quailed before it. Like a cobra stretching before it struck, the deathwurm bobbed for a moment, then lunged, mouth gaping.

It grabbed the head of a giant serpent. Teeth crunched, piercing the brain pan.

The snake writhed, its body lashing and crushing nearby warriors.

The deathwurm gulped, peristalsis dragging the serpent deeper into its throat. The creature did not die. Its spasms continued as it descended. The sides of the wurm bulged, showing the blind contours of the snake's head. With a final lurching gulp, the wurm swallowed the shuddering tail.

Another wurm lunged. It caught a rhino in its vicious mouth, and the pachyderm disappeared. The wurm withdrew, swallowing, and more of its kind reared up to feast.

The allied legions withdrew. They had stood in the face of shape shifters, crabmen, jellyfish, and even their worst nightmares, but these wurms . . .

Kamahl bowed, scooping Jeska in his one good arm. His wounded arm hung useless at his side, but he had the strength to lift his sister. She was as light as a fallen sparrow. Cradling her to his chest, Kamahl staggered up.

The motion caught the eye of a deathwurm. It rose, swaying hypnotically. Its mouth edged open, and saliva the color of ink slipped from between its teeth.

Kamahl turned and ran across the killing field. Clambering over the corpse of a gigantipithicus, Kamahl rushed amid the still jittering parts of a zombie platoon.

Air whistled. The wurm was lunging for them.

"Hang on!" Kamahl shouted. He pulled Jeska all the tighter to him, and she clung to his neck. His eyes were pinned to the corpse of a giant centaur just ahead. If only he could reach it—

A blast of grave breath plumed over them.

Kamahl leapt. He and Jeska barely cleared the massive corpse, tumbling over it. They landed in a sprawl on the ground just beyond.

The deathwurm's mouth smashed down around the giant centaur. Its teeth bit like shovels into the ground. A snout of rubbery black flesh impacted beside Kamahl's leg. The thing's bubble eyes stared hungrily at him. Jaw muscles flexed, and teeth descended through the ground, scooping up tons of soil. A strange hiss began around the massive head, and dust fled in under it. As the wurm lifted its head, the suction only grew stronger. Winds raced into the hole it had bitten.

The wurm had chomped through the very fabric of the nightmare lands. It had left a sucking pit. Within lay nothingness.

Kamahl hunkered down, holding himself against the ravenous winds. Jeska clung to him though her hands were growing weak. Clutching the ground, Kamahl waited for the wind to abate.

A rising shadow told him he could wait no longer. Another wurm rose.

Still holding his sister, Kamahl crawled away from the sucking hole. Once he had gotten beyond the worst winds, he clambered to his feet and ran.

Kamahl dodged beside a shorn rhino just before a death-wurm struck and ate it. A gaping hole opened where it had been, and air sucked down through it. Kamahl kept his feet, running ahead.

The whistling sound came again. It rose in pitch, and Kamahl leaped the other way. With a profound concussion, the deathwurm smashed against the corpses just beside Kamahl.

He only ran. Holes opened across the ground, dragging bodies into them. Another wurm struck, and another, and Kamahl evaded each by a narrower margin.

A hundred more running steps and he would be beyond the nightmare lands, where perhaps he could fall and rest. . . . But even then, Jeska would die.

He couldn't think of that now. He could only run.

All around him, deathwurms crashed.

* * * * *

Braids crowed in mad delight. "Death! Carnage! Destruction!" She turned a back flip atop the caravan. "Amazing! Incredible! Inescapable!"

She was right. A deathwurm crashed down atop a nearby wagon, gobbling up the conveyance and the noble within.

"Who wants to take odds on survival?" Braids shouted, bounding down onto the sands. She leaped along the curve of caravans as more deathwurms snatched up her patrons. "I'll give any of you fifty to one against. If you survive, you'll be rich. If not, it won't matter!"

It was an excellent wager, but no one seemed interested. The nobles were scampering everywhere. Folk who had not taken a single step this whole trip now took hundreds. No longer did they cower in their wagons.

They ran.

They fell.

They died.

Braids shook her head in a paroxysm of sadness. All that money lost. If only they had taken the bet!

"Where are you going? This is the payoff! This is what you came for! You wanted death! I give you death!" Braids grew angrier and angrier as she ran beside the wagons, overturned and half-chewed, spilling bodies both living and dead. Didn't they understand? This had ceased to be mere entertainment. This was art. "So few people appreciate art."

Braids did. She gave up on her patrons—after all, she'd gotten enough money out of them. Instead, she turned to the wurms and watched as they ate.

"Beautiful!"

Their flesh was like hers, their appetites—these were friends, things she understood. Surely, they understood her.

One of the huge beasts lunged down to snatched a man beside

her. Braids took the opportunity to leap onto its head. While the wurm munched, she settled in, grasping its fleshy spikes. She would ride the wurm right through this war. She only hoped its appetite would hold.

"Come one, come all! Death calls everyone! Experience the thrill of a lifetime—the end of a lifetime!" cried Braids as she rode the darting wurm.

* * * * *

Zagorka lashed Chester, though the mule needed no encouragement to run.

A deathwurm thudded to ground behind them. The monster rose, leaving a pit that sucked wind like the moaning of the damned. Another wurm crashed down nearby, sinking its teeth into a platoon of goblins.

"Death bites!" shrieked Zagorka.

Chester snorted his agreement.

The wurm yanked its head free, opening a roaring pit.

"Death sucks!"

Chester shook his head bitterly.

"I thought we'd already faced down our worst nightmare!"

They had. Chester's worst nightmare was an enormously fat man who kept trying to mount him. Zagorka's was, interestingly, the same man trying to do the same thing to her. They double-teamed him. The mule's hooves pummeled the man's backside while Zagorka's boots pummeled his front. In short order, he pleaded for mercy, fell dead, and disappeared entirely.

It would be an absolute irony to have survived that atrocity only to die now.

A deathwurm surged down, mouth agape, and slammed over

the rushing pair. The hot, bright battlefield was swallowed in cold blackness.

"We've been ate!" Zagorka shouted, glancing around at the jaws. She stared up the gullet of doom and saw a big flap of blackness. "A uvula!"

The pendulous thing struck Chester's backside, and he kicked. A pair of giant hooves struck the dangling flesh.

The wurm gagged. Its sinews convulsed. From its cold, cavernous gullet came a deep gurgle. Things flooded down—living vomit. A mass of struggling limbs and gaping mouths came tumbling out the wurm's throat. The glutinous tide struck Zagorka and Chester, flinging them to the ground. The wurm recoiled and left them there.

For a shocked moment, the creatures in that oozy mound looked around, stunned. Then they struggled up and began to run.

Somehow, Zagorka had remained atop Chester. The huge mule bolted full-out toward the desert.

Another hoofed creature thundered up to run beside them. Only when Zagorka flung the muck out of her eyes did she recognize the centaur. "General Stonebrow! You were one of those in the belly of the beast?"

The horse-man didn't answer, keeping his famous pate turned toward the open spaces beyond.

Zagorka let out a barking laugh. "Even the mighty Stonebrow runs!"

The general grunted irritably.

"Don't be ashamed. Nobody can blame you for running from death."

"I'm not ashamed," rumbled the gigantic centaur.

Nothing remained to be said. The crone, the mule, and the horseman ran for their lives in companionable silence.

* * * * *

Kamahl stumbled out of the nightmare lands. He took ten staggering steps in the sand before he could go no farther. Falling to his knees, Kamahl lowered Jeska gently to the ground. He crouched above her, spreading his good arm protectively. It was a futile gesture, for if a rhino wanted to run over them, it would.

The allied legions were in full rout, stampeding back toward the desert. Goblins, slaves, serpents, squirrels, elves, dwarves, and every other creature fled past Kamahl and Jeska. Feet and hooves beat the ground, their clamor punctuated by the profound boom of deathwurms. They rose, snapped, and advanced. No one could stand against them. Every living thing fled and hoped that Ixidor's nightmares could not escape the dreamlands.

Kamahl clung to his sister and said, "We'll be fine. We'll be fine."

Jeska shook her head weakly. "You go. Go. You shouldn't die."

Heaving a sigh, Kamahl said, "The brother who would have left you is dead already. I'll not leave you this time, even if we must die together. I came back to save you."

Jeska's eyes brimmed. "You have saved me. I used to think that dying in Krosan would be the worst fate I could suffer. Now I know there are worse things. Much worse."

Nodding, Kamahl glanced over his shoulder. The battlefield was emptying. Only a few hundred souls remained between them and the ravenous wurms. "Do you think you could run?"

Jeska shook her head sadly.

"Walk?"

"I don't think so."

He smiled tightly. "At least we will be together." He looked down into her eyes and saw there affection and something else—a bright presence that looked like hope. "What is it?"

She pointed. "Look."

There, above the riling mound of deathwurms, a vision floated—a marvelous creature in white, bearing a great and shining lance.

Together, brother and sister said, "Akroma!"

CHAPTER TWENTY-THREE

PALLAS AND JOVE

Absolute darkness could not exist without absolute light. Anyone who stared on the deathwurms in their convoluted mass would have known that a pure light was coming: the angel Akroma.

Wide wings spread above the tangled wurms. Perfect pinions flashed the sunlight as they bore her above the swarm. The wings sprouted from feline shoulders, and a spotted tail lashed the air as she came. In one muscular arm, Akroma bore a staff like a jag of lightning. The other arm pointed down into the mess of monsters. Within a mane of flesh, the woman's serene face stared at the darkness, her white eyes intense.

"I see what you are. Deaths. Terrible deaths. One of you is the death of Nivea, the birth of me. One of you."

Akroma pivoted into a dive. She tucked her wings and held the lightning lance foremost. From blue skies, she shrieked down upon the wurms. In a riven second, she reached them.

Her lance stabbed one beast in the back, just above a lump where living creatures struggled. Muscle burst open. The lightning staff pierced the bolus and burned away flesh. Snarling like a jaguar, Akroma yanked the lance upward. The wurm's flesh peeled open. Terrified creatures boiled up and out.

Covered in digestive slime, elves and goblins clawed their way out of the belly of death. They slid down the thing's flanks and fetched up against adjacent wurms. Gasping, they turned to see their deliverer but winced away in terror.

Above Akroma loomed the gargantuan head of the deathwurm she had pierced. It reared up to block the sun. She was just lifting her face to see it when the horrid jaws roared down to snap her up. Translucent teeth gleamed around a black gullet.

With a single stroke of her wings, Akroma shot upward. She was not fast enough to fully evade the darting head of the wurm, but she hadn't meant to escape. She lifted the lightning lance high and rammed it down through the snout of the worm. It pierced the palate, jagged through the mouth, and pinned its lower jaw.

The wurm shrieked, pitching its head back and forth.

Akroma rode that convulsing head, all the while twisting her lance, stirring it through wider rings of flesh. In time, she would reach brain, burn through it, and kill the beast. This particular wurm was not the death of Nivea: Akroma would have sensed it. Still, it was an abomination, and soon it would be dead.

A shadow loomed above the impaled head. Akroma did not even look up. She hurled herself into the air, dragging the lightning lance out of the hole it had burned. Eagle wings caught the air, and feline claws leaped free of the wurm. Akroma soared away just as the second deathwurm clamped its head on the first. With a swift crunch, it bit through skin, sinew, and bone. Even as it swallowed, the headless body shivered miserably.

Akroma rose above the horrid battle. From here, the mass of worms seemed a huge, dark brain. It spread across an imagined world and disbelieved all. It left nothingness in its wake. Akroma hefted her lightning lance. She would move like a brainstorm across that evil mind.

Two surges of her wings sent her strafing above the wurms.

Without slowing, she jabbed the lance in, stabbing one monster after another. She impaled a creature's head, another's back, and a third's belly, stitching agony across the mound of death.

She sought a particular death. If she could find the death of Nivea, could slay it and gut it from gullet to anus, perhaps she would find Nivea yet alive within. Her lightning lance came down twice more, and again, tasting the deathwurms but finding no trace of Nivea.

* * * * *

One wurm did not remain with the others. It was driven by a strange instinct. The souls of the dead naturally gravitate toward their homes, to linger and haunt, to greet loved ones and terrify hated ones. This wurm homed in.

It plunged through the jungle, snapping up the occasional great cat along the way. The scent of clear waters and limestone came from up ahead. Mixed with those odors was the taste of the soul who had made this place. The wurm drove toward that soul to which it was bound.

Here was the incarnate death of Nivea, and it would be the death of Ixidor too.

The wurm moved rapidly, toppling trees and leaving a mucus trail behind. Birds pecked at its flesh as it went, ripping off hunks of black and gobbling them down—only to gasp and die. Landbound creatures recoiled from the seeking beast. It drove a small stampede of them right out of the forest and onto the shore of a blue lake. Next moment, the wurm itself arrived.

From the waters ahead rose a glorious palace, white marble above and white reflection below. The wurm was home, gazing upon the outward manifestation of the beloved mind.

The great black beast scuttled down the sands and waded out

upon the waves. From its skin, darkness spread in the water. As more of its vast bulk ventured out, inky waves spread from either side. It slithered back and forth, its movements churning the once-placid lake. Soon, a hundred tons of wurm traveled weightlessly across the waves.

Ahead stood a shimmering man on a broad raft. He seemed like Ixidor. He poled away in terror.

The wurm merely opened its mouth and swallowed a few thousand gallons and the man and the raft. It wasn't him, but it tasted like him.

It reached the foundations, pylons sinking into the waters and holding aloft the palace. Even these massive drums of stone smelled of Ixidor. With wet sucker feet, the wurm gripped the smooth stone and climbed. Its weight made the massive walls grind and creak. As it went, the wurm cracked stone, and grit dropped away, pattering into the lake.

The wurm climbed up a long column, across the pediment, over a flying buttress, and atop a roof that buckled and fell. Through a hanging garden, over an aerial bridge, across a broad dome, and up another tower the wurm smelled its quarry. Ixidor was within.

Its black head craned up over the balustrade of a broad balcony. It oozed over the rail, bashing aside the chairs and table that waited there. Beyond the arched doorway opened a grand bedchamber, and in the center of that space stood Ixidor.

He trembled. There was something defective in his eyes, as if he were mad or wounded or both. The man sucked a breath, drawing in the dark spores that wafted from the wurm's flesh. He smelled it, too, for he said sadly, "Nivea."

That name energized the great wurm. It hunched forward. Its head jabbed beneath the balcony's arch, and its tail dragged slime along the tower wall. Caterpillar feet slapped the floor and drove the beast toward Ixidor. The wurm's mouth gaped for its long-awaited meal.

Ixidor wasn't alone. Around him stood six shadows, his own shadows, but living. He turned to one of them and dived into it, slipping away, as though it were a hole in the air. In rapid succession, the other shadows followed. Two, three, four, they were gone, then the fifth.

The wurm lunged.

The sixth dissolved to nothing.

Translucent teeth snapped down on emptiness. Ixidor was gone. He had escaped.

The wurm thrashed, crushing the grand canopied bed and tearing down the curtains. Its head was a mallet in that place of glass and silk. Its teeth tore the guts out of Ixidor's bedchamber. The space smelled fragrant of Ixidor, and destroying it was the second best thing to destroying him.

Only when the chamber was entirely gutted did the furious creature slide back out. Its flanged head slipped beneath the archway, and it reared out on the wind. The scent was faint here, but it remained. Ixidor was still in his palace. It would find him and destroy him, as it had destroyed Nivea.

At last, they would be together.

* * * * *

Akroma flew low above the tangled wurms and stabbed down with her lightning staff. She ripped open the back of another beast. Even as half-living creatures spilled from its wound, the death-wurm reared angrily. Its head rose just beneath Akroma. Her wings surged, flinging her beyond the reach of that ravenous mouth and out to soar over empty ground.

The wurm lunged after her, missed, ripped open a sucking hole in the nightmare lands, and flung itself onward, relentless. It gnashed again and tore open the world. Three pits and four opened beneath the monster. It rushed on after Akroma.

Her wings beat with almost frantic speed, flinging her along. A succession of pits opened behind her. The wind ripped feathers from her wings, and she was losing her hold on the air. Just behind her claws, the mouth of the wurm crashed closed. One more bite, and she would be destroyed.

The wurm pounced. Akroma hurled herself skyward. Glassy teeth snapped closed, scraping her hind paws. Trailing blood, Akroma climbed into the heavens.

The sucking wind was suddenly gone.

Reaching the apex of her flight, Akroma glanced down.

The wurm was stuck tight atop the series of pits it had chewed in the world. Its rubbery body had been sucked down into them in five places. The creature struggled to pull itself free, but the sound of ripping sinews told what would come next. With five greasy pops, the deathwurm tore into sections and disappeared down through the holes.

It was Akroma's fifth kill. Still perhaps a thousand monsters remained. They had uncoiled, no longer lying in a great mound atop each other but spreading out across the land. Most feasted on those who lay wounded on the battlefield—easy kills and readily available. Others pursued the fleeing armies across the nightmare lands, toward the desert.

The creator had mandated that Akroma kill all the wurms. So far she had destroyed only a handful.

Even as she hung above them, a new tactic came to her. Gathering her wings, Akroma stooped down from the sky. She dived toward the head of a wurm, though she held her lightning staff behind her, not before. Swooping in front of the huge thing's eyes, she rose to land lightly on the head of a nearby creature. It did not know she was there, but the first wurm did.

It rose, mouth gaping, and waggled back and forth, expecting her to leap away. Akroma only stood, returning its soulless stare. The rearing wurm struck. Its jaws spread wide so that its teeth seemed a giant bear trap. They clamped down but caught only a few of Akroma's darting feathers. Still, the fangs cut a huge chunk out of the other wurm's head.

Recoiling, the beast swallowed the gobbet. It gasped and choked, death eating death, and thrashed its life away. It rolled in agony atop the split skull of its victim. Together, the killers perished.

Those were the sixth and seventh kills for Akroma. Flapping conspicuously past the eyes of her next victim, she lighted on the neck of a nearby beast. It was not the way she was designed to fight—bait to make one wurm food for another. Still, with each attack, she could slay two of the monsters. At this rate, she would have them defeated in a few weeks.

By then, they might have spread through all of Otaria.

Akroma shrugged away the thought, hurling herself into the air.

Teeth clamped down on the flesh where she had been, and a pair of wurms began to die.

Perhaps Akroma could not slay them all. Perhaps she would be killed herself the next time she tried. Until she discovered a more lethal technique, though, she would flit from head to head and destroy.

* * * * *

Ixidor landed on his side in a broad courtyard of Locus. Gritting his teeth, he glanced up through the glimmering air.

His unmen followed, vaulting one after another overhead. Five of them escaped through the sixth, who closed forever, keeping the wurm away.

Not for long.

Shifting his focus, Ixidor saw the monstrous beast. Twisted, titanic, evil, it clung to the highest tower of his palace. Its black bulk dripped ooze down the white walls. Its head rooted through the chamber above—Ixidor's bedchamber.

Staring up at the grotesque creature, Ixidor awakened from his stupor. Since the beetles had first poured in their ravenous swarm from Phage, he had reeled like a man suffering a stroke. Part of his mind had been eaten away. All the thoughts that had dwelt therein had vanished. At first, Ixidor had been unable to move or think. Now, he could do both. Anger awakened him.

Locus was his tribute to Nivea: beauty defying ugliness, life defying death. Now death's ugly parasite clung to it.

Ixidor rose. His five remaining unmen did so as well, standing in the center of a beautiful garden. Beneath their feet, four paths diverged, each leading outward to one of the white walls. At the terminus of each path stood a huge frieze of Nivea's face. Four Niveas peered inward.

"My north, south, east, and west."

The flowers of each season were planted around her faces so that as the fickle year turned, she would never be without adornment. This was Locus at its finest—beautifully defiant. It was the perfect place for Ixidor to battle the wurm.

On the tower above, it finished its depredations and withdrew from the ravaged bedchamber. Its head waggled in the air, seeming to sniff, then, with slow magnificence, that sinewy thing turned toward Ixidor. Recognition glinted in its ink-ball eyes. Shifting feet on the stony side of the tower, the wurm wound its slimy way down the tower.

Ixidor strode to gather his weapons. He would not wield

killing things, for the wurm embodied every killing thing. Ixidor would fight only with life, with beauty—the essence of Nivea.

He started small, gathering a broad bouquet of fresh blooms. His arm was its vase, and his life energy was its water. It was a work of art, his greatest weapon.

The wurm slithered over the courtyard wall. It was quick. Extending its rubbery form down to the river-stone walk, the wurm wound toward Ixidor.

The man only stood and waited, his unmen surrounding him. He held his bouquet ready as if the wurm were a coming bride. The flowers were no longer mere flowers, though. They had transcended their material forms. Ixidor had infused each stem, leaf, and petal with his life essence. The bouquet solidified in this precise form, this exact orientation. He completed his creation by extending the flowers toward the wurm. He said, "These are for you, Nivea—my love. For you alone."

Wet and lunging, the wurm flopped up the trail and opened its black mouth.

Ixidor leaned forward like a man flinging flowers into a grave. He opened his arm, hurling the bouquet into the jaws of death.

The wurm snapped closed on the flowers. When its mouth opened again, the blooms were gone. It leaped on Ixidor.

He flung himself sideways through one of his unmen. The other four followed. Ixidor left the bright garden and the black wurm and landed in a long art gallery. The remaining unmen tumbled down around him, while their comrade vanished in the face of the wurm.

Ixidor stood, feeling the thick woolen rug beneath his feet. He wished he could have remained to watch what his bouquet did. It would tumble intact through the monster's gut and seek out whatever essence of Nivea remained there. It would find her, and he would find it.

Or perhaps the bouquet was a foolish fancy, and Ixidor was simply mad.

He peered around at the gallery, and his misgivings deepened. Perhaps he *was* mad. He'd only half imagined this space. The long rug beneath his feet was extraordinarily detailed, but the paintings on the wall were indistinct, the sculptures shapeless, the ceiling irregularly bossed and in places receding into misty uncertainty. Ixidor had known he wanted an art gallery in his palace, but had been so busy creating living art that he had neglected dead art.

It was just as well. He could finish the gallery now and finish off the wurm.

Even as he stood there among his unmen, the rose window at the end of the gallery shattered. Where once bright panes welcomed the sun, now jagged fangs of glass ringed the frame. The wurm broke through. Glass cut long furrows in its sinewy flesh as it squeezed in.

Ixidor turned away from the coming beast. He lifted his hand toward the empty frames on the walls and sent out mental images of himself. Each painting became a precise portrait of him—so precise that it lived and moved. Ixidors stepped from their frames and mingled upon the floor. Death would have to eat them all before it could find him.

Lowering his hand, Ixidor flung it out toward the sculptures. They too took shape, life-sized images of him. They jumped down from their bases and stood staring at the monster that flopped toward them.

"All for you, Nivea. I give these folk only to you."

Just like the immutable flowers, these works of art would not dissolve in the tract of the beast. They would climb through it, giving Nivea company and killing the monster from within.

Or Ixidor was mad.

The wurm would not be stopped. It smelled the true Ixidor

among all these false ones and bashed the creatures aside. They scrambled up along its muzzle, and when the beast gnashed at them, the Ixidors leaped into its mouth. An army of semblances invaded the monster and ripped out fistfuls of flesh as they went.

Ixidor laughed. He had reached the farthest vestibule in his gallery, and the wurm thundered angrily toward him. It swallowed its killers obliviously—deadly portraits, beauty against ugliness. Ixidor laughed.

The great beast lunged.

Ixidor hurled himself through another unman. The final three followed. They and their master tumbled to the ground elsewhere in the palace, and the one who had been their portal snapped shut.

Air hissed into Ixidor's inner ears. He clutched his head while the pressure equalized and then looked around at the deep chamber, stony and dark. Though he had created this windowless space, he had never been here before. There was no way into this deep sanctum except through a single stair that wound down within one of the foundation pylons. They were fifty feet beneath the bottom of the lake. Even if the wurm could smell him under stone and silt and water, it could not hope to squeeze down the pylon to reach him. Here he would be safe.

Ixidor smiled. He snapped his fingers. Lights flickered into being along the stony walls. They showed an opulent chamber with thick red carpets. Before him, a long and elegant dining table stood in the midst of tall seats. To one side, a canopy bed waited, and next to it stood a giant wardrobe. With a huge and well-stocked pantry, a deep cesspit, and burgeoning bookshelves, Ixidor could remain in this room forever.

He had forgotten about this place. He should have come here first. Let Topos take care of itself. Let mortals ravage his world, and when they were done, he would rise to live again.

Ixidor strode toward the canopy bed, and his three remaining unmen followed. Heaving an exhausted sigh, Ixidor climbed onto the silken sheets and laid himself out flat. He would wait out the war here with his unmen.

He must have slept. He had right and reason to.

Ixidor awoke to see an unman grasping at him. It tried to shake him, but its empty hands laid hold of nothing. Its silent shouts had not awakened Ixidor either. He rose because of the steady trickle of water off the canopy onto the carpet.

"What is it?" Ixidor asked.

In reply, a deep whuffling noise came from the stone ceiling.

Ixidor stood and stared at the great slab. It had cracked. Water traced out the jag and dripped down to strike the peak of the canopy. Even as Ixidor watched, the drops grew larger, and the crack began to spray.

"What's happening?" Ixidor wondered again. It sounded like something massive was burrowing into the silty bottom of the lake. . . .

A chunk of stone bounded free of the crack. Water poured down in a white shaft and spread across the floor. The shaft widened, and the ceiling cracked out in the precise diameter of the deathwurm's head.

Ixidor turned and took a step, trying to spot the stairway out.

The wurm broke through.

Massive blocks shattered and fell. In their midst came a true horror. Where once a slender column of water rushed down, now a fat and meaty wurm crashed through the ceiling. Water poured in a roaring cascade all around it. Its jaws snapped up the canopy bed, crunching it to splinters and feathers. Down stuck to its translucent teeth as it turned its head. Stupid little eyes fixed on Ixidor.

"I should have known. There is no safe place, not even in my mind. Especially not in my mind."

With one last, longing look at the deep sanctum, Ixidor hurled himself through the unman who had awakened him.

He landed on his side in another corner of Locus—a private theater that had never held a play. Ixidor lay there panting. That had been a close one. Would he be running forever?

Water poured out around him, sluicing through the legs of the unman. Ixidor blinked, seeing twin floods gush across the ground. The unman hadn't closed. He yet stood there, a portal between the deep sanctum and the theater. Why hadn't he closed? And where were the other unmen?

Ixidor hadn't seen them since he fell asleep. They should have been incapable of leaving him, for he had never granted them free will.

Two of his unmen had abandoned him. The third remained open, waiting for its companions to jump through. The open gate would allow any creature to pass—

Ixidor lurched backward—

Through the unman burst the head of the wurm. Its mouth gaped, teeth spread, and jaws snapped.

Ixidor could not get out of the way.

The thing's mouth closed around him, and its cold gullet swallowed. All was darkness and agony.

The wurm withdrew its head through the unman.

Deprived of its master, the unman only stood and trembled, water pouring through shuddering legs.

He was gone.

* * * * *

Above the ravenous wurms and the sucking pits, Akroma somehow sensed it. The creator was gone.

"Ixidor."

She could do no more. Battered and weary, Akroma had killed fifty deathwurms. More than a thousand remained. She had fought because she knew Ixidor wished it. Now he was gone.

Akroma labored into the uncaring sky.

Beneath her feline feet, wurms bounded across the nightmare lands and entered the sandy desert. They continued on, gobbling up folk as they went. They could not bite through the world anymore, but they would scour it of all life.

Akroma hung in the sky and watched the end of Otaria.

CHAPTER TWENTY-FOUR

THE SAVED AND THE DAMNED

Kamahl knelt before Jeska. She lay limp in his arms, panting miserably. She was dying once again, dying of the old, unhealing wound. An identical injury crossed his own belly and made him weak. It would kill him too, if he and Jeska and Otaria somehow survived the third laceration—a wound on the world.

Like giant black maggots, deathwurms galloped across the nightmare lands. They had already scoured the battlefield of all living things and left the soil itself riddled with holes. The infection spread. Many wurms had plunged onto the desert, pursuing the routed troops. No one would survive this battle—not warriors, not countryfolk, not anything on Otaria.

A deathwurm bounded straight toward Kamahl and Jeska, its mucousy muzzle homing on their scent.

"Go, Brother," Jeska said faintly. "They cannot kill me."

Clenching his jaw, Kamahl stood, a bulwark of flesh between his sister and the monster that thundered down on them. "They will not."

Jeska shook her head fiercely. "They *cannot*. They did not kill me from the inside, and they cannot kill me from the outside."

Kamahl turned away and said to himself, "Delirious." He faced down the wurm.

It was lunacy. The thing's head was the size of a house, and its body was a league long. Kamahl did not even have a weapon. Still, rage and desperation had been Kamahl's greatest weapons in the past. He smiled. Of all the deaths that he and his sister could suffer, at least this one could be punched in the face.

The wurm pounded the ground, almost flinging Kamahl off his feet. One more leap and it would be upon them.

Kamahl clenched his hand into a fist, and he reared it back. "Good-bye, Sister."

He swung. His fist crashed into the black nose of the beast, but it in turn smashed into him, hurling him back. Kamahl flew over Jeska. The wurm plunged atop her, its mouth agape.

Tumbling, Kamahl realized he had done it again—had survived the death that would take her. He hit the ground just as the wurm did and rolled miserably, knowing his sister was gone. Kamahl spread his arms, heels digging in, and flopped to a stop on his back. He flipped over, a shout of grief erupting from him.

Jeska yet lay there, trembling. The wurm was nowhere to be seen.

Staggering to his feet, Kamahl scrambled toward her. "What happened? What did you do?"

Jeska smiled wanly up at him. She seemed somehow stronger, her skin less pale. "I told you it could not kill me."

Falling to his knees at her side, Kamahl saw the dark glint in her eyes, the gray tinge to her flesh. "It is within you, isn't it? You absorbed it back into yourself."

"I once held thousands. There is room enough in me for all of them."

"What are you talking about?" Kamahl blurted.

"I have made these deathwurms. I made them by killing—"

"You didn't kill. It was Phage."

"I am Phage. She is the dark side of me."

The ground thundered with impacts coming straight toward them.

Clenching his fists, Kamahl rose to meet the new menace.

It wasn't a menace at all, though. Eight hooves pounded the ground—a giant centaur galloping beside a giant mule and its rider.

"Stonebrow!" Kamahl gasped in relief. "And . . . and—"

"Zagorka," Jeska said softly.

The centaur and mule galloped up and skidded to a halt. Dust rose in clouds around them and continued on over the desert sands.

Stonebrow extended his hand to Kamahl. "We must flee! It is death to remain."

"Yes!" Kamahl said. "Carry me away, and Zaborra can take Jeska."

"Zagorka," the old woman corrected.

"She cannot take me," Jeska said. "I'm staying."

Kamahl's mouth hung open. "There isn't time for this!"

"If I flee," Jeska said, breathing slowly, "we all will die. There is one way for Otaria to survive this day. . . . There is only one way for me to survive."

Kamahl shook his head. "You can't do it, Jeska. You can't take them back into you."

"They didn't kill me before. I can bear it again."

"That's not you speaking," Kamahl said. He gripped her arm and felt the first tingle of hostility beneath her skin. "That's Phage. She doesn't want you to live, Jeska. She wants herself to live again."

Her eyes met his, and for a moment the darkness retreated. She was Jeska again. "There is only one way, Kamahl."

His brow beetled. "But all of this—I did this to save you."

Jeska shook her head and stroked his jaw. "No. You did this to save yourself."

He could only stare in amazement at her.

"You *have* saved yourself. You killed the man you once were and saved the woman I once was. Your journey is done, but mine only begins. These deathwurms arise from the murders I have committed, starting with Seton—"

"Seton!"

"Braids killed him, but I took his life force into me. I took his life! That's where all the blackness began. You cannot destroy these wurms. Only I can. You cannot save me. I must save myself, and to do so, I must take these things back into me."

"No, Jeska."

"I will find my way out again," Jeska said, "or die trying. Better that than to die without trying."

Stonebrow's eyes glinted with fear. "We must go now!"

"Last chance," Zagorka said, reining in her champing mule.

Kamahl drew a deep breath. He looked about. Wurms vaulted everywhere.

"Go, Kamahl," Jeska said. "I will stay. It's the only way to save Otaria."

Kamahl's nostrils flared. "Stonebrow," he said, his voice a low growl. "Get out of here. That's an order."

Nodding his noble head, Stonebrow said, "As you wish."

"I could use an order here, myself," Zagorka broke in.

"Go," Jeska said simply.

It was all the old woman needed. She dug her heels into Chester, and they dashed away. Stonebrow galloped beside her. In moments, they were lost behind twin clouds of dust and sand.

"What are we going to do, then," Kamahl wondered incredulously, "lie here and wait for a thousand beasts to attack, and then absorb them one by one?" He stared out across the desert, where hundreds of wurms already charged. "It will be too late."

Jeska blinked. "We need Ixidor. To reach him, we must reach her."

"Who?"

"Akroma," Jeska said, pointing toward the sky.

Kamahl sat back on his heels, stunned. Above the thundering wurms hung a single point of light, a star beaming down on an abandoned world. "She is sworn to kill you."

"She does not fight me, but the deathwurms. She will help us," Jeska said. "Call her."

Standing, Kamahl lifted his arms and his voice. "Akroma! Protector! We call you. Come to us!" Above the battling beasts, the angel hovered. No longer did she fight. She only hung there. "We wish to ally, to save your land and ours! Akroma! Come to us!"

His summons did not bring the angel but only another wurm. It roared toward them across the same path of compression left by the last beast.

Kamahl turned desperate eyes toward Jeska.

"Step aside," she hissed. "I'll take this one in as well. Call her!"

"Akroma! Come to us!" Kamahl shouted into the literal teeth of the deathwurm. At the last moment, he hurled himself aside.

The black beast pounded down upon Jeska, its mouth wide. Instead of swallowing her, it was swallowed by her. The head was gone, and then the lashing neck of the thing. A half mile of wurm sank into her body as if she herself were a pit. A mile.

At first, Kamahl could only gape at the strange spectacle, but then he lifted his hands again. "Akroma! Help us! Akroma!"

* * * * *

Above the roar of black wurms came a tiny keen: gnat song. It broke through the lethargy of Akroma's mind.

Someone called her. It was not the creator—Ixidor was gone—but it was someone like the creator.

"Akroma! Come to us!"

She stared down toward the sound and saw a strange thing: a deathwurm disappearing. It seemed to plunge down one of the sucking pits. It tail flipped once, and it was gone. Instead of leaving behind a round hole, though, it vanished through the shape of a woman.

Not just a woman. *The* woman. Phage. She had been the bringer of all this evil. She lay on the desert, and her brother stood above her, calling out in his minuscule voice. Akroma cared nothing for the man, but the woman she wanted dead.

Akroma gathered her wings and dived. It felt good to move again. It felt good to have something to fight. She brought her lightning lance out before her and prepared to kill Phage.

How like the coliseum battle this was—Akroma stooping down from the air, Kamahl guarding his evil sister, and Phage lying, near-slain, on the sands. Only the deathwurms were different, ravaging all the world.

One wurm veered toward them. In two more bounds, it reached Kamahl. He leaped aside, allowing the monster to devour his sister. Its jaws never snapped closed, though. The monster plunged into her, slipping to nothingness. Phage was destroying the deathwurms. She was fighting the same battle that the creator had assigned to Akroma.

It didn't matter. Akroma was made to destroy Phage. With her lightning lance foremost, she plunged from the sky upon her greatest foe. In moments, she was there.

It was so easy. Phage didn't even flinch. The avenging angel rammed her staff down into the unmoving form—

Except that something hit Akroma and knocked her aside. The lance missed Phage. It pierced the ground deeply enough that the weapon was ripped from Akroma's hands. Careening out of control, the angel crashed down, along with the thing that had hit her: Kamahl. The two of them rolled together in the desert sands.

Snarling, Akroma raked his chest with her claws. Kamahl shouted and tumbled free. Akroma spun once more and rose from the sands.

Already, the barbarian had scrambled to his feet. Deep gouges crossed his chest, and blood poured across a wound on his belly. He crouched at the ready for attack, but his hands were empty as he lifted them. "You cannot kill her."

"You are not my creator," she said, stalking toward her lightning shaft, which shuddered in the ground.

Kamahl shifted before her. "Only Jes—only Phage can stop the deathwurms."

Growling angrily, Akroma backhanded the barbarian, knocking him aside. She grasped her lightning lance and strode toward Phage.

The woman placidly watched her approach. "Unless the wurms return into me, all of us will die. Tell your creator—"

Akroma's eyes grew flinty. "The creator is gone."

"Gone . . ." Phage echoed incredulously.

Akroma lifted the lightning lance. "He sent me to fight the wurms, and now he is gone."

The lance glinted in Phage's eyes. "It was his last command, that you fight the wurms," she said. "Then why do you disobey him? Why are you destroying your one chance to kill the wurms?"

The staff trembled in Akroma's hand. Her angelic features were as hard as granite. "I am sworn to kill you."

"Once the wurms are gone, you can kill me," Phage said serenely.

"First, I must seek my master."

"Whatever. Finish the wurms, find your master, and then finish me," Phage replied. "Do it however you want—but first, help me defeat the wurms."

Akroma's eyes blazed, but she lowered the staff. "What must I do to shunt these wurms into you?"

"The blue sparks," Phage said, struggling to sit up. "They brought the wurms out. They can gather them in again."

"I will summon them," Akroma said. A new resolve straightened her back. "Until the creator returns, I will command his disciples. I will protect his creation."

Her wings spread and surged. The blast of air threw Kamahl to the ground and whipped up a stinging cloud of sand. Plumes beat again, and Akroma's feet lifted into the air. A third surge, and she was flying away above their heads.

"For the creator," Akroma said to herself as she vaulted into the sky.

With each stroke of her massive wings, she climbed higher above the sullen world. She was ascending, and not simply in body. Until Akroma could find the creator, she had to assume his mantle. Ixidor had brought this dream into being, and Akroma would keep dreaming it lest it disappear. Such was her destiny.

Piercing the endless blue, Akroma reached the apex of the sky. She held the lightning lance high overhead and sang.

Never before had a star sung above the world. It drew the ear of every creature below. In their pell-mell flight, the routed armies looked back. The creatures of the jungle poked heads from their lairs. Even deathwurms paused to crane oozy necks skyward. It was right that they should witness the ascension of this new god over Topos.

Akroma sang again. Her wordless tone was filled with longing for the creator. All of Ixidor's creatures heard and yearned skyward, though most were land-bound and could not rise. The birds in their chromatic choruses flashed above the treetops, but their wings were insufficient in the vast blue. Only quintessential creatures could join the singer, only beings that were kin to the stars.

The disciples came. They seemed faerie fire emerging from the windows of Locus and scintillating along rails and pilasters. The sparks gathered above onion domes and swarmed together into the sky. Following paths through the air, they soared toward the angel.

Akroma's song resonated in them, and the skies sang with dread and longing.

Motes reached her and coursed about her. They traced her face, lingered along her wings, and pierced her mind. In moments, they knew what distressed her and what they must do.

Stars slowly peeled from their angel-god. At first, they came away as one, a glittering veil of energy that retained her shape, but then the gossamer sheet spread. Disciples tumbled down blue stairways of sky, out across the nightmare lands, and toward the deathwurms.

Flickering like candle flames, Ixidor's disciples dropped into the brows of the beasts. Their radiance was snuffed in black folds of flesh, but their spirits reached on through lightless innards. There, the disciples encountered hunger, hatred, and rage, but they continued on, seeking the essence of the beasts. It would be the darkest corner, the most heartless desire.

One by one, the sparks found it: the death wish. They sank their hooks in that horrible desire and streamed backward.

From the snapping mouths of the beasts, the disciples emerged, drawing black strands behind them. They soared into the sky and converged, weaving together their webs of power. En masse, the disciples turned and plunged toward a single target.

Jeska.

* * * * *

"Here they come," Kamahl said quietly.

Blue points of light traced lines across his eyes. He knelt, holding his sister despite the virulent poison beneath her skin. He could only just bear to hold her, with three wurms within. In moments, when the blue sparks arrived, her touch would be death.

"You're getting your wish," he said.

Jeska's eyes were hard, but her voice pleaded. "Remember me, Kamahl. Remember what I do today, even if I never emerge again."

"Don't say that. You'll—"

A blue light soared in, smacked her forehead, and disappeared, dragging a black filament after it.

Jeska shuddered as the darkness drilled into her mind. A spark fled from between her lips.

Kamahl gaped, watching the line sink deeper. "No, Jeska . . . no!"

With a shriek of tortured air, the slender thread widened into a huge beast. It poured itself into Jeska. She convulsed and grew pale, and her flesh stung like nettles in Kamahl's hands.

He did not let her go. He would cling to her as long as she was Jeska.

Another blue spark impacted, and a third.

She thrashed her head, as if to break the black threads. They only plunged faster into her. Her limbs trembled, and her eyes glowed with evil flame. Two more sparks fled from her howling mouth.

Swallowing, she gasped out, "One more . . . and I will be gone, Kamahl. . . . One more . . ."

The tails of the two wurms slipped into her brow.

Kamahl leaned over Jeska, tears streaming down his face. He embraced her one last time and kissed her pale cheek. "Good-bye, Sister." Laying her gently on the ground, Kamahl backed away.

A fourth spark struck, and a fifth, a sixth. Glowing creatures cascaded from the sky. They made Jeska bounce, writhe, and kick. The wurms were filling her, possessing her, but also healing her wound.

Jeska stood, her hands open wide to the influx of the monsters. She seemed a worshiper invoking a god.

Kamahl could not bear the sight. He turned away.

No wurms remained on the corpse-strewn battlefield. Few fought on in jungle and desert. All those that were left were connected by black threads to Jeska . . . to Phage. They drained across astral channels into her.

She was doing it. She was saving Otaria and damning herself.

In a flash of blue and white and black, it was done.

The wurms were gone.

Jeska was gone.

Only Phage remained.

* * * * *

Akroma saw it all. How she wished to kill that witch, and yet, Phage had saved Topos and Locus and Otaria.

Turning in the sky, Akroma winged toward Topos. If Ixidor was anywhere, he was there. She would seek him, find him, and turn her wrath on the one named Phage.

* * * * *

Kamahl sat in that sandy waste, the birthplace of a goddess.

Phage stood with her back to him. Her hands were yet lifted to the heavens, though they had poured out all their damnation already.

"Phage," Kamahl said reverently.

She turned. Her eyes were dark, no longer the eyes of Jeska. Without saying a word, she walked away.

"Don't waste yourself on the fights, on the Cabal," said Kamahl. "I won your freedom from all that. You can do anything you want, wander free. Why don't you come with me to Krosan? We can make a home for you there."

"We are enemies," she replied over her shoulder, "the saved and the damned."

JOURNEYS END AND BEGIN

Akroma flew above Topos and sought signs of Ixidor. Her paws dragged over the fronds of the forest and startled birds, red and gold among leaf shadows. They darted away, their cries silencing the howl of monkeys. Akroma spread her wings and soared out above a trampled trail.

A deathwurm had passed here, heading toward the lake.

Akroma followed the path. In two strokes, she reached the shore.

Once the lake had been sky-blue, but now it was gray, its bottom torn up. In the midst of the tainted waters, Locus rose. Its arches and towers gleamed despite the gray ooze that draped them, despite the failing mortar and crumbled ramparts. The deathwurm had climbed all across that glorious palace.

Akroma had never noticed how beautiful Topos had been.

Rising on heated air, she soared along the front gate. The slime trail led her up the wall, around the central tower, and to the master's balcony. With a final surge of her wings, Akroma vaulted over the dripping balustrade and landed.

The balcony was crossed with stress fractures. Beyond shattered glass doors lay a bedchamber in utter ruins. It seemed a gaping mouth. Ceiling, walls, and floor ran with gray ooze.

"Did you die here, Master?" wondered Akroma.

Never before had she allowed the thought that he might be dead. She knew he was gone, yes, but dead? It is a very different thing to serve a departed god than a dead one.

Leaping into the air, Akroma followed a second slime trail that spiraled down the wall. The path led through a ravaged garden, across rooftops to a shattered rose window. Akroma dived through the circle of shards and into a long gallery. Her breath caught. In the carnage of toppled statues and torn paintings, Ixidor was everywhere. His head lay here in stone, his arm there on canvas, his spirit throughout the chamber.

Lighting on the runner, Akroma took a deep breath. "This will be a shrine to you, Master. I will clean it and save every fragment of you, so that future generations will glimpse your face in the pieces."

The far wall of the gallery had been shattered by the wurm. Akroma winged through. The trail led across more rooftops and then precipitously down a wall and into the gray lake. A black hole lay in the bed below.

If the wurm had gone there, it must have followed Ixidor.

Akroma tucked her wings and dived. Air shrieked across her pinions, and then she clove into the water. The impact was like thunder. Waves opened around her and then clapped closed.

Akroma swam to the bottom of the lake and into the pit that the wurm had dug. It was a cold black throat. As she descended, walls of sand gave way to walls of mud, then to rock.

Akroma entered a wide, flooded chamber, its magic lamps gleaming eerily through the gray water. The place had been ravaged, ruined furniture trapped against the ceiling—

Someone stood there.

Master!

Akroma swam toward the silhouette of Ixidor, shimmering in

the murk. As she neared, though, she realized it was not the creator but an unman. He was the doorway to where the creator had gone.

Using her wings like fins, Akroma propelled herself to the unman, and through him.

She spilled with tons of water out the other side and into an upper chamber of the palace. It was half-flooded. Its furnishings had already washed out the door. Water rushed into the corridor beyond and down the nearby stairs.

Ixidor was not here, nor the wurm. The unman would have closed if the creator had made it safely through.

He was gone. It was a certainty. He was dead. Her god was dead.

Akroma stood amid the shoving waters and wept.

* * * * *

Your journey is done. Mine only begins.

Jeska had said that. She was wise—wise and damned.

Kamahl sat in the ravaged ziggurat of Krosan. No one else ventured here, so near the rapacious heart of the forest, but to Kamahl, this spot was sacred. He came here to think.

His journey was finished and his wound only a healed-over scar, a testament to all he had done.

Kamahl had slain his former self and saved his former sister. He had even saved the forest, pouring the darkness from his own soul into the Mirari sword.

How strange. His salvation had come by emptying himself of evil. Jeska's had come by filling herself with it.

He glanced toward the thistle wall, beyond which General Stonebrow waited. The giant centaur guarded his master and wished for more wars.

Let him wait. He could learn something in waiting.

Kamahl had a waking dream: A deathwurm chased him to the edge of a cliff. He climbed halfway down it and clung to a tree that grew there. Another deathwurm waited at the bottom of the cliff. Death above and death below. As Kamahl held onto the tree, he realized it was an apple tree. It bore a single huge apple, the roundest and reddest he had ever seen. He reached out and plucked it and ate.

Life was no longer about running from death. It was about eating apples.

Poor Jeska. She could not run from death, for one can't run from oneself.

"My journey is done. Yours, Sister, only begins."

* * * * *

"Behold the glories of the Nightmare War!" the man shouted. He was not Braids—no one would ever truly replace Braids, leaping like a manic goat around the rim of the coliseum. But she had not returned from Topos, and the show must go on. The man's shout reverberated among a hundred thousand spectators. They avidly cheered the reenactment.

On the sands below, a dementia summoner played Phage. She brought giant, undead serpents from her mind and piled them in a coiling mound at the center of the arena.

"Behold, the deathwurms!" The crowd loved the gnarly pile. "Remember, all bets on individual warriors pay three to one for survival! Who will live? Kamahl? Ixidor? Braids? Phage?"

The true Phage did not fight this time. She was too grand a personage to engage in such vulgar sports. She sat where she belonged, in the royal box beside the First.

Black robes and black silk, seats of iron and the best views in the coliseum—Phage and the First stared unblinking at the battle. In their eyes, the whole deadly drama played out in miniature.

An undead serpent attacked the summoner who had created it. The beast ate her to nothing, to the delight of the audience.

"That would never happen," said Phage quietly.

"Of course not, my love," replied the First. He reached his hand to hers.

She took that killing grasp and squeezed.

"We are the eaters of death," he said, eyes still on the melee.

Phage nodded. "We are the dreamers of nightmare."

* * * * *

In the belly of the beast, Ixidor finally found Nivea.